P9-CEI-829

ACCLAIMED BESTSELLERS
BY DEAN KOONTZ

DRAGON TEARS

His newest novel—available from G. P. Putnam's Sons.

SHADOWFIRES

"Koontz is a master storyteller."   —*Wichita Falls Times*

HIDEAWAY

"Not just a thriller, but a meditation on the nature of evil."   —*Lexington Herald-Leader*

COLD FIRE

"An extraordinary piece of fiction . . . It will be a classic."   —*UPI*

THE HOUSE OF THUNDER

"Koontz is brilliant."   —*Chicago Sun-Times*

THE VOICE OF THE NIGHT

"A fearsome tour of an adolescent's psyche. Terrifying, knee-knocking suspense."   —*Chicago Sun-Times*

continued . . .

THE BAD PLACE

"A new experience in breathless terror." —UPI

THE SERVANTS OF TWILIGHT

"A great storyteller." —*New York Daily News*

MIDNIGHT

"A triumph." —*New York Times*

LIGHTNING

"Brilliant . . . a spine-tingling tale . . . both challenging and entertaining." —Associated Press

THE MASK

"Koontz hones his fearful yarns to a gleaming edge." —*People*

WATCHERS

"A breakthrough for Koontz . . . his best ever."
—*Kirkus Reviews*

TWILIGHT EYES

"A spine-chilling adventure . . . will keep you turning pages to the very end."   —*Rave Reviews*

STRANGERS

"A unique spellbinder that captures the reader on the first page. Exciting, enjoyable, and an intensely satisfying read."   —Mary Higgins Clark

PHANTOMS

"First-rate suspense, scary and stylish."
—*Los Angeles Times*

WHISPERS

"Pulls out all the stops . . . an incredible, terrifying tale."   —*Publishers Weekly*

continued . . .

NIGHT CHILLS

"Will send chills down your back."   —*New York Times*

DARKFALL

"A fast-paced tale . . . one of the scariest chase scenes ever."   —*Houston Post*

SHATTERED

"A chilling tale . . . sleek as a bullet."
                              —*Publishers Weekly*

THE VISION

"Spine-tingling—it gives you an almost lethal shock."   —*San Francisco Chronicle*

THE FACE OF FEAR

"Real suspense . . . tension upon tension."
                              —*New York Times*

DEAN KOONTZ

SHADOW FIRES

Previously published under the pseudonym Leigh Nichols

BERKLEY BOOKS, NEW YORK

If you purchased this book without a cover, you should be aware that this book is stolen property. It was reported as "unsold and destroyed" to the publisher, and neither the author nor the publisher has received any payment for this "stripped book."

Originally published under the pseudonym Leigh Nichols.

SHADOWFIRES

A Berkley Book / published by arrangement with
Nkui, Inc.

PRINTING HISTORY
Dark Harvest edition published 1990
Berkley edition / June 1993

All rights reserved.
Copyright © 1987 by Nkui, Inc.
Back cover photograph © Jerry Bauer.
This book may not be reproduced in
whole or in part, by mimeograph or any other
means, without permission. For information
address: The Berkley Publishing Group,
200 Madison Avenue, New York, New York 10016.

ISBN: 0-425-13698-1

A BERKLEY BOOK ® ™ 757,375
Berkley Books are published by The Berkley Publishing Group,
200 Madison Avenue, New York, New York 10016.
The name "BERKLEY" and the "B" logo
are trademarks belonging to Berkley Publishing Corporation.

PRINTED IN THE UNITED STATES OF AMERICA

10 9 8 7 6 5 4 3 2 1

This book is dedicated to
Dick and Ann Laymon
who simply can't be as nice
as they seem.
And a special hello
to Kelly.

A gasp of breath,
a sudden death:
the tale begun.

The Hulk

—*The Book of Counted Sorrows*

SHADOW FIRES

PART ONE

DARK

To know the darkness is to love the light,
to welcome dawn and fear the coming night.

—*The Book of Counted Sorrows*

1989 Good 88

◊ 1 ◊

SHOCK

Brightness fell from the air, nearly as tangible as rain. It rippled down windows, formed colorful puddles on the hoods and trunks of parked cars, and imparted a wet sheen to the leaves of trees and to the chrome on the bustling traffic that filled the street. Miniature images of the California sun shimmered in every reflective surface, and downtown Santa Ana was drenched in the clear light of a late-June morning.

When Rachael Leben exited the lobby doors of the office building and stepped onto the sidewalk, the summer sunshine felt like warm water on her bare arms. She closed her eyes and, for a moment, turned her face to the heavens, bathing in the radiance, relishing it.

"You stand there smiling as if nothing better has ever happened to you or ever will," Eric said sourly when he followed her out of the building and saw her luxuriating in the June heat.

"Please," she said, face still tilted to the sun, "let's not have a scene."

"You made a fool of me in there."

"I certainly did not."

"What the hell are you trying to prove, anyway?"

She did not respond; she was determined not to let him spoil the lovely day. She turned and started to walk away.

Eric stepped in front of her, blocking her way. His gray-blue eyes usually had an icy aspect, but now his gaze was hot.

"Let's not be childish," she said.

"You're not satisfied just to leave me. You've got to let the world know you don't need me or any damn thing I can give you."

"No, Eric. I don't care what the world thinks of you— one way or the other."

"You want to rub my face in it."

"That's not true, Eric."

"Oh, yes," he said. "Hell, yes. You're just reveling in my humiliation. Wallowing in it."

She saw him as she had never seen him before: a pathetic man. Previously he'd seemed strong to her: physically, emotionally, and mentally strong; strong-willed; strongly opinionated. He was aloof, too, and sometimes cold. He could be cruel. And there had been times during their seven years of marriage when he had been as distant as the moon. But until this moment, he'd never seemed weak or pitiable.

"Humiliation?" she said wonderingly. "Eric, I've done you an enormous favor. Any other man would buy a bottle of champagne to celebrate."

They had just left the offices of Eric's attorneys, where their divorce settlement had been negotiated with a speed that had surprised everyone but Rachael. She had startled them by arriving without an attorney of her own and by failing to press for everything to which she was entitled under California's community-property laws. When Eric's attorney presented a first offer, she had insisted it was too generous and had given them another set of figures that had seemed more reasonable to her.

"Champagne, huh? You're going to be telling everyone you took twelve and a half million less than you deserved just so you could get a quick divorce and be done with me fast, and I'm supposed to stand here grinning? ▬▬▬"

"Eric—"

"Couldn't *wait* to be done with me. Cut off a ▬ damn *arm* to be done with me. And I'm supposed to celebrate my humiliation?"

"It's a matter of principle with me not to take more than—"

"Principle, my ass."

"Eric, you know I wouldn't—"

"Everyone'll be looking at me and saying, '▬▬▬ just how insufferable must the guy have been if it was worth twelve and a half million to be rid of him!'"

"I'm not going to tell anyone what we settled for," Rachael said.

"Bullshit."

"If you think I'd ever talk against you or gossip about you, then you know even less about me than I'd thought."

Eric, twelve years her senior, had been thirty-five and worth four million when she'd married him. Now he was forty-two, and his fortune totaled more than thirty million, and by any interpretation of California law, she was entitled to thirteen million dollars in the divorce settlement—half the wealth accumulated during their marriage. Instead, she insisted on settling for her red Mercedes 560 SL sports car, five hundred thousand dollars, and no alimony—which was approximately one twenty-sixth of what she could have claimed. She had calculated that this nest egg would give her the time and resources to decide what to do with the rest of her life and to finance whatever plans she finally made.

Aware that passersby were staring as she and Eric confronted each other on the sun-splashed street, Rachael said quietly, "I didn't marry you for your money."

"I wonder," he said acidly and irrationally. His bold-featured face wasn't handsome at the moment. Anger had carved it into an ugly mask—all hard, deep, down-slashing lines.

Rachael spoke calmly, with no trace of bitterness, with no desire to put him in his place or to hurt him in any way. It was just over. She felt no rage. Only mild regret. "And now that it's finally over, I don't expect to be supported in high style and great luxury for the rest of my days. I don't want your millions. You earned them, not me. Your genius, your iron determination, your endless hours in the office and the lab. You built it all, you and you alone, and you alone deserve what you've built. You're an important man, maybe even a great man in your field, Eric, and I am only me, Rachael, and I'm not going to pretend I had anything to do with your triumphs."

The lines of anger in his face deepened as she complimented him. He was accustomed to occupying the dominant role in all relationships, professional and private. From his position of absolute dominance, he relentlessly forced submission to his wishes—or crushed anyone who would not submit. Friends, employees, and business associates always did things Eric Leben's way, or they were history. Submit or be rejected and destroyed—those were their only choices. He enjoyed the exercise of power, thrived on conquests as major as million-dollar deals and as minor as winning domestic arguments. Rachael had done as he wished for seven years, but she would not submit any longer.

The funny thing was that, by her docility and reasonableness, she had robbed him of the power on which he thrived. He had been looking forward to a protracted battle over the division of spoils, and she had walked away from it. He relished the prospect of acrimonious squabbling over alimony payments, but she thwarted him by rejecting all such assistance. He had pleasurably anticipated a court fight in which he would make her look like a gold-digging bitch and reduce her, at last, to a creature without dignity who would be willing to settle for far less than was her due. Then, although leaving her rich, he would have felt that the war had been won and he had beaten her into submission. But when she made it clear that his millions were of no importance to her, she had eliminated the one power he still had over her. She had cut him off at the knees, and his anger arose from his realization that, by her docility, she had somehow made herself his equal—if not his superior—in any further contact they might have.

She said, "Well, the way I see it, I've lost seven years, and all I want is reasonable compensation for that time. I'm twenty-nine, almost thirty, and in a way, I'm just beginning my life. Starting out later than other people. This settlement will give me a terrific start. If I lose the bundle, if someday I have reason to wish I'd gone for the whole thirteen million . . . well, then that's my tough luck, not yours. We've been through all this, Eric. It's finished."

She stepped around him, trying to walk away, but he grabbed her arm, halting her.

"Please let me go," she said evenly.

Glaring at her, he said, "How could I have been so wrong about you? I thought you were sweet, a bit shy, an unworldly little fluff of a girl. But you're a nasty little ball-buster, aren't you?"

"Really, this is an absolutely crazy attitude. And this crude behavior isn't worthy of you. Now let me go."

He gripped her even tighter. "Or is this all just a negotiating ploy? Huh? When the papers are drawn up, when we come back to sign everything on Friday, will you suddenly have a change of heart? Will you want more?"

"No, I'm not playing any games."

His grin was tight and mean. "I'll bet that's it. If we agree to such a ridiculously low settlement and draw up the papers, you'll refuse to sign them, but you'll use them in court to try to prove we were going to give you the shaft. You'll pretend the offer was *ours* and that we tried to strong-arm you into signing it. Make me look bad. Make me look as if I'm a real hard-hearted bastard. Huh? Is that the strategy? Is that the game?"

"I told you, there's no game. I'm sincere."

He dug his fingers into her upper arm. "The truth, Rachael."

"Stop it."

"Is that the strategy?"

"You're hurting me."

"And while you're at it, why don't you tell me all about Ben Shadway, too?"

She blinked in surprise, for she had never imagined that Eric knew about Benny.

His face seemed to harden in the hot sun, cracking with more deep lines of anger. "How long was he fucking you before you finally walked out on me?"

"You're disgusting," she said, immediately regretting the harsh words because she saw that he was pleased to have broken through her cool facade at last.

"How long?" he demanded, tightening his grip.

"I didn't meet Benny till six months after you and I separated," she said, striving to keep a neutral tone that would deny him the noisy confrontation he apparently desired.

"How long was he poaching on me, Rachael?"

"If you know about Benny, you've had me watched, something you've no right to do."

"Yeah, you want to keep your dirty little secrets."

"If you *have* hired someone to watch me, you know I've been seeing Benny for just five months. Now let go. You're still hurting me."

A young bearded guy, passing by, hesitated, stepped toward them, and said, "You need help, lady?"

Eric turned on the stranger in such a rage that he seemed to spit the words out rather than speak them: "Butt out, mister. This is my wife, and it's none of your goddamn business."

Rachael tried to wrench free of Eric's iron grip without success.

The bearded stranger said, "So she's your wife—that doesn't give you the right to hurt her."

Letting go of Rachael, Eric fisted his hands and turned more directly toward the intruder.

Rachael spoke quickly to her would-be Galahad, eager to defuse the situation. "Thank you, but it's all right. Really. I'm fine. Just a minor disagreement."

The young man shrugged and walked away, glancing back as he went.

The incident had at last made Eric aware that he was in danger of making a spectacle of himself, which a man of his high position and self-importance was loath to do. However, his temper had not cooled. His face was flushed, and his lips were bloodless. His eyes were the eyes of a dangerous man.

She said, "Be happy, Eric. You've saved millions of dollars and God knows how much more in attorneys' fees. You won. You didn't get to crush me or muddy my reputation in court the way you had hoped to, but you still won. Be happy with that."

With a seething hatred that shocked her, he said, "You stupid, rotten bitch. The day you walked out on me, I wanted to knock you down and kick your stupid face in. I should've done it. Wish I had. But I thought you'd come crawling back, so I didn't. I should've. Should've kicked your stupid face in." He raised his hand as if to slap her. But he checked himself even as she flinched from the expected blow. Furious, he turned and hurried away.

As she watched him go, Rachael suddenly understood that his sick desire to dominate everyone was a far more fundamental need than she'd realized. By stripping him of his power over her, by turning her back on both him and his money, she had not merely reduced him to an equal but had, in his eyes, *unmanned* him. That had to be the case, for nothing else explained the degree of his rage or his urge to commit violence, an urge he had barely controlled.

She had grown to dislike him intensely, if not hate him, and she had feared him a little, too. But until now, she had not been fully aware of the immensity and intensity of the rage within him. She had not realized how thoroughly dangerous he was.

Although the golden sunshine still dazzled her eyes and forced her to squint, although it still baked her skin, she felt a cold shiver pass through her, spawned by the realization that she'd been wise to leave Eric when she had—and perhaps fortunate to escape with no more physical damage than the bruises his fingers were certain to have left on her arm.

Watching him step off the sidewalk into the street, she was relieved to see him go. A moment later, relief turned to horror.

He was heading toward his black Mercedes, which was parked along the other side of the avenue. Perhaps he actually was blinded by his anger. Or maybe it was the brilliant June sunlight flashing on every shiny surface that interfered with his vision. Whatever the reason, he dashed across the southbound lanes of Main Street, which were at the moment without traffic, and kept on going into the northbound lanes, directly into the path of a city garbage truck that was doing forty miles an hour.

Too late, Rachael screamed a warning.

The driver tramped his brake pedal to the floorboards. But the shriek of the truck's locked wheels came almost simultaneously with the sickening sound of impact.

Eric was hurled into the air and thrown back into the southbound lanes as if by the concussion wave of a bomb blast. He crashed into the pavement and tumbled twenty feet, stiffly at first, then with a horrible looseness, as if he were constructed of string and old rags. He came to rest facedown, unmoving.

A southbound yellow Subaru braked with a banshee screech and a hard flat wail of its horn, halting only two feet from him. A Chevy, following too close, rammed into the back of the Subaru and pushed it within a few inches of the body.

Rachael was the first to reach Eric. Heart hammering, shouting his name, she dropped to her knees and, by instinct, put one hand to his neck to feel for a pulse. His skin was wet with blood, and her fingers slipped on the slick flesh as she searched desperately for the throbbing artery.

Then she saw the hideous depression that had reshaped his skull. His head had been staved in along the right side, above the torn ear, and all the way forward past the temple to the edge of his pale brow. His head was turned so she could see one eye, which was open wide, staring in shock, though sightless now. Many wickedly sharp fragments of bone must have been driven deep into his brain. Death had been instantaneous.

She stood up abruptly, tottering, nauseated. Dizzy, she might have fallen if the driver of the garbage truck had not grabbed hold of her, provided support, and escorted her around the side of the Subaru, where she could lean against the car.

"There was nothin' I could do," he said miserably.

"I know," she said.

"Nothin' at all. He run in front of me. Didn't look. Nothin' I could do."

At first Rachael had difficulty breathing. Then she realized she was absentmindedly scrubbing her blood-covered hand on her sundress, and the sight of those damp rusty-scarlet stains on the pastel-blue cotton made her breath come quicker, too quick. Hyperventilating, she slumped against the Subaru, closed her eyes, hugged herself, and clenched her teeth. She was determined not to faint. She strove to hold in each shallow breath as long as possible, and the very process of changing the rhythm of her breathing was a calming influence.

Around her she heard the voices of motorists who had left their cars in the snarl of stalled traffic. Some of them asked her if she was all right, and she nodded; others asked if she needed medical attention, and she shook her head—no.

If she had ever loved Eric, that love had been ground to dust beneath his heel. It had been a long time since she'd even *liked* him. Moments before the accident, he'd revealed a pure and terrifying hatred of her, so she supposed she should have been utterly unmoved by his death. Yet she was badly shaken. As she hugged herself and shivered, she was aware of a cold emptiness within, a hollow sense of loss that she could not quite understand. Not grief. Just . . . loss.

She heard sirens in the distance.

Gradually she regained control of her breathing.

Her shivering grew less violent, though it did not stop entirely.

The sirens grew nearer, louder.

She opened her eyes. The bright June sunshine no longer seemed clean and fresh. The darkness of death had passed through the day, and in its wake, the morning light had acquired a sour yellow cast that reminded her more of sulfur than of honey.

Red lights flashing, sirens dying, a paramedic van and a police sedan approached along the northbound lanes.

"Rachael?"

She turned and saw Herbert Tuleman, Eric's personal attorney, with whom she had met only minutes ago. She had always liked Herb, and he had liked her as well. He was a grandfatherly man with bushy gray eyebrows that were now drawn together in a single bar.

"One of my associates . . . returning to the office . . . saw it happen," Herbert said, "hurried up to tell me. My God."

"Yes," she said numbly.

"My God, Rachael."

"Yes."

"It's too . . . crazy."

"Yes."

"But . . ."

"Yes," she said.

And she knew what Herbert was thinking. Within the past hour, she had told them she would not fight for a large share of Eric's fortune but would settle for, proportionately, a pittance. Now, by virtue of the fact that Eric had no family and no children from his first marriage, the entire thirty million plus his currently unvalued stock in the company would almost certainly, by default, come into her sole possession.

◊ 2 ◊

SPOOKED

The hot, dry air was filled with the crackle of police radios, a metallic chorus of dispatchers' voices, and the smell of sun-softened asphalt.

The paramedics could do nothing for Eric Leben except convey his corpse to the city morgue, where it would lie in a refrigerated room until the medical examiner had time to attend to it. Because Eric had been killed in an accident, the law required an autopsy.

"The body should be available for release in twenty-four hours," one of the policemen had told Rachael.

While they had filled out a brief report, she had sat in the back of one of the patrol cars. Now she was standing in the sun again.

She no longer felt sick. Just numb.

They loaded the draped cadaver into the van. In spots, the shroud was dark with blood.

Herbert Tuleman felt obliged to comfort Rachael and repeatedly suggested that she return with him to his law office. "You need to sit down, get a grip on yourself," he said, one hand on her shoulder, his kindly face wrinkled with concern.

"I'm all right, Herb. Really, I am. Just a little shaken."

"Some cognac. That's what you need. I've got a bottle of Rémy Martin in the office bar."

"No, thank you. I guess it'll be up to me to handle the funeral, so I've got things to attend to."

The two paramedics closed the rear doors on the van and walked unhurriedly to the front of the vehicle. No need for sirens and flashing red emergency beacons. Speed would not help Eric now.

Herb said, "If you don't want brandy, then perhaps coffee. Or just come and sit with me for a while. I don't think you should get behind a wheel right away."

Rachael touched his leathery cheek affectionately. He was a weekend sailor, and his skin had been toughened and creased less by age than by his time upon the sea. "I appreciate your concern. I really do. But I'm fine. I'm almost ashamed of how well I'm taking it. I mean . . . I feel no grief at all."

He held her hand. "Don't be ashamed. He was my client, Rachael, so I'm aware that he was . . . a difficult man."

"Yes."

"He gave you no reason to grieve."

"It still seems wrong to feel . . . so little. Nothing."

"He wasn't just a difficult man, Rachael. He was also a fool for not recognizing what a jewel he had in you and for not doing whatever was necessary to make you want to stay with him."

"You're a dear."

"It's true. If it weren't *very* true, I wouldn't speak of a client like this, not even when he was . . . deceased."

The van, bearing the corpse, pulled away from the accident scene. Paradoxically, there was a cold, wintry quality to the way the summer sun glimmered in the white paint and in the polished chrome bumpers, making it appear as if Eric were being borne away in a vehicle carved from ice.

Herb walked with her, through the gathered onlookers, past his office building, to her red 560 SL. He said, "I could have someone drive Eric's car back to his house, put it in the garage, and leave the keys at your place."

"That would be helpful," she said.

When Rachael was behind the wheel, belted in, Herb leaned down to the window and said, "We'll have to talk soon about the estate."

"In a few days," she said.

"And the company."

"Things will run themselves for a few days, won't they?"

"Certainly. It's Monday, so shall we say you'll come see me Friday morning? That gives you four days to . . . adjust."

"All right."

"Ten o'clock?"

"Fine."

"You sure you're okay?"

"Yes," she said, and she drove home without incident, though she felt as though she were dreaming.

She lived in a quaint three-bedroom bungalow in Placentia. The neighborhood was solidly middle-class and friendly, and the house had loads of charm: French windows, window seats, coffered ceilings, a used-brick fireplace, and more. She'd made the down payment and moved a year ago, when she left Eric. Her house was far different from the place in Villa Park, which was set on an acre of manicured grounds and which boasted every luxury; however, she liked her cozy bungalow better than his Spanish-modern mansion, not merely because the scale seemed more human here but also because the Placentia house was not tainted by countless bad memories as was the house in Villa Park.

She took off her bloodstained blue sundress. She washed her hands and face, brushed her hair, and reapplied what little makeup she wore. Gradually the mundane task of grooming herself had a calming effect. Her hands stopped trembling. Although a hollow coldness remained at the core of her, she stopped shivering.

After dressing in one of the few somber outfits she owned—a charcoal-gray suit with a pale gray blouse, slightly too heavy for a hot summer day—she called Attison Brothers, a firm of prestigious morticians. Having ascertained that they could see her immediately, she drove directly to their imposing colonial-style funeral home in Yorba Linda.

She had never made funeral arrangements before, and she had never imagined that there would be anything amusing about the experience. But when she sat down with Paul Attison in his softly lighted, darkly paneled, plushly carpeted, uncannily quiet office and listened to him call himself a "grief counselor," she saw dark humor in the situation. The atmosphere was so meticulously somber and so self-consciously reverent that it was stagy. His proffered sympathy was oily yet ponderous, relentless and calculated, but surprisingly she found herself playing along with him, responding to his condolences and platitudes with clichés of her own. She felt as if she were an actor trapped in a bad play by an incompetent playwright, forced to deliver her wooden lines of dialogue because it was less embarrassing to persevere to the end of the third act than to stalk off the stage in the middle of the performance. In addition to identifying himself as a grief counselor, Attison referred to a casket as an "eternal bower." A suit of burial clothes, in which the corpse would be dressed, was called "the final raiments." Attison said "preparations for preservation" instead of "embalming," and "resting place" instead of "grave."

Although the experience was riddled with macabre humor, Rachael was not able to laugh even when she left the funeral home after two and a half hours and was alone in her car again. Ordinarily she had a special fondness for black humor, for laughter that mocked the grim, dark aspects of life. Not today. It was neither grief nor any kind of sadness that kept her in a gray and humorless mood. Nor worry about widowhood. Nor shock. Nor the morbid recognition of Death's lurking presence in even the sunniest day. For a while, as she tended to other details of the funeral, and later, at home once more, as she called Eric's friends and business associates to convey the news, she could not quite understand the cause of her unremitting solemnity.

Then, late in the afternoon, she could no longer fool herself. She knew that her mental state resulted from fear. She tried to deny what was coming, tried not to think about it, and she had some success at not thinking, but in her heart she knew. She knew.

She went through the house, making sure that all the doors and windows were locked. She closed the blinds and drapes.

◑   ◑

At five-thirty, Rachael put the telephone on the answering machine. Reporters had begun to call, wanting a few words with the widow of the Great Man, and she had no patience whatsoever for media types.

The house was a bit too cool, so she reset the air conditioner. But for the susurrant sound of cold air coming through the wall vents and the occasional single ring the telephone made before the machine answered it, the house was as silent as Paul Attison's gloom-shrouded office.

Today, deep silence was intolerable; it gave her the creeps. She switched on the stereo, tuned to an FM station playing easy-listening music. For a moment, she stood before the big speakers, eyes closed, swaying as she listened to Johnny Mathis singing "Chances Are." Then she turned up the volume so the music could be heard throughout the house.

In the kitchen, she cut a small piece of semisweet dark chocolate from a bar and put it on a white saucer. She opened a split of fine, dry champagne. She took the chocolate, the champagne, and a glass into the master bathroom.

On the radio, Sinatra was singing "Days of Wine and Roses."

Rachael drew a tub of water as hot as she could tolerate, added a drizzle of jasmine-scented oil, and undressed. Just as she was about to settle in to soak, the pulse of fear which had been beating quietly within her suddenly began to throb hard and fast. She tried to calm herself by closing her eyes and breathing deeply, tried telling herself that she was being childish, but nothing worked.

Naked, she went into the bedroom and got the .32-caliber pistol from the top drawer of the nightstand. She checked the magazine to be sure it was fully loaded. Switching off both safeties, she took the thirty-two into the bathroom and put it on the deep blue tile at the edge of the sunken tub, beside the champagne and chocolate.

Andy Williams was singing "Moon River."

Wincing, she stepped into the hot bath and settled down until the water had slipped most of the way up the slopes of her breasts. It stung at first. Then she became accustomed to the temperature, and the heat was good, penetrating to her bones and finally dispelling the chill that had plagued her ever since Eric had dashed in front of the truck almost seven and a half hours ago.

She nibbled at the candy, taking only a few shavings from the edge of the piece. She let them melt slowly on her tongue.

She tried not to think. She tried to concentrate on just the mindless pleasure of a good hot steep. Just drift. Just *be*.

She leaned back in the tub, savoring the taste of chocolate, relishing the scent of jasmine in the rising steam.

After a couple of minutes, she opened her eyes and poured a glass of champagne from the ice-cold bottle. The crisp taste was a perfect complement to the lingering trace of chocolate and to the voice of Sinatra crooning the nostalgic and sweetly melancholy lines of "It Was a Very Good Year."

For Rachael, this relaxing ritual was an important part of the day, perhaps the *most* important. Sometimes she nibbled at a small wedge of sharp cheese instead of chocolate and sipped a single glass of chardonnay instead of champagne. Sometimes it was an extremely cold bottle of dark beer—Heineken or Beck's—and a handful of the special plump peanuts that were sold by an expensive nut shop in Costa Mesa. Whatever her choice of the day, she consumed it with care and slow delight, in tiny bites and small sips, relishing every nuance of taste and scent and texture.

She was a "present-focused" person.

Benny Shadway, the man Eric had thought was Rachael's lover, said there were basically four types of people: past-, present-, future-, and omni-focused. Those focused primarily on the future had little interest in the past or present. They were often worriers, peering toward tomorrow to see what crisis or insoluble problem might be hurtling toward them—although some were shiftless dreamers rather than worriers, always looking ahead because they were unreasonably certain they were due for great good fortune of one kind or another. Some were also workaholics, dedicated achievers who believed that the future and opportunity were the same thing.

Eric had been such a one, forever brooding about and eagerly anticipating new challenges and conquests. He had been utterly bored with the past and impatient with the snail's pace at which the present sometimes crept by.

A present-focused person, on the other hand, expended most of his energy and interest in the joys and tribulations of the moment. Some present-focused types were merely sluggards, too lazy to prepare for tomorrow or even to contemplate it. Strokes of bad luck often caught them unaware, for they had difficulty accepting the possibility that the pleasantness of the moment might not go on forever. And when they found themselves mired in misfortune, they usually fell into ruinous despair, for they were incapable of embarking upon a course of action that would, at some point in the future, free them from their troubles. However, another type of present-focused person was the hard worker who could involve himself in the task at hand with a single-mindedness that made for splendid efficiency and craftsmanship. A first-rate cabinetmaker, for example, had to be a present-focused person, one who did not look forward impatiently to the final assembly and completion of a piece of furniture but who directed his attention entirely and lovingly to the meticulous shaping and finishing of each rung and arm of a chair, to each drawer face and knob and doorframe of a china hutch, taking his greatest satisfaction in the *process* of creation rather than in the culmination of the process.

Present-focused people, according to Benny, are more likely to find obvious solutions to problems than are other people, for they are not preoccupied with either what was or what might come to pass but only with what *is*. They are also the people most sensuously connected with the physical realities of life—therefore the most perceptive in some ways—and they most likely have more sheer pleasure and fun than any dozen past- or future-oriented citizens.

"You're the best kind of present-oriented woman," Benny had once told her over a Chinese dinner at Peking Duck. "You prepare for the future but never at the expense of losing touch with *now*. And you're so admirably able to put the past behind you."

She had said, "Ah, shut up and eat your moo goo gai pan."

Essentially, what Benny said was true. Since leaving Eric, Rachael had taken five courses in business management at a Pepperdine extension, for she intended to launch a small business. Perhaps a clothing store for upscale women. A place that would be dramatic and fun, the kind of shop that people talked about as not only a source of well-made clothes but an experience. After all, she'd attended UCLA, majoring in dramatic arts, and had earned her bachelor's degree just before meeting Eric at a university function; and though she had no interest in acting, she had real talent for costume and set design, which might serve her well in creating an unusual decor for a clothing store and in acquiring merchandise for sale. However, she had not yet gone so far as to commit herself to the acquisition of an M.B.A. degree nor to choosing a particular enterprise. Rooted in the present, she proceeded to gather knowledge and ideas, waiting patiently for the moment when her plans would simply . . . crystallize. As for the past—well, to dwell on yesterday's pleasures was to risk missing out on pleasures of the moment, and to dwell on past pains and tragedies was a pointless waste of energy and time.

Now, resting languorously in her steaming bath, Rachael drew a deep breath of the jasmine-scented air.

She hummed along softly with Johnny Mathis as he sang "I'll Be Seeing You."

She tasted the chocolate again. She sipped the champagne.

She tried to relax, to drift, to go with the flow and embrace the mellow mood in the best California tradition.

For a while she pretended to be completely at ease, and she did not entirely realize that her detachment was only pretense until the doorbell rang. The instant the bell sounded above the lulling music, she sat up in the water, heart hammering, and grabbed for the pistol with such panic that she knocked over her champagne glass.

When she had gotten out of the tub and put on her blue robe, she held the gun at her side, with the muzzle pointed at the floor, and walked slowly through the shadowy house to the front door. She was filled with dread at the prospect of answering the bell; at the same time, she was irresistibly drawn to the door as if in a trance, as if compelled by the mesmeric voice of a hypnotist.

She paused at the stereo to switch it off. The ensuing silence had an ominous quality.

In the foyer, with her hand upon the knob, she hesitated as the bell rang again. The front door had no window, no sidelights. She had been meaning to have a fish-eye security lens installed, through which she would be able to study the person on the doorstep, and now she ardently wished that she had not procrastinated. She stared at the dark oak before her, as if she might miraculously acquire the power to see through it and clearly identify the caller beyond. She was trembling.

She did not know why she faced the prospect of a visitor with such unmitigated dread.

Well, perhaps that was not exactly true. Deep down—or even not so deep—she knew why she was afraid. But she was reluctant to admit the source of her fear, as if admission would transform a horrible possibility into a deadly reality.

The bell rang again.

◦ 3 ◦

JUST VANISHED

While listening to news on the radio during the drive home from his office in Tustin, Ben Shadway heard about Dr. Eric Leben's sudden death. He wasn't sure how he felt. Shocked, yes. But he wasn't saddened, even though the world had lost a potentially great man. Leben had been brilliant, indisputably a genius, but he had also been arrogant, self-important, perhaps even dangerous.

Ben mostly felt relieved. He had been afraid that Eric, finally aware that he could never regain his wife, would harm her. The man hated to lose. There was a dark rage in him usually relieved by his obsessive commitment to his work, but it might have found expression in violence if he had felt deeply humiliated by Rachael's rejection.

Ben kept a cellular phone in his car—a meticulously restored 1956 Thunderbird, white with blue interior—and he immediately called Rachael. She had her answering machine on, and she did not pick up the receiver when he identified himself.

At the traffic light at the corner of Seventeenth Street and Newport Avenue, he hesitated, then turned left instead of continuing on to his own house in Orange Park Acres. Rachael might not be home right now, but she would get there eventually, and she might need support. He headed for her place in Placentia.

The June sun dappled the Thunderbird's windshield and made bright rippling patterns when he passed through the inconstant shadows of overhanging trees. He switched off the news and put on a Glenn Miller tape. Speeding through the California sun, with "String of Pearls" filling the car, he found it hard to believe that anyone could die on such a golden day.

◊　　◊

By his own system of personality classification, Benjamin Lee Shadway was primarily a past-focused man. He liked old movies better than new ones. De Niro, Streep, Gere, Field, Travolta, and Penn were of less interest to him than Bogart, Bacall, Gable, Lombard, Tracy, Hepburn, Cary Grant, William Powell, Myrna Loy. His favorite books were from the 1920s, 1930s, and 1940s: hard-boiled stuff by Chandler and Hammett and James M. Cain, and the early Nero Wolfe novels. His music of choice was from the swing era: Tommy and Jimmy Dorsey, Harry James, Duke Ellington, Glenn Miller, the incomparable Benny Goodman.

For relaxation, he built working models of locomotives from kits, and he collected all kinds of railroad memorabilia. There are no hobbies so reeking with nostalgia or more suited to a past-focused person than those dealing with trains.

He was not focused *entirely* on the past. At twenty-four, he had obtained a real-estate license, and by the time he was thirty-one, he had established his own brokerage. Now, at thirty-seven, he had six offices with thirty agents working under him. Part of the reason for his success was that he treated his employees and customers with a concern and courtesy that were old-fashioned and enormously appealing in the fast-paced, brusque, and plastic world of the present.

Lately, in addition to his work, there was one other thing that could distract Ben from railroads, old movies, swing music, and his general preoccupation with the past: Rachael Leben. Titian-haired, green-eyed, long-limbed, full-bodied Rachael Leben.

She was somehow both the girl next door and one of those elegant beauties to be found in any 1930s movie about high society, a cross between Grace Kelly and Carole Lombard. She was sweet-tempered. She was amusing. She was smart. She was everything Ben Shadway had ever dreamed about, and what he wanted to do was get in a time machine with her, travel back to 1940, take a private compartment on the Superchief, and cross the country by rail, making love for three thousand miles in time with the gently rocking rhythm of the train.

She'd come to his real-estate agency for help in finding a house, but the house had not been the end of it. They had been seeing each other frequently for five months. At first he had been fascinated by her in the same way any man might be fascinated by any exceptionally attractive woman, intrigued by the thought of what her lips would taste like and of how her body would fit against his, thrilled by the texture of her skin, the sleekness of her legs, the curve of hip and breast. However, soon after he got to know her, he found her sharp mind and generous heart as appealing as her appearance. Her intensely sensuous appreciation for the world around her was wondrous to behold; she could find as much pleasure in a red sunset or in a graceful configuration of shadows as in a hundred-dollar, seven-course dinner at the county's finest restaurant. Ben's lust had quickly turned to infatuation. And sometime within the past two months—he could not pinpoint the date—infatuation had turned to love.

Ben was relatively confident that Rachael loved him, too. They had not yet quite reached the stage where they could forthrightly and comfortably declare the true depth of their feelings for each other. But he felt love in the tenderness of her touch and in the weight of her gaze when he caught her looking secretly at him.

In love, they had not yet *made* love. Although she was a present-focused woman with the enviable ability to wring every last drop of pleasure from the moment, that did not mean she was promiscuous. She didn't speak bluntly of her feelings, but he sensed that she wanted to progress in small, easy steps. A leisurely romance provided plenty of time for her to explore and savor each new strand of affection in the steadily strengthening bond that bound them to each other, and when at last they succumbed to desire and surrendered to complete intimacy, sex would be all the sweeter for the delay.

He was willing to give her as much time as she required. For one thing, day by day he felt their need growing, and he derived a special thrill from contemplating the tremendous power and intensity of the lovemaking when they finally unleashed their desire. And through her, he had come to realize that they would be cheating themselves out of the more innocent pleasures of the moment if they rushed headlong through the early stages of courtship to satisfy a libidinal urge.

Also, as a man with an affinity for better and more genteel ages, Ben was old-fashioned about these matters and preferred not to jump straight into bed for quick and easy gratification. Neither he nor Rachael was a virgin, but he found it emotionally and spiritually satisfying— and erotic as hell—to wait until the many threads linking them had been woven tightly together, leaving sex for the last strand in the bond.

◊   ◊

He parked the Thunderbird in Rachael's driveway, beside her red 560 SL, which she had not bothered to put in the garage.

Thick bougainvillea, ablaze with thousands of red blossoms, grew up one wall of the bungalow and over part of the roof. With the help of a latticework frame, it formed a living green-and-scarlet canopy above the front stoop.

Ben stood in cool bougainvillea shadows, with the warm sun at his back, and rang the bell half a dozen times, growing concerned when Rachael took so long to respond.

Inside, music was playing. Suddenly, it was cut off.

When at last Rachael opened the door, she had the security chain in place, and she looked warily through the narrow gap. She smiled when she saw him, though it seemed as much a smile of nervous relief as of pleasure. "Oh, Benny, I'm so glad it's you."

She slipped the brass chain and let him in. She was barefoot, wearing a tightly belted silky blue robe—and carrying a gun.

Disconcerted, he said, "What're you doing with that?"

"I didn't know who it might be," she said, switching on the two safeties and putting the pistol on the small foyer table. Then, seeing his frown and realizing that her explanation was inadequate, she said, "Oh, I don't know. I guess I'm just . . . shaky."

"I heard about Eric on the radio. Just minutes ago."

She came into his arms. Her hair was partially damp. Her skin was sweet with the fragrance of jasmine, and her breath smelled of chocolate. He knew she must have been taking one of her long lazy soaks in the tub.

Holding her close, he felt her trembling. He said, "According to the radio, you were there."

"Yes."

"I'm sorry."

"It was horrible, Benny." She clung to him. "I'll never forget the sound of the truck hitting him. Or the way he bounced and rolled along the pavement." She shuddered.

"Easy," he said, pressing his cheek against her damp hair. "You don't have to talk about it."

"Yes, I do," she said. "I've got to talk it out if I'm ever going to get it off my mind."

He put a hand under her chin and tilted her lovely face up to him. He kissed her once, gently. Her mouth tasted of chocolate.

"Okay," he said. "Let's go sit down, and you can tell me what happened."

"Lock the door," she said.

"It's okay," he said, leading her out of the foyer.

She stopped and refused to move. "Lock the door," she insisted.

Puzzled, he went back and locked it.

She took the pistol from the foyer and carried it with her.

Something was wrong, something more than Eric's death, but Ben did not understand what it was.

The living room was shrouded in deep shadows, for she had drawn all the drapes. That was distinctly odd. Ordinarily she loved the sun and reveled in its warm caress with the languid pleasure of a cat sunning on a windowsill. He had never seen the drapes drawn in this house until now.

"Leave them closed," Rachael said when Ben started to unveil the windows.

She switched on a single lamp and sat in its amber glow, in the corner of a peach-colored sofa. The room was very modern, all in shades of peach and white with dark blue accents, polished bronze lamps, and a bronze-and-glass coffee table. In her blue robe she was in harmony with the decor.

She put the pistol on the table beside the lamp. Near to hand.

Ben retrieved her champagne and chocolate from the bathroom and brought them to her. In the kitchen, he got another cold split of champagne and a glass for himself.

When he joined her on the living-room sofa, she said, "It doesn't seem right. The champagne and chocolate, I mean. It looks as if I'm celebrating his death."

"Considering what a bastard he was to you, perhaps a celebration would be justified."

She shook her head adamantly. "No. Death is never a cause for celebration, Benny. No matter what the circumstances. Never."

But she unconsciously ran her fingertips back and forth along the pale, pencil-thin, barely visible three-inch scar that followed the edge of her delicate jawline on the right side of her face. A year ago, in one of his nastier moods, Eric had thrown a glass of Scotch at her. It had missed, hitting the wall and shattering, but a sharp fragment had caught her on the rebound, slicing her cheek, requiring fifteen expertly sewn little stitches to avoid a prominent scar. That was the day she finally walked out on him. Eric would never hurt her again. She had to be relieved by his death even if only on a subconscious level.

Pausing now and then to sip champagne, she told Ben about this morning's meeting in the attorney's office and about the subsequent altercation on the sidewalk when Eric took her by the arm and seemed on the verge of violence. She recounted the accident and the hideous condition of the corpse in vivid detail, as if she had to put every terrible, bloody image into words in order to be free of it. She told him about making the funeral arrangements as well, and as she spoke, her shaky hands gradually grew steadier.

He sat close, turned sideways to face her, with one hand on her shoulder. Sometimes he moved his hand to gently massage her neck or to stroke her copper-brown hair.

"Thirty million dollars," he said when she had finished, shaking his head at the irony of her getting everything when she had been willing to settle for so little.

"I don't really want it," she said. "I've half a mind to give it away. A large part of it, anyway."

"It's yours to do with as you wish," he said. "But don't make any decisions now that you'd regret later."

She looked down into the champagne glass that she held in both hands. Frowning worriedly, she said, "Of course, he'd be furious if I gave it away."

"Who?"

"Eric," she said softly.

Ben thought it odd that she should be concerned about Eric's disapproval. Obviously she was still shaken by events and not yet quite herself. "Give yourself time to adjust to the circumstances."

She sighed and nodded. "What time is it?"

He looked at his watch. "Ten minutes till seven."

"I called a lot of people earlier this afternoon and told them what happened, let them know about the funeral.

But there must be thirty or forty more to get in touch with. He had no close relatives—just a few cousins. And an aunt he loathed. Not many friends, either. He wasn't a man who cared much for friends, and he didn't have much talent for making them. But lots of business associates, you know. God, I'm not looking forward to the chore."

"I have my cellular phone in the car," Ben said. "I can help you call them. We'll get it done fast."

She smiled vaguely. "And just how would that look— the wife's boyfriend helping her contact the bereaved?"

"They don't have to know who I am. I'll just say I'm a friend of the family."

"Since I'm all that's left of the family," Rachael said, "I guess that wouldn't be a lie. You're my best friend in the world, Benny."

"More than just a friend."

"Oh, yes."

"Much more, I hope."

"I hope," she said.

She kissed him lightly and, for a moment, rested her head upon his shoulder.

◊   ◊

They contacted all of Eric's friends and business associates by eight-thirty, at which time Rachael expressed surprise that she was hungry. "After a day like this and everything that I saw . . . isn't it sort of hard-boiled of me to have an appetite?"

"Not at all," Ben said gently. "Life goes on, babe. The living have got to live. Fact is, I read somewhere that witnesses to sudden and violent death usually experience a sharp increase in all their appetites during the days and weeks that follow."

"Proving to themselves that they're alive."

"Trumpeting it."

She said, "I can't offer much of a dinner, I'm afraid. I have the makings of a salad. And we could cook up a pot of rigatoni, open a jar of Ragú sauce."

"A veritable feast fit for a king."

She brought the pistol with her to the kitchen and put it down on the counter near the microwave oven.

She had closed the Levolor blinds. Tight. Ben liked the view from those rear windows—the lushly planted backyard with its azalea beds and leafy Indian laurels, the property wall that was completely covered by a riotously bright tangle of red and yellow bougainvillea—and he reached for the control rod to open the slats.

"Please don't," she said. "I want . . . the privacy."

"No one can see in from the yard. It's walled and gated."

"Please."

He left the blinds as she wanted them.

"What are you afraid of, Rachael?"

"Afraid? But I'm not."

"The gun?"

"I told you—I didn't know who was at the door, and since it's been such an upsetting day . . ."

"Now you know it was me at the door."

"Yes."

"And you don't need a gun to deal with me. Just the promise of another kiss or two will keep me in line."

She smiled. "I guess I should put it back in the bedroom where it belongs. Does it make you nervous?"

"No. But I—"

"I'll put it away as soon as we've got dinner cooking," she said, but there was a tone in her voice that made her statement seem less like a promise than a delaying tactic.

Intrigued and somewhat uneasy, he opted for diplomacy and said no more for the moment.

She put a big pot of water on the stove to boil while he emptied the jar of Ragú into a smaller pot. Together, they chopped lettuce, celery, tomatoes, onions, and black olives for the salad.

They talked as they worked, primarily about Italian food. Their conversation was not quite as fluid and natural as usual, perhaps because they were trying too hard to be lighthearted and to put all thoughts of death aside.

Rachael mostly kept her eyes on the vegetables as she prepared them, bringing her characteristically effortless concentration to the task, rendering each rib of celery into slices that were all precisely the same width, as if symmetry were a vital element in a successful salad and would enhance the taste.

Distracted by her beauty, Ben looked at her as much as at the culinary work before him. She was almost thirty, appeared to be twenty, yet had the elegance and poise of a grande dame who'd had a long lifetime in which to learn the angles and attitudes of perfect gracefulness. He never grew tired of looking at her. It wasn't just that she, excited him. By some magic that he could not understand, the sight of her also relaxed him and made him feel that all was right with the world and that he, for the first time in his often lonely life, was a complete man with a hope of lasting happiness.

Impulsively he put down the knife with which he had been slicing a tomato, took the knife from her hand and set it aside, turned her toward him, pulled her against him, slipped his arms around her, and kissed her deeply. Now her soft mouth tasted of champagne instead of chocolate. She still smelled faintly of jasmine, though beneath that fragrance was her own clean and appealing scent. He moved his hands slowly down her back, tracing the concave arc to her bottom, feeling the firm and exquisitely sculpted contours of her body through the silky robe. She was wearing nothing underneath. His warm hands grew hot—then much hotter—as the heat of her was transmitted through the material to his own flesh.

She clung to him for a moment with what seemed like desperation, as if she were shipwrecked and he were a raft in a tossing sea. Her body was stiff. Her hands clutched tensely, fingers digging into him. Then, after a moment, she relaxed against him, and her hands began to move over his back and shoulders and upper arms, testing and kneading his muscles. Her mouth opened wider, and their kiss became hungrier. Her breathing quickened.

He could feel her full breasts pressing against his chest. As if with a will and intention of their own, his hands moved more urgently in exploration of her.

The phone rang.

Ben remembered at once that they had forgotten to put it on the answering machine again when they had finished contacting people with the news of Eric's death and funeral, and in confirmation it rang again, stridently.

"Damn," Rachael said, pulling back from him.

"I'll get it."

"Probably another reporter."

He took the call on the wall phone by the refrigerator, and it was not a reporter. It was Everett Kordell, chief medical examiner for the city of Santa Ana, phoning from the morgue. A serious problem had arisen, and he needed to speak to Mrs. Leben.

"I'm a family friend," Ben said. "I'm taking all calls for her."

"But I've got to speak to her personally," the medical examiner insisted. "It's urgent."

"Surely you can understand that Mrs. Leben has had a difficult day. I'm afraid you'll simply have to deal with me."

"But she's got to come downtown," Kordell said plaintively.

"Downtown? You mean to the morgue? Now?"

"Yes. Right away."

"Why?"

Kordell hesitated. Then: "This is embarrassing and frustrating, and I assure you that it'll all be straightened out sooner or later, probably very soon, but . . . well, Eric Leben's corpse is missing."

Certain that he'd misunderstood, Ben said, "Missing?"

"Well . . . perhaps misplaced," Everett Kordell said nervously.

"Perhaps?"

"Or perhaps . . . stolen."

Ben got a few more details, hung up, and turned to Rachael.

She was hugging herself, as if in the grip of a sudden chill. "The morgue, you said?"

He nodded. "The damn incompetent bureaucrats have apparently lost the body."

Rachael was very pale, and her eyes had a haunted look. But, curiously, she did not appear to be surprised by the startling news.

Ben had the strange feeling that she had been waiting for this call all evening.

◊ 4 ◊

DOWN WHERE THEY KEEP THE DEAD

To Rachael, the condition of the medical examiner's office was evidence that Everett Kordell was an obsessive-compulsive personality. No papers, books, or files cluttered his desk. The blotter was new, crisp, unmarked. The pen-and-pencil set, letter opener, letter tray, and silver-framed pictures of his family were precisely arranged. On the shelves behind his desk were two hundred or three hundred books in such pristine condition and so evenly placed that they almost appeared to be part of a painted backdrop. His diplomas and two anatomy charts were hung on the walls with an exactitude that made Rachael wonder if he checked their alignment every morning with ruler and plumb line.

Kordell's preoccupation with neatness and orderliness was also evident in his appearance. He was tall and almost excessively lean, about fifty, with a sharp-featured ascetic face and clear brown eyes. Not a strand of his graying, razor-cut hair was out of place. His long-fingered hands were singularly spare of flesh, almost skeletal. His white shirt looked as if it had been laundered only five minutes ago, and the straight creases in each leg of his dark brown trousers were so sharp they almost glinted in the fluorescent light.

When Rachael and Benny were settled in a pair of dark pine chairs with forest-green leather cushions, Kordell went around the desk to his own chair. "This is most distressing to me, Mrs. Leben—to add this burden to what you've already been through today. It's quite inexcusable. I apologize again and extend my deepest sympathies, though I know nothing I say can make the matter any less disturbing. Are you all right? Can I get you a glass of water or anything?"

"I'm okay," Rachael said, though she could not remember ever feeling worse.

Benny reached out and squeezed her shoulder reassuringly. Sweet, reliable Benny. She was so glad he was with her. At five eleven and a hundred fifty pounds, he was not physically imposing. With brown hair, brown eyes, and a pleasing but ordinary face, he seemed like a man who would vanish in a crowd and be virtually invisible at a party. But when he spoke in that soft voice of his, or moved with his uncanny grace, or just looked hard at you, his sensitivity and intelligence were instantly discernible. In his own quiet way, he had the impact of a lion's roar. Everything would be easier with Benny at her side, but she worried about getting him involved in this.

To the medical examiner, Rachael said, "I just want to understand what's happened."

But she was afraid that she understood more than Kordell.

"I'll be entirely candid, Mrs. Leben," Kordell said. "No point in being otherwise." He sighed and shook his head as if he still had difficulty believing such a screwup had happened. Then he blinked, frowned, and turned to Benny. "You're not Mrs. Leben's attorney, by any chance?"

"Just an old friend," Benny said.

"Really?"

"I'm here for moral support."

"Well, I'm hoping we can avoid attorneys," Kordell said.

"I've absolutely no intention of retaining legal counsel," Rachael assured him.

The medical examiner nodded glumly, clearly unconvinced of her sincerity. He said, "I'm not ordinarily in the office at this hour." It was nine-thirty Monday night. "When work unexpectedly backs up and it's necessary to schedule late autopsies, I leave them to one of the assistant medical examiners. The only exceptions are when the deceased is a prominent citizen or the victim of a particularly bizarre and complex homicide. In that case, when there's certain to be a lot of heat involved— the media and politicians, I mean—then I prefer not to put the burden on my subordinates, and if a night autopsy is unavoidable, I stay after hours. Your husband was, of course, a very prominent citizen."

As he seemed to expect a response, she nodded. She didn't trust herself to speak. Fear had risen and fallen in her ever since she had received the news of the body's disappearance, and at the moment it was at high tide.

"The body was delivered to the morgue and logged in at 12:14 this afternoon," Kordell continued. "Because we were already behind schedule and because I had a speaking engagement this afternoon, I ordered my assistants to proceed with the cadavers in the order of their log entries, and I arranged to handle your husband's body myself at 6:30 this evening." He put his fingertips to his temples, massaging lightly and wincing as if merely recounting these events had given him an excruciating headache. "At that time, when I'd prepared the autopsy chamber, I sent an assistant to bring Dr. Leben's body from the morgue . . . but the cadaver couldn't be found."

"Misplaced?" Benny asked.

"That's rarely happened during my tenure in this office," Kordell said with a brief flash of pride. "And on those few occasions when a cadaver has been misplaced—sent to a wrong autopsy table, stored in the wrong drawer, or left on a gurney with an improper ID tag—we've always located it within five minutes."

"But tonight you couldn't find it," Benny said.

"We looked for nearly an hour. Everywhere. Everywhere," Kordell said with evident distress. "It makes no sense. No sense whatsoever. Given our procedures, it's an impossibility."

Rachael realized that she was clutching the purse in her lap so tightly that her knuckles were sharp and white. She tried to relax her hands, folded them. Afraid that either Kordell or Benny would suddenly read a fragment of the monstrous truth in her unguarded eyes, she closed them and lowered her head, hoping the men would think she was simply reacting to the dreadful circumstances that had brought them here.

From within her private darkness, Rachael heard Benny say, "Dr. Kordell, is it possible that Dr. Leben's body was released in error to a private mortuary?"

"We'd been informed earlier today that the Attison Brothers' firm was handling funeral arrangements, so of course we called them when we couldn't find the body. We suspected they'd come for Dr. Leben and that a day employee of the morgue had mistakenly released the cadaver without authorization, prior to autopsy. But they tell us they never came to collect, were in fact waiting for a call from us, and don't have the deceased."

"What I meant," Benny said, "was that perhaps Dr. Leben's body was released in error to another mortician who had come to collect someone else."

"That, of course, was another possibility that we explored with, I assure you, considerable urgency. Subsequent to the arrival of Dr. Leben's body at 12:14 this afternoon, four other bodies were released to private mortuaries. We sent employees to all of those funeral homes to confirm the identity of the cadavers and to make sure none of them was Dr. Leben. None of them was."

"Then what do you suppose has happened to him?" Benny asked.

Eyes closed, Rachael listened to their macabre conversation in darkness, and gradually it began to seem as if she were asleep and as if their voices were the echoey phantom voices of characters in a nightmare.

Kordell said, "Insane as it seems, we were forced to conclude the body's been stolen."

In her self-imposed blackness, Rachael tried unsuccessfully to block out the gruesome images that her imagination began to supply.

"You've contacted the police?" Benny asked the medical examiner.

"Yes, we brought them into it as soon as we realized theft was the only remaining explanation. They're downstairs right now, in the morgue, and of course they want to speak with you, Mrs. Leben."

A soft rhythmic rasping noise was coming from Everett Kordell's direction. Rachael opened her eyes. The medical examiner was nervously sliding his letter opener in and out of its protective sheath. Rachael closed her eyes again.

Benny said, "But are your security measures so inadequate that someone could waltz right in off the street and steal a corpse?"

"Certainly not," Kordell said. "Nothing like this has happened before. I tell you, it's inexplicable. Oh, yes, a determined person might be clever enough to find a way through our security, but it wouldn't be an easy job. Not easy at all."

"But not impossible," Benny said.

The rasping noise stopped. From the new sounds that followed, Rachael figured that the medical examiner must be compulsively rearranging the silver-framed photographs on his desk.

She concentrated on that image to counteract the mad scenes that her darkly cunning imagination had conjured up for her horrified consideration.

Everett Kordell said, "I'd like to suggest that both of you accompany me to the morgue downstairs, so you can see firsthand exactly how tight our security is and how very difficult it would be to breach it. Mrs. Leben? Do you feel strong enough to take a tour of the facility?"

Rachael opened her eyes. Both Benny and Kordell were watching her with concern. She nodded.

"Are you sure?" Kordell asked, rising and coming out from behind his desk. "Please understand that I'm not insisting on it. But it would make me feel ever so much better if you would let me show you how careful we are, how responsibly we fulfill our duties here."

"I'm okay," she said.

Picking at a tiny piece of dark lint that he had just spotted on his sleeve, the medical examiner headed toward the door.

As Rachael got up from her chair and turned to follow Kordell, she was swept by a wave of dizziness. She swayed.

Benny took her arm, steadied her. "This tour isn't necessary."

"Yes," she said grimly. "Yes, it is. I've got to see. I've got to know."

Benny looked at her strangely, and she couldn't meet his eyes. He knew something was wrong, something more than Eric's death and disappearance, but he didn't know what. He was unabashedly curious.

Rachael had intended to conceal her anxiety and keep him out of this hideous affair. But deceit was not one of her talents, and she knew he had been aware of her fear from the moment he'd stepped into her house. The dear man was both intrigued and concerned, staunchly determined to stay by her side, which was exactly what she didn't want, but she couldn't help that now. Later, she would have to find a way to get rid of Benny because, much as she needed him, it was not fair to drag him into this mess, not fair to put his life in jeopardy the way hers was.

Right now, however, she had to see where Eric's battered corpse had lain, for she hoped a better understanding of the circumstances surrounding the body's disappearance would allay her worst fears. She needed all her strength for the tour of the morgue.

They left the office and went down where the dead waited.

◑　◑

The broad, tile-floored, pale gray corridor ended at a heavy metal door. A white-uniformed attendant sat at a desk in an alcove to the right, this side of the door. When he saw Kordell approaching with Rachael and Benny, he got up and fished a set of bright jangling keys from the pocket of his uniform jacket.

"This is the only interior entrance to the morgue," Kordell said. "The door is always locked. Isn't that right, Walt?"

"Absolutely," the attendant said. "You did want to go in, Dr. Kordell?"

"Yes."

When Walt slid the key into the lock, Rachael saw a tiny spark of static electricity.

Kordell said, "There's an attendant—Walt or someone else—on duty at this desk twenty-four hours a day, seven days a week. No one can get in without his assistance. And he keeps a registry of all visitors."

The wide door was unlocked, and Walt was holding it open for them. They went inside, where the cool air smelled of antiseptics and of something unidentifiable that was less pungent and less clean. The door closed behind them with a faint creak of hinges that seemed to echo through Rachael's bones. The lock engaged automatically with a hollow thunk.

Two sets of double doors, both open, led to big rooms on both sides of the morgue corridor. A fourth windowless metal portal, like that through which they had just entered, lay at the far end of the chilly hallway.

"Now please let me show you the only exterior entrance, where the morgue wagons and the morticians' vehicles pull up," Kordell said, leading the way toward the distant barrier.

Rachael followed him, though just being in this repository of the dead, where Eric had so recently lain, made her knees weak and broke her out in a sweat along the back of her neck and all over her scalp.

"Wait a second," Benny said. He turned to the door through which they had come, pushed down on the bar handle, and opened it, startling Walt, who was just returning to his desk on the other side. Letting the heavy door fall shut again, Benny looked at Kordell and said, "Although it's always locked from the outside, it's always open from the inside?"

"That's right, of course," Kordell said. "It'd be too much trouble to have to summon the attendant to be let out as well as in. Besides, we can't risk having someone accidentally locked in here during an emergency. Fire or earthquake, for example."

Their footsteps echoed eerily off the highly polished tile floor as they continued along the corridor toward the exterior service door at the far end. When they passed the two large rooms, Rachael saw several people in the chamber on the left, standing and moving and talking softly in a glare of crisp, cold fluorescent light. Morgue workers wearing hospital whites. A fat man in beige slacks and a beige-yellow-red-green madras sports jacket. Two men in dark suits looked up as Rachael walked by.

She also saw three dead bodies: still, shrouded shapes lying on stainless-steel gurneys.

At the end of the hall, Everett Kordell pushed open the wide metal door. He stepped outside and beckoned them.

Rachael and Benny followed. She expected to find an alleyway beyond, but though they had left the building, they were not actually outside. The exterior morgue door opened onto one of the underground levels of an adjacent multistory parking garage. It was the same garage in which she'd parked her 560 SL just a short while ago, though she'd left it a few levels above this one.

The gray concrete floor, the blank walls, and the thick pillars holding up the gray concrete ceiling made the subterranean garage seem like an immense, starkly modernistic, Western version of a pharaoh's tomb. The sodium-vapor ceiling lights, widely spaced, provided a jaundice-yellow illumination that Rachael found fitting for a place that served as an antechamber to the hall of the dead.

The area around the morgue entrance was a no-parking zone. But a score of cars were scattered farther out in the vast room, half in the crepuscular bile-yellow light and half in purple-black shadows that had the velvet texture of a casket lining.

Looking at the cars, she had the extraordinary feeling that something was hiding among them, watching.

Watching her in particular.

Benny saw her shiver, and he put his arm around her shoulders.

Everett Kordell closed the heavy morgue door, then tried to open it, but the bar handle could not be depressed. "You see? It locks automatically. Ambulances, morgue wagons, and hearses drive down that ramp from the street and stop here. The only way to get in is to push this button." He pushed a white button in the wall beside the door. "And speak into this intercom." He brought his mouth close to a wire speaker set flush in the concrete. "Walt? This is Dr. Kordell at the outer door. Will you buzz us back in, please?"

Walt's voice came from the speaker. "Right away, sir."

A buzzer sounded, and Kordell was able to open the door again.

"I assume the attendant doesn't just open for anyone who asks to be let in," Benny said.

"Of course not," Kordell said, standing in the open doorway. "If he's sure he recognizes the voice and if he knows the person, he buzzes him through. If he doesn't recognize the voice, or if it's someone new from a private mortuary, or if there's any reason to be suspicious, the attendant walks through the corridor that we just walked, all the way from the front desk, and he inspects whoever's seeking admittance."

Rachael had lost all interest in these details and was concerned only about the gloom-mantled garage around them, which provided a hundred excellent hiding places.

Benny said, "At that point the attendant, not expecting violence, could be overpowered, and the intruder could force his way inside."

"Possibly," Kordell said, his thin face drawing into a sharp scowl. "But that's never happened."

"The attendants on duty today swear that they logged in everyone who came and went—and allowed only authorized personnel to enter?"

"They swear," Kordell said.

"And you trust them all?"

"Implicitly. Everyone who works here is aware that the bodies in our custody are the remains of other people's loved ones, and we know we have a solemn—even sacred—responsibility to protect those remains while we're in charge of them. I think that's evident in the security arrangements I've just shown you."

"Then," Benny said, "someone either had to pick the lock—"

"It's virtually unpickable."

"Or someone slipped into the morgue while the outer door was open for legitimate visitors, hid out, waited until he was the only living person inside, then spirited Dr. Leben's body away."

"Evidently yes. But it's so unlikely that—"

Rachael said, "Could we go back inside, please?"

"Certainly," Kordell said at once, eager to please. He stepped out of her way.

She returned to the morgue corridor, where the cold air carried a faint foul smell beneath the heavy scent of pine disinfectant.

◊ 5 ◊

UNANSWERED
QUESTIONS

In the holding room where the cadavers awaited autopsy, the air was even colder than in the morgue's corridor. Glimmering strangely in all metal surfaces, the stark fluorescent light imparted a wintry sheen to the stainless-steel gurneys and to the bright stainless-steel handles and hinges on the cabinets along the walls. The glossy white enamel finish of the chests and cabinets, though surely no thicker than an eighth of an inch, had a curiously deep—even bottomless—appearance similar to the mysterious, lustrous depth of a landscape of moon-washed snow.

She tried not to look at the shrouded bodies and refused to think about what might lie in some of the enormous cabinet drawers.

The fat man in the madras jacket was Ronald Tescanet, an attorney representing the city's interests. He had been called away from dinner to be on hand when Rachael spoke with the police and, afterward, to discuss the disappearance of her husband's body. His voice was too mellifluous, almost greasy, and he was so effusively sympathetic that his condolences poured forth like warm oil from a bottle. While the police questioned

Rachael, Tescanet paced in silence behind them, frequently smoothing his thick black hair with his plump
white hands, each of which was brightened by two gold
and diamond rings.

As she had suspected, the two men in dark suits were
plainclothes police. They showed Rachael their ID cards
and badges. Refreshingly, they did not burden her with
unctuous sympathy.

The younger of the two, beetle-browed and burly, was
Detective Hagerstrom. He said nothing at all, leaving the
questioning entirely to his partner. He stood unmoving,
like a rooted oak, in contrast to the attorney's ceaseless
roaming. He watched with small brown eyes that gave
Rachael the impression of stupidity at first; but after a
while, on reconsideration, she realized that he possessed
a higher than average intelligence which he kept carefully veiled.

She worried that somehow Hagerstrom, by virtue of
a cop's almost magical sixth sense, would pierce her
deception and see the knowledge that she was concealing. As inconspicuously as possible, she avoided meeting
his gaze.

The older cop, Detective Julio Verdad, was a small
man whose complexion was the shade of cinnamon and
whose black eyes had a vague trace of purple like the
skins of ripe plums. He was a sharp dresser: a well-
tailored blue suit, dark but summerweight; a white shirt
that might have been silk, with French cuffs held together by gold and pearl cuff links; a burgundy necktie with
a gold tie chain instead of a clip or tack; dark burgundy
Bally loafers.

Although Verdad spoke in clipped sentences and was
almost curt, his voice was unfailingly quiet and gentle.
The contrast between his lulling tone and his brisk manner was disconcerting. "You've seen their security, Mrs.
Leben."

"Yes."

"And are satisfied?"

"I suppose."

To Benny, Verdad said, "You are?"

"Ben Shadway. An old friend of Mrs. Leben's."

"Old school friend?"

"No."

"A friend from work?"

"No. Just a friend."

The plum-dark eyes gleamed. "I see." To Rachael, Verdad said, "I have a few questions."

"About what?"

Instead of answering at once, Verdad said, "Like to sit down, Mrs. Leben?"

Everett Kordell said, "Yes, of course, a chair," and both he and the fat attorney, Ronald Tescanet, hurried to draw one away from a corner desk.

Seeing that no one else intended to sit, concerned about being placed in a position of inferiority with the others peering down at her, Rachael said, "No, thank you. I'll stand. I can't see why this should take very long. I'm certainly in no mood to linger here. What is it you want to ask me, anyway?"

Verdad said, "An unusual crime."

"Body snatching," she said, pretending to be both baffled and sickened by what had happened. The first emotion had to be feigned; the second was more or less genuine.

"Who might have done it?" Verdad asked.

"I've no idea."

"You know no one with a reason?"

"Someone with a motive for stealing Eric's body? No, of course not," she said.

"He had enemies?"

"In addition to being a genius in his field, he was a successful businessman. Geniuses often unwittingly arouse jealousy on the part of colleagues. And, inevitably, some people envied his wealth. And some felt he'd . . . wronged them on his climb up the ladder."

"*Had* he wronged people?"

"Yes. A few. He was a driven man. But I strongly doubt that any of his enemies are the type to take satisfaction from a revenge as pointless and macabre as this."

"He was not just driven," Verdad said.

"Oh?"

"He was ruthless."

"Why do you say that?"

"I've read about him," Verdad said. "Ruthless."

"All right, yes, perhaps. And difficult. I won't deny it."

"Ruthlessness makes passionate enemies."

"You mean so passionate that body snatching would make sense?"

"Perhaps. I'll need the names of his enemies, people who might have reason to hold a grudge."

"You can get that information from the people he worked with at Geneplan," she said.

"His company? But you're his wife."

"I knew very little about his business. He didn't want me to know. He had very strong opinions about . . . my proper place. Besides, for the past year I've been separated from him."

Verdad looked surprised, but somehow Rachael sensed that he had already done some background work and knew what she was telling him.

"Divorcing?" he asked.

"Yes."

"Bitter?"

"On his part, yes."

"So this explains it."

"Explains what?" she asked.

"Your utter lack of grief."

She had begun to suspect that Verdad was twice as dangerous as the silent, motionless, watchful Hagerstrom. Now she was sure of it.

"Dr. Leben treated her abominably," Benny said in her defense.

"I see," Verdad said.

"She had no reason to grieve for him," Benny said.

"I see."

Benny said, "You're acting as if this is a murder case, for God's sake."

"Am I?" Verdad said.

"You're treating her as if she's a suspect."

"Do you think so?" Verdad asked quietly.

"Dr. Leben was killed in a freak accident," Benny said, "and if anyone was at fault, it was Leben himself."

"So we understand."

"There were at least a dozen witnesses."

"Are you Mrs. Leben's attorney?" Verdad inquired.

"No, I told you—"

"Yes, the old friend," Verdad said, making his point subtly.

"If you were an attorney, Mr. Shadway," Ronald Tescanet said, stepping forward so quickly that his jowls trembled, "you'd understand why the police have no choice but to pursue this unpleasant line of questioning. They must, of course, consider the possibility that Dr. Leben's body was stolen to prevent an autopsy. To *hide* something."

"How melodramatic," Benny said scornfully.

"But conceivable. Which would mean that his death was not as cut-and-dried as it appeared to be," Tescanet said.

"Exactly," Verdad said.

"Nonsense," Benny said.

Rachael appreciated Benny's determination to protect her honor. He was unfailingly sweet and supportive. But she was willing to let Verdad and Hagerstrom regard her as a possible murderess or at least an accomplice to murder. She was incapable of killing anyone, and Eric's death was entirely accidental, and in time that would be clear to the most suspicious homicide detective. But while Hagerstrom and Verdad were busy satisfying themselves on those points, they would not be free to pursue other avenues of inquiry closer to the terrible truth. They were in the process of dragging their own red herring across the trail, and she would not take offense at their misdirected suspicion as long as it kept them baying after the wrong scent.

She said, "Lieutenant Verdad, surely the most logical explanation is that, in spite of Dr. Kordell's assertions, the body has simply been misplaced." Both the stork-thin medical examiner and Ronald Tescanet protested. She quietly but firmly cut them off. "Or maybe it was kids playing an elaborate joke. College kids. An initiation rite of some sort. They've been known to do worse."

"I think I already know the answer to this question," Benny said. "But is it possible that Eric Leben was not dead after all? Could his condition have been misjudged? Is it possible that he walked out of here in a daze?"

"No, no, no!" Tescanet said, blanching and suddenly sweating in spite of the cold air.

"Impossible," Kordell said simultaneously. "I saw him. Massive head injuries. No vital signs whatsoever."

But this off-the-wall theory seemed to intrigue Verdad. He said, "Didn't Dr. Leben receive medical attention immediately after the accident?"

"Paramedics," Kordell said.

"Highly trained, reliable men," Tescanet said, mopping his doughy face with a handkerchief. He had to be doing rapid mental arithmetic right now, calculating the difference between the financial settlement that might be necessitated by a morgue screwup and the far more major judgment that might be won against the city for the incompetence of its paramedics. "They would never, regardless of circumstances, *never* mistakenly pronounce a man dead when he wasn't."

"One—there was no heartbeat whatsoever," Kordell said, counting the proofs of death on fingers so long and supple that they would have served him equally well if he had been a concert pianist instead of a pathologist. "The paramedics had a perfectly flat line on the small EKG unit in their van. Two—no respiration. Three—steadily falling body temperature."

"Unquestionably dead," Tescanet murmured.

Lieutenant Verdad now regarded the attorney and the chief medical examiner with the same flat expression and hawkish eyes that he had turned on Rachael. He probably didn't think Tescanet and Kordell—or the paramedics—were covering up malpractice or malfeasance. But his nature and experience ensured his willingness to suspect anyone of anything at any time, given even the poorest reason for suspicion.

Scowling at Tescanet's interruption, Everett Kordell continued, "Four—there was absolutely no perceptible electrical activity in the brain. We have an EEG machine here in the morgue. We frequently use it in accident cases as a final test. That's a safety procedure I've instituted since taking this position. Dr. Leben was attached to the EEG the moment he was brought in, and we could find no perceptible brain waves. I was present. I saw the graph. Brain death. If there is any single, universally accepted standard for declaring a man dead, it's when the attending physician encounters a condition of full and irreversible cardiac arrest coupled with brain death. The pupils of Dr. Leben's eyes wouldn't dilate in bright light. And no respiration. With all due respect, Mrs. Leben, your husband was as dead as any man I've ever seen, and I will stake my reputation on that."

Rachael had no doubt that Eric had been dead. She had seen his sightless, unblinking eyes as he lay on the blood-spattered pavement. She had seen, too well, the deep concavity running from behind his ear all the way to the curve of his brow: the crushed and splintered bone. However, she was thankful that Benny had unwittingly confused things and had given the detectives yet another false trail to pursue.

She said, "I'm sure he was dead. I've no doubt of it. I saw him at the scene of the accident, and I know there could have been no mistaken diagnosis."

Kordell and Tescanet looked immeasurably relieved.

With a shrug, Verdad said, "Then we discard the hypothesis."

But Rachael knew that, once the possibility of misdiagnosis had been planted in the cops' minds, they would expend time and energy in the exploration of it, which was all that mattered. Delay. That was the name of the game. Delay, stall, confuse the issue. She needed time to confirm her own worst suspicions, time to decide what must be done to protect herself from various sources of danger.

Lieutenant Verdad led Rachael past the three draped bodies and stopped with her at an empty gurney that was bedecked with rumpled shrouds. On it lay a thick paper tag trailing two strands of plastic-coated wire. The tag was crumpled.

"That's all we've got to go on, I'm afraid. The cart that the corpse once occupied and the ID tag that was once tied to its foot." Only inches from Rachael, the detective looked hard at her, his intense dark eyes as flat and unreadable as his face. "Now, why do you suppose a body snatcher, whatever his motivation, would take the time to untie the tag from the dead man's toe?"

"I don't have the slightest idea," she said.

"The thief would be worried about getting caught. He'd be in a hurry. Untying the tag would take precious seconds."

"It's crazy," she said shakily.

"Yes, crazy," Verdad said.

"But then the whole thing's crazy."

"Yes."

She stared down at the wrinkled and vaguely stained shroud, thinking of how it had wrapped her husband's cold and naked cadaver, and she shuddered uncontrollably.

"Enough of this," Benny said, putting his arm around her for warmth and support. "I'm getting you the hell out of this place."

◊   ◊

Everett Kordell and Ronald Tescanet accompanied Rachael and Benny to the elevator in the parking garage, continuing to make a case for the morgue's and the city's complete lack of culpability in the body's disappearance. They were not convinced by her repeated assurances that she did not intend to sue anyone. There were so many things for her to think and worry about that she had neither the energy nor the inclination to persuade them that her intentions were benign. She just wanted to be rid of them so she could get on with the urgent tasks that awaited her.

When the elevator doors closed, finally separating her and Benny from the lean pathologist and the corpulent attorney, Benny said, "If it was me, I think I *would* sue them."

"Lawsuits, countersuits, depositions, legal strategy meetings, courtrooms—boring, boring, boring," Rachael said. She opened her purse as the elevator rose.

"Verdad is a cool son of a bitch, isn't he?" Benny said.

"Just doing his job, I guess." Rachael took the thirty-two pistol out of her purse.

Benny, watching the light move on the board of numbers above the lift's doors, did not immediately see the gun. "Yeah, well, he could do his job with a little more compassion and a little less machinelike efficiency."

They had risen one and a half floors from the basement. On the indicator panel, the 2 was about to light. Her Mercedes was one level farther up.

Benny had wanted to bring his car, but Rachael had insisted on driving her own. As long as she was behind the wheel, her hands were occupied and her attention was partly on the road, so she couldn't become morbidly preoccupied with the frightening situation in which she found herself. If she had nothing to do but brood about recent developments, she would very likely lose the tenuous self-control she now possessed. She had to remain busy in order to hold terror at arm's length and stave off panic.

They reached the second floor and kept going up.

She said, "Benny, step away from the door."

"Huh?" He looked down from the lightboard, blinked in surprise when he saw the pistol. "Hey, where the hell did you get that?"

"Brought it from home."

"Why?"

"Please step back. Quickly now, Benny," she said shakily, aiming at the doors.

Still blinking, confused, he got out of the way. "What's going on? You're not going to shoot anybody."

Her thunderous heartbeat was so loud that it muffled his voice and made it sound as if he were speaking to her from a distance.

They arrived at the third floor.

The indicator board went *ping!* The 3 lighted. The elevator stopped with a slight bounce.

"Rachael, answer me. What is this?"

She did not respond. She had gotten the gun after leaving Eric. A woman alone ought to have a gun . . . especially after walking out on a man like him. As the doors rolled open, she tried to remember what her pistol instructor had said: Don't jerk the trigger; squeeze it slowly, or you'll pull the muzzle off target and miss.

But no one was waiting for them, at least not in front of the elevator. The gray concrete floor, walls, pillars, and ceiling looked like those in the basement from which they'd begun their ascent. The silence was the same, too: sepulchral and somehow threatening. The air was less dank and far warmer than it had been three levels below, though it was every bit as still. A few of the ceiling lights were burned out or broken, so a greater number of shadows populated the huge room than had darkened the basement, and they seemed deeper as well, better suited for the complete concealment of an attacker, though perhaps her imagination painted them blacker than they really were.

Following her out of the elevator, Benny said, "Rachael, who are you afraid of?"

"Later. Right now let's just get the hell out of here."

"But—"

"Later."

Their footsteps echoed and reechoed hollowly off the concrete, and she felt as if they were walking not through an ordinary parking garage in Santa Ana but through the chambers of an alien temple, under the eye of an unimaginably strange deity.

At that late hour, her red 560 SL was one of only three cars parked on the entire floor. It stood alone, gleaming, a hundred feet from the elevator. She walked directly toward it, circled it warily. No one crouched on the far side. Through the windows, she could see that no one was inside, either. She opened the door, got in quickly. As soon as Benny climbed in and closed his door, she hit the master lock switch, started the engine, threw the car in gear, popped the emergency brake, and drove too fast toward the exit ramp.

As she drove, she engaged the safeties on her pistol and, with one hand, returned it to her purse.

When they reached the street, Benny said, "Okay, now tell me what this cloak-and-dagger stuff is all about."

She hesitated, wishing she had not brought him this far into it. She should have come to the morgue alone. She'd been weak, needed to lean on him, but now if she didn't break her dependency on him, if she drew him further into it, she would without doubt be putting his life in jeopardy. She had no right to endanger him.

"Rachael?"

She stopped at a red traffic light at the intersection of Main Street and Fourth, where a hot summer wind blew a few scraps of litter into the center of the crossroads and spun them around for a moment before sweeping them away.

"Rachael?" Benny persisted.

A shabbily dressed derelict stood at the corner, only a few feet away. He was filthy, unshaven, and drunk. His nose was gnarled and hideous, half eaten away by melanoma. In his left hand he held a wine bottle imperfectly concealed in a paper bag. In his grubby right paw he gripped a broken alarm clock—no glass covering the face of it, the minute hand missing—as if he thought he possessed a great treasure. He stooped down, peered in at her. His eyes were fevered, blasted.

Ignoring the derelict, Benny said, "Don't withdraw from me, Rachael. What's wrong? Tell me. I can help."

"I don't want to get you involved," she said.

"I'm already involved."

"No. Right now you don't know anything. And I really think that's best."

"You promised—"

The traffic light changed, and she tramped the accelerator so suddenly that Benny was thrown against his seat belt and cut off in midsentence.

Behind them, the drunk with the clock shouted: *"I'm Father Time!"*

Rachael said, "Listen, Benny, I'll take you back to my place so you can get your car."

"Like hell."

"Please let me handle this myself."

"Handle *what*? What's going on?"

"Benny, don't interrogate me. Just please don't do that. I've got a lot to think about, a lot to do . . ."

"Sounds like you're going somewhere else tonight."

"It doesn't concern you," she said.

"Where are you going?"

"There're things I've got to . . . check out. Never mind."

Getting angry now, he said, "You going to shoot someone?"

"Of course not."

"Then why're you packing a gun?"

She didn't answer.

He said, "You got a permit for a concealed weapon?"

She shook her head. "A permit, but just for home use."

He glanced behind to see if anyone was near them, then leaned over from his seat, grabbed the steering wheel, and jerked it hard to the right.

The car whipped around with a screech of tires, and she hit the brakes, and they slid sideways six or eight yards, and when she tried to straighten the wheel he grabbed it again, and she shouted at him to stop it, and he let go of the wheel, which spun through her hands for a moment, but then she was firmly in control once more, pulled to the curb, stopped, looked at him, said, "What are you—crazy?"

"Just angry."

"Let it be," she said, staring out at the street.

"I want to help you."

"You can't."

"Try me. Where do you have to go?"

She sighed. "Just to Eric's place."

"His house? In Villa Park? Why?"

"I can't tell you."

"After his house, where?"

"Geneplan. His office."

"Why?"

"I can't tell you that, either."

"Why not?"

"Benny, it's dangerous. It could get violent."

"So what the fuck am I—porcelain? Crystal? Shit, woman, do you think I'm going to fly into a million goddamn pieces at the tap of a goddamn finger?"

She looked at him. The amber glow of the streetlamp came through only her half of the windshield, leaving him in darkness, but his eyes shone in the shadows. She said, "My God, you're furious. I've never heard you use that kind of language before."

He said, "Rachael, do we have something or not? I think we have something. Special, I mean."

"Yes."

"You really think so?"

"You know I do."

"Then you can't freeze me out of this. You can't keep me from helping you when you need help. Not if we're to go on from here."

She looked at him, feeling very tender toward him, wanting more than anything to bring him into her confidence, to have him as her ally, but involving him would be a rotten thing to do. He was right now thinking what kind of trouble she might be in, his mind churning furiously, listing possibilities, but nothing he could imagine would be half as dangerous as the truth. If he knew the truth, he might not be so eager to help, but she dared not tell him.

He said, "I mean, you know I'm a pretty old-fashioned guy. Not very with it by most standards. Staid in some ways. Hell, half the guys in California real estate wear white cords and pastel blazers when they go to work on a summer day like this, but I don't feel comfortable in less than a three-piece suit and wing tips. I may be the last guy in a real-estate office who even knows what a goddamn vest *is*. So when someone like me sees the woman he cares about in trouble, he has to help, it's the only thing he *can* do, the plain old-fashioned thing, the right thing, and if she won't let him help, then that's pretty much a slap in the face, an affront to all his values, a rejection of what he *is*, and no matter how much he likes her, he's got to walk, it's as simple as that."

She said, "I never heard you make a speech before."

"I never had to before."

Both touched and frustrated by his ultimatum, Rachael closed her eyes and leaned back in the seat, unable to decide what to do. She kept her hands on the steering wheel, gripping it tightly, for if she let go, Benny would be sure to see how badly her hands were shaking.

He said, "Who are you afraid of, Rachael?"

She didn't answer.

He said, "You know what happened to his body, don't you?"

"Maybe."

"You know who took it."

"Maybe."

"And you're afraid of them. Who are they, Rachael? For God's sake, who would do something like that—and why?"

She opened her eyes, put the car in gear, and pulled away from the curb. "Okay, you can come along with me."

"To Eric's house, the office? What're we looking for?"

"That," she said, "I'm not prepared to tell you."

He was silent for a moment. Then he said, "Okay. All right. One step at a time. I can live with that."

She drove north on Main Street to Katella Avenue, east on Katella to the expensive community of Villa Park, into the hills toward her dead husband's estate. In the upper reaches of Villa Park, the big houses, many priced well over a million dollars, were less than half visible beyond screens of shrubbery and the gathered cloaks of night. Eric's house, looming beyond a row of enormous Indian laurels, seemed darker than any other, a cold place even on a June night, the many windows like sheets of some strange obsidian that would not permit the passage of light in either direction.

◊ **6** ◊

THE TRUNK

The long driveway, made of rust-red Mexican paving tiles, curved past Eric Leben's enormous Spanish-modern house before finally turning out of sight to the garages in back. Rachael parked in front.

Although Ben Shadway delighted in authentic Spanish buildings with their multiplicity of arches and angles and deep-set leaded windows, he was no fan of Spanish *modern*. The stark lines, smooth surfaces, big plate-glass windows, and total lack of ornamentation might seem stylish and satisfyingly clean to some, but he found such architecture boring, without character, and perilously close to the cheap-looking stucco boxes of so many southern California neighborhoods.

Nevertheless, as he got out of the car and followed Rachael down a dark Mexican-tile walkway, across an unlighted veranda where yellow-flowering succulents and bloom-laden white azaleas glowed palely in enormous clay pots, to the front door of the house, Ben was impressed by the place. It was massive—certainly ten thousand square feet of living space—set on expansive, elaborately landscaped grounds. From the property, there was a view of most of Orange County to the west, a vast carpet of light stretching fifteen miles to the pitch-black ocean; in daylight, in clear weather, one could probably see all the way to Catalina. In spite of the spareness of the architecture, the Leben house reeked of wealth. To Ben, the crickets singing in the bushes even sounded different from those that chirruped in more modest neighborhoods, less shrill and more melodious, as if their minuscule brains encompassed awareness of—and respect for—their surroundings.

Ben had known that Eric Leben was a very rich man, but somehow that knowledge had had no impact until now. Suddenly he sensed what it meant to be worth tens of millions of dollars. Leben's wealth pressed on Ben, like a very real weight.

Until he was nineteen, Ben Shadway had never given much thought to money. His parents were neither rich enough to be preoccupied with investments nor poor enough to worry about paying next month's bills, nor had they much ambition, so wealth—or lack of it—had not been a topic of conversation in the Shadway household. However, by the time Ben completed two years of military service, his primary interest was money: making it, investing it, accumulating ever-larger piles.

He did not love money for its own sake. He did not even care all that much for the finer things that money could buy; imported sports cars, pleasure boats, Rolex watches, and two-thousand-dollar suits held no great appeal for him. He was happier with his meticulously restored 1956 Thunderbird than Rachael was with her new Mercedes, and he bought his suits off the rack at Harris & Frank. Some men loved money for the power it gave them, but Ben was no more interested in exercising power over others than he was in learning Swahili.

To him, money was primarily a time machine that would eventually allow him to do a lot of traveling back through the years to a more appealing age—the 1920s, 1930s, and 1940s, which held so much interest for him. Thus far, he had worked long hours with a few days off. But he intended to build the company into one of the top real-estate powerhouses in Orange

County within the next five years, then sell out and take a capital gain large enough to support him comfortably for most—if not the rest—of his life. Thereafter, he could devote himself almost entirely to swing music, old movies, the hard-boiled detective fiction he loved, and his miniature trains.

Although the Great Depression extended through more than a third of the period to which Ben was attracted, it seemed to him like a far better time than the present. During the twenties, thirties, and forties, there had been no terrorists, no end-of-the-world atomic threat, no street crime to speak of, no frustrating fifty-five-mile-per-hour speed limit, no polyester or lite beer. Television, the moron box that is the curse of modern life, was not a major social force by the end of the forties. Currently, the world seemed a cesspool of easy sex, pornography, illiterate fiction, witless and graceless music. The second, third, and fourth decades of the century were so fresh and innocent by comparison with the present that Ben's nostalgia sometimes deepened into a melancholy longing, into a profound desire to have been born before his own time.

Now, as the respectful crickets offered trilling songs to the otherwise peaceful silence of the Leben estate, as a warm wind scented with star jasmine blew across the sea-facing hills and through the long veranda, Ben could almost believe that he had, in fact, been transported back in time to a more genteel, less hectic age. Only the architecture spoiled the halcyon illusion.

And Rachael's pistol.

That spoiled things, too.

She was an extraordinarily easygoing woman, quick to laugh and slow to anger, too self-confident to be easily frightened. Only a very real and very serious threat could compel her to arm herself.

Before getting out of the car, she had withdrawn the gun from her purse and had clicked off the safeties. She warned Ben to be alert and cautious, though she refused to say exactly what it was that he should be alert to and cautious of. Her dread was almost palpable, yet she declined to share her worry and thus relieve her mind; she jealously guarded her secret as she had done all evening.

He suppressed his impatience with her—not because he had the forbearance of a saint but simply because he had no choice but to let her proceed with her revelations at her own pace.

At the door of the house, she fumbled with her keys, trying to find the lock and keyhole in the gloom. When she had walked out a year ago, she'd kept her house key because she'd thought she would need to return later to collect some of her belongings, a task that had become unnecessary when Eric had everything packed and sent to her along with, she said, an infuriatingly smug note expressing his certainty that she would soon realize how foolish she had been and seek reconciliation.

The cold, hard scrape of key metal on lock metal gave rise to an unfortunate image in Ben's mind: a pair of murderously sharp and gleaming knives being stropped against each other.

He noticed a burglar-alarm box with indicator lights by the door, but the system was evidently not engaged because none of the bulbs on the panel was lit.

While Rachael continued to poke at the lock with the key, Ben said, "Maybe he had the locks changed after you moved out."

"I doubt it. He was *so* confident that I'd move back in with him sooner or later. Eric was a very confident man."

She found the keyhole. The key worked. She opened the door, nervously reached inside, snapped on the lights in the foyer, and went into the house with the pistol held out in front of her.

Ben followed, feeling as if the male and female roles had been wrongly reversed, feeling as if he ought to have the gun, feeling a bit foolish when you came right down to it.

The house was perfectly still.

"I think we're alone," Rachael said.

"Who did you expect to find?" he asked.

She did not answer.

Although she had just expressed the opinion that they were alone, she advanced with her pistol ready.

They went slowly from room to room, turning on every light, and each new revelation of the interior made the house more imposing. The rooms were large, high-ceilinged, white-walled, airy, with Mexican-tile floors and lots of big windows; some had massive fireplaces of either stone or ceramic tile; a few boasted oak cabinets of superb craftsmanship. A party for two hundred guests would not have strained the capacity of the living room and adjacent library.

The furniture was as starkly modern and functional as the rather forbidding architecture. The upholstered white sofas and chairs were utterly free of ornamentation. Coffee tables, end tables, and all the occasional tables were also quite plain, finished in mirror-bright high-gloss enamel, some black and some white.

The only color and drama were provided by an eclectic group of paintings, antiques, and objets d'art. The bland decor was intended to serve as an unobtrusive backdrop against which to display those items of surpassing quality and value, each of which was artfully illuminated by indirect lighting or tightly focused overhead minispots. Over one fireplace was a tile panel of birds by William de Morgan, which had been done (Rachael said) for Czar Nicholas I. Here, a blazing Jackson Pollock canvas. There, a Roman torso carved from marble, dating to the first century B.C. The ancient was intermixed with the new in wildly unconventional but striking arrangements. Here, a nineteenth-century Kirman panel recording the lives of the greatest shahs of Persia. Here, a bold Mark Rothko canvas featuring only broad bands of color. There, a pair of Lalique crystal-deer consoles, each holding an exquisite Ming vase. The effect was both breathtaking and jarring—and altogether more like a museum than a real home.

Although he had known Rachael was married to a wealthy man, and although he had known that she had become a very wealthy widow as of this morning, Ben had given no thought to what her wealth might mean to their relationship. Now her new status impinged upon him like an elbow in his side, making him uncomfortable. *Rich.* Rachael was very damn rich. For the first time, that thought had meaning for him.

He realized he'd need to sit down and think about it at length, and he would need to talk with her forthrightly about the influence of so much money, about the changes for better and worse that it might cause between them. However, this was neither the time nor the place to pursue the matter, and he decided to put it out of his mind for the moment. That was not easy. A fortune in tens of millions was a powerful magnet relentlessly drawing the mind regardless of how many other urgent matters required attention.

"You lived here six years?" he asked disbelievingly as they moved through the cool sterile rooms, past the precisely arranged displays.

"Yes," she said, relaxing slightly as they roamed deeper into the house without encountering a threat of any kind. "Six long years."

As they inspected the white vaulted chambers, the place began to seem less like a house and more like a great mass of ice in which some primeval catastrophe had embedded scores of gorgeous artifacts from another, earlier civilization.

He said, "It seems . . . forbidding."

"Eric didn't care about having a real home—a cozy, livable home, I mean. He never was much aware of his surroundings anyway. He lived in the future, not the present. All he wanted of his house was that it serve as a monument to his success, and that's what you see here."

"I'd expect to see your touch—your sensual style— everywhere, *somewhere,* but it's nowhere in sight."

"Eric allowed no changes in decor," she said.

"And you could live with that?"

"I did, yes."

"I can't picture you being happy in such a chilly place."

"Oh, it wasn't that bad. Really, it wasn't. There *are* many amazingly beautiful things here. Any one of them can occupy hours of study . . . contemplation . . . and provide great pleasure, even spiritual pleasure."

He always marveled at how Rachael routinely found the positive aspect of even difficult circumstances. She wrung every drop of enjoyment and delight from a situation and did her best to ignore the unpleasant aspects. Her present-focused, pleasure-oriented personality was an effective armor against the vicissitudes of life.

At the rear of the ground floor, in the billiards room that looked out upon the swimming pool, the largest object on display was an intricately carved, claw-footed, late-nineteenth-century billiards table that boasted teak rails inlaid with semiprecious stones.

"Eric never played," Rachael said. "Never held a cue stick in his hands. All he cared about was that the table is one of a kind and that it cost more than thirty thousand dollars. The overhead lights aren't positioned to facilitate play; they're aimed to present the table to its best advantage."

"The more I see of this place, the better I understand him," Ben said, "but the less able I am to grasp why you ever married him."

"I was young, unsure of myself, perhaps looking for the father figure that'd always been missing in my life. He was so calm. He had such tremendous self-assurance. In him, I saw a man of power, a man who could carve out a niche for himself, a ledge on the mountainside where I could find stability, safety. At the time, I thought that was all I wanted."

Implicit in those words was the admission that her childhood and adolescence had been difficult at best, confirming a suspicion Ben had harbored for months. She seldom spoke of her parents or of her school years, and Ben believed that those formative experiences had been so negative as to leave her with a loathing for the past, a distrust of the uncertain future, and a defensive ability to focus intently upon whatever great or meager joys the moment offered.

He wanted to pursue that subject now, but before he could say anything, the mood abruptly changed. A sense of imminent danger had hung heavy in the air upon their entrance, then had faded as they progressed from one deserted white room to another with the growing conviction that no intruder lurked within the house. Rachael had stopped pointing the pistol ahead of her and had been holding it at her side with the muzzle aimed at the floor. But now the threatening atmosphere clouded the air again when she spotted three distinct fingerprints and a portion of a palmprint on one arm of a sofa, etched into the snowy fabric in a burgundy-dark substance which, on closer inspection, looked as if it might be blood.

She crouched beside the sofa, peering closely at the prints, and Ben saw her shiver. In a tremulous whisper she said, "Been here, damn it. I was afraid of this. Oh, God. Something's happened here." She touched one finger to the ugly stain, instantly snatched her hand away, and shuddered. "Damp. My God, it's *damp*."

"*Who's* been here?" Ben asked. "What's happened?"

She stared at the tip of her finger, the one with which she had touched the stain, and her face was distorted with horror. Slowly she raised her eyes and looked at Ben, who had stooped beside her, and for a moment he thought her terror had reached such a peak that she was prepared, at last, to tell him everything and seek his help. But after a moment he could see the resolve and self-control flooding back into her gaze and into her lovely face.

She said, "Come on. Let's check out the rest of the house. And for God's sake, be careful."

He followed her as she resumed her search. Again she held the pistol in front of her.

In the huge kitchen, which was nearly as well equipped as that of a major restaurant, they found broken glass scattered across the floor. One pane had been smashed out of the French door that opened onto the patio.

"An alarm system's no good if you don't use it," Ben said. "Why would Eric go off and leave a house like this unprotected?"

She didn't answer.

He said, "And doesn't a man like him have servants in residence?"

"Yes. A nice live-in couple with an apartment over the garage."

"Where are they? Wouldn't they have heard a break-in?"

"They're off Monday and Tuesday," she said. "They often drive up to Santa Barbara to spend the time with their daughter's family."

"Forced entry," Ben said, lightly kicking a shard of glass across the tile floor. "Okay, now hadn't we better call the police?"

She merely said, "Let's look upstairs." As the sofa had been stained with blood, so her voice was stained with anxiety. But worse: there was a bleakness about her, a grim and sombrous air, that made it easy to believe she might never laugh again.

The thought of Rachael without laughter was unbearable.

They climbed the stairs with caution, entered the upstairs hall, and checked out the second-floor rooms with the wariness they might have shown if unraveling a mile of tangled rope with the knowledge that a poisonous serpent lay concealed in the snarled line.

At first nothing was out of order, and they discovered nothing untoward—until they entered the master bedroom, where all was chaos. The contents of the walk-in closet—shirts, slacks, sweaters, shoes, suits, ties, and more—lay in a torn and tangled mess. Sheets, a white quilted spread, and feather-leaking pillows were strewn across the floor. The mattress had been heaved off the springs, which had been knocked halfway off the frame. Two black ceramic lamps were smashed, the shades ripped and then apparently stomped. Enormously valuable paintings had been wrenched from the walls and slashed to ribbons, damaged beyond repair. Of a pair of graceful Klismos-style chairs, one was upended, and the other had been hammered against a wall until it had gouged out big chunks of plaster and was itself reduced to splintered rubble.

Ben felt the skin on his arms puckering with gooseflesh, and an icy current quivered along the back of his neck.

Initially he thought that the destruction had been perpetrated by someone engaged upon a methodical search for something of value, but on taking a second look, he realized that such was not the case. The guilty party had unquestionably been in a blind rage, violently trashing the bedroom with malevolent glee or in a frenzy of hatred. The intruder had been someone possessed of considerable strength and little sanity. Someone strange. Someone infinitely dangerous.

With a recklessness evidently born of fear, Rachael plunged into the adjacent bathroom, one of only two places in the house that they had not yet searched, but the intruder was not there, either. She stepped back into the bedroom and surveyed the ruins, shaky and pale.

"Breaking and entering, now vandalism," Ben said. "You want me to call the cops, or should you do it?"

She did not reply but entered the last of the unsearched places, the enormous walk-in closet, returning a moment later, scowling. "The wall safe's been opened and emptied."

"Burglary too. Now we've got to call the cops, Rachael."

"No," she said. The bleakness that had hung about her like a gray and sodden cloak now became a specific presence in her gaze, a dull sheen in those usually bright green eyes.

Ben was more alarmed by that dullness than he had been by her fear, for it implied fading hope. Rachael, *his* Rachael, had never seemed capable of despair, and he couldn't bear to see her in the grip of that emotion.

"No cops," she said.

"Why not?" Ben said.

"If I bring the cops into it, I'll be killed for sure."

He blinked. "What? Killed? By the police? What on earth do you mean?"

"No, not by the cops."

"Then who? Why?"

Nervously chewing on the thumbnail of her left hand, she said, "I should never have brought you here."

"You're stuck with me. Rachael, really now, isn't it time you told me more?"

Ignoring his plea, she said, "Let's check the garage, see if one of the cars is missing," and she dashed from the room, leaving him no choice but to hurry after her with feeble protests.

◊   ◊

A white Rolls-Royce. A Jaguar sedan the same deep green as Rachael's eyes. Then two empty stalls. And in the last space, a dusty, well-used, ten-year-old Ford with a broken radio antenna.

Rachael said, "There should be a black Mercedes 560 SEL." Her voice echoed off the walls of the long garage. "Eric drove it to our meeting with the lawyers this morning. After the accident . . . after Eric was killed, Herb Tuleman—the attorney—said he'd have the car driven back here and left in the garage. Herb is reliable. He always does what he says. I'm sure it was returned. And now it's gone."

"Car theft," Ben said. "How long does the list of crimes have to get before you'll agree to calling the cops?"

She walked to the last stall, where the battered Ford was parked in the harsh bluish glare of a fluorescent ceiling strip. "And this one doesn't belong here at all. It's not Eric's."

"It's probably what the burglar arrived in," Ben said. "Decided to swap it for the Mercedes."

With obvious reluctance, with the pistol raised, she opened one of the Ford's front doors, which squeaked, and looked inside. "Nothing."

He said, "What did you expect?"

She opened one of the rear doors and peered into the back seat.

Again there was nothing to be found.

"Rachael, this silent sphinx act is irritating as hell."

She returned to the driver's door, which she had opened first. She opened it again, looked in past the wheel, saw the keys in the ignition, and removed them.

"Rachael, damn it."

Her face was not simply troubled. Her grim expression looked as if it had been carved in flesh that was really stone and would remain upon her visage from now until the end of time.

He followed her to the trunk. "What are you looking for now?"

At the back of the Ford, fumbling with the keys, she said, "The intruder wouldn't have left this here if it could be traced to him. A burglar wouldn't leave such an easy clue. No way. So maybe he came here in a stolen car that *couldn't* be traced to him."

Ben said, "You're probably right. But you're not going to find the registration slip in the trunk. Let's try the glove compartment."

Slipping a key into the trunk lock, she said, "I'm not looking for the registration slip."

"Then what?"

Turning the key, she said, "I don't really know. Except . . ."

The lock clicked. The trunk lid popped up an inch.

She opened it all the way.

Inside, blood was puddled thinly on the floor of the trunk.

Rachael made a faint mournful sound.

Ben looked closer and saw that a woman's blue high-heeled shoe was on its side in one corner of the shallow compartment. In another corner lay a woman's eyeglasses, the bridge of which was broken, one lens missing and the other lens cracked.

"Oh, God," Rachael said, "he not only stole the car. He killed the woman who was driving it. Killed her and stuffed the body in here until he had a chance to dispose of it. And now where will it end? Where will it end? Who will stop him?"

Badly shocked by what they'd found, Ben was nevertheless aware that when Rachael said "him," she was talking about someone other than an unidentified burglar. Her fear was more specific than that.

◦ 7 ◦

NASTY
LITTLE GAMES

Two snowflake moths swooped around the overhead fluorescent light, batting against the cool bulbs, as if in a frustrated suicidal urge to find the flame. Their shadows, greatly enlarged, darted back and forth across the walls, over the Ford, across the back of the hand that Rachael held to her face.

The metallic odor of blood rose out of the open trunk of the car. Ben took a step backward to avoid the noxious scent.

He said, "How did you know?"

"Know what?" Rachael asked, eyes still closed, head still bowed, coppery red-brown hair falling forward and half concealing her face.

"You knew what you might find in the trunk. How?"

"No. I didn't know. I was half afraid I'd find . . . something. Something else. But not this."

"Then what *did* you expect?"

"Maybe something worse."

"Like what?"

"Don't ask."

"I have asked."

The soft bodies of the moths tapped against the fire-filled tubes of glass above. *Tap-tap-tick-tap.*

Rachael opened her eyes, shook her head, started walking away from the battered Ford. "Let's get out of here."

He grabbed her by the arm. "We have to call the cops now. And you'll have to tell them whatever it is you know about what's going on here. So you might as well tell me first."

"No police," she said, either unwilling or unable to look at him.

"I was ready to go along with you on that. Until now."

"No police," she insisted.

"But someone's been killed!"

"There's no body."

"Christ, isn't the blood enough?"

She turned to him and finally met his eyes. "Benny, please, please, don't argue with me. There's no time to argue. If that poor woman's body were in the trunk, it might be different, and we might be able to call the cops, because with a body they'd have something to work on and they'd move a lot faster. But without a body to focus on, they'll ask a lot of questions, endless questions, and they won't believe the answers I could give them, so they'll waste a lot of time. But there's none to waste because soon there're going to be people looking for me . . . dangerous people."

"Who?"

"If they aren't already looking for me. I don't think they could've learned that Eric's body is missing, not yet, but if they have heard about it, they'll be coming here. We've got to go."

"Who?" he demanded exasperatedly. "Who are they? What are they after? What do they want? For God's sake, Rachael, let me in on it."

She shook her head. "Our agreement was that you could come with me but that I wasn't going to answer questions."

"I made no such promises."

"Benny, damn it, my *life* is on the line."

She was serious; she really meant it; she was desperately afraid for her life, and that was sufficient to break Ben's resolve and make him cooperate. Plaintively he said, "But the police could provide protection."

"Not from the people who may be coming after me."

"You make it sound as if you're being pursued by demons."

"At least."

She quickly embraced him, kissed him lightly on the mouth.

She felt good in his arms. He was badly shaken by the thought of a future without her.

Rachael said, "You're terrific. For wanting to stand by me. But go home now. Get out of it. Let me handle things myself."

"Not very damn likely."

"Then don't interfere. Now let's *go*."

Pulling away from him, she headed back across the five-car garage toward the door that led into the house.

A moth dropped from the light and fluttered against his face, as if his feelings for Rachael were, at the moment, brighter than the fluorescent bulbs. He batted it away.

He slammed the lid on the Ford's trunk, leaving the wet blood to congeal and the gruesome smell to thicken.

He followed Rachael.

At the far end of the garage, near the door that led into the house through the laundry room, she stopped, staring down at something on the floor. When Ben caught up with her, he saw some clothes that had been discarded in the corner, which neither he nor she had noticed when they had entered the garage. There were a pair of soft white vinyl shoes with white rubber soles and heels, wide white laces. A pair of baggy pale green cotton pants with a drawstring waist. And a loose short-sleeve shirt that matched the pants.

Looking up from the clothes, he saw that Rachael's face was no longer merely pale and waxen. She appeared to have been dusted with ashes. Gray. Seared.

Ben looked down at the suit of clothes again. He realized it was an outfit of the sort surgeons wore when they went into an operating theater, what they called hospital whites. Hospital whites had once actually been white, but these days they were usually this soft shade of green. However, not only surgeons wore them. Many other hospital employees preferred the same basic uniform. Furthermore, he had seen the assistant pathologists and attendants dressed in exactly the same kind of clothes at the morgue, only a short while ago.

Rachael drew a deep hissing breath through clenched teeth, shook herself, and went into the house.

Ben hesitated, staring intently at the discarded pair of shoes and rumpled clothes. Riveted by the soft green hue. Half mesmerized by the random patterns of gentle folds and creases in the material. His mind spinning. His heart pounding. Breathlessly considering the implications.

When at last he broke the spell and hurried after Rachael, Ben discovered that sweat had popped out all over his face.

◑   ◑

Rachael drove much too fast to the Geneplan building in Newport Beach. She handled the car with considerable skill, but Ben was glad to have a seat belt. Having ridden with her before, he knew she enjoyed driving even more than she enjoyed most other things in life; she was exhilarated by speed, delighted by the SL's maneuverability. But tonight she was in too much of a hurry to take any pleasure from her driving skill, and although she was not exactly reckless, she took some turns at such high speed and changed lanes so suddenly that she could not be accused of timidity.

He said, "Are you in some kind of trouble that rules out turning to the police? Is that it?"

"Do you mean—am I afraid the cops would get something on me?"

"Are you?"

"No," she said without hesitation, in a tone that seemed devoid of deception.

" 'Cause if somehow you've gotten in deep with the wrong kind of people, it's never too late to turn back."

"Nothing like that."

"Good. I'm glad to hear it."

The backsplash of dim light from the dashboard meters and gauges was just bright enough to softly illuminate her face but not bright enough to reveal the tension in her or the unhealthy grayness that fear had brought to her complexion. She looked now as Ben always thought of her when they were separated: breathtaking.

In different circumstances, with a different destination, the moment would have been like something from a perfect dream or from one of those great old movies. After all, what could be more thrilling or exquisitely erotic than being with a gorgeous woman in a sleek sports car, barreling through the night toward some romantic destination, where they could forsake the snug contours of bucket seats for cool sheets, the excitement of high-speed travel having primed them for fiercely passionate lovemaking.

She said, "I've done nothing wrong, Benny."

"I didn't really think you had."

"You implied . . ."

"I had to ask."

"Do I look like a villain to you?"

"You look like an angel."

"There's no danger I'll land in jail. The worst that can happen to me is that I'll wind up a victim."

"Damned if I'll let that happen."

"You're really very sweet," she said. She glanced away from the road and managed a thin smile. "Very sweet."

The smile was confined to her lips and did not chase the fear from the rest of her face, did not even touch her troubled eyes. And no matter how sweet she thought he was, she was still not prepared to share any of her secrets with him.

◊   ◊

They reached Geneplan at eleven-thirty.

Dr. Eric Leben's corporate headquarters was a four-story, glass-walled building in an expensive business park off Jamboree Road in Newport Beach, stylishly irregular in design with six sides that were not all of equal length, and with a modernistic polished marble and glass porte cochere. Ben usually despised such architecture, but he grudgingly had to admit that the Geneplan headquarters had a certain appealing boldness. The parking lot was divided into sections by long planters overflowing with vine geraniums heavily laden with wine-red and white blooms. The building was surrounded by an impressive amount of green space as well, with artfully arranged palm trees. Even at this late hour, the trees, grounds, and building were lit by cunningly placed spotlights that imparted a sense of drama and importance to the place.

Rachael pulled her Mercedes around to the rear of the building, where a short driveway sloped down to a large bronze-tinted door that evidently rolled up to admit delivery trucks to an interior loading bay on the basement level. She drove to the bottom and parked at the door, below ground level, with concrete walls rising on both sides. She said, "If anyone gets the idea I might come to Geneplan, and if they drive by looking for my car, they won't spot it down here."

Getting out of the car, Ben noticed how much cooler and more pleasant the night was in Newport Beach, closer to the sea, than it had been in either Santa Ana or Villa Park. They were much too far from the ocean— a couple of miles—to hear the waves or to smell the salt and seaweed, but the Pacific air nevertheless had an effect.

A smaller, man-size door was set in the wall beside the larger entrance and also opened into the basement level. It had two locks.

Living with Eric, Rachael had run errands to and from Geneplan when he hadn't the time himself and when, for whatever reason, he did not trust a subordinate with the task, so she'd once possessed keys. But the day she walked out on him, she put the keys on a small table in the foyer of the Villa Park house. Tonight, she had found them exactly where she'd left them a year ago, on the table beside a tall nineteenth-century Japanese cloisonné vase, dust-filmed. Evidently Eric had instructed the maid not to move the keys even an inch. He must have intended that their undisturbed presence should be a subtle humiliation for Rachael when she came crawling back to him. Happily, she had denied him that sick satisfaction.

Clearly, Eric Leben had been a supremely arrogant bastard, and Ben was glad that he had never met the man.

Now Rachael opened the steel door, stepped into the building, and switched on the lights in the small underground shipping bay. An alarm box was set in the concrete wall. She tapped a series of numbers on its keyboard. The pair of glowing red lights winked out, and a green bulb lit up, indicating that the system was deactivated.

Ben followed her to the end of the chamber, which was sealed off from the rest of the subterranean level for security reasons. At the next door there was another alarm box for another system independent of that which had guarded the exterior door. Ben watched her switch it off with another number code.

She said, "The first one is based on Eric's birthday, this one on mine. There're more ahead."

They proceeded by the beam of the flashlight that Rachael had brought from the house in Villa Park, for she did not want to turn on any lights that might be spotted from outside.

"But you've a perfect right to be here," Ben said. "You're his widow, and you've almost certainly inherited everything."

"Yes, but if the wrong people drive by and see lights on, they'll figure it's me, and they'll come in to get me."

He wished to God she'd tell him who these "wrong people" were, but he knew better than to ask. Rachael was moving fast, eager to put her hands on whatever had drawn her to this place, then get out. She would have no more patience for his questions here than she'd had in the house in Villa Park.

As he accompanied her through the rest of the basement to the elevator, up to the second floor, Ben was increasingly intrigued by the extraordinary security system in operation after normal business hours. There was a third alarm to be penetrated before the elevator could be summoned to the basement. On the second floor, they debarked from the elevator into a reception lounge also designed with security in mind. In the searching beam of Rachael's flashlight, Ben saw a sculpted beige carpet, a striking desk of brown marble and brass for the receptionist, half a dozen brass and leather chairs for visitors, glass and brass coffee tables, and three large and ethereal paintings that might have been by Martin Green, but even if the flashlight had been switched off, he would have seen the blood-red alarm lights in the darkness. Three burnished brass doors—probably solid-core and virtually impenetrable—led out of the lounge, and alarm lights glowed beside each of them.

"This is nothing compared to the precautions taken on the third and fourth levels," Rachael said.

"What's up there?"

"The computers and duplicate research data banks. Every inch is covered by infrared, sonic, and visual-motion detectors."

"We going up there?"

"Fortunately, we don't have to. And we don't have to go out to Riverside County, either, thank God."

"What's in Riverside?"

"The actual research labs. The entire facility is underground, not just for biological isolation but for better security against industrial espionage, too."

Ben was aware that Geneplan was a leader in the most fiercely competitive and rapidly developing industry in the world. The frantic race to be first with a new product, when coupled with the natural competitiveness of the kind of men drawn into the industry, made it necessary to guard trade secrets and product development with a care that was explicitly paranoid. Still, he was not quite prepared for the obvious siege mentality that lay behind the design of Geneplan's electronic security.

Dr. Eric Leben had been a specialist in recombinant DNA, one of the most brilliant figures in the rapidly expanding science of gene splicing. And Geneplan was one of the companies on the cutting edge of the extremely profitable bio-business that had grown out of this new science since the late 1970s.

Eric Leben and Geneplan held valuable patents on a variety of genetically engineered microorganisms and new strains of plant life, including but not limited to: a microbe that produced an extremely effective hepatitis vaccine, which was currently undergoing the process of acquiring the FDA seal but was now only a year away from certain approval and marketing; another man-made microbe "factory" that produced a supervaccine against all types of herpes; a new variety of corn that could flourish even if irrigated with salt water, making it possible for farmers to cultivate abundant crops in arid lands within pumping distance of the seacoast, where nothing had previously grown; a new family of slightly altered oranges and lemons genetically modified to be impervious to fruit flies, citrus canker, and other diseases, thus eliminating the need for pesticides in a large portion of the citrus-fruit industry. Any one such patent might be worth tens or even hundreds of millions of dollars, and Ben supposed it was only prudent for Geneplan to be paranoid and to spend a small fortune to guard the research data that led to the creation of each of these living gold mines.

Rachael went to the middle of the three doors, deactivated the alarm, and used another key to disengage the lock.

When Ben went through the door behind her and eased it shut, he discovered that it was enormously heavy and would have been immovable if it had not been hung in perfect balance on cunningly designed ball-bearing hinges.

She led him along a series of dark and silent corridors, through additional doors to Eric's private suite. There she required one more code for a final alarm box.

Inside the sanctum sanctorum at last, she quickly crossed a vast expanse of antique Chinese carpet in rose and beige to Eric's massive desk. It was as ultramodern as that of the company's front-lounge receptionist but even more stunning and expensive, constructed of rare gold-veined marble and polished malachite.

The bright but narrowly focused lance of the flashlight beam revealed only the middle of the big room as Rachael advanced through it, so Ben had only glimpses and shadowy impressions of the decor. It seemed even more determinedly modern than Eric Leben's other haunts, downright futuristic.

She put her purse and pistol on the desk as she passed it, went to the wall behind, where Ben joined her. She played the flashlight over a four-foot-square painting: broad bands of sombrous yellow and a particularly depressing gray separated by a thin swath of blood-dark maroon.

"Another Rothko?" Ben asked.

"Yeah. And with an important function besides just being a piece of art."

She slipped her fingers under the burnished steel frame, feeling along the bottom. A latch clicked, and the big painting swung away from the wall, to which it had been firmly fixed rather than hung on wire. Behind the hinged Rothko was a large wall safe with a circular door about two feet in diameter. The steel face, dial, and handle gleamed.

"Trite," Ben said.

"Not really. Not your ordinary wall safe. Four-inch-thick steel casing, six-inch face and door. Not just set in the wall but actually welded to the steel beams of the building itself. Requires not one but two combinations, the first forward, the second reverse. Fireproof and virtually blastproof, too."

"What's he keep in there—the meaning of life?"

"Some money, I guess, like in the safe at the house," she said, handing Ben the flashlight. She turned the dial and began to put in the first combination. "Important papers."

He aimed the light at the safe door. "Okay, so what're we after exactly? The cash?"

"No. A file folder. Maybe a ring-binder notebook."

"What's in it?"

"The essentials of an important research project. More or less an abstract of the developments to date, including copies of Morgan Lewis's regular reports to Eric. Lewis is the project head. And with any luck, Eric's personal project diary is in here, too. All of his practical and philosophical thoughts on the subject."

Ben was surprised that she had answered. Was she finally prepared to let him in on at least some of her secrets?

"What subject?" he asked. "What's this particular research project all about?"

She did not respond but blotted her sweat-damp fingers on her blouse before easing the safe's dial backward toward the first number of the second combination.

"Concerning what?" he pressed.

"I have to concentrate, Benny," she said. "If I overshoot one of these numbers, then I'll have to start all over and put the first set in again."

He had gotten all he was going to get, the one little scrap about the file. But, not caring to stand idly by, having nothing else to do but pressure her, he said, "There must be hundreds of research files on scores of projects, so if he keeps just one of them here, it's got to involve the most important thing Geneplan's currently working on."

Squinting, and with her tongue poked out between her teeth, she brought all of her attention to bear on the dial.

"Something big," he said.

She said nothing.

He said, "Or it's research they're doing for the government, the military. Something extremely sensitive."

Rachael put in the final number, twisted the handle, opened the small steel door, and said, "Oh, damn."

The safe was empty.

"They got here before us," she said.

"Who?" Ben demanded.

"They must've suspected that I knew."

"Who suspected?"

"Otherwise, they wouldn't have been so quick to get rid of the file," she said.

"Who?" Ben said.

"Surprise," said a man behind them.

As Rachael gasped, Ben was already turning, seeking the intruder. The flashlight beam caught a tall, bald man in a tan leisure suit and a green-and-white-striped shirt. His head was so completely hairless that he must have shaved it. He had a square face, wide mouth, proud nose, Slavic cheekbones, and gray eyes the shade of dirty ice. He was standing on the other side of the desk. He resembled the late Otto Preminger, the film director. Sophisticated in spite of his leisure suit. Obviously intelligent. Potentially dangerous. He had confiscated the pistol that Rachael had put down with her purse when she had come into the office.

Worse, the guy was holding a Smith & Wesson Model 19 Combat Magnum. Ben was familiar with—and deeply respected—that revolver. Meticulously constructed, it had a four-inch barrel, was chambered for the .357 Magnum cartridge, weighed a moderate thirty-five ounces, and was so accurate and so powerful that it could even be used for deer hunting. Loaded with hollow-point expanding cartridges or with armor-piercing rounds, it was as deadly a handgun as any in the world, deadlier than most.

In the beam of the Eveready, the intruder's gray eyes glistened strangely.

"Lights on," the bald man said, raising his voice slightly, and immediately the room's overhead lights blinked to life, evidently engaged by a voice-activated switch, a trick that suited Eric Leben's preference for ultramodern design.

Rachael said, "Vincent, put the gun away."

"Not possible, I'm afraid," the bald man said. Though his head was quite naked, the back of his big hand had plenty of hair, almost like a pelt, and it even bristled on his fingers between the knuckles.

"There's no need for violence," Rachael said.

Vincent's smile was sour, imparting a cold viciousness to his broad face. "Indeed? No need for violence? I suppose that's why you brought a pistol," he said, holding up the thirty-two that he had snatched off the desk.

Ben knew the S&W Combat Magnum had twice the recoil of a forty-five, which was why it featured large hand-filling stocks. In spite of the superb accuracy built into it, the weapon could be wildly inaccurate in the hands of an inexperienced shooter unprepared for the hard kick it delivered. If the bald man did not appreciate the tremendous power of the gun, if he were inexperienced, he would almost certainly fire the first couple of shots high into the wall, over their heads, which might give Ben time to reach him and take him out.

"We didn't really believe Eric would've been reckless enough to tell you about Wildcard," Vincent said. "But apparently he did, the poor damn fool, or you wouldn't be here, rummaging in his office safe. No matter how badly he treated you, Rachael, he still had a weakness for you."

"He was too proud," she said. "Always was. He liked to brag about his accomplishments."

"Ninety-five percent of Geneplan's staff is in the dark about the Wildcard Project," Vincent said. "It's that sensitive. Believe me, no matter how much you may have hated him, he thought you were special, and he wouldn't have bragged about it to anyone else."

"I didn't hate him," she said. "I pity him. Especially now. Vincent, did you know he'd broken the cardinal rule?"

Vincent shook his head. "Not until . . . tonight. It was a mad thing to do."

Intently watching the bald man, Ben reluctantly decided that the guy was experienced with the Combat Magnum and would not be startled by its recoil.

His grip on it was not at all casual; his right hand was clenched tightly. His aim was not casual, either; his right arm was extended, stiff and straight, elbow locked, with the muzzle lined up between Rachael and Ben. He would only have to swing it a couple of inches in either direction to blow one or both of them away.

Unaware that Ben could be of more use in such a situation than he'd ever given her reason to believe, Rachael said, "Forget the damn gun, Vincent. We don't need guns. We're all in this together now."

"No," Vincent said. "No, as far as the rest of us are concerned, you're not in this. Never should've been. We simply don't trust you, Rachael. And this friend of yours . . ."

The dirty-gray eyes shifted focus from Rachael to Ben. His gaze was piercing, disconcerting. Although his eyes lingered on Ben only a second or two, there was an iciness in them that was transmitted to Ben, sending a chill along his spine.

Then, having failed to detect that he was dealing with someone far less innocent than appearances indicated, Vincent looked away from Ben, back at Rachael, and said, "He's a complete outsider. If we don't want you in this, then we certainly aren't about to make room for *him.*"

To Ben, that statement sounded ominously like a death sentence, and at last he moved with a sinuosity and lightning speed worthy of a striking snake. Taking a big chance that the second command to the voice-activated switch would be as simple as the first, he said, "Lights *off!*" The room instantly went dark as he simultaneously threw the flashlight at Vincent's head, but, Jesus, the guy was already turning to fire at him, and Rachael was screaming—Ben hoped she was diving for the floor—and the sudden darkness was cast into confusion by the whipping beam of the tumbling Eveready, which he hoped would be enough to give him the edge, an edge he badly needed because, just a fraction of a second after the lights went out and the flashlight left his hand, he was already pitching forward, onto the malachite desk in a sliding belly flop that ought to carry him across and into Vincent, committed to action, no turning back now, all of this like a film run at twice its normal speed, yet with an eerie objective time sense so slowed down that each second seemed like a minute, which was just the old program taking control of his brain, the fighting animal taking charge of the body. In the next single second a hell of a lot happened all at once: Rachael was still screaming shrilly, and Ben was sliding, and the flashlight was tumbling, and the muzzle of the Magnum flashed blue-white, and Ben sensed a slug passing over him so close it might have singed his hair, heard the whine of its passage even above the thunderous roar of the shot itself—*skeeeeeeeen*—felt the coldness of the polished malachite through his shirt, and the flashlight struck Vincent as the shot exploded and as Ben was crossing the desk, Vincent grunted from the blow, the flash rebounded and fell to the floor, its lance of light coming to rest on a six-foot piece of abstract bronze sculpture, and Ben was off the desk by then, colliding with his adversary, both of them going down hard. The gun fired again. The shot went into the ceiling. Ben was sprawled on top of Vincent in the darkness, but with a perfect intuitive sense of the relationship of their bodies, which made it possible for him to bring a knee up between the man's thighs, smashing it into the unprotected crotch, and Vincent screamed louder than Rachael, so Ben rammed his knee up again, showing no mercy, daring no mercy, chopped him in the throat, too, which cut off the scream, then hit him along the right temple, hit him again, hard, harder, and a third shot rang out, deafening, so Ben chopped him once more, harder still, then the gun fell out of Vincent's suddenly limp hand, and gaspingly Ben said, "Lights on!"

Instantly the room brightened.

Vincent was out cold, making a slight wet rattling noise as slow inhalations and exhalations passed through his injured throat.

The air stank of gunpowder and hot metal.

Ben rolled off the unconscious man and crawled to the Combat Magnum, taking possession of it with more than a little relief.

Rachael had ventured from behind the desk. Stooping, she picked up her thirty-two pistol, which Vincent had also dropped. The look she gave Ben was part shock, part astonishment, part disbelief.

He crawled back to Vincent and examined him. Thumbed up one eyelid and then the other, checking for the uneven dilation that might indicate a severe concussion or other brain injury. Gently inspected the man's right temple, where two edge-of-the-hand chops had landed. Felt his throat. Made sure his breathing, though hampered, was not too badly obstructed. Took his wrist, located his pulse, timed it.

He sighed and said, "He won't die, thank God. Sometimes it's hard to judge how much force is enough . . . or too much. But he won't die. He'll be out for a while, and when he comes around he'll need medical attention, but he'll be able to get to a doctor on his own."

Speechless, Rachael stared at him.

He took a cushion from a chair and used it to prop up Vincent's head, which would help keep the trachea open if there was some bleeding in the throat.

He quickly searched Vincent but did not find the Wildcard file. "He must have come here with others. They opened the safe, took the contents, while he stayed behind to wait for us."

She put a hand on his shoulder, and he raised his head to meet her eyes. She said, "Benny, for God's sake, you're just a real-estate salesman."

"Yeah," he said, as if he didn't understand the implied question, "and I'm a damn good one, too."

"But . . . the way you handled him . . . the way you . . . so fast . . . violent . . . so sure of yourself . . ."

With satisfaction so intense it almost hurt, he watched her as she grappled with the realization that she was not the only one with secrets.

Showing her no more mercy than she'd thus far shown him, letting her stew in her curiosity, he said, "Come on. Let's get the hell out of here before someone else shows up. I'm good at these nasty little games, but I don't particularly enjoy them."

◊ 8 ◊

DUMPSTER

When an old wino in soiled pants and a ragged Hawaiian shirt wandered into the alley, stacked some crates, and climbed up to search in the garbage dumpster for God knows what treasures, two rats had leaped from the bin, startling him. He had fallen off his makeshift ladder—just as he'd caught a glimpse of the dead woman sprawled in the garbage. She wore a cream-colored summer dress with a blue belt.

The wino's name was Percy. He couldn't remember his last name. "Not really sure I ever had one," he said when Verdad and Hagerstrom questioned him in the alley a short while later. "For a fact, I ain't used a last name since I can remember. Guess maybe I did have one sometime, but my memory ain't what it used to be on account of the damn cheap wine, barf brew, which is the only rot I can pay for."

"You think this slimeball killed her?" Hagerstrom asked Verdad, as if the alky couldn't hear them unless they spoke directly to him.

Studying Percy with extreme distaste, Verdad replied in the same tone of voice. "Not likely."

"Yeah. And even if he saw anything important, he wouldn't know what it meant, and he won't remember it anyway."

Lieutenant Verdad said nothing. As an immigrant born and raised in a far less fortunate and less just country than that to which he now willingly pledged his allegiance, he had little patience and no understanding for lost cases like Percy. Born with the priceless advantage of United States citizenship, how could a man turn from all the opportunities around him and *choose* degradation and squalor? Julio knew he ought to have more compassion for self-made outcasts like Percy. He knew this ruined man might have suffered, might have endured tragedy, been broken by fate or by cruel parents. A graduate of the police department's awareness programs, Julio was well versed in the psychology and sociology of the outcast-as-victim philosophy. But he would have had less trouble understanding the alien thought processes of a man from Mars than he had trying to get a handle on wasted men like this one. He just sighed wearily, tugged on the cuffs of his white silk shirt, and adjusted his pearl cuff links, first the right one, then the left.

Hagerstrom said, "You know, sometimes it seems like a law of nature that any potential witness to a homicide in this town has got to be drunk and about three weeks away from his last bath."

"If the job was easy," Verdad said, "we wouldn't like it so much, would we?"

"I would. Jesus, this guy stinks."

As they talked about him, Percy did, in fact, seem oblivious. He picked at an unidentifiable piece of crud that had crusted to one of the sleeves of his Hawaiian shirt, and after a deep rumbling burp, he returned to the subject of his burnt-out cerebellum. "Cheap hootch fuzzies up your brain. I swear Christ, I think my brain's shrinkin' a little bit more every day, and the empty spaces is fillin' up with hairballs and old wet newspapers. I think a cat sneaks up on me and spits the hairballs in my ears when I'm asleep." He sounded entirely serious, even a bit afraid of such a bold and invasive feline.

Although he wasn't able to remember his last name or much of anything else, Percy had enough brain tissue left—in there among the hairballs and old wet newspapers—to know that the proper thing to do upon finding a corpse was to call the police. And though he was not exactly a pillar of the community with much respect for the law or any sense of common decency, he had hurried immediately in search of the authorities. He thought that reporting the body in the dumpster might earn him a reward.

Now, after arriving with the technicians from the Scientific Investigation Division more than an hour ago, and after fruitlessly questioning Percy while the SID men strung their cables and switched on their lights, Lieutenant Verdad saw another rat explode in panic from the garbage as the coroner's men, having overseen the extensive photographing of the corpse in situ, began to haul the dead woman out of the dumpster. Pelt matted with filth, tail long and pink and moist, the disgusting rodent scurried along the wall of the building toward the mouth of the alley. Julio required every bit of his self-control to keep from drawing his gun and firing wildly at the creature. It dashed to a storm drain with a broken grating and vanished into the depths.

Julio hated rats. The mere sight of a rat robbed him of the self-image he had painstakingly constructed during more than nineteen years as an American citizen and police officer. When he glimpsed a rat, he was instantly stripped of all that he had accomplished and become in nearly two decades, was transformed into pathetic little Julio Verdad of the Tijuana slums, where he had been born in a one-room shack made of scrap lumber and rusting barrels and tar paper. If the right of tenancy had been predicated upon mere numbers, the rats would have owned that shack, for the seven members of the Verdad clan were far outnumbered by vermin.

Watching *this* rat scramble out of the portable floodlights and into shadows and down the alley drain, Julio felt as if his good suit and custom-made shirt and Bally loafers were sorcerously transformed into thirdhand jeans, a tattered shirt, and badly worn sandals. A shudder passed through him, and for a moment he was five years old again, standing in that stifling shack on a blistering August day in Tijuana, staring down in paralyzed horror at the two rats that were chewing busily at the throat of the four-month-old baby, Ernesto. Everyone else was outside, sitting in patches of shade along the dusty street, fanning themselves, the children playing at quiet games and sipping at water, the adults cooling off with the beer they'd purchased cheap from two young *ladrones* who had successfully broken into a brewery warehouse the night before. Little Julio tried to scream, tried to call for help, but no sound would escape him, as if words and cries could not rise because of the heavy, humid August air. The rats, aware of him, turned boldly upon him, hissing, and even when he lunged forward, swatting furiously at them, they backed off only with great reluctance and only after one of them had tested his mettle by biting the meatiest part of his left hand. He screamed and struck out in even greater fury, routing the rats at last, and he was still screaming when his mother and his oldest sister, Evalina, rushed in from the sun-scorched day to find him weeping blood from his hand as if from stigmata—and his baby brother dead.

Reese Hagerstrom—having been partners with Julio long enough to know about his dread of rats, but too considerate ever to mention that fear directly or even indirectly—put one of his enormous hands on Julio's slender shoulder and said, by way of distraction, "I think I'll give Percy five bucks and tell him to get lost. He had nothing to do with this, and we're not going to get anything more out of him, and I'm sick of the stink of him."

"Go ahead," Julio said. "I'm in for two-fifty of it."

While Reese dealt with the wino, Julio watched the dead woman being hauled out of the dumpster. He tried to distance himself from the victim. He tried to tell himself she didn't look real, looked more like a big rag doll, and maybe even was a doll, or a mannequin, just a mannequin. But it was a lie. She looked real enough.

Hell, she looked *too* real. They deposited her on a tarp that had been spread on the pavement for that purpose.

In the glare of the portable lights, the photographer took a few more pictures, and Julio moved in for a closer look. The dead woman was young, in her early twenties, a black-haired and brown-eyed Latino. In spite of what the killer had done to her, and in spite of the garbage and the industrious rats, there was reason to believe that she had been at least attractive and perhaps beautiful. She had gone to her death in a summery cream-colored dress with blue piping on the collar and sleeves, a blue belt, and blue high-heeled shoes.

She was only wearing one shoe. No doubt the other was in the dumpster.

There was something unbearably sad about her gay dress and her one bare foot with its meticulously painted toenails.

At Julio's direction, two uniformed men donned rubber boots, put on scented surgical masks, and climbed into the dumpster to go through every piece of rubbish. They were searching for the other shoe, the murder weapon, and anything else that might pertain to the case.

They found the dead woman's purse. She had not been robbed, for her wallet contained forty-three dollars. According to her driver's license, she was Ernestina Hernandez, twenty-four, of Santa Ana.

Ernestina.

Julio shivered. The similarity between her name and that of his long-dead little brother, Ernesto, gave him a chill. Both the child and the woman had been left for the rats, and though Julio had not known Ernestina, he felt an instant, profound, and only partially explicable obligation to her the moment he learned her name.

I will find your killer, he promised her silently. You were so lovely, and you died before your time, and if there is any justice in the world, any hope of making sense out of life, then your murderer cannot go unpunished. I swear to you, even if I have to go to the ends of the earth, I will find your killer.

Two minutes later, they found a blood-spattered lab

coat of the kind doctors wore. Four words were stitched on the breast pocket: SANTA ANA CITY MORGUE.

"What the hell?" Reese Hagerstrom said. "You think someone from the morgue cut her throat?"

Frowning at the lab coat, Julio Verdad said nothing.

A lab man carefully folded the coat, trying not to shake loose any hairs or fibers that might be clinging to it. He put it into a plastic bag, which he sealed tightly.

Ten minutes later, the officers in the dumpster found a sharp scalpel with traces of blood on the blade. An expensive, finely crafted instrument of surgical quality. Similar to those used in hospital operating rooms. Or in a medical examiner's pathology lab.

The scalpel, too, was put in a plastic bag, then laid beside the lab coat, which lay beside the now-draped body.

By midnight, they had not found the dead woman's other blue shoe. But there was still about sixteen inches of garbage in the dumpster, and the missing item was almost certain to turn up in that last layer of refuse.

◊ 9 ◊

SUDDEN DEATH

Bulleting through the hot June night, from the Riverside Freeway to I-15 East, then east on I-10, past Beaumont and Banning, skirting the Morongo Indian Reservation, to Cabazon and beyond, Rachael had plenty of time to think. Mile by mile, the metropolitan sprawl of southern California fell behind; the lights of civilization grew sparser, dimmer. They headed deeper into the desert, where vast stretches of empty darkness opened on all sides, and where often the only things to be seen on the plains and hills were a few toothy rock formations and scattered Joshua trees limned by frost-pale moonlight that waxed and waned as it was screened by the thin and curling clouds that filigreed the night sky. The barren landscape said all that could be said about solitude, and it encouraged introspection, as did the lulling hum of the Mercedes's engine and the whisper of its spinning tires on the pavement.

Slumped in the passenger's seat, Benny was stubbornly silent for long periods, staring at the black ribbon of highway revealed in the headlights. A few times, they engaged in short conversations, though the topic was always so light and inconsequential that, under the circumstances, it seemed surreal. They discussed Chinese food for a while, subsided into a deep and mutual silence, then talked of Clint Eastwood movies, followed by another and longer silence.

She was aware that Benny was paying her back for her refusal to share her secrets with him. He surely knew that she was stunned by the ease with which he had disposed of Vincent Baresco in Eric's office and that she was dying to know where he had learned to handle himself so well. By turning cool on her, by letting the brooding silences draw out, he was telling her that she was going to have to give him some information in order to get some in return.

But she could not give. Not yet. She was afraid he had already been drawn too far into this deadly business, and she was angry with herself for letting him get involved. She was determined not to drag him deeper into the nightmare—unless his survival depended upon a complete understanding of what was happening and of what was at stake.

As she turned off Interstate 10 onto State Highway 111, now only eleven miles from Palm Springs, she wondered if she could have done more to dissuade him from coming with her to the desert. But upon leaving Geneplan's offices in Newport Beach, he had been quietly adamant, and attempting to change his mind had seemed as fruitless as standing on the shore of the Pacific and commanding an incoming tide to reverse itself immediately.

Rachael deeply regretted the awkwardness between them. In the five months since they had met, this was the first time they had been uneasy with each other, the first time that their relationship had been touched by even a hint of anger or had been in any way less than entirely harmonious.

Having departed Newport Beach at midnight, they arrived in Palm Springs and drove through the heart of town on Palm Canyon Drive at one-fifteen Tuesday morning. That was ninety-nine miles in only an hour and fifteen minutes, for an average speed of eighty miles an hour, which should have given Rachael a sense of speed.

But she continued to feel that she was creeping snail-slow, falling farther and farther behind events, losing ground by the minute.

Summer, with its blazing desert heat, was a somewhat less busy tourist season in Palm Springs than other times of the year, and at one-fifteen in the morning the main street was virtually deserted. In the hot and windless June night, the palm trees stood as still as images painted on canvas, illuminated and slightly silvered by the streetlights. The many shops were dark. The sidewalks were empty. The traffic signals still cycled from green to yellow to red to green again, although hers was the only car passing through most of the intersections.

She almost felt as if she were driving through a post-Armageddon world, depopulated by disease. For a moment she was half convinced that if she switched on the radio, there would be no music—only the cold empty hiss of static all the way across the dial.

Since receiving the news of Eric's missing corpse, she had known that something terrible had come into the world, and hour by hour she had grown more bleak. Now even an empty street, which would have looked peaceful to anyone else, stirred ominous thoughts in her. She knew she was overreacting. No matter what happened in the next few days, this was not the end of the world.

On the other hand, she thought, it might be the end of *me,* the end of *my* world.

Driving from the commercial district into residential areas, from neighborhoods of modest means into wealthier streets, she encountered even fewer signs of life, until at last she pulled into a Futura Stone driveway and parked in front of a low, sleek, flat-roofed stucco house that was the epitome of clean-lined desert architecture. The lush landscaping was distinctly not of the desert—ficus trees, benjamina, impatiens, begonias, beds of marigolds and Gerber daisies—green and thick and flower-laden in the soft glow of a series of Malibu lights. Those were the only lights burning; all the front windows were dark.

She had told Benny that this was another of Eric's houses—though she had been closemouthed about the reason she had come. Now, as she switched off the headlights, he said, "Nice little vacation retreat."

She said, "No. This is where he kept his mistress."

Enough soft light fell from the Malibu fixtures, rebounded from the lawn and from the edge of the driveway, penetrated the windows of the car, and touched Benny's face to reveal his look of surprise. "How did you know?"

"A little over a year ago, just a week before I left him, she—Cindy Wasloff was her name—she called the house in Villa Park. Eric had told her never to phone there except in the direst emergency, and if she spoke with anyone but him, she was supposed to say she was the secretary of some business associate. But she was furious with him because, the night before, he'd beaten her pretty badly, and she was leaving him. First, however, she wanted to let me know he'd been keeping her."

"Had you suspected?"

"That he had a mistress? No. But it didn't matter. By then I'd already decided to call it quits. I listened to her and commiserated, got the address of the house, because I thought maybe the day would come when I might be able to use the fact of Eric's adultery to pry myself loose from him if he wouldn't cooperate in the divorce. Even as ugly as it got, it never got quite *that* tawdry, thank God. And it would have been exceedingly tawdry indeed if I'd had to go public with it . . . because the girl was only sixteen."

"What? The mistress?"

"Yes. Sixteen. A runaway. One of those lost kids, from the sound of her. You know the type. They start doing drugs in junior high and just seem to . . . burn away too many gray cells. No, that's not right, either. The drugs don't destroy brain cells so much as they . . . eat away at their souls, leave them empty and purposeless. They're pathetic."

"Some are," he said. "And some are scary. Bored and listless kids who've tried everything. They either become amoral sociopaths as dangerous as rattlesnakes—or they become easy prey. I gather you're telling me that Cindy Wasloff was easy prey and that Eric swept her in out of the gutter for some fun and games."

"And apparently she wasn't the first."

"He had a thing for teenage girls, huh?"

Rachael said, "What he had a thing about was getting old. It terrified him. He was only forty-one when I left him, still a young man, but every year when his birthday rolled around he was crazier about it than the year before, as if at any moment he'd blink and find himself in a nursing home, decrepit and senile. He had an irrational fear of growing old and dying, and the fear expressed itself in all sorts of ways. For one thing, year by year, *newness* in everything became increasingly important to him: new cars every year, as if a twelve-month-old Mercedes was ready for the scrap heap; a constant change of wardrobe, out with the old and in with the new . . ."

"And the modern art, modern architecture, all the ultramodern furniture."

"Yes. And the latest electronic gadgetry. And I guess teenage girls were just another part of his obsession with staying young and . . . cheating death. I guess, in his twisted mind, being with young girls kept him young, too. When I learned about Cindy Wasloff and this house in Palm Springs, I realized that one of the main reasons he'd married me was because I was twelve years younger than him, twenty-three to his thirty-five. I was just one more means of slowing down the flow of time for him, and when I started to get into my late twenties, when he could see me getting a little older, then I no longer served that purpose quite as well for him, so he needed younger flesh like Cindy."

She opened her door and got out of the car, and Benny got out on his side. He said, "So exactly what're we looking for here? Not just his current mistress; you wouldn't have rocketed out here like a race-car driver just to get a peek at his latest bimbo."

Closing her door, withdrawing the thirty-two pistol from her purse, and heading toward the house, Rachael did not—could not—answer.

The night was warm and dry. The vault of the clear desert sky was spangled with an incredibility of stars. The air was still, and all was silent but for crickets singing in the shrubbery.

Too much shrubbery. She looked around nervously at all the looming dark forms and black spaces beyond the glow of the Malibu lights. Lots of hiding places. She shivered.

The door was ajar, which seemed an ominous sign. She rang the bell, waited, rang again, waited, rang and rang, but no one responded.

At her side, Benny said, "It's probably your house now. You inherited it with everything else, so I don't think you need an invitation to go in."

The door, ajar as it was, provided more invitation than she would have liked. It looked as if it were the open door on a trap. If she went inside in search of the bait, the trap might be sprung, and the door might slam behind her.

Rachael took a step back, kicked out with one foot, knocking the door inward. It swung back hard against the wall of the foyer with a shuddering crash.

"So you don't expect to be welcomed with open arms," Benny said.

The exterior light above the door shed pale beams a few feet into the foyer, though not as far as she had hoped. She could see that no one lurked in the first six or eight feet, but beyond lay darkness that might shelter an assailant.

Because he didn't know everything she knew and therefore didn't appreciate the true extent of the danger, because he expected nothing worse than another Vincent Baresco with another revolver, Benny was bolder than Rachael. He stepped past her into the house, found the wall switch in the foyer, and snapped on the lights.

Rachael went inside and moved past him. "Damn it, Benny, don't be so quick to step through a doorway. Let's be slow and careful."

"Believe it or not, I can handle just about any teenage girl who wants to throw a punch at me."

"It's not the mistress I'm worried about," she said sharply.

"Then who?"

Tight-lipped, holding her pistol at the ready, she led the way through the house, turning on lights as they went.

The uncluttered ultramodern decor—more futuristic than in any of Eric's other habitats—bordered on starkness and sterility. A highly polished terrazzo floor that looked as cold as ice, no carpet anywhere. Levolor metal blinds instead of drapes. Hard-looking chairs. Sofas that, if moved to the depths of a forest, might have passed for giant fungi. Everything was in pale gray, white, black, and taupe, with no color except for scattered accent pieces all in shades of orange.

The kitchen had been wrecked. The white-lacquered breakfast table and two chairs were overturned. The other two chairs had been hammered to pieces against everything else in sight. The refrigerator was badly dented and scraped; the tempered glass in the oven door was shattered; the counters and cabinets were gouged and scratched, edges splintered. Dishes and drinking glasses had been pulled from the cupboards and thrown against the walls, and the floor was prickled and glinting with thousands of sharp shards. Food had been swept off the shelves of the refrigerator onto the floor: Pickles, milk, macaroni salad, mustard, chocolate pudding, maraschino cherries, a chunk of ham, and several unidentifiable substances were congealing in a disgusting pool. Beside the sink, above the cutting board, all six knives had been removed from their rack and, with tremendous force, had been driven into the wall; some of the blades were buried up to half their lengths in the drywall, while two had been driven in to their hilts.

"You think they were looking for something?" Benny asked.

"Maybe."

"No," he said, "I don't think so. It's got the same look as the bedroom in the Villa Park house. Weird. Creepy. This was done in a rage. Out of fierce hatred, in a frenzy, a fury. Or by someone who takes pure, unadulterated pleasure in destruction."

Rachael could not take her eyes off the knives embedded in the wall. A deep sick quivering filled her stomach. Her chest and throat tightened with fear.

The gun in her hand felt different from the way it had felt just a moment ago. Too light. Too small. Almost like a toy. If she had to use it, would it be effective? Against *this* adversary?

They continued through the silent house with considerably greater caution. Even Benny had been shaken by the psychopathic violence that had been unleashed here. He no longer taunted her with his boldness, but stayed close at her side, warier than he had been.

In the large master bedroom, there was more destruction, though it was not as extensive or as indicative of insane fury as the damage in the kitchen. Beside the king-size bed of black-lacquered wood and burnished stainless steel, a torn pillow leaked feathers. The bedsheets were strewn across the floor, and a chair was overturned. One of the two black ceramic lamps had been knocked off a nightstand and broken, and the shade had been crushed. The shade on the other lamp was cocked, and the paintings hung askew on the walls.

Benny stooped and carefully lifted a section of one of the sheets to have a closer look at it. Small reddish spots and a single reddish smear shone with almost preternatural brilliance on the white cotton.

"Blood," he said.

Rachael felt a cold sweat suddenly break out on her scalp and along the back of her neck.

"Not much," Benny said, standing again, his gaze traveling over the tangled sheets. "Not much, but definitely blood."

Rachael saw a bloody handprint on the wall beside the open door that led into the master bedroom. It was a man's print, and large—as if a butcher, exhausted from his hideous labors, had leaned there for a moment to catch his breath.

The lights were on in the large bathroom, the only chamber in the house that had not been dark when they'd reached it. Through the open door, Rachael could see virtually everything either directly or in the mirrors covering one wall: gray tile with a burnt-yellow border, big sunken tub, shower stall, toilet, one edge of the counter that held the sinks, bright brass towel racks and brass-rimmed recessed ceiling lamps. The bathroom appeared deserted. However, when she crossed the threshold, she heard someone's quick, panicked breathing, and her own heartbeat, already trotting, *raced.*

Close behind her, Benny said, "What's wrong?"

She pointed to the opaque shower stall. The glass was so heavily frosted that nothing could be seen of the person on the other side, not even a tenebrous form. "Somebody's in there."

Benny leaned forward, listening.

Rachael had backed against the wall, the muzzle of the thirty-two aimed at the shower door.

"Better come out of there," Benny said to the person in the stall.

No answer. Just quick, thin wheezing.

"Better come out right now," Benny said.

"Come out, damn you!" Rachael said, her raised voice echoing harshly off the gray tile and the bright mirrors.

From the stall came an unexpectedly woeful mewling that was the very essence of terror. It sounded like a child.

Shocked, concerned, but still wary, Rachael edged toward the frosted glass.

Benny stepped past her, took hold of the brass handle, and pulled the door open. "Oh, my God."

Rachael saw a nude girl huddled pathetically on the tile floor of the shadowy stall, her back pressed into the corner. She looked no older than fifteen or sixteen and must be the current mistress in residence, the latest—and last—of Eric's pitiable "conquests." Her slender arms were crossed over her breasts more in fear and self-defense than in modesty. She was trembling uncontrollably, and her eyes were wide with terror, and her face was pale, sickly, waxen.

She was probably quite pretty, but it was difficult to tell for sure, not because of the gloominess of the enclosed shower stall but because she had been badly beaten. Her right eye was blackened and beginning to swell. Another ugly bruise was forming on her right cheek, from the corner of the eye all the way down to the jaw. Her upper lip had been split; blood still oozed from it, and blood covered her chin. There were bruises on her arms as well, and a big one on her left thigh.

Benny turned away, clearly as embarrassed for the girl as he was alarmed by her condition.

Lowering her pistol, stooping at the shower door, Rachael said, "Who did this to you, honey? Who did this?" She already knew what the answer must be, dreaded hearing it, but was morbidly compelled to ask the question.

The girl could not respond. Her bleeding lips moved, and she tried to form words, but all that came out was that thin grievous whining, broken into chords by an especially violent siege of the shivers. Even if she had spoken, she would most likely not have answered the question, for she was obviously in shock and to some degree disassociated from reality. She seemed only partially aware of Rachael and Benny, with the larger part of her attention focused on some private horror. She met Rachael's eyes but didn't really seem to see her.

Rachael reached into the stall with one hand. "Honey, it's all right. Everything's all right. No one's going to hurt you anymore. You can come out now. We won't let anyone hurt you anymore."

The girl stared through Rachael, murmuring softly but urgently to herself, shaken by a wind of fear that blew through some grim inner landscape in which she seemed trapped.

Rachael handed her gun to Benny. She stepped into the big shower stall and knelt beside the girl, speaking softly and reassuringly to her, touching her gently on the face and arms, smoothing her tangled blond hair. At the first few touches, the girl flinched as if she'd been struck, though the contact briefly broke her trance. She looked *at* Rachael for a moment instead of through her, and she allowed herself to be coaxed to her feet and out of the shadowy stall, though by the time she crossed the sill of the shower into the bathroom, she was already retreating once more into her semicatatonic state, unable to answer questions or even to respond with a nod when spoken to, unable to meet Rachael's eyes.

"We've got to get her to a hospital," Rachael said, wincing when she got a better look at the poor child's injuries in the brighter light of the bathroom. Two fingernails on the girl's right hand had been broken back almost to the cuticle and were bleeding; one finger appeared to be broken.

Rachael sat with her on the edge of the bed while Benny went through the closets and various dresser drawers, looking for clothes.

She listened for strange noises elsewhere in the house.

She heard none.

Still, she listened attentively.

In addition to panties, faded blue jeans, a blue-checkered blouse, peds, and a pair of New Balance running shoes, Benny found a trove of illegal drugs. The bottom drawer of one of the nightstands contained fifty or sixty hand-rolled joints, a plastic bag full of unidentified brightly colored capsules, and another plastic bag containing about two ounces of white powder. "Probably cocaine," Benny said.

Eric had not used drugs; he had disdained them. He had always said that drugs were for the weak, for the losers who could not cope with life on its own terms. But obviously he had not been averse to supplying all sorts of illicit substances to the young girls he kept, ensuring their docility and compliance at the expense of further corrupting them. Rachael had never loathed him as much as she did at that moment.

She found it necessary to dress the naked girl as she would have had to dress a very small child, although the teenager's helpless daze—marked by spells of shivers and occasional whimpering—was caused by shock and terror rather than by the illegal chemicals that Benny had found in the nightstand.

As Rachael quickly dressed the girl, chivalrous Benny kept his eyes discreetly averted. Having found her purse while searching for her clothes, he now went through it, seeking identification. "Her name's Sarah Kiel, and she turned sixteen just two months ago. Looks like she's come west from . . . Coffeyville, Kansas."

Another runaway, Rachael thought. Maybe fleeing an intolerable home life. Maybe just a rebellious type who chafed at discipline and entertained the illusion that life on her own, without restrictions, would be pure bliss. Off to L.A., the Big Orange, to take a shot at the movie business, dreaming of stardom. Or maybe just seeking some excitement, an escape from the boredom of the vast and slumbering Kansas plains.

Instead of the expected romance and glamour, Sarah Kiel had found what most girls like her found at the end of the California rainbow: a hard and homeless life on the streets—and eventually the solicitous attention of a pimp. Eric must have either bought her from a pimp or found her himself while on the prowl for the kind of fresh meat that would keep him feeling young. Ensconced in an expensive Palm Springs house, supplied with all the drugs she wanted, plaything of a very rich man, Sarah had surely begun to convince herself that she was, after all, destined for a fairy-tale life. The naive child could not have guessed the true extent of the danger into which she had stepped, could not have conceived of the horror that would one day pay a visit and leave her dazed and mute with terror.

"Help me get her out to the car," Rachael said as she finished dressing Sarah Kiel.

Benny put an arm around the girl from one side, and Rachael held her from the other side, and although Sarah shuffled along under her own power, she would have collapsed several times if they had not provided support. Her knees kept buckling.

The night smelled of star jasmine stirred by a breeze that also rustled shrubbery, causing Rachael to glance nervously at the shadows.

They put Sarah in the car and fastened her seat belt for her, whereupon she slumped against the restraining straps and let her head fall forward. It was possible for a third person to ride in the 560 SL, although it was necessary for the extra passenger to sit sideways in the open storage space behind the two bucket seats and endure a bit of squeezing. Benny was too big to fit, so Rachael got behind the seats, and he took the wheel for the trip to the hospital.

As they pulled out of the driveway, a car turned the corner, headlights washing over them, and when they entered the street, the other car suddenly surged forward, fast, coming straight at them.

Rachael's heart stuttered, and she said, "Oh, hell, it's *them!*"

The oncoming car angled across the narrow street, intending to block it. Benny wasted no time asking questions, immediately changed directions, pulling hard on the wheel, putting the other car behind them. He tramped the accelerator; tires squealed; the Mercedes leaped forward with dependable quickness, racing past the low dark houses. Ahead, the street ended in a cross street, forcing them to turn either left or right, so Benny had to slow down, and Rachael lowered her head and peered through the rear window against which she was crammed, and she saw that the other car—a Cadillac of some kind, maybe a Seville—was following close, very close, closer.

Benny took the corner wide, at a frightening slant, and Rachael would have been thrown by the sudden force of the turn if she hadn't been wedged tightly in the storage space behind the seats. There was nowhere for her to be thrown *to,* and she didn't even have to hold on to anything, but she did hold on to the back of Sarah Kiel's seat because she felt as if the world were about to fall

out from under her, and she thought, *God, please, don't
let the car roll over.*

The Mercedes didn't roll, hugged the road beautifully,
came out into a straight stretch of residential street, and
accelerated. But behind them, the Cadillac almost went
over on its side, and the driver overcompensated, which
made the Caddy swing so dangerously wide that it side-
swiped a Corvette parked at the curb. Sparks showered
into the air, cascaded along the pavement. The Caddy
lurched away from the impact and looked like it would
veer across the street and into the cars along the other
curb, but then it recovered. It had lost some ground, but
it came after them again, its driver undaunted.

Benny whipped the little 560 SL into another turn,
around another corner, holding it tighter this time, then
stood on the accelerator for a block and a half, so it
seemed as if they were in a rocket ship instead of an
automobile. Just when Rachael felt herself pressed back
with a force of maybe 4.5 Gs, just when it seemed they
would break the chains of gravity and explode straight
into orbit, Benny manipulated the brakes with all the
style of a great concert pianist executing "Moonlight
Sonata," and as he came up on another stop sign with
no intention of obeying it, he spun the wheel as hard as
he dared, so from behind it must have looked as if the
Mercedes had just *popped* off that street onto the street
that intersected from the left.

He was as expert at evasive driving as he had proved
to be at hand-to-hand combat, and Rachael wanted to say,
*Who the hell are you, anyway, not just a placid real-estate
salesman with a love of trains and swing music, damned
if you are,* but she didn't say anything because she was
afraid she would distract him, and if she distracted him
at this speed, they would inevitably roll—or worse—
and be killed for sure.

◗   ◗

Ben knew that the 560 SL could easily win a speed
contest with the Cadillac out on the open roads, but it
was a different story on streets like these, which were

narrow and occasionally bisected by speed bumps to prevent drag racing. Besides, there were traffic lights as they drew nearer the center of town, and even at this dead hour of the morning he had to slow for those main intersections, at least a little, or risk plowing broadside into a rare specimen of crosstown traffic. Fortunately, the Mercedes cornered about a thousand times better than the Cadillac, so he didn't have to slow down nearly as much as his pursuers, and every time he switched streets he gained a few yards that the Caddy could not entirely regain on the next stretch of straightaway. By the time he had zigzagged to within a block of Palm Canyon Drive, the main drag, the Caddy was more than a block and a half behind and losing ground, and he was finally confident that he would shake the bastards, whoever they were—

—and that was when he saw the police car.

It was parked at the front of a line of curbed cars, at the corner of Palm Canyon, a block away, and the cop must have seen him coming in the rearview mirror, coming like a bat out of hell, because the flashing red and blue beacons on the roof of the cruiser came on, bright and startling, ahead on the right.

"Hallelujah!" Ben said.

"No," Rachael said from her awkward seat in the open storage space behind him, shouting though her mouth was nearly at his ear. "No, you can't go to the cops! We're dead if you go to the cops."

Nevertheless, as he rocketed toward the cruiser, Ben started to brake because, damn it, she'd never told him *why* they couldn't rely on the police for protection, and he was not a man who believed in taking the law into his own hands, and surely the guys in the Cadillac would back off fast if the cops came into it.

But Rachael shouted, "No! Benny, for Christ's sake, trust me, why don't you? We're dead if you stop. They'll blow our brains out, sure as hell."

Being accused of not trusting her—that hurt, stung. He trusted her, by God, trusted her implicitly because he loved her. He didn't *understand* her worth shit, not tonight he didn't, but he did trust her, and it was like a knife twisting in his heart to hear that note of disappointment and accusation in her voice. He took his foot off the brake and put it back on the accelerator, swept right past the black-and-white so fast that the light from its swiveling emergency beacons flashed through the Mercedes only once and then were behind. When he'd glanced over, he'd seen two uniformed officers looking astonished. He figured they'd wait for the Caddy and then give chase to both cars, which would be fine, just fine, because the guys in the Caddy couldn't catch up with him and blow his brains out if they had the police on their tail.

But to Ben's surprise and dismay, the cops pulled out right after him, siren screaming. Maybe they had been so shocked by the sight of the Mercedes coming at them like a jet that they hadn't noticed the Cadillac farther back. Or maybe they'd seen the Caddy but had been so startled by the Mercedes that they hadn't realized the second car was approaching at almost the same high speed. Whatever their reasoning, they shot away from the curb and fell in behind him as he hung a right onto Palm Canyon Drive.

Ben made that turn with the reckless aplomb of a stunt driver who knows that his roll bars and special stabilizers and heavy duty hydraulic shock absorbers and other sophisticated equipment remove most of the danger from such risky maneuvers—except he didn't have roll bars and special stabilizers. He realized he'd miscalculated and was about to turn Rachael and Sarah and himself into canned meat, three lumps of imitation Spam encased in expensive German steel, Jesus, and the car tilted onto two tires, he smelled smoking rubber, it seemed an hour they teetered on edge, but by the grace of God and the brilliance of the Benz designers they came down again onto all fours with a jolt and crash that, by virtue of another miracle, did not blow out any tires, though Rachael hit her head on the ceiling and let out her breath in a whoosh that he felt on the back of his neck.

He saw the old man in the yellow Banlon shirt and the cocker spaniel even before the car stopped bouncing on its springs. They had been crossing the street in the middle of the block when he had come around the corner like a fugitive from a demolition derby. He was bearing down on them at a frightening speed, and they were frozen in surprise and fear, both dog and man, heads up, eyes wide. The guy looked ninety, and the dog seemed decrepit, too, so it didn't make sense for them to be out on the street at nearly two o'clock in the morning. They ought to have been home in bed, occupied with dreams of fire hydrants and well-fitted false teeth, but here they were.

"Benny!" Rachael shouted.

"I see, I see!"

He had no hope of stopping in time, so he not only jumped on the brakes but turned across Palm Canyon, a combination of forces that sent the Mercedes into a full spin combined with a slide, so they went around a full hundred and eighty degrees and wound up against the far curb. By the time he peeled rubber, roared back across the street, and was headed north again, the old man and the cocker had finally tottered for the safety of the sidewalk—and the police cruiser was no more than ten yards behind him.

In the mirror, he could see that the Caddy had also turned the corner and was still giving chase, undeterred by the presence of the police. Crazily the Caddy pulled out around the black-and-white, trying to pass it.

"They're lunatics," Ben said.

"Worse," Rachael said. "Far worse."

In the passenger seat, Sarah Kiel was making urgent noises, but she did not appear to be frightened by the current danger. Instead, it seemed as if the violence of the chase had stirred the sediment of memory, recalling for her the other—and worse—violence that she had endured earlier in the night.

Picking up speed as he headed north on Palm Canyon, Ben glanced again at the mirror and saw that the Cadillac had pulled alongside the police cruiser. They appeared to be drag racing back there, just a couple of carloads of guys out for some fun. It was . . . well, it was downright silly was what it was. Then suddenly it wasn't silly at all because the intentions of the men in the Caddy became horribly clear with the repeated winking of muzzle flashes and the *tat-tat-tat-tat-tat-tat* of automatic weapons fire. They had opened up on the cops with a submachine gun, as if this weren't Palm Springs but Chicago in the Roaring Twenties.

"They shot the cops!" he said, as astonished as he had ever been in his life.

The black-and-white went out of control, jumped the curb, crossed the sidewalk, and rammed through the plate-glass window of an elegant boutique, but still a guy in the back seat of the Cadillac continued to lean out the window, spraying bullets back at the cruiser until it was out of range.

In the seat beside Ben, Sarah said, "Uh, uh, uh, uh, uh, uh," and she twitched and spasmed as if someone were raining blows on her. She seemed to be reliving the beating she had taken, oblivious of the immediate danger.

"Benny, you're slowing down," Rachael said urgently.

Overcome by shock, he had relaxed his foot on the accelerator.

The Cadillac was closing on them as hungrily as any shark had ever closed on any swimmer.

Ben tried to press the gas pedal through the floorboards, and the Mercedes reacted as if it were a cat that had just been kicked in the butt. They exploded up Palm Canyon Drive, which was relatively straight for a long way, so he could even put some distance between them and the Cadillac before he made any turns. And he did make turns, one after the other, off into the west side of town now, up into the hills, back down, working steadily south, through older residential streets where trees arched overhead to form a tunnel, then through newer neighborhoods where the trees were small and the shrubbery too sparse to conceal the reality of the desert on which the town had been built. With every corner he rounded, he widened the gap between them and the killers in the Cadillac.

Stunned, Ben said, "They wasted two cops just because the poor bastards got in the way."

"They want us real bad," Rachael said. "That's what I've tried to tell you. They want us so very bad."

The Caddy was two blocks behind now, and within five or six more turns, Ben would lose them because they wouldn't have him in sight and wouldn't know which way he had gone.

Hearing a tremor in his voice that surprised him, a quavering note that he didn't like, he said, "But, damn it, they never really had much of a chance of catching us. Not with us in this little beauty and them in a lumbering Caddy. They had to see that. They had to. One chance in a hundred. At best. One chance in a hundred, but they still wasted the cops."

He half wheeled and half slid around another turn, onto a new street.

"Ohmygod, ohmygod, ohmygod," Sarah said softly, frantically, drawing down in the seat as far as the safety harness would allow, crossing her arms over her breasts as she had done in the shower stall when she had been naked.

Behind Ben, sounding as shaky as he did, Rachael said, "They probably figured the police had gotten our license number—and theirs, too—and were about to call them in for identification."

The Cadillac headlights turned the corner far back, losing ground more rapidly now. Ben took another turn and sped along another dark and slumbering street, past older houses that had gotten a bit seedy and no longer measured up to the Chamber of Commerce's fantasy image of Palm Springs.

"But you've implied that the guys in the Caddy would get their hands on you even quicker if you went to the police."

"Yes."

"So why wouldn't they want the police to nab us?"

Rachael said, "It's true that in police custody I'd be even easier to nail. I'd have no chance at all. But killing me then will be a lot messier, more public. The people in that Cadillac . . . and their associates . . . would prefer to keep this private if they can, even if that means they'll need more time to get their hands on me."

Before the Cadillac headlights could appear again, Ben executed yet another turn. In a minute he would finally slip away from their pursuers for good. He said, "What the hell do they want from you?"

"Two things. For one . . . a secret they think I have."

"But you don't have it?"

"No."

"What's the second thing?"

"Another secret that I *do* know. I share it with them. They already know it, and they want to stop me from telling anyone else."

"What is it?"

"If I told you, they'd have as much reason to kill you as me."

"I think they *already* want my butt," Ben said. "I'm in too deep already. So tell me."

"Keep your mind on your driving," she said.

"Tell me."

"Not now. You've got to concentrate on getting away from them."

"Don't worry about that, and don't try to use it as an excuse to clam up on me, damn it. We're already out of the woods. One more turn, and we'll have lost them for good."

The right front tire blew out.

◊ **10** ◊

NAILS

It was a long night for Julio and Reese.

By 12:32, the last of the garbage in the dumpster had been inspected, but Ernestina Hernandez's blue shoe had not been found.

Once the trash had been searched and the corpse had been moved to the morgue, most detectives would have decided to go home to get some shut-eye and start fresh the next day—but not Lieutenant Julio Verdad. He was aware the trail was freshest in the twenty-four hours after the discovery of the body. Furthermore, for at least a day following assignment to a new case, he had difficulty sleeping, for then he was especially troubled by a sense of the horror of murder.

Besides, this time, he had a special obligation to the victim. For reasons which might have seemed inadequate to others but which were compelling to him, he felt a deep commitment to Ernestina. Bringing her killer to justice was not just his job but a point of honor with Julio.

His partner, Reese Hagerstrom, accompanied him without once commenting on the lateness of the hour. For Julio and for no one else, Reese would work around the clock, deny himself not only sleep but days off and regular meals, and make any sacrifice required. Julio knew, if it ever became necessary for Reese to step into the path of a bullet and *die* for Julio, the big man would make that ultimate sacrifice as well, and without the slightest hesitation. It was something which they both understood in their hearts, in their bones, but of which they had never spoken.

At 12:41 in the morning, they took the news of Ernestina's brutal death to her parents, with whom she had lived, a block east of Main Street in a modest house flanked by twin magnolias. The family had to be awakened, and at first they were disbelieving, certain that Ernestina had come home and gone to bed by now. But, of course, her bed was empty.

Though Juan and Maria Hernandez had six children, they took this blow as hard as parents with one precious child would have taken it. Maria sat on the rose-colored sofa in the living room, too weak to stand. Her two youngest sons—both teenagers—sat beside her, red-eyed and too shaken to maintain the macho front behind which Latino boys of their age usually hid. Maria held a framed photograph of Ernestina, alternately weeping and tremulously speaking of good times shared with the beloved daughter. Another daughter, nineteen-year-old Laurita, sat alone in the dining room, unapproachable, inconsolable, clutching a rosary. Juan Hernandez paced agitatedly, jaws clenched, blinking furiously to repress his tears. As patriarch, it was his duty to provide an example of strength to his family, to be unshaken and unbroken by this visitation of *muerta*. But it was too much for him to bear, and twice he retreated to the kitchen where, behind the closed door, he made soft strangled sounds of grief.

Julio could do nothing to relieve their anguish, but he inspired trust and hope for justice, perhaps because his special commitment to Ernestina was clear and convincing. Perhaps because, in his soft-spoken way, he conveyed a hound-dog perseverance that lent conviction to promises of swift justice. Or perhaps his smoldering fury at the very *existence* of death, all death, was painfully evident in his face and eyes and voice. After all, that fury had burned in him for many years now, since the afternoon when he had discovered rats chewing out the throat of his baby brother, and by now the fire within him must have grown bright enough to show through for all to see.

From Mr. Hernandez, Julio and Reese learned that Ernestina had gone out for an evening on the town with her best girlfriend, Becky Klienstad, with whom she worked at a local Mexican restaurant, where both were waitresses. They had gone in Ernestina's car: a powder-blue, ten-year-old Ford Fairlane.

"If this has happened to my Ernestina," Mr. Hernandez said, "then what's happened to poor Becky? Something must have happened to her, too. Something very terrible."

From the Hernandez kitchen, Julio telephoned the Klienstad family in Orange. Becky—actually Rebecca—was not yet home. Her parents had not been worried because she was, after all, a grown woman, and because some of the dance spots that she and Ernestina favored were open until two in the morning. But now they were very worried indeed.

◗   ◗

1:20 A.M.

In the unmarked sedan in front of the Hernandez house, Julio sat behind the wheel and stared bleakly out at the magnolia-scented night.

Through the open windows came the susurration of leaves stirring in the vague June breeze. A lonely, cold sound.

Reese used the console-mounted computer terminal to generate an APB and pickup order on Ernestina's powder-blue Ford. He'd obtained the license number from her parents.

"See if there're any messages on hold for us," Julio said.

At the moment he did not trust himself to operate the keyboard. He was full of anger and wanted to pound on something—anything—with both fists, and if the computer gave him any trouble or if he hit one wrong key by mistake, he might take out his frustration on the machine merely because it was a convenient target.

Reese accessed the police department's data banks at headquarters and requested on-file messages. Softly glowing green letters scrolled up on the video display. It was a report from the uniformed officers who'd gone to the morgue, at Julio's direction, to ascertain if the scalpel and bloodstained morgue coat found in the dumpster could be traced to a specific employee on the coroner's staff. Officials at the coroner's office were able to confirm that a scalpel, lab coat, set of hospital whites, surgical cap, and a pair of antistatic lab shoes were missing from the morgue's supplies closet. However, no specific employee could be linked with the theft of those items.

Looking up from the VDT, gazing at the night, Julio said, "This murder is somehow tied to the disappearance of Eric Leben's body."

"Could be coincidence," Reese said.

"You believe in coincidence?"

Reese sighed. "No."

A moth fluttered against the windshield.

"Maybe whoever stole the body also killed Ernestina," Julio said.

"But why?"

"That's what we must find out."

Julio drove away from the Hernandez house.

He drove away from the fluttering moth and the whispering leaves.

He turned north and drove away from downtown Santa Ana.

However, although he followed Main Street, where closely spaced streetlamps blazed, he could not drive away from the deep darkness, not even temporarily, for the darkness was within him.

◊   ◊

1:38 A.M.

They reached Eric Leben's Spanish-modern house quickly, for there was no traffic. Night in that wealthy neighborhood was respectfully still. Their footsteps clicked hollowly on the tile walkway, and when they rang the doorbell, it sounded as if it were echoing back to them from the bottom of a deep well.

Julio and Reese had no authority whatsoever in Villa Park, which was two towns removed from their own jurisdiction. However, in the vast urban sprawl of Orange County, which was essentially one great spread-out city divided into many communities, a lot of crimes were not conveniently restricted to a single jurisdiction, and a criminal could not be allowed to gain time or safety by simply crossing the artificial political boundary between one town and another. When it became necessary to pursue a lead into another jurisdiction, one was required to seek an escort from the local authorities or obtain their approval or even enlist them to make the inquiries themselves, and these requests were routinely honored.

But because time was wasted going through proper channels, Julio and Reese frequently skipped the protocol. They went where they needed to go, talked with whomever they needed to talk, and only informed local authorities when and if they found something pertinent to their case—or if a situation looked as if it might turn violent.

Few detectives operated that boldly. Failure to follow standard procedures might result in a reprimand. Repeated violations of the rules might be viewed as a dismal lack of respect for the command structure, resulting in disciplinary suspension. Too much of that, and even the finest cop could forget about further promotions—and might have to worry about hanging on to collect his pension.

The risks did not particularly concern Julio or Reese. They wanted promotions, of course. And they wanted their pensions. But more than career advancement and financial security, they wanted to solve cases and put murderers in prison. Being a cop was pointless if you weren't willing to put your life on the line for your ideals, and if you *were* willing to risk your life, then it made no sense to worry about small stuff like salary increases and retirement funds.

When no one responded to the bell, Julio tried the door, but it was locked. He didn't attempt to void the lock or force it. In the absence of a court order, what they needed to get them into the Leben house was probable cause to believe that criminal activity of some kind was under way on the premises, that innocent people might be harmed, and that there was nothing less than a public emergency.

When they circled to the back of the house, they found what they needed: a broken pane of glass in the French door that led from the patio into the kitchen. They would have been remiss if they had not assumed the worst: that an armed intruder had forced his way into the house to commit burglary or to harm whoever resided legally within.

Drawing their revolvers, they entered cautiously. Shards of broken glass crunched underfoot.

As they moved from room to room, they turned on lights and saw enough to justify intrusion. The bloody palmprint etched into the arm of the white sofa in the family room. The destruction in the master bedroom. And in the garage . . . Ernestina Hernandez's powder-blue Ford.

Inspecting the car, Reese found bloodstains on the back seat and floor mats. "Some of it's still a little sticky," he told Julio.

Julio tried the trunk of the car and found it unlocked. Inside, there was more blood, a pair of broken eyeglasses—and one blue shoe.

The shoe was Ernestina's, and the sight of it caused Julio's chest to tighten.

As far as Julio knew, the Hernandez girl had not worn glasses. In photographs he had seen at the Hernandez home, however, Becky Klienstad, friend and fellow waitress, had worn a pair like these. Evidently, both women had been killed and stuffed into the Ford's trunk. Later, Ernestina's corpse had been heaved into the dumpster. But what happened to the other body?

"Call the locals," Julio said. "It's time for protocol."

◑   ◑

1:52 A.M.

When Reese Hagerstrom returned from the sedan, he paused to put up the electric garage doors to air out the smell of blood that had risen from the open trunk of the Ford and reached into every corner of the long room. As the doors rolled up, he spotted a discarded set of hospital whites and a pair of antistatic shoes in one corner. "Julio? Come here and look at this."

Julio had been staring intently into the bloody trunk of the car, unable to touch anything lest he ruin precious evidence, but hoping to spot some small clue by sheer dint of intense study. He joined Reese at the discarded clothes.

Reese said, "What the hell is going on?"

Julio did not reply.

Reese said, "The evening started out with one missing corpse. Now two are missing—Leben and the Klienstad girl. And we've found a third we wish we hadn't. If someone's collecting dead bodies, why wouldn't they keep Ernestina Hernandez, too?"

Puzzling over these bizarre discoveries and the baffling link between the snatching of Leben's corpse and the murder of Ernestina, Julio unconsciously straightened his necktie, tugged on his shirt sleeves, and adjusted his cuff links. Even in summer heat, he would not forsake a tie and long-sleeve shirt, the way some detectives did. Like a priest, a detective held a sacred office, labored in the service of the gods of Justice and Law, and to dress any less formally would have seemed, to him, as disrespectful as a priest celebrating the Mass in jeans and a T-shirt.

"Are the locals coming?" he asked Reese.

"Yes. And as soon as we've had a chance to explain the situation to them, we've got to go up to Placentia."

Julio blinked. "Placentia? Why?"

"I checked messages when I got to the car. HQ had an important one for us. The Placentia police have found Becky Klienstad."

"Where? Alive?"

"Dead. In Rachael Leben's house."

Astonished, Julio repeated the question that Reese had asked only a few minutes ago: "What the hell is going on?"

◊   ◊

1:58 A.M.

To get to Placentia, they drove from Villa Park through part of Orange, across a portion of Anaheim, over the Tustin Avenue bridge of the Santa Ana River, which was only a river of dust during this dry season. They passed oil wells where the big pumps, like enormous praying mantises, worked up and down, a shade lighter than the night around them, identifiable and yet somehow mysterious shapes that added one more ominous note to the darkness.

Placentia was usually one of the quietest communities in the county, neither rich nor poor, just comfortable and content, with no terrible drawbacks, with no great advantages over other nearby towns except, perhaps, for the enormous and beautiful date palms which lined some of its streets. Palms of remarkable lushness and stature lined the street on which Rachael Leben lived, and their dense overhanging fronds appeared to be afire in the flickering reflection of the red emergency beacons on the clustered police cars parked under them.

Julio and Reese were met at the front door by a tall uniformed Placentia officer named Orin Mulveck. He was pale. His eyes looked strange, as if he had just seen something he would never choose to remember but would also never be able to forget. "Neighbor called us because she saw a man leaving the house in a hurry, and she thought there was something suspicious about him. When we came to check the place out, we found the front door standing wide open, lights on."

"Mrs. Leben wasn't here?"

"No."

"Any indication where she is?"

"No." Mulveck had taken off his cap and was compulsively combing his fingers through his hair. "Jesus," he said more to himself than to Julio or Reese. Then: "No, Mrs. Leben is gone. But we found the dead woman in Mrs. Leben's bedroom."

Entering the cozy house behind Mulveck, Julio said, "Rebecca Klienstad."

"Yeah."

Mulveck led Julio and Reese across a charming living room decorated in shades of peach and white with dark blue accents and brass lamps.

Julio said, "How'd you identify the deceased?"

"She was wearing one of those medical-alert medallions," Mulveck said. "Had several allergies, including one to penicillin. You seen those medallions? Name, address, medical condition on it. Then, how we got onto you so fast—we asked our computer to check the Klienstad woman through Data Net, and it spit out that you were looking for her in Santa Ana in connection with the Hernandez killing."

The Law Enforcement Data Net, through which the county's many police agencies shared information among their computers, was a new program, a natural outgrowth of the computerization of the sheriff's department and all local police. Hours, sometimes days, could be saved with the use of Data Net, and this was not the first time Julio found reason to be thankful that he was a cop in the Microchip Age.

"Was the woman killed here?" Julio asked as they circled around a burly lab technician who was dusting furniture for fingerprints.

"No," Mulveck said. "Not enough blood." He was still combing one hand through his hair as he walked. "Killed somewhere else and . . . and brought here."

"Why?"

"You'll see why. But damned if you'll *understand* why."

Puzzling over that cryptic statement, Julio trailed Mulveck down a hallway into the master bedroom. He gasped at the sight awaiting him and for a moment could not breathe.

Behind him, Reese said, "Holy shit."

Both bedside lamps were burning, and though there were still shadows around the edges of the room, Rebecca Klienstad's corpse was in the brightest spot, mouth open, eyes wide with a vision of death. She had been stripped naked and nailed to the wall, directly over the big bed. One nail through each hand. One nail just below each elbow joint. One in each foot. And a large spike through the hollow of the throat. It was not precisely the classic pose of crucifixion, for the legs were immodestly spread, but it was close.

A police photographer was still snapping the corpse from every angle. With each flash of his strobe unit, the dead woman seemed to move on the wall; it was only an illusion, but she appeared to twitch as if straining at the nails that held her.

Julio had never seen anything as savage as the crucifixion of the dead woman, yet it had obviously been done not in a white-hot madness but with cold calculation. Clearly, the woman had already been dead when brought here, for the nail holes weren't bleeding. Her slender throat had been slashed, and that was evidently the mortal wound. The killer—or killers—had expended considerable time and energy finding the nails and the hammer (which now lay on the floor in one corner of the room), hoisting the corpse against the wall, holding it in place, and precisely driving the impaling spikes through the cool dead flesh. Apparently the head had drooped down, chin to chest, and apparently the killer had wanted the dead woman to be staring at the bedroom door (a grisly surprise for Rachael Leben), so he had looped a wire under the chin and had tied it tautly to a nail driven into the wall above her skull, to keep her facing out. Finally he had taped her eyes open—so she would be staring sightlessly at whomever discovered her.

"I understand," Julio said.

"Yes," Reese Hagerstrom said shakily.

Mulveck blinked in surprise. Pearls of sweat glistened on his pale forehead, perhaps not because of the June heat. "You've got to be joking. You understand this . . . madness? You see a *reason* for it?"

Julio said, "Ernestina and this girl were murdered primarily because the killer needed a car, and they *had* a car. But when he saw what the Klienstad woman looked like, he dumped the other one and brought the second body here to leave this message."

Mulveck nervously combed one hand through his hair. "But if this psycho intended to kill Mrs. Leben, if she was his primary target, why not just come here and get her? Why just leave a . . . a message?"

"The killer must have had reason to suspect that she wouldn't be at home. Maybe he even called first," Julio said.

He was remembering Rachael Leben's extreme nervousness when he had questioned her at the morgue earlier this evening. He had sensed that she was hiding something and that she was very much afraid. Now he knew that, even then, she had realized her life was in danger.

But who was she afraid of, and why couldn't she turn to the police for help? What was she hiding?

The police photographer's camera click-flashed.

Julio continued: "The killer knew he wouldn't be able to get his hands on her right away, but he wanted her to know she could expect him later. He—or they—wanted to scare her witless. And when he took a good look at this Klienstad woman he had killed, he knew what he must do."

"Huh?" Mulveck said. "I don't follow."

"Rebecca Klienstad was voluptuous," Julio said, indicating the crucified woman. "So is Rachael Leben. Very similar body types."

"And Mrs. Leben has hair much the same as the Klienstad girl's," Reese said. "Coppery brown."

"Titian," Julio said. "And although this woman isn't nearly as lovely as Mrs. Leben, there's a vague resemblance, a similarity of facial structure."

The photographer paused to put new film in his camera.

Officer Mulveck shook his head. "Let me get this straight. The way it was supposed to work—Mrs. Leben would eventually come home and when she walked into this room she would see this woman crucified and know, by the similarities, that it was *her* this psycho really wanted to nail to the wall."

"Yes," Julio said, "I think so."

"Yes," Reese agreed.

"Good God," Mulveck said, "do you realize how black, how bitter, how deep this hatred must be? Whoever he is, what could Mrs. Leben possibly have done to make him hate her like that? What sort of enemies does she have?"

"Very dangerous enemies," Julio said. "That's all I know. And . . . if we don't find her quickly, we won't find her alive."

The photographer's camera flashed.

The corpse seemed to twitch.

Flash, twitch.

Flash, twitch.

◊ 11 ◊

GHOST STORY

When the right front tire blew, Benny hardly slowed. He wrestled with the wheel and drove another half block. The Mercedes thumped and shuddered and rocked along, crippled but cooperative.

No headlights appeared behind them. The pursuing Cadillac had not yet turned the corner two blocks back. But it would. Soon.

Benny kept looking desperately left and right.

Rachael wondered what sort of bolthole he was searching for.

Then he found it: a one-story stucco house with a FOR SALE sign in the front yard, set on a big half-acre lot, grass unmown, separated from its neighbors by an eight-foot-high concrete-block wall that was also finished in stucco and that afforded some privacy. There were lots of trees on the property as well, and overgrown shrubbery in need of a gardener's attention.

"Eureka," Benny said.

He swung into the driveway, then pulled across one corner of the lawn and around the side of the house. In back, he parked on a concrete deck, under a redwood patio cover. He switched off the headlights, the engine.

Darkness fell over them.

The car's hot metal made soft pinging sounds as it cooled.

The house was unoccupied, so no one came out to see what was happening. And because the place was screened from the neighbors on both sides by the wall and trees, no alarm was raised from those sources, either.

Benny said, "Give me your gun."

From her perch behind the seats, Rachael handed over the pistol.

Sarah Kiel was watching them, still trembling, still afraid, but no longer in a trance of terror. The violence of the chase seemed to have jolted her out of her preoccupation with her memories of other, earlier violence.

Benny opened his door and started to get out.

Rachael said, "Where are you going?"

"I want to make sure they go past and don't double back. Then I've got to find another car."

"We can change the tire—"

"No. This heap's too easy to spot. We need something ordinary."

"But where will you get another car?"

"Steal it," he said. "You just sit tight, and I'll be back as soon as I can."

He closed his door softly, sprinted back the way they had come, slipped around the corner of the house, and was gone.

◊   ◊

Scuttling in a half crouch along the side of the house, Ben heard a chorus of distant sirens. Police cars and ambulances were probably still converging on Palm Canyon Drive, a mile or two away, where the bullet-riddled cops had ridden their cruiser through the windows of a boutique.

Ben reached the front of the house and saw the Cadillac coming along the street. He dove into a lush planting bed at the corner and cautiously peered between branches of the overgrown oleander bushes, which were heavily laden with pink flowers and poisonous berries.

The Caddy cruised slowly by, giving him a chance to ascertain that there were three men inside. He could see only one clearly—the guy in the front passenger's seat, who had a receding hairline, a mustache, blunt features, and a mean slash of a mouth.

They were looking for the red Mercedes, of course, and they were smart enough to know that Ben might have tried to slip into a shadowy niche and wait until they had gone past. He hoped to God that he had not left obvious tire tracks across the short stretch of unmown lawn that he'd traversed between the driveway and the side of the house. It was dense Bermuda grass, highly resilient, and it hadn't been watered as regularly as it should have been, so it was badly blotched with brown patches, which provided a natural camouflage to further conceal the marks of the Mercedes's passage. But the men in the Caddy might be trained hunters who could spot the most subtle signs of their quarry's trail.

Hunkering in the bushy oleander, still wearing his thoroughly inappropriate suit trousers, vest, white shirt, and tie with the knot askew, Ben felt ridiculous. Worse, he felt hopelessly inadequate to meet the challenge confronting him. He'd been a real-estate salesman too long. He was not up to this sort of thing anymore, not for an extended length of time. He was thirty-seven, and he'd last been a man of action when he'd been twenty-one, which seemed a date lost in the mists of the Paleolithic era. Although he had kept in shape over the years, he was rusty. To Rachael, he had looked formidable when he'd gone after the man named Vincent Baresco in Eric Leben's Newport Beach office, and his handling of the car had no doubt impressed her, but he knew his reflexes weren't what they had once been. And he knew these people, his nameless enemies, were deadly serious.

He was scared.

They had blown away those two cops as if swatting a couple of annoying flies. Jesus.

What secret did they share with Rachael? What could be so damn important that they would kill anyone, even cops, to keep a lid on it?

If he lived through the next hour, he would get the truth out of her one way or another. Damned if he would let her keep stalling.

The Caddy's engine sort of purred and sort of rumbled, and the car moved past at a crawl, and the guy with the mustache looked right at Ben for a moment, or seemed to, stared right between the oleander branches that Ben was holding slightly apart. Ben wanted to let the branches close up, but he was afraid the movement would be seen, slight as it was, so he just looked back into the other man's eyes, expecting the Caddy to stop and the doors to fly open, expecting a submachine gun to start crackling, shredding the oleander leaves with a thousand bullets. But the car kept moving past the house and on down the street. Watching its taillights dwindle, Ben let out his breath with a shudder.

He crept free of the shrubbery, went out to the street, and stood in the shadows by a tall jacaranda growing near the curb. He stared after the Cadillac until it had traveled three blocks, climbed a small hill, and disappeared over the crest.

In the distance, there were still sirens, though fewer. They had sounded angry before. Now they sounded mournful.

Holding the thirty-two pistol at his side, he hurried off into the night-cloaked neighborhood in search of a car to steal.

◊   ◊

In the 560 SL, Rachael had moved up front to the driver's seat. It was more comfortable than the cramped storage space, and it was a better position from which to talk with Sarah Kiel. She switched on the little overhead light provided for map reading, confident it would not be seen past the property's thick screen of trees. The moon-pale glow illuminated a portion of the dashboard, the console, Rachael's face, and Sarah's stricken countenance.

The battered girl, having been shaken from her catatonic state, was at last capable of responding to questions.

She was holding her curled right hand protectively against her breast, which somehow gave her the look of a small, injured bird. Her torn fingernails had stopped bleeding, but her broken finger was grotesquely swollen. With her left hand, she tenderly explored her blackened eye, bruised cheek, and split lip, frequently wincing and making small, thin sounds of pain. She said nothing, but when her frightened eyes met Rachael's, awareness glimmered in them.

Rachael said, "Honey, we'll get you to a hospital in just a few minutes. Okay?"

The girl nodded.

"Sarah, do you have any idea who I am?"

The girl shook her head.

"I'm Rachael Leben, Eric's wife."

Fear seemed to darken the blue of Sarah's eyes.

"No, honey, it's all right. I'm on your side. Really. I was in the process of divorcing him. I knew about his young girls, but that has nothing to do with why I left him. The man was sick, honey. Twisted and arrogant and sick. I learned to despise and fear him. So you can speak freely with me. You've got a friend in me. You understand?"

Sarah nodded.

Pausing to look around at the darkness beyond the car, at the blank black windows and patio doors of the house on one side and the untended shrubbery and trees on the other, Rachael locked both doors with the master latch. It was getting warm inside the car. She knew she should open the windows, but she felt safer with them closed.

Returning her attention to the teenager, Rachael said, "Tell me what happened to you, honey. Tell me everything."

The girl tried to speak, but her voice broke. Violent shivers coursed through her.

"Take it easy," Rachael said. "You're safe now." She hoped that was true. "You're safe. Who did this to you?"

In the frosty glow of the map light, Sarah's skin looked as pallid as carved bone. She cleared her throat and whispered, "Eric. Eric b-beat me."

Rachael had known this would be the answer, yet it chilled her to the marrow and, for a moment, left her speechless. At last she said, "When? When did he do this to you?"

"He came . . . at half past midnight."

"Dear God, not even an hour before we got there! He must've left just before we arrived."

From the time she'd left the city morgue earlier this evening, she had hoped to catch up with Eric, and she should have been pleased to learn they were so close behind him. Instead, her heart broke into hard drumlike pounding and her chest tightened as she realized how closely they had passed by him in the warm desert night.

"He rang the bell, and I answered the door, and he just . . . he just . . . hit me." Sarah carefully touched her blackened eye, which was now almost swollen shut. "Hit me and knocked me down and kicked me twice, kicked my legs . . ."

Rachael remembered the ugly bruises on Sarah's thighs.

" . . . grabbed me by the hair . . ."

Rachael took the girl's left hand, held it.

" . . . dragged me into the bedroom . . ."

"Go on," Rachael said.

" . . . just *tore* my pajamas off, you know, and . . . and kept yanking on my hair and hitting me, hitting, punching me . . ."

"Has he ever beaten you before?"

"N-no. A few slaps. You know . . . a little roughhouse. That's all. But tonight . . . tonight he was wild . . . so full of *hatred.*"

"Did he say anything?"

"Not much. Called me names. Awful names, you know. And his speech—it was funny, slurred."

"How did he look?" Rachael asked.

"Oh God . . ."

"Tell me."

"A couple teeth busted out. Bruised up. He looked bad."

"How bad?"

"*Gray.*"

"What about his head, Sarah?"

The girl gripped Rachael's hand very tightly. "His face . . . all gray . . . like, you know, like ashes."

"What about his head?" Rachael repeated.

"He . . . he was wearing a knitted cap when he came in. He had it pulled way down, you know what I mean, like a toboggan cap. But when he was beating me . . . when I tried to fight back . . . the cap came off."

Rachael waited.

The air in the car was stuffy and tainted by the acid stink of the girl's sweat.

"His head was . . . it was all banged up," Sarah said, her voice thickening with terror, horror, and disgust.

"The side of his skull?" Rachael asked. "You saw that?"

"All broken, punched in . . . terrible, terrible."

"His eyes. What about his eyes?"

Sarah tried to speak, choked. She lowered her head and closed her eyes for a moment, struggling to regain control of herself.

Seized by the irrational but quite understandable feeling that someone—or some*thing*—was stealthily creeping up on the Mercedes, Rachael surveyed the night again. It seemed to pulse against the car, seeking entrance at the windows.

When the brutalized girl raised her head again, Rachael said, "Please, honey, tell me about his eyes."

"Strange. Hyper. Spaced out, you know? And . . . clouded . . ."

"Sort of muddy-looking?"

"Yeah."

"His movements. Was there anything odd about the way he moved?"

"Sometimes . . . he seemed jerky . . . you know, a little spastic. But most of the time he was quick, too quick for me."

"And you said his speech was slurred."

"Yeah. Sometimes it didn't make any sense at all. And a couple times he stopped hitting me and just stood there, swaying back and forth, and he seemed . . . confused, you know, as if he couldn't figure where he was or who he was, as if he'd forgotten all about me."

Rachael found that she was trembling as badly as Sarah—and that she was drawing as much strength from the contact with the girl's hand as the girl was drawing from her.

"His touch," Rachael said. "His skin. What did he *feel* like?"

"You don't even have to ask, do you? 'Cause you already know what he felt like. Huh?" the girl said. "Don't you? Somehow . . . you already know."

"But tell me anyway."

"Cold. He felt too cold."

"And moist?" Rachael asked.

"Yeah . . . but . . . not like sweat."

"Greasy," Rachael said.

The memory was so vivid that the girl gagged on it and nodded.

Ever so slightly greasy flesh, like the first stage—the very earliest stage—of putrefaction, Rachael thought, but she was too sick to her stomach and too sick at heart to speak that thought aloud.

Sarah said, "Tonight I watched the eleven o'clock news, and that's when I first heard he'd been killed, hit by a truck earlier in the day, yesterday morning, and I'm wondering how long I can stay in the house before someone comes to put me out, and I'm trying to figure what to do, where to go from here. But then little more than an hour after I see the story about him on the news, he shows up at the door, and at first I think the story must've been all wrong, but then . . .oh, Christ . . . then I knew it wasn't wrong. He . . . he really was killed. He *was*."

"Yes."

The girl tenderly licked her split lip. "But somehow . . ."

"Yes."

" . . . he came back."

"Yes," Rachael said. "He came back. In fact, he's still *coming* back. He's not made it all the way back yet and probably won't ever make it."

"But how—"

"Never mind how. You don't want to know."

"And who—"

"You don't want to *know* who! Believe me, you don't want to know, can't afford to know. Honey, you've got to listen closely now, and I want you to take to heart what I'm saying to you. You can't tell anyone what you've seen. Not anyone. Understand? If you do . . . you'll be in terrible danger. There're people who'd kill you in a minute to keep you from talking about Eric's resurrection. There's more involved here than you can ever know, and they'll kill as many people as necessary to keep their secrets."

A dark, ironic, and not entirely sane laugh escaped the girl. "Who could I tell that would believe me, anyway?"

"Exactly," Rachael said.

"They'd think I was crazy. It's nuts, the whole thing, just plain impossible."

Sarah's voice had a bleak edge, a haunted note, and it was clear that what she had seen tonight had changed her forever, perhaps for the better, perhaps for the worse. She would never be the same again. And for a long time, perhaps for the rest of her life, sleep would not be easily attained, for she would always fear what dreams might come.

Rachael said, "All right. Now, when we get you to a hospital, I'll pay all your bills. And I'm going to give you a check for ten thousand dollars as well, which I hope to God you won't throw away on drugs. And if you want me to, I'll call your parents out there in Kansas and ask them to come for you."

"I . . . I think I'd like that."

"Good. I think that's very good, honey. I'm sure they've been worried about you."

"You know . . . Eric would've killed me. I'm sure that's what he wanted. To kill me. Maybe not me in particular. Just someone. He just felt like he *had* to kill someone, like it was a *need* in him, in his blood. And I was there. You know? Convenient."

"How did you get away from him?"

"He . . . he sort of *phased out* for a couple of minutes. Like I told you, he seemed confused at times. And then at one point his eyes just sort of clouded up even worse, and he started making this funny little wheezing noise. He turned away from me and looked around, as if he was really mixed up . . . you know, bewildered. He seemed to get weak, too, because he leaned against the wall there by the bathroom door and hung his head down."

Rachael remembered the bloody palmprint on the bedroom wall, beside the bathroom door.

"And when he was like that," Sarah said, "when he was distracted, I was flat on the bathroom floor, hurt real bad, hardly able to move, and so the best I could do was crawl into the shower stall, and I was sure he'd come in after me when he got his senses back, you know, but he didn't. Like he forgot me. Came to his senses and either didn't remember I'd been there or couldn't figure out where I'd gone to. And then, after a while, I heard him farther back in the house, pounding things, breaking things."

"He pretty much wrecked the kitchen," Rachael said, and in a dark corner of her memory was the image of the knives driven deep into the kitchen wall.

Tears slid first from Sarah's good eye, then from the blackened and swollen one, and she said, "I can't figure . . ."

"What?" Rachael asked.

"Why he'd come after *me*."

"He probably didn't come after you specifically," Rachael said. "If there was a wall safe in the house, he would've wanted the money from it. But basically, I think he's just . . . looking for a place to go to ground for a while, until the process . . . runs its course. Then, when he blanked out for a moment and you hid from him, and when he came around again and didn't see you, he probably figured you'd gone for help, so he had to get out of there fast, go somewhere else."

"The cabin, I'll bet."

"What cabin?"

"You don't know about his cabin up at Lake Arrowhead?"

"No," Rachael said.

"It's not on the lake, really. Farther up there on the mountain. He took me up to it once. He owns a couple of acres of woods and this neat cabin—"

Someone tapped on the window.

Rachael and Sarah cried out in surprise.

It was only Benny. He pulled open Rachael's door and said, "Come on. I've got us a new set of wheels. It's a gray Subaru—one hell of a lot less conspicuous than this buggy."

Rachael hesitated, catching her breath, waiting for her drumming heartbeat to slow down. She felt as if she and Sarah were kids who'd been sitting at a camp fire, telling ghost stories, trying to spook each other and succeeding all too well. For an instant, crazily, she had been certain that the tapping at the window was the hard, bony *click-click-click* of a skeletal finger.

◦ 12 ◦

SHARP

From the moment Julio met Anson Sharp, he disliked the man. Minute by minute, his dislike intensified.

Sharp came into Rachael Leben's house in Placentia in more of a swagger than a walk, flashing his Defense Security Agency credentials as if ordinary policemen were expected to fall to their knees and venerate a federal agent of such high position. He looked at Becky Klienstad crucified on the wall, shook his head, and said, "Too bad. She was a nice-looking piece, wasn't she?" With an authoritarian briskness that seemed calculated to offend, he told them that the murders of the Hernandez and Klienstad women were now part of an extremely sensitive federal case, removed from the jurisdiction of local police agencies, for reasons that he could not—or would not—divulge. He asked questions and demanded answers, but he would give no answers of his own. He was a big man, even bigger than Reese, with chest and shoulders and arms that looked as if they had been hewn from immense timbers, and his neck was almost as thick as his head. Unlike Reese, he enjoyed using his size to intimidate others and had a habit of standing too close, intentionally violating your space, *looming* over you when he talked to you, looking down with a vague, barely perceptible, yet nevertheless infuriating smirk. He had a handsome face and seemed vain about his looks, and he had thick blond hair expensively razor-cut, and his jewel-bright green eyes said, *I'm better than you, smarter than you, more clever than you, and I always will be.*

Sharp told Orin Mulveck and the other Placentia police officers that they were to vacate the premises and immediately desist in their investigation. "All of the evidence you've collected, photographs you've taken, and paperwork you've generated will be turned over to my own team at once. You will leave one patrol car and two officers at the curb and assign them to assist us in any way we see fit."

Clearly, Orin Mulveck was no happier with Sharp than Julio and Reese were. Mulveck and his people had been reduced to the role of the federal agent's glorified messenger boys, and none of them liked it, though they would have been considerably less offended if Sharp had handled them with more tact—hell, with any tact at all.

"I'll have to check your orders with my chief," Mulveck said.

"By all means," Sharp said. "Meanwhile, please get all your people out of this house. And you are all under orders not to speak of anything you've seen here. Is that understood?"

"I'll check with my chief," Mulveck said. His face was red and the arteries were pounding in his temples when he stalked out.

Two men in dark suits had come with Sharp, neither as large as he, neither as imposing, but both of them cool and smug. They stood just inside the bedroom, one on each side of the door, like temple guards, watching Julio and Reese with unconcealed suspicion.

Julio had never encountered Defense Security Agency men before. They were far different from the FBI agents that he had sometimes worked with, less like policemen than FBI men were. They wore elitism as if it were a pungent cologne.

To Julio and Reese, Sharp said, "I know who you are, and I know a little bit about your reputations—two hound dogs. You bite into a case and you just never let go. Usually that's admirable. This time, however, you've got to unclench your teeth and let go. I can't make it clear enough. Understand me?"

"It's basically our case," Julio said tightly. "It started in our jurisdiction, and we caught the first call."

Sharp frowned. "I'm telling you it's over and you're out. As far as your department's concerned, there *is* no case for you to work on here. The files on Hernandez, Klienstad, and Leben have all been pulled from your records, as if they never existed, and from now on *we* handle everything. I've got my own forensics team driving in from L.A. right now. We don't need or want anything you can provide. *Comprende, amigo?* Listen, Lieutenant Verdad, you're *gone.* Check with your superiors if you don't believe me."

"I don't like it," Julio said.

"You don't have to like it," Sharp said.

◊   ◊

Julio drove only two blocks from Rachael Leben's house before he had to pull over to the curb and stop. He threw the car into park with a violent swipe at the gearshift and said, "Damn! Sharp's so sold on himself he probably thinks someone ought to bottle his piss and sell it as perfume."

During the ten years Reese had worked with Julio, he had never seen his partner this angry. Furious. His eyes looked hard and hot. A tic in his right cheek made half his face twitch. The muscles in his jaws clenched and unclenched, and the cords in his neck were taut. He looked like he wanted to break something in half. Reese was struck by the weird thought that if Julio had been a cartoon character, steam would have been pouring from his ears.

Reese said, "He's an asshole, sure, but he's an asshole with a lot of authority and connections."

"Acts like a damn storm trooper."

"I suppose he's got his job to do."

"Yeah, but it's *our* job he's doing."

"Let it go," Reese said.

"I can't."

"Let it go."

Julio shook his head. "No. This is a special case. I feel a special obligation to that Hernandez girl. Don't ask me to explain it. You'd think I was getting sentimental in my old age. Anyway, if it was just an ordinary case, just the usual homicide, I'd let it go in a minute, I would, I really would, but this one is special."

Reese sighed.

To Julio, nearly every case was special. He was a small man, especially for a detective, but he was *committed*, damned if he wasn't, and one way or another he found an excuse for persevering in a case when any other cop would have given up, when common sense said there was no point in continuing, and when the law of diminishing returns made it perfectly clear that the time had come to move on to something else. Sometimes he said, "Reese, I feel a special commitment to this victim 'cause he was so young, never had a chance to know life, and it isn't fair, it *eats* at me." And sometimes he said, "Reese, this case is personal and special to me because the victim was so old, so old and defenseless, and if we don't go an extra mile to protect our elderly citizens, then we're a very sick society; this *eats* at me, Reese." Sometimes the case was special to Julio because the victim was pretty, and it seemed such a tragedy for any beauty to be lost to the world that it just *ate* at him. But he could be equally eaten because the victim was ugly, therefore already disadvantaged in life, which made the additional curse of death too unfair to be borne. This time, Reese suspected that Julio had formed a special attachment to Ernestina because her name was similar to that of his long-dead little brother. It didn't take much to elicit a fierce commitment from Julio Verdad. Almost any little thing would do. The problem was that Julio had such a deep reservoir of compassion and empathy that he was always in danger of drowning in it.

Sitting rigidly behind the steering wheel, lightly but repeatedly thumping one fist against his thigh, Julio said, "Obviously, the snatching of Eric Leben's corpse and the murders of these two women are connected. But how? Did the people who stole his body kill Ernestina and Becky? And why? And why nail her to the wall in Mrs. Leben's bedroom? That's so grotesque!"

Reese said, "Let it go."

"And where's Mrs. Leben? What's she know about this? Something. When I questioned her, I sensed she was holding something back."

"Let it go."

"And why would this be a national security matter requiring Anson Sharp and his damn Defense Security Agency?"

"Let it go," Reese said, sounding like a broken record, aware that it was useless to attempt to divert Julio, but making the effort anyway. It was their usual litany; he would have felt incomplete if he had not upheld his end of it.

Less angry now than thoughtful, Julio said, "It must have something to do with work Leben's company is doing for the government. A defense contract of some kind."

"You're going to keep poking around, aren't you?"

"I told you, Reese, I feel a special connection with that poor Hernandez girl."

"Don't worry; they'll find her killer."

"Sharp? We're supposed to rely on *him?* He's a jack-ass. You see the way he dresses?" Julio, of course, was always impeccably dressed. "The sleeves on his suit jacket were about an inch too short, and it needed to be let out along the back seam. And he doesn't polish his shoes often enough; they looked like he'd just been hiking in them. How can he find Ernestina's killer if he can't even keep his shoes properly polished?"

"I have a feeling of my own about this one, Julio. I think they'll have our scalps if we don't just let it go."

"I can't walk away," Julio said adamantly. "I'm still in. I'm in for the duration. You can opt out if you want."

"I'll stay."

"I'm putting no pressure on you."

"I'm in," Reese said.

"You don't have to do anything you don't want to do."

"I said I was in, and I'm in."

Five years ago, in an act of unparalleled bravery, Julio Verdad had saved the life of Esther Susanne Hagerstrom, Reese's daughter and only child, who had then been just four years old and achingly small and very helpless. In the world according to Reese Hagerstrom, the seasons changed and the sun rose and the sun set and the sea rose and the sea fell all for one reason: to please Esther Susanne. She was the center, the middle, the ends, and the circumference of his life, and he had almost lost her, but Julio had saved her, had killed one man and nearly killed two others in order to rescue her, so now Reese would have walked away from a million-dollar inheritance sooner than he would have walked away from his partner.

"I can handle everything on my own," Julio said. "Really."

"Didn't you hear me say I was in?"

"We're liable to screw ourselves into disciplinary suspensions."

"I'm in."

"Could be kissing good-bye to any more promotions."

"I'm in."

"You're in, then?"

"I'm in."

"You're sure?"

"I'm sure."

Julio put the car in gear, pulled away from the curb, and headed out of Placentia. "All right, we're both a little whacked out, need some rest. I'll drop you off at your place, let you get a few hours in the sack, and pick you up at ten in the morning."

"And where will you be going while I'm sleeping?"

"Might try to get a few winks myself," Julio said.

Reese and his sister, Agnes, lived with Esther Susanne on East Adams Avenue in the town of Orange, in a pleasant house that Reese had rather substantially remodeled himself during his days off. Julio had an apartment in an attractive Spanish-style complex just a block off Fourth Street, way out at the east end of Santa Ana.

Both of them would be going home to cold and lonely beds. Julio's wife had died of cancer seven years ago. Reese's wife, Esther's mother, had been shot and killed during the same incident in which he had almost lost his little girl, so he had been a widower five years, only two less than Julio.

On the 57 Freeway, shooting south toward Orange and Santa Ana, Reese said, "And if you can't sleep?"

"I'll go into the office, nose around, try to see if anyone knows anything about this Sharp and why he's so damned hot to run the show. Maybe ask around here and there about Dr. Eric Leben, too."

"What're we going to do exactly when you pick me up at ten in the morning?"

"I don't know yet," Julio said. "But I'll have figured out something by then."

◊ 13 ◊

REVELATIONS

They took Sarah Kiel to the hospital in the stolen gray Subaru. Rachael arranged to pay the hospital bills, left a ten-thousand-dollar check with Sarah, called the girl's parents in Kansas, then left the hospital with Ben and went looking for a suitable place to hole up for the rest of the night.

By 3:35 Tuesday morning, grainy-eyed and exhausted, they found a large motel on Palm Canyon Drive with an all-night desk clerk. Their room had orange and white drapes that almost made Ben's eyes bleed, and Rachael said the bedspread pattern looked like yak puke, but the shower and air-conditioning worked, and the two queen-size beds had firm mattresses, and the unit was at the back of the complex, away from the street, where they could expect quiet even after the town came alive in the morning, so it wasn't exactly hell on earth.

Leaving Rachael alone for ten minutes, Ben drove the stolen Subaru out the motel's rear exit, left it in a supermarket parking lot several blocks away, and returned on foot. Both going and coming, he avoided passing the windows of the motel office and therefore did not stir the curiosity of the night clerk. Tomorrow, with the need for wheels less urgent, they could take time to rent a car.

In his absence, Rachael had visited the ice-maker and the soda-vending machine. A plastic bucket brimming with ice cubes stood on the small table by the window, plus cans of Diet Coke and regular Coke and A&W Root Beer and Orange Crush.

She said, "I thought you might be thirsty."

He was suddenly aware that they were smack in the middle of the desert and that they had been moving in a sweat for hours. Standing, he drank an Orange Crush in two swallows, finished a root beer nearly as fast, then sat down and popped the tab on a Diet Coke. "Even with the hump, how do camels do it?"

As if dropping under an immense weight, she sat down on the other side of the table, opened a Coke, and said, "Well?"

"Well what?"

"Aren't you going to ask?"

He yawned, not out of perversity, and not because he wanted to irritate her, but because at that moment the prospect of sleep was more appealing than finally learning the truth of her circumstances. He said, "Ask what?"

"The same questions you've been asking all night."

"You made it clear you wouldn't give answers."

"Well, now I will. Now there's no keeping you out of it."

She looked so sad that Ben felt a cold premonition of death in his bones and wondered if he had, indeed, been foolish to involve himself even to help the woman he loved. She was looking at him as if he were already dead—as if they were *both* dead.

"So if you're ready to tell me," he said, "then I don't need to ask questions."

"You're going to have to keep an open mind. What I'm about to tell you might seem unbelievable . . . damn strange."

He sipped the Diet Coke and said, "You mean about Eric dying and coming back from the dead?"

She jerked in surprise and gaped at him. She tried to speak but couldn't get any words out.

He had never in his life elicited such a rewarding reaction from anyone else, and he took enormous pleasure in it.

At last she said, "But . . . but how . . . when . . . what . . ."

He said, "How do I know what I know? When did I figure it out? What clued me in?"

She nodded.

He said, "Hell, if someone had stolen Eric's body, they'd surely have come with a car of their own to haul it away. They wouldn't have had to kill a woman and steal *her* car. And there were those discarded hospital whites in the garage in Villa Park. Besides, you were scared witless from the moment I showed up at your door last evening, and you aren't easily spooked. You're a very competent and self-sufficient woman, not the type to get the willies. In fact, I've never seen you scared of anything except maybe . . . Eric."

"He really was killed by that truck, you know. It isn't just that they misdiagnosed his condition."

The desire for sleep retreated a bit, and Ben said, "His business—and genius—was genetic engineering. And the man was obsessed with staying young. So I figure he found a way to edit out the genes linked to aging and death. Or maybe he edited *in* an artificially constructed gene for swift healing, tissue stasis . . . immortality."

"You endlessly amaze me," she said.

"I'm quite a guy."

Her own weariness gave way to nervous energy. She could not keep still. She got up and paced.

He remained seated, sipping his Diet Coke. He had been badly rattled all night; now it was her turn.

Her bleak voice was tinted by dread, resignation. "When Geneplan patented its first highly profitable artificial microorganisms, Eric could've taken the company public, could've sold thirty percent of his stock and made a hundred million overnight."

"A hundred? Jesus!"

"His two partners and three of the research associates, who also had pieces of the company, half wanted him to do just that because they'd have made a killing, too. Everyone else but Vincent Baresco was leaning toward going for the gold. Eric refused."

"Baresco," Ben said. "The guy who pulled the Magnum on us, the guy I trashed in Eric's office tonight—is he a partner?"

"It's *Dr.* Vincent Baresco. He's on Eric's handpicked research staff—one of the few who know about the Wildcard Project. In fact, only the six of them knew everything. Six plus me. Eric loved to brag to me. Anyway, Baresco sided with Eric, didn't want Geneplan to go public, and he convinced the others. If it remained a privately held company, they didn't have to please stockholders. They could spend money on unlikely projects without defending their decisions."

"Such as a search for immortality or its equivalent."

"They didn't expect to achieve full immortality—but longevity, regeneration. It took a *lot* of funds, money that stockholders would've wanted to see paid out in dividends. Eric and the others were getting rich, anyway, from the modest percentage of corporate profits they distributed to themselves, so they didn't desperately need the capital they'd get by going public."

"Regeneration," Ben said thoughtfully.

At the window, Rachael stopped pacing, cautiously drew back the drape, and peered out at the night-cloaked motel parking lot.

She said, "God knows, I'm no expert in recombinant DNA. But . . . well, they hoped to develop a benign virus that'd function as a 'carrier' to convey new genetic material into the body's cells and precisely place the new bits on the chains of chromosomes. Think of the virus as a sort of living scalpel that does genetic surgery. Because it's microscopic, it can perform minute operations no real scalpel ever could. It can be designed to seek out—and attach itself to—a certain portion of a chromosomal chain, either destroying the gene already there or inserting a new one."

"And they *did* develop it?"

"Yes. Then they needed to positively identify genes associated with aging and edit them out—*and* develop artificial genetic material for the virus to carry into the cells. Those new genes would be designed to halt the aging process and tremendously boost the natural immune system by cuing the body to produce vastly larger quantities of interferon and other healing substances. Follow me?"

"Mostly."

"They even believed they could give the human body the ability to regenerate ruined tissue, bone, and vital organs."

She still stared out at the night, and she appeared to have gone pale—not at something she had seen but at the consideration of what she was slowly revealing to him.

Finally she continued: "Their patents were bringing in a river of money, a flood. So they spent God knows how many tens of millions, farming out pieces of the research puzzle to geneticists not in the company, keeping the work fragmented so no one was likely to realize the true intent of their efforts. It was like a privately financed equivalent of the Manhattan Project—and maybe even more secret than the development of the atomic bomb."

"Secret . . . because if they succeeded, they wanted to keep the blessing of an extended life span for themselves?"

"Partly, yes." Letting the drape fall in place, she turned from the window. "And by holding the secret, by dispensing the blessing only to whomever they chose—just imagine the *power* they'd wield. They could essentially create a long-lived elite master race that owed its existence to them. And the threat of withholding the gift would be a bludgeon that could make virtually anyone cooperate with them. I used to listen to Eric talk about it, and it sounded like nonsense, pipe dreams, even though I knew he was a genius in his field."

"Those men in the Cadillac who pursued us and shot the cops—"

"From Geneplan," she said, still full of nervous energy, pacing again. "I recognized the car. It belongs to Rupert Knowls. Knowls supplied the initial venture capital that got Eric started. After Eric, he's the chief partner."

"A rich man . . . yet he's willing to risk his reputation and his freedom by gunning down two cops?"

"To protect this secret, yeah, I guess he is. He's not exactly a scrupulous man to begin with. And confronted with *this* opportunity, I suppose he'll stretch his scruples even further than usual."

"Okay. So they developed the technique to prolong life and promote incredibly rapid healing. Then what?"

Her lovely face had been pale. Now it darkened as if a shadow had fallen across it, though there was no shadow. "Then . . . they began experiments on lab animals. Primarily white mice."

Ben sat up straighter in his chair and put the can of Diet Coke aside, because from Rachael's demeanor he sensed that she was reaching the crux of the story.

She paused for a moment to check the dead bolt on the room door, which opened onto a covered breezeway that flanked the parking lot. The lock was securely engaged, but after a moment's hesitation she took one of the straight-backed chairs from the table, tipped it onto two legs, and braced it under the doorknob for extra protection.

He was sure she was being overly cautious, treading the edge of paranoia. On the other hand, he didn't object.

She returned to the edge of the bed. "They injected the mice, *changed* the mice, working with mouse genes instead of human genes, of course, but applying the same theories and techniques they intended to use to promote human longevity. And the mice, a short-lived variety, survived longer . . . twice as long as usual and still kicking. Then three times as long . . . four times . . . and still young. Some mice were subjected to injuries of various kinds—everything from contusions and abrasions to punctures, broken bones, serious burns—and they healed at a remarkable rate. They recovered and flourished after their kidneys were virtually destroyed.

Lungs eaten half away by acid fumes were regenerated. They actually regained their vision after being blinded. And then . . ."

Her voice trailed away, and she glanced at the fortified door, then at the window, lowered her head, closed her eyes.

Ben waited.

Eyes still closed, she said, "Following standard procedure, they killed some mice and put them aside for dissection and for thorough tissue tests. Some were killed with injections of air—embolisms. Killed others with lethal injections of formaldehyde. And there was no question they were dead. Very dead. But those that weren't yet dissected . . . they came back. Within a few hours. Lying there in the lab trays . . . they just . . . started twitching, squirming. Bleary-eyed, weak at first . . . *but they came back.* Soon they were on their feet, scurrying about their cages, eating—fully alive. Which no one had anticipated, not at all. Oh, sure, before the mice were killed, they'd had tremendously enhanced immune systems, truly astonishing capacity to heal, and life spans that had been dramatically increased, but . . ." Rachael raised her head, opened her eyes, looked at Ben. "But once the line of death is crossed . . . who'd imagine it could be *re*crossed?"

Ben's hands started shaking, and a wintry shiver followed the track of his spine, and he realized that the true meaning and power of these events had only now begun to sink in.

"Yes," Rachael said, as if she knew what thoughts and emotions were racing through his mind and heart.

He was overcome by a strange mixture of terror, awe, and wild joy: terror at the idea of anything, mouse or man, returning from the land of the dead; awe at the thought that humankind's genius had perhaps shattered nature's dreadful chains of mortality; joy at the prospect of humanity freed forever from the loss of loved ones, freed forever from the great fears of sickness and death.

And as if reading his mind, Rachael said, "Maybe one day . . . maybe even one day soon, the threat of the grave will pass away. But not yet. Not quite yet. Because the Wildcard Project's breakthrough is not entirely successful. The mice that came back were . . . strange."

"Strange?"

Instead of elaborating on that freighted word, she said, "At first the researchers thought the mice's odd behavior resulted from some sort of brain damage—maybe not to cerebral tissues but to the fundamental *chemistry* of the brain—that couldn't be repaired even by the mice's enhanced healing abilities. But that wasn't the case. They could still run difficult mazes and repeat other complex tricks they'd been taught before they'd died—"

"So somehow the memories, knowledge, probably even personality survives the brief period of lifelessness between death and rebirth."

She nodded. "Which would indicate that some small current still exists in the brain for a time after death, enough to keep memory intact until . . . resurrection. Like a computer during a power failure, barely holding on to material in its short-term memory by using the meager flow of current from a standby battery."

Ben wasn't sleepy anymore. "Okay, so the mice could run mazes, but there was something strange about them. What? How strange?"

"Sometimes they became confused—more frequently at first than after they'd been back with the living awhile—and they repeatedly rammed themselves against their cages or ran in circles chasing their tails. That kind of abnormal behavior slowly passed. But another, more frightening behavior emerged . . . and endured."

Outside a car pulled into the motel parking lot and stopped.

Rachael glanced worriedly at the barricaded door.

In the still desert air, a car door opened, closed.

Ben sat up straighter in his chair, tense.

Footsteps echoed softly through the empty night. They were heading away from Rachael's and Ben's room. In another part of the motel, the door to another room opened and closed.

With visible relief Rachael let her shoulders sag. "Mice are natural-born cowards, of course. They never fight their enemies. They're not equipped to. They survive by running, dodging, hiding. They don't even fight among themselves for supremacy or territory. They're meek, timid. But the mice who came back weren't meek at all. They fought one another, and they attacked mice that had *not* been resurrected—and they even tried to nip at the researchers handling them, though a mouse has no hope of hurting a man and is ordinarily acutely aware of that. They flew into rages, clawing at the floors of their cages, pawing at the air as if fighting imaginary enemies, sometimes even clawing at themselves. Occasionally these fits lasted less than a minute, but more often went on until the mouse collapsed in exhaustion."

For a moment, neither spoke.

The silence in the motel room was sepulchral, profound.

At last Ben said, "In spite of this strangeness in the mice, Eric and his researchers must've been electrified. Dear God, they'd hoped to extend the life span—and instead they defeated death altogether! So they were eager to move on to development of similar methods of genetic alteration for human beings."

"Yes."

"In spite of the mice's unexplained tendency to frenzies, rages, random violence."

"Yes."

"Figuring that problem might never arise in a human subject . . . or could be dealt with somewhere along the way."

"Yes."

Ben said, "So . . . slowly the work progressed, but too slowly for Eric. Youth-oriented, youth-*obsessed,* and inordinately afraid of dying, he decided not to wait for a safe and proven process."

"Yes."

"That's what you meant in Eric's office tonight, when you asked Baresco if he knew Eric had broken the cardinal rule. To a genetics researcher or other specialist in

biological sciences, the cardinal rule would be—what?—
that he should never experiment with human beings until
all encountered problems and unanswered questions are
dealt with at the test-animal level or below."

"Exactly," she said. She had folded her hands in her
lap to keep them from shaking, but her fingers kept
picking at one another. "And Vincent didn't know Eric
had broken the cardinal rule. *I* knew, but it must've come
as a nasty shock to them when they heard Eric's body was
missing. The moment they heard, they knew he'd done
the craziest, most reckless, most unforgivable thing he
possibly could've done."

"And now what?" Ben asked. "They want to help
him?"

"No. They want to kill him. Again."

"Why?"

"Because he won't come back all the way, won't
ever be exactly like he was. This stuff wasn't *perfected* yet."

"He'll be like the lab animals?"

"Probably. Strangely violent, dangerous."

Ben thought of the mindless destruction in the Villa
Park house, the blood in the trunk of the car.

Rachael said, "Remember—he was a ruthless man all
his life and troubled by barely suppressed violent urges
even before this. The mice started out meek, but Eric
didn't, so what might he be like now? Look what he
did to Sarah Kiel."

Ben remembered not only the beaten girl but the
wrecked kitchen in the Palm Springs house, the knives
driven into the wall.

"And if Eric murders someone in one of these rages,"
Rachael said, "the police are more likely to learn he's
alive, and Wildcard will be blown wide open. So his
partners want to kill him in some *very* final manner that'll
rule out another resurrection. I wouldn't be surprised if
they dismembered the corpse or burned it to ashes and
then disposed of the remains in several locations."

Good God, Ben thought, is this reality or Chiller
Theater?

He said, "They want to kill you because you know about Wildcard?"

"Yes, but that's not the only reason they'd like to get their hands on me. They've got two others at least. For one thing, they probably think I know where Eric will go to ground."

"But you don't?"

"I had some ideas. And Sarah Kiel gave me another one. But I don't know for sure."

"You said there's a third reason they'd want you?"

She nodded. "I'm first in line to inherit Geneplan, and they don't trust me to continue pumping enough money into Wildcard. By removing me, they stand a much better chance of retaining control of the corporation and of keeping Wildcard secret. If I could've gotten to Eric's safe ahead of them and could've put my hands on his project diary, I would've had solid proof that Wildcard exists, and then they wouldn't have dared touch me. Without proof, I'm vulnerable."

Ben rose and began to move restlessly around the room, thinking furiously.

Somewhere in the night, not far beyond the motel walls, a cat cried either in anger or in passion. It went on a long time, rising and falling, an eerie ululation.

Finally Ben said, "Rachael, why are *you* pursuing Eric? Why this desperate rush to reach him before the others? What'll you do if you find him?"

"Kill him," she said without hesitation, and the bleakness in her green eyes was now complemented by a Rachael-like determination and iron resolve. "Kill him for good. Because if I don't kill him, he's going to hide out until he's in better condition, until he's a bit more in control of himself, and then he's going to come kill me. He died furious with me, consumed by such hatred for me that he dashed blindly out into traffic, and I'm sure that same hatred was seething in him the moment awareness returned to him in the county morgue. In his clouded and twisted mind, I'm very likely his primary obsession, and I don't think he'll rest until I'm dead. Or until he's dead, really dead this time."

He knew she was right. He was deeply afraid for her.

His preference for the past was as strong in him now as it had ever been, and he longed for simpler times. How mad had the modern world become? Criminals owned the city streets at night. The whole planet could be utterly destroyed in an hour with the pressing of a few buttons. And now . . . *now* dead men could be reanimated. Ben wished for a time machine that could carry him back to a better age: say the early 1920s, when a sense of wonder was still alive and when faith in the human potential was unsullied and unsurpassed.

Yet . . . he remembered the joy that had surged in him when Rachael had first said that death had been beaten, before she had explained that those who came back from beyond were frighteningly changed. He had been *thrilled.* Hardly the response of a genuine stick-in-the-mud reactionary. He might peer back at the past and long for it with full-blown sentimentalism, but in his heart he was, like others of his age, undeniably attracted to science and its potential for creating a brighter future. Maybe he was not such a misfit in the modern world as he liked to pretend. Maybe this experience was teaching him something about himself that he would have preferred not to learn.

He said, "Could you really pull the trigger on Eric?"

"Yes."

"I'm not sure you could. I suspect you'd freeze up when you were really confronted with the moral implications of murder."

"This wouldn't be murder. He's no longer a human being. He's already dead. The living dead. The walking dead. He's not a man anymore. He's different. *Changed.* Just as those mice were changed. He's only a thing now, not a man, a dangerous *thing,* and I wouldn't have any qualms about blowing his head off. If the authorities ever found out, I don't think they'd even try to prosecute me. And I see no moral questions that would put me on trial in my own mind."

"You've obviously thought hard about this," he said. "But why not hide out, keep a low profile, let Eric's partners find him and kill him for you?"

She shook her head. "I can't bet everything on their success. They might fail. They might not get to him before he finds me. This is *my* life we're talking about, and by God I'm not trusting in anyone but me to protect it."

"And me," he said.

"And you, yes. And you, Benny."

He came to the bed and sat down on the edge of it, beside her. "So we're chasing a dead man."

"Yes."

"But we've got to get some rest now."

"I'm beat," she agreed.

"Then where will we go tomorrow?"

"Sarah told me about a cabin Eric has in the mountains near Lake Arrowhead. It sounded secluded. Just what he needs now, for the next few days, while the initial healing's going on."

Ben sighed. "Yeah, I think we might find him in a place like that."

"You don't have to come with me."

"I will."

"But you don't *have* to."

"I know. But I will."

She kissed him lightly on the cheek.

Though she was weary, sweaty, and rumpled, with lank hair and bloodshot eyes, she was beautiful.

He had never felt closer to her. Facing death together always forged a special bond between people, drew them even closer regardless of how very close they might have been before. He knew, for he had been to war in the Green Hell.

Tenderly she said, "Let's get some rest, Benny."

"Right," he said.

But before he could lie down and turn off the lights, he had to break out the magazine of the Smith & Wesson Combat Magnum that he had taken off Vincent Baresco several hours ago and count the remaining cartridges. Three. Half the magazine's load had been expended in Eric's office, when Baresco had fired wildly in the darkness as Ben attacked him. Three left. Not much. Not nearly enough to make Ben feel secure, even though Rachael had her own thirty-two pistol. How many bullets were required to stop a walking dead man? Ben put the Combat Magnum on the nightstand, where he could reach out and lay his hand on it in an instant if he needed it during what remained of the night.

In the morning, he would buy a box of ammunition. Two boxes.

◦ 14 ◦

LIKE A NIGHT BIRD

Leaving two men behind at Rachael Leben's house in Placentia—where the crucified corpse of Rebecca Klienstad had finally been taken down from the bedroom wall—and leaving other men at the Leben house in Villa Park and still others at the Geneplan offices, Anson Sharp of the Defense Security Agency choppered through the desert darkness with two more agents, flying low and fast, to Eric Leben's stylish yet squalid love nest in Palm Springs. The pilot put the helicopter down in a bank parking lot less than a block off Palm Canyon Drive, where a nondescript government car was waiting. The chuffling rotors of the aircraft sliced up the hot dry desert air and flung slabs of it at Sharp's back as he dashed to the sedan.

Five minutes later, they arrived at the house where Dr. Leben had kept his string of teenage girls. Sharp wasn't surprised to find the front door ajar. He rang the bell repeatedly, but no one answered. Drawing his service revolver, a Smith & Wesson Chief's Special, he led the way inside, in search of Sarah Kiel who, according to the most recent report on Leben, was the current piece of fluff in residence.

The Defense Security Agency knew about Leben's lechery because it knew *everything* about people engaged in top-secret contract work with the Pentagon. That was something civilians like Leben just could never seem to understand: Once they accepted the Pentagon's money and undertook highly sensitive research work, they had absolutely no privacy. Sharp knew all about Leben's fascination with modern art, modern design, and modern architecture. He knew about Eric Leben's marital problems in detail. He knew what foods Leben preferred, what music he liked, what brand of underwear he wore; so of course he also knew every little thing about the teenage girls because the potential for blackmail that they presented was related to national security.

When Sharp stepped into the kitchen and saw the destruction, especially the knives driven into the wall, he figured he would not find Sarah Kiel alive. She would be nailed up in another room, or maybe bolted to the ceiling, or maybe hacked to pieces and hung on wire to form a bloody mobile, maybe even worse. You couldn't guess what might happen next in this case. *Anything* could happen.

Weird.

Gosser and Peake, the two young agents with Sharp, were startled and made uneasy by the mess in the kitchen and by the psychopathic frenzy it implied. Their security clearance and need to know were as high as Sharp's, so they were aware that they were hunting for a walking dead man. They knew Eric Leben had risen from a morgue slab and escaped in stolen hospital whites, and they knew a half-alive and deranged Eric Leben had killed the Hernandez and Klienstad women to obtain their car, so Gosser and Peake held their service revolvers as tightly and cautiously as Sharp held his.

Of course, the DSA was fully aware of the nature of the work Geneplan was doing for the government: biological warfare research, the creation of deadly man-made viruses. But the agency also knew the details of other projects under way within the company, including the Wildcard Project, although Leben and his associates had labored under the delusion that the secret of Wildcard was theirs alone. They were unaware of the federal agents and stoolies among them. And they did not realize how quickly government computers had ascertained their intentions merely by surveying the research they farmed out to other companies and extrapolating the purpose of it all.

These civilian types just could not understand that when you bargained with Uncle Sam and eagerly took his money, you couldn't sell only a small piece of your soul. You had to sell it all.

Anson Sharp usually enjoyed bringing that bit of nasty news to people like Eric Leben. They thought they were such big fish, but they forgot that even big fish are eaten by bigger fish, and there was no bigger fish in the sea than the whale called Washington. Sharp loved to watch that realization sink in. He relished seeing the self-important hotshots break into a sweat and quiver. They usually tried to bribe him or reason with him, and sometimes they begged, but of course he could not let them off the hook. Even if he could have let them off, he would not have done it, because he liked nothing more than seeing them squirm before him.

Dr. Eric Leben and his six cronies had been permitted to proceed unhampered with their revolutionary research into longevity. But if they had solved all the problems and achieved a useful breakthrough, the government would have moved in on them and would have absorbed the project by one means or another, through the swift declaration of a national defense emergency.

Now Eric Leben had screwed up everything. He administered the faulty treatment to himself and then accidentally put it to the test by walking in front of a damn garbage truck. No one could have anticipated such a turn of events because the guy had seemed too smart to risk his own genetic integrity.

Looking at the broken china and the trampled food that littered the floor, Gosser wrinkled his choirboy face and said, "The guy's a real berserker."

"Looks like the work of an animal," Peake said, frowning.

Sharp led them out of the kitchen, through the rest of the house, finally to the master bedroom and bath, where more destruction had been wrought and where there was also some blood, including a bloody palmprint on the wall. It was probably Leben's print: proof that the dead man, in some strange fashion, lived.

No cadaver could be found in the house, neither Sarah Kiel's nor anybody else's, and Sharp was disappointed. The nude and crucified woman in Placentia had been unexpected and kinky, a welcome change from the corpses he usually saw. Victims of guns, knives, plastique, and the garroting wire were old news to Sharp; he had seen them in such plenitude over the years that he no longer got a kick out of them. But he had sure gotten a kick out of that bimbo nailed to the wall, and he was curious to see what Leben's deranged and rotting mind might come up with next.

Sharp checked the hidden safe in the floor of the bedroom closet and found that it had been emptied.

Leaving Gosser behind to house-sit in case Leben returned, Sharp took Peake along on a search of the garage, expecting to find Sarah Kiel's body, which they did not. Then he sent Peake into the backyard with a flashlight to examine the lawn and flower beds for signs of a freshly dug grave, though it seemed unlikely that Leben, in his current condition, would have the desire or the foresight to bury his victims and cover his tracks.

"If you don't find anything," Sharp told Peake, "then start checking the hospitals. In spite of the blood, maybe the Kiel girl wasn't killed. Maybe she managed to run away from him and get medical attention."

"If I find her at some hospital?"

"I'll need to know at once," Sharp said, for he would have to prevent Sarah Kiel from talking about Eric Leben's return. He would try to use reason, intimidation, and outright threats to ensure her silence. If that didn't work, she would be quietly removed.

Rachael Leben and Ben Shadway also had to be found soon and silenced.

As Peake set out on his assigned tasks—and while Gosser waited alertly inside the house—Sharp climbed into the unmarked sedan at the curb and had the driver return him to the bank parking lot off Palm Canyon Drive, where the helicopter was still waiting for him.

Airborne again, heading for the Geneplan labs in Riverside, Anson Sharp stared out at the night landscape as it rushed past below the chopper, his eyes narrowed as if he were a night bird seeking prey.

◊ 15 ◊

LOVING

Ben's dreams were dark and full of thunder, blasted by strange lightning that illuminated nothing in a landscape without form, inhabited by an unseen but fearful creature that stalked him through the shadows, where all was vast and cold and lonely. It was—and yet was not—the Green Hell where he had spent more than three years of his youth, a familiar yet unfamiliar place, the same as it had been, yet changed as landscapes can be only in dreams.

Shortly after dawn, he came awake with bird-thin cries, full of dread, shuddering, and Rachael was with him. She had moved from the other bed and had drawn him to her, comforting him. Her warm tender touch dispelled the cold and lonely dream. The rhythmic thumping of her heart seemed like the steady throbbing of a bright lighthouse beacon along a fogbound coast, each pulse a reassurance.

He believed she had intended to offer nothing more than the comfort that a good friend could provide, though perhaps unconsciously she brought the greater gift of love and sought it in return. In the half-awake state following sleep, when his vision seemed filtered by a semitransparent cloth, when an invisible thinness of warm silk seemed to interpose itself between his hands and everything he touched, and while sounds were still dream-muffled, his perceptions were not sharp enough to determine how and when her offered comfort became offered—and accepted—love. He only knew that it happened and that, when he drew her unclothed body to his, he felt a *rightness* that he had never felt before in his thirty-seven years.

He was at last within her, and she was filled with him. It was fresh and wondrous, yet they did not have to search for the rhythms and patterns that pleased them, because they knew what was perfect for them as lovers of a decade might know.

Although the softly rumbling air conditioner kept the room cool, Ben had an almost psychic awareness of desert heat pressing at the windows. The cool chamber was a bubble suspended outside the reality of the harsh land, just as their special moment of tender coupling was a bubble drifting outside the normal flow of seconds and minutes.

Only one opaque window of frosted glass—high in the kitchenette wall—was not covered with a drape, and upon it the rising sun built a slowly growing fire. Outside, palm fronds, fanning lazily in a breeze, filtered the beams of the sun; feathery tropical shadows and frost-pale light fell on their nude bodies, rippling as they moved.

Ben saw her face clearly even in that inconstant light. Her eyes were shut, mouth open. She drew deep breaths at first, then breathed more quickly. Every line of her face was exquisitely sensuous—but also infinitely precious. His perception of her preciousness mattered more to him than the shatteringly sensuous vision she presented, for it was an emotional rather than physical response, a result of their months together and of his great affection for her. Because she was so special to him, their coupling was not merely an act of sex but an immeasurably more gratifying act of love.

Sensing his examination, she opened her eyes and looked into his, and he was electrified by that new degree of contact.

The palm-patterned morning light grew rapidly brighter, changing hue as well, from frost-pale to lemon-yellow to gold. It imparted those colors to Rachael's face, slender throat, full breasts. As the richness of the light increased, so did the pace of their lovemaking, till both were gasping, till she cried out and cried out again, at which moment the breeze outside became a sudden energetic wind that whipped the palm fronds, casting abruptly frantic shadows through the milky window, upon the bed. At precisely the moment when the wind-sculpted shadows leaped and shuddered, Ben thrust deep and shuddered too, emptying copious measures of himself into Rachael, and just when the last rush of his seed had streamed from him, the spill of wind was also depleted, flowing away to other corners of the world.

In time he withdrew from her, and they lay on their sides, facing each other, heads close, their breath mingling. Still, neither spoke nor needed to, and gradually they drifted toward sleep again.

He had never before felt as fulfilled and contented as this. Even in the good days of his youth, before the Green Hell, before Vietnam, he had never felt half this fine.

She slept before Ben did, and for a long pleasant moment he watched as a bubble of saliva slowly formed between her parted lips, and popped. His eyes grew heavy, and the last thing he saw before he closed them was the vague—almost invisible—scar along her jawline, where she had been cut when Eric had thrown a glass at her.

Drifting down into a restful darkness, Ben almost felt sorry for Eric Leben, because the scientist had never realized love was the closest thing to immortality that men would ever know and that the only—and best— answer to death was loving. Loving.

◊ 16 ◊

IN THE
ZOMBIE ZONE

For part of the night he lay fully clothed on the bed in the cabin above Lake Arrowhead, in a condition deeper than sleep, deeper than coma, his body temperature steadily declining, his heart beating only twenty times a minute, blood barely circulating, drawing breath shallowly and only intermittently. Occasionally his respiration and heartbeat stopped entirely for periods as long as ten or fifteen minutes, during which the only life within him was at a cellular level, though even that was not life as much as stasis, a strange twilight existence that no other man on earth had ever known. During those periods of suspended animation, with cells only slowly renewing themselves and performing their functions at a greatly reduced pace, the body was gathering energy for the next period of wakefulness and accelerated healing.

He *was* healing, and at an astonishing rate. Hour by hour, almost visibly, his multitude of punctures and lacerations were scabbing over, closing up. Beneath the ugly bluish blackness of the bruises that he had suffered from the brutal impact with the garbage truck, there was already a visible yellow hue arising as the blood from crushed capillaries was leeched from the tissues. When he was awake, he could feel fragments of his broken skull pressing insistently into his brain, even though medical wisdom held that tissue of the brain was without nerve endings and therefore insensate; it was not a pain as much as a pressure, like a Novocaine-numbed tooth registering the grinding bit of a dentist's drill. And he could sense, without understanding how, that his genetically improved body was methodically dealing with that head injury as surely as it was closing up its other wounds. For a week he would need much rest, but during that time the periods of stasis would grow shorter, less frequent, less frightening. That was what he wanted to believe. In two or three weeks, his physical condition would be no worse than that of a man leaving the hospital after major surgery. In a month he might be fully recovered, although he'd always have a slight—or even pronounced—depression along the right side of his skull.

But mental recovery was not keeping pace with the rapid physical regeneration of tissues. Even when awake, heartbeat and respiration close to normal, he was seldom fully alert. And during those brief periods when he possessed approximately the same intellectual capacity he had known before his death, he was acutely and dismally aware that for the most part he was functioning in a robotic state, with frequent lapses into a confused and, at times, virtually animalistic condition.

He had strange thoughts.

Sometimes he believed himself to be a young man again, recently graduated from college, but sometimes he recognized that he was actually past forty. Sometimes he did not know exactly where he was, especially when he was out on the road, driving, with no familiar reference points to his own past life; overcome by confusion, feeling lost and sensing that he would *forever* be lost, he had to pull over to the edge of the highway until the panic passed. He knew that he had a great goal, an important mission, though he was never quite able to define his purpose or destination. Sometimes he thought he was dead and making his way through the levels of hell on a Dantean journey. Sometimes he thought he had killed people, although he could not remember who, and then he *did* briefly remember and shrank from the memory, not only shrank from it but convinced himself that it was not a memory at all but a fantasy, for of course he was incapable of cold-blooded murder. Of course. Yet at other times he thought about how exciting and satisfying it would be to kill someone, anyone, everyone, because in his heart he knew they were after him, all of them, out to get him, the rotten bastards, as they had always been out to get him, though they were even more determined now than ever. Sometimes he thought urgently, *Remember the mice, the mice, the deranged mice bashing themselves to pieces against the walls of their cages,* and more than once he even said it aloud, "Remember the mice, the mice," but he had no idea what those words meant: what mice, where, when?

He saw strange things, too.

Sometimes he saw people who could not possibly be there: his long-dead mother, a hated uncle who had abused him when he had been a little boy, a neighborhood bully who had terrorized him in grade school. Now and then, as if suffering from the delirium tremens of a chronic alcoholic, he saw things crawling out of the walls, bugs and snakes and more frightening creatures that defied definition.

Several times, he was certain that he saw a path of perfectly black flagstones leading down into a terrible darkness in the earth. Always compelled to follow those stones, he repeatedly discovered the path was illusory, a figment of his morbid and fevered imagination.

Of all the apparitions and illusions that flickered past his eyes and through his damaged mind, the most unusual and the most disturbing were the shadowfires. They leaped up unexpectedly and made a crackling sound that he not only heard but *felt* in his bones. He would be moving right along, walking with reasonable sure-footedness, passing among the living with some conviction, functioning better than he dared believe he could—when suddenly a fire would spring up in the shadowed corners of a room or in the shadows clustered beneath a tree, in any deep pocket of gloom, flames the shade of wet blood with hot silvery edges, startling him. And when he looked close, he could see that nothing was burning, that the flames had erupted out of thin air and were fed by nothing whatsoever, as if the shadows themselves were burning and made excellent fuel in spite of their lack of substance. When the fires faded and were extinguished, no signs of them remained—no ashes, charred fragments, or smoke stains.

Though he had never been afraid of fire before he died, had never entertained the pyrophobic idea that he was destined to die in flames, he was thoroughly terrified of these hungry phantom fires. When he peered into the flickering brightness, he felt that just beyond lay a mystery he must solve, though the solution would bring him unimaginable anguish.

In his few moments of relative lucidity, when his intellectual capacity was nearly what it once had been, he told himself that the illusions of flames merely resulted from misfiring synapses in his injured brain, electrical pulses shorting through the damaged tissues. And he told himself that the illusions frightened him because, above all else, he was an intellectual, a man whose life had been a life of the mind, so he had every *right* to be frightened by signs of brain deterioration. The tissues would heal, the shadowfires fade forever, and he would be all right. That was also what he told himself. But in his less lucid moments, when the world turned tenebrous and eerie, when he was gripped by confusion and animal fear, he looked upon the shadowfires with unalloyed horror and was sometimes reduced to paralysis by something he thought he glimpsed within—or beyond—the dancing flames.

Now, as dawn insistently pressed upon the resistant darkness of the mountains, Eric Leben ascended from stasis, groaned softly for a while, then louder, and finally woke. He sat up on the edge of the bed. His mouth was stale; he tasted ashes. His head was filled with pain. He touched his broken pate. It was no worse; his skull was not coming apart.

The meager glow of morning entered by two windows, and a small lamp was on—not sufficient illumination to dispel all the shadows in the bedroom, but enough to hurt his extremely sensitive eyes. Watery and hot, his eyes had been less able to adapt to brightness since he had risen from the cold steel gurney in the morgue, as if darkness were his natural habitat now, as if he did not belong in a world subject either to sun or to man-made light.

For a couple of minutes he concentrated on his breathing, for his rate of respiration was irregular, now too slow and deep, now too fast and shallow. Taking a stethoscope from the nightstand, he listened to his heart as well. It was beating fast enough to assure that he would not soon slip back into a state of suspended animation, though it was unsettlingly arrhythmic.

In addition to the stethoscope, he had brought other instruments with which to monitor his progress. A sphygmomanometer for measuring his blood pressure. An ophthalmoscope which, in conjunction with a mirror, he could use to study the condition of his retinas and the pupil response. He had a notebook, too, in which he had intended to record his observations of himself, for he was aware—sometimes only dimly aware but always aware—that he was the first man to die and come back from beyond, that he was making history, and that such a journal would be invaluable once he had fully recovered.

Remember the mice, the mice . . .

He shook his head irritably, as if that sudden baffling thought were a bothersome gnat buzzing around his face. *Remember the mice, the mice:* He had not the slightest idea what it meant, yet it was an annoyingly repetitive and peculiarly urgent thought that had assailed him frequently last night. He vaguely suspected that he did, in fact, know the meaning of the mice and that he was suppressing the knowledge because it frightened him. However, when he tried to focus on the subject and force an understanding, he had no success but became increasingly frustrated, agitated, and confused.

Returning the stethoscope to the nightstand, he did not pick up the sphygmomanometer because he did not have the patience or the dexterity required to roll up his shirt sleeve, bind the pressure cuff around his arm, operate the bulb-type pump, and simultaneously hold the gauge so he could read it. He had tried last night, and his clumsiness had finally driven him into a rage. He did not pick up the ophthalmoscope, either, for to examine his own eyes he would have to go into the bathroom and use the mirror. He could not bear to see himself as he now appeared: gray-faced, muddy-eyed, with a slackness in his facial muscles that made him look . . . half dead.

The pages of his small notebook were mostly blank, and now he did not attempt to add further observations to his recovery journal. For one thing, he had found that he was not capable of the intense and prolonged concentration required to write either intelligibly or legibly. Besides, the sight of his sloppily scrawled handwriting, which previously had been precise and neat, was yet another thing that had the power to excite a vicious rage in him.

Remember the mice, the mice bashing themselves against the walls of their cages, chasing their tails, the mice, the mice . . .

Putting both hands to his head as if to physically suppress that unwanted and mysterious thought, Eric Leben lurched out of bed, onto his feet. He needed to piss, and he was hungry. Those were two good signs, two indications that he was alive, at least more alive than dead, and he took heart from those simple biological needs.

He started toward the bathroom but stopped suddenly when fire leaped up in a corner of the room. Not real flames but shadowfire. Blood-red tongues with silver edges. Crackling hungrily, consuming the shadows from which they erupted yet in no way reducing that darkness.

Squinting his light-stung eyes, Eric found that, as before, he was compelled to peer into the flames, and within them he thought he saw strange forms writhing and . . . and beckoning to him . . .

Though he was unaccountably terrified of these shadowfires, a part of him, perverse beyond his understanding, longed to go within the flames, pass through them as one might pass through a door, and learn what lay beyond.

No!

As he felt that longing grow into an acute need, he desperately turned away from the fire and stood swaying in fear and bewilderment, two feelings that, in his current fragile state, quickly metamorphosed into anger, the anger into rage. Everything seemed to lead to rage, as if it were the ultimate and inevitable distillate of all other emotions.

A brass-and-pewter floor lamp with a frosted crystal shade stood beside an easy chair, within his reach. He seized it with both hands, lifted it high above his head, and threw it across the room. The shade shattered against the wall, and gleaming shards of frosted crystal fell like cracking ice. The metal base and pole hit the edge of the white-lacquered dresser and rebounded with a clang, clattered to the floor.

The thrill of destruction that shivered through him was of a dark intensity akin to a sadistic sexual urge, and its power was nearly as great as orgasm. Before his death, he had been an obsessive achiever, a builder of empires, a compulsive acquirer of wealth, but following his death he had become an engine of destruction, as fully compelled to smash property as he had once been compelled to acquire it.

The cabin was decorated in ultramodern with accents of art deco—like the ruined floor lamp—not a style particularly well suited to a five-room mountain cabin but one which satisfied Eric's need for a sense of newness and modernity in all things. In a frenzy, he began to reduce the trendy decor to piles of bright rubble. He picked up the armchair as if it weighed only a pound or two and heaved it at the three-panel mirror on the wall behind the bed. The tripartite mirror exploded, and the armchair fell onto the bed in a rain of silvered glass. Breathing hard, Eric seized the damaged floor lamp, held it by the pole, swung it at a piece of bronze sculpture that stood on the dresser, using the heavy base of the lamp as a huge hammer—*bang!*—knocking the sculpture to the floor, swung the lamp-hammer twice at the dresser mirror—*bang, bang!*—smashing, smashing, swung it at a painting hanging on the wall near the door to the bathroom, brought the picture down, hammered the artwork where it lay on the floor. He felt good, so good, never better, *alive*. As he gave himself entirely and joyfully to his berserker rage, he snarled with animal ferocity or shrieked wordlessly, though he was able to form one special word with unmistakable clarity, "Rachael," spoke it with unadulterated hatred, spittle spraying, "Rachael, Rachael." He pounded the makeshift hammer into a white-lacquered occasional table that had stood beside the armchair, pounded and pounded until the table was reduced to splinters—"Rachael, Rachael"—struck the smaller lamp on the nightstand and knocked it to the floor. *Bang!* Arteries pounding furiously in his neck and temples, blood singing in his ears, he hammered the nightstand itself until he had broken the handles off the drawers, hammered the wall, "Rachael," hammered until the pole lamp was too bent to be of any further use, angrily tossed it aside, grabbed the drapes and ripped them from their rods, tore another painting from the wall and put his foot through the canvas, "Rachael, Rachael, Rachael." He staggered wildly now and flailed at the air with his big arms and turned in circles, a crazed bull, and he abruptly found it hard to breathe, felt the insane strength drain out of him, felt the mad destructive urge flowing away, away, and he dropped to the floor, onto his knees, stretched flat out on his chest, head turned to one side, face in the deep-pile carpet, gasping. His confused thoughts were even muddier than the strange and clouded eyes that he could not bear to look at in a mirror, but though he no longer possessed demonic energy, he had the strength to mutter that special name again and again while he lay on the floor: "Rachael . . . Rachael . . . Rachael . . ."

PART TWO

◊◊

DARKER

Night has patterns that can be read
less by the living than by the dead.

—*The Book of Counted Sorrows*

• 17 •

PEOPLE
ON THE MOVE

Choppering in from Palm Springs, Anson Sharp had arrived before dawn at Geneplan's bacteriologically secure underground research laboratories near Riverside, where he had been greeted by a contingent of six Defense Security Agency operatives, four U.S. marshals, and eight of the marshals' deputies, who had arrived minutes before him. Under the pretense of a national defense emergency, fully supported by valid court orders and search warrants, they identified themselves to Geneplan's night security guards, entered the premises, applied seals to all research files and computers, and established an operations headquarters in the rather sumptuously appointed offices belonging to Dr. Vincent Baresco, chief of the research staff.

As dawn dispelled the night and as day took possession of the world above the subterranean laboratories, Anson Sharp slumped in Baresco's enormous leather chair, sipped black coffee, and received reports, by phone, from subordinates throughout southern California, to the effect that Eric Leben's coconspirators in the Wildcard Project were all under house arrest. In Orange County, Dr. Morgan Eugene Lewis, research coordinator of Wildcard, was being detained with his wife at his home in North Tustin. Dr. J. Felix Geffels was being held at his house right there in Riverside. Dr. Vincent Baresco, head of all research for Geneplan, had been found by DSA agents in Geneplan's Newport Beach headquarters, unconscious on the floor of Eric Leben's office, amidst indications of gunplay and a fierce struggle.

Rather than take Baresco to a public hospital and even partially relinquish control of him, Sharp's men transported the bald and burly scientist to the U.S. Marine Corps Air Station at El Toro, where he was seen by a Marine physician in the base infirmary. Having received two hard blows to the throat that made it impossible for him to speak, Baresco used a pen and notepad to tell DSA agents that he had been assaulted by Ben Shadway, Rachael Leben's lover, when he had caught them in the act of looting Eric's office safe. He was disgruntled when they refused to believe that was the whole story, and he was downright shocked to discover they knew about Wildcard and were aware of Eric Leben's return from the dead. Using pen and notepad again, Baresco had demanded to be transferred to a civilian hospital, demanded to know what possible charges they could lodge, demanded to see his lawyer. All three demands were, of course, ignored.

Rupert Knowls and Perry Seitz, the money men who had supplied the large amount of venture capital that had gotten Geneplan off the ground nearly a decade ago, were at Knowls's sprawling ten-acre estate, Havenhurst, in Palm Springs. Three Defense Security Agency operatives had arrived at the estate with arrest warrants for Knowls and Seitz and with a search warrant. They had found an illegally modified Uzi submachine gun, doubtless the weapon with which two Palm Springs policemen had been murdered only a couple of hours earlier.

Currently and indefinitely under detention at Havenhurst, neither Knowls nor Seitz was raising objections. They knew the score. They would receive an unattractive offer to convey to the government all research, rights, and title to the Wildcard enterprise, without a shred of compensation, and they would be required to remain for-ever silent about that undertaking and about Eric Leben's resurrection. They would also be required to sign murder confessions which could be used to keep them acquiescent the rest of their lives. Although the offer had no legal basis or force, although the DSA was violating every tenet of democracy and breaking innumerable laws, Knowls and Seitz would accept the terms. They were worldly men, and they knew that failure to cooperate—and especially any attempt to exercise their constitutional rights—would be the death of them.

Those five were sitting on a secret that was potentially the most powerful in history. The immortality process was currently imperfect, true, but eventually the problems would be solved. Then whoever controlled the secrets of Wildcard would control the world. With so much at stake, the government was not concerned about observing the thin line between moral and immoral behavior, and in this very special case, it had no interest whatsoever in the niceties of due process.

After receiving the report on Seitz and Knowls, Sharp put down the phone, got up from the leather chair, and paced the windowless subterranean office. He rolled his big shoulders, stretched, and tried to work a kink out of his thick, muscular neck.

He had begun with eight people to worry about, eight possible leaks to plug, and now five of those eight had been dealt with quickly and smoothly. He felt pretty good about things in general and about himself in particular. He was damned good at his job.

At times like this, he wished he had someone with whom to share his triumphs, an admiring assistant, but he could not afford to let anyone get close to him. He was the deputy director of the Defense Security Agency, the number two man in the whole outfit, and he was determined to become director by the time he was forty. He intended to secure that position by collecting sufficient damaging material about the current director— Jarrod McClain—to force him out *and* to blackmail McClain into writing a wholehearted recommendation that Anson Sharp replace him. McClain treated Sharp like a son, making him privy to every secret of the agency, and already Sharp possessed most of what he needed to destroy McClain. But, as he was a careful man, he would not move until there was no possibility whatsoever of his coup failing. And when he ascended to the director's chair, he would not make the mistake of taking a subordinate to his bosom, as McClain had embraced him. It would be lonely at the top, *must* be lonely if he were to survive up there a long time, so he made himself get used to loneliness now: though he had protégés, he did not have friends.

Having worked the stiffness out of his thick neck and immense shoulders, Sharp returned to the chair behind the desk, sat down, closed his eyes, and thought about the three people who remained on the loose and who must be apprehended. Eric Leben, Mrs. Leben, Ben Shadway. They would not be offered a deal, as the other five had been. If Leben could be taken "alive," he would be locked away and studied as if he were a lab animal. Mrs. Leben and Shadway would simply be terminated and their deaths made to look accidental.

He had several reasons for wanting them dead. For one thing, they were both independent-minded, tough, and honest—a dangerous mixture, volatile. They might blow the Wildcard story wide open for the pure hell of it or out of misguided idealism, thus dealing Sharp a major setback on his climb to the top. The others—Lewis, Geffels, Baresco, Knowls, and Seitz—would knuckle under out of sheer self-interest, but Rachael Leben and Ben Shadway could not be counted on to put their own best interests first. Besides, neither had committed a criminal act, and neither had sold his soul to the government as the men of Geneplan had done, so no swords hung over their heads; there were no credible threats by which they could be controlled.

But most important of all, Sharp wanted Rachael Leben dead simply because she was Shadway's lover, because Shadway cared for her. He wanted to kill her first, in front of Ben Shadway. And he wanted Shadway dead because he had hated the man for almost seventeen years.

Alone in that underground office, eyes closed, Sharp smiled. He wondered what Ben Shadway would do if he knew that his old nemesis, Anson Sharp, was hunting for him. Sharp was almost painfully eager for the inevitable confrontation, eager to see the astonishment on Shadway's face, eager to waste the son of a bitch.

◊   ◊

Jerry Peake, the young DSA agent assigned by Anson Sharp to find Sarah Kiel, carefully searched for a freshly dug grave on Eric Leben's walled property in Palm Springs. Using a high-intensity flashlight, being diligent and utterly thorough, Peake tramped through flower beds, struggled through shrubbery, getting his pant legs damp and his shoes muddy, but he found nothing suspicious.

He turned on the pool lights, half expecting to find a dead woman either floating there—or weighted to the blue bottom and peering up through chlorine-treated water. When the pool proved to be free of corpses, Peake decided he had been reading too many mystery novels; in mystery novels, swimming pools were always full of bodies, but never in real life.

A passionate fan of mystery fiction since he was twelve, Jerry Peake had never wanted to be anything other than a detective, and not just an ordinary detective but something special, like a CIA or FBI or DSA man, and not just an ordinary DSA man but an investigative genius of the sort that John Le Carré, William F. Buckley, or Frederick Forsythe might write about. Peake wanted to be a legend in his own time. He was only in his fifth year with the DSA, and his reputation as a whiz was nonexistent, but he was not worried. He had patience. No one became a legend in just five years. First, you had to spend a lot of hours doing dog's work—like tramping through flower beds, snagging your best suits on thorny shrubbery, and peering hopefully into swimming pools in the dead of night.

When he did not turn up Sarah Kiel's body on the Leben property, Peake made the rounds of the hospitals, hoping to find her name on a patient roster or on a list of recently treated outpatients. He had no luck at his first two stops. Worse, even though he had his DSA credentials, complete with photograph, the nurses and physicians with whom he spoke seemed to regard him with skepticism. They cooperated, but guardedly, as if they thought he might be an imposter with hidden—and none too admirable—intentions.

He knew he looked too young to be a DSA agent; he was cursed with a frustratingly fresh, open face. And he was less aggressive in his questioning than he should be. But this time, he was sure the problem was not his baby face or slightly hesitant manner. Instead, he was greeted with doubt because of his muddy shoes, which he had cleaned with paper towels but which remained smeary-looking. And because of his trouser legs: Having gotten wet, the material had dried baggy and wrinkled. You could not be taken seriously, be respected, or become a legend if you looked as if you'd just slopped pigs.

An hour after dawn, at the third hospital, Desert General, he hit pay dirt in spite of his sartorial inadequacies. Sarah Kiel had been admitted for treatment during the night. She was still a patient.

The head nurse, Alma Dunn, was a sturdy white-haired woman of about fifty-five, unimpressed with Peake's credentials and incapable of being intimidated. After checking on Sarah Kiel, she returned to the nurses' station, where she'd made Peake wait, and she said, "The poor girl's still sleeping. She was . . . sedated only a few hours ago, so I don't expect she'll be awake for another few hours."

"Wake her, please. This is an urgent national security matter."

"I'll do no such thing," Nurse Dunn said. "The girl was hurt. She needs her rest. You'll have to wait."

"Then I'll wait in her room."

Nurse Dunn's jaw muscles bulged, and her merry blue eyes turned cold. "You certainly will not. You'll wait in the visitors' lounge."

Peake knew he would get nowhere with Alma Dunn because she looked like Jane Marple, Agatha Christie's indomitable amateur detective, and no one who looked like Miss Marple would be intimidated. "Listen, if you're going to be uncooperative, I'll have to talk to your superior."

"That's fine with me," she said, glancing down disapprovingly at his shoes. "I'll get Dr. Werfell."

◊   ◊

Beneath the earth in Riverside, Anson Sharp slept for one hour on the Ultrasuede sofa in Vincent Baresco's office, showered in the small adjacent bathroom, and changed into a fresh suit of clothes from the suitcase that he had kept with him on every leg of his zigzagging route through southern California the previous night. He was blessed with the ability to fall asleep at will in a minute or less, without fail, and to feel rested and alert after only a nap. He could sleep anywhere he chose, regardless of background noise. He believed this ability was just one more proof that he was destined to climb to the top, where he longed to be, proof that he was superior to other men.

Refreshed, he made a few calls, speaking with agents guarding the Geneplan partners and research chiefs at various points in three counties. He also received reports from other men at the Geneplan offices in Newport Beach, Eric Leben's house in Villa Park, and Mrs. Leben's place in Placentia.

From the agents guarding Baresco at the U.S. Marine Air Station in El Toro, Sharp learned that Ben Shadway had taken a Smith & Wesson .357 Magnum off the scientist in the Geneplan office last night, and that the revolver could not be located anywhere in that building. Shadway had not left it behind, had not disposed of it in a nearby trash container or hallway, but apparently had chosen to hold on to it. Furthermore, agents in Placentia reported that a .32-caliber semiautomatic pistol, registered to Rachael Leben, could be found nowhere in her house, and the assumption was that she was carrying it, though she did not possess a permit to carry.

Sharp was delighted to learn that both Shadway and the woman were armed, for that contributed to the justification of an arrest warrant. And when he cornered them, he could shoot them down and claim, with a measure of credibility, that they had opened fire on him first.

◑   ◑

As Jerry Peake waited at the nurses' station for Alma Dunn to return with Dr. Werfell, the hospital came alive for the day. The empty halls grew busy with nurses conveying medicines to patients, with orderlies transporting patients in wheelchairs and on gurneys to various departments and operating theaters, and with a few doctors making very early rounds. The pervading scent of pine disinfectant was increasingly overlaid with others—alcohol, clove oil, urine, vomit—as if the busily scurrying staff had stirred stagnant odors out of every corner of the building.

In ten minutes, Nurse Dunn returned with a tall man in a white lab coat. He had handsome hawkish features, thick salt-and-pepper hair, and a neat mustache. He seemed familiar, though Peake was not sure why. Alma Dunn introduced him as Dr. Hans Werfell, supervising physician of the morning shift.

Looking down at Peake's muddy shoes and badly wrinkled trousers, Dr. Werfell said, "Miss Kiel's physical condition is not grave by any means, and I suppose she'll be out of here today or tomorrow. But she suffered severe emotional trauma, so she needs to be allowed to rest when she can. And right now she's resting, sound asleep."

Stop looking at my shoes, damn you, Peake thought. He said, "Doctor, I understand your concern for the patient, but this is an urgent matter of national security."

Finally raising his gaze from Peake's shoes, Werfell frowned skeptically and said, "What on earth could a sixteen-year-old girl have to do with national security?"

"That's classified, strictly classified," Peake said, trying to pull his baby face into a suitably serious and imposing expression that would convince Werfell of the gravity of the situation and gain his cooperation.

"No point waking her, anyway," Werfell said. "She'd still be under the influence of the sedative, not in any condition to give accurate answers to your questions."

"Couldn't you give her something to counteract the drug?"

With only a frown, Werfell registered severe disapproval. "Mr. Peake, this is a hospital. We exist to help people get well. We wouldn't be helping Miss Kiel to get well if we pumped her full of drugs for no other purpose than to counteract *other* drugs and please an impatient government agent."

Peake felt his face flush. "I wasn't suggesting you violate medical principles."

"Good." Werfell's patrician face and manner were not conducive to debate. "Then you'll wait until she wakes naturally."

Frustrated, still trying to think why Werfell looked familiar, Peake said, "But we think she can tell us where to find someone whom we desperately *must* find."

"Well, I'm sure she'll cooperate when she's awake and alert."

"And when will that be, Doctor?"

"Oh, I imagine . . . another four hours, maybe longer."

"What? Why that long?"

"The night physician gave her a very mild sedative, which didn't suit her, and when he refused to give her anything stronger, she took one of her own."

"One of her own?"

"We didn't realize until later that she had drugs in her purse: a few Benzedrine tablets wrapped in one small packet of foil—"

"Bennies, uppers?"

"Yes. And a few tranquilizers in another packet, and a couple of sedatives. Hers was much stronger than the one we gave her, so she's pretty deep under at the moment. We've confiscated her remaining drugs, of course."

Peake said, "I'll wait in her room."

"No," Werfell said.

"Then I'll wait just outside her room."

"I'm afraid not."

"Then I'll wait right here."

"You'll be in the way here," Werfell said. "You'll wait in the visitors' lounge, and we'll call you when Miss Kiel is awake."

"I'll wait here," Peake insisted, scrunching his baby face into the sternest, toughest, most hard-boiled look he could manage.

"The visitors' lounge," Werfell said ominously. "And if you do not proceed there immediately, I'll have hospital security men escort you."

Peake hesitated, wishing to God he could be more aggressive. "All right, but you damn well better call me the *minute* she wakes up."

Furious, he turned from Werfell and stalked down the hall in search of the visitors' lounge, too embarrassed to ask where it was. When he glanced back at Werfell, who was now in deep conversation with another physician, he realized the doctor was a dead ringer for Dashiell Hammett, the formidable Pinkerton detective and mystery novelist, which was why he had looked familiar to a dedicated reader like Peake. No wonder Werfell had such a tremendous air of authority. Dashiell Hammett, for God's sake. Peake felt a little better about having deferred to him.

◐   ◐

They slept another two hours, woke within moments of each other, and made love again in the motel bed. For Rachael, it was even better this time than it had been before: slower, sweeter, with an even more graceful and fulfilling rhythm. She was sinewy, supple, taut, and she took enormous and intense pleasure in her superb physical condition, drew satisfaction from each flexing and gentle thrusting and soft lazy grinding of her body, not merely the usual pleasure of male and female organs mating, but the more subtle thrill of muscle and tendon and bone functioning with the perfect oiled smoothness that, like nothing else, made her feel young, healthy, *alive*.

With her special gift for fully experiencing the moment, she let her hands roam over Benny's body, marveling over his leanness, testing the rock-hard muscles of his shoulders and arms, kneading the bunched muscles of his back, glorying in the silken smoothness of his skin, the rocking motion of his hips against hers, pelvis to pelvis, the hot touch of his hands, the branding heat of his lips upon her cheeks, her mouth, her throat, her breasts.

Until this interlude with Benny, Rachael had not made love in almost fifteen months. And never in her life had she made love like this: never this good, this tender or exciting, never this satisfying. She felt as if she had been half dead heretofore and this was the hour of her resurrection.

Finally spent, they lay in each other's arms for a while, silent, at peace, but the soft afterglow of lovemaking slowly gave way to a curious disquiet. At first she was not certain what disturbed her, but soon she recognized it as that rare and peculiar feeling that someone had just walked over her grave, an irrational but convincingly instinctive sensation that brought a vague chill to her bare flesh and a colder shiver to her spine.

She looked at Benny's gentle smile, studied every much-loved line of his face, stared into his eyes—and had the shocking, unshakable feeling that she was going to lose him.

She tried to tell herself that her sudden apprehension was the understandable reaction of a thirty-year-old woman who, having made one bad marriage, had at last miraculously found the right man. Call it the I-don't-deserve-to-be-this-happy syndrome. When life finally hands us a beautiful bouquet of flowers, we usually peer cautiously among the petals in expectation of a bee. Superstition—evinced especially in a distrust of good fortune—was perhaps the very core of human nature, and it was natural for her to fear losing him.

That was what she tried to tell herself, but she knew her sudden terror was something more than superstition, something darker. The chill along her spine deepened until she felt as if each vertebra had been transformed into a lump of ice. The cool breath that had touched her skin now penetrated deeper, down toward her bones.

She turned from him, swung her legs out of the bed, stood up, naked and shivering.

Benny said, "Rachael?"

"Let's get moving," she said anxiously, heading toward the bathroom through the golden light and palm shadows that came through the single, undraped window.

"What's wrong?" he asked.

"We're sitting ducks here. Or might be. We've got to keep moving. We've got to keep on the offensive. We've got to find him before he finds us—or before anyone else finds us."

Benny got out of bed, stepped between her and the bathroom door, put his hands on her shoulders. "Everything's going to be all right."

"Don't say that."

"But it will."

"Don't tempt fate."

"We're strong together," he said. "Nothing's stronger."

"Don't," she insisted, putting a hand to his lips to silence him. "Please. I . . . I couldn't bear losing you."

"You won't lose me," he said.

But when she looked at him, she had the terrible feeling that he was already lost, that death was very near to him, inevitable.

The I-don't-deserve-to-be-this-happy syndrome.

Or maybe a genuine premonition.

She had no way of knowing which it was.

◊   ◊

The search for Dr. Eric Leben was getting nowhere.

The grim possibility of failure was, for Anson Sharp, like a great pressure pushing in on the walls of Geneplan's underground labs in Riverside, compressing the windowless rooms, until he felt as if he were being slowly crushed. He could not abide failure; he was a winner, always a winner, superior to all other men, and that was the only way he cared to think of himself, the only way he could *bear* to think of himself, as the sole member of a superior species, for that image of himself justified anything he wished to do, anything at all, and he was a man who simply could not live with the moral and ethical limitations of ordinary men.

Yet field agents were filing negative reports from every place that the walking dead man might have been expected to show up, and Sharp was getting angrier and more nervous by the hour. Perhaps their knowledge of Eric Leben was not quite as thorough as they thought. In anticipation of these events, perhaps the geneticist had prepared a place where he could go to ground, and had managed to keep it secret even from the DSA. If that were the case, the failure to apprehend Leben would be seen as Sharp's personal failure, for he had identified himself too closely with the operation in expectation of taking full credit for its success.

Then he got a break. Jerry Peake called to report that Sarah Kiel, Eric Leben's underage mistress, had been located in a Palm Springs hospital. "But the damn medical staff," Peake explained in his earnest but frustratingly wimpy manner, "isn't cooperative."

Sometimes Anson Sharp wondered if the advantages of surrounding himself with weaker—and therefore unthreatening—young agents were outweighed by the disadvantage of their inefficiency. Certainly none of them would pose a danger to him once he had ascended to the director's chair, but neither were they likely to do anything on their own hook that would reflect positively on him as their mentor.

Sharp said, "I'll be there before she shakes off the sedative."

The investigation at the Geneplan labs could proceed without him for a while. The researchers and technicians had arrived for the day and had been sent home with orders not to report back until notified. Defense Security Agency computer mavens were seeking the Wildcard files hidden in the Geneplan data banks, but their work was so highly specialized that Sharp could neither supervise nor understand it.

He made a few telephone calls to several federal agencies in Washington, seeking—and obtaining—information about Desert General Hospital and Dr. Hans Werfell that might give him leverage with them, then boarded his waiting chopper and flew back across the desert to Palm Springs, pleased to be on the move again.

◊   ◊

Rachael and Benny taxied to the Palm Springs airport, rented a clean new Ford from Hertz, and drove back into town in time to be the first customers at a clothing store that opened at nine-thirty. She bought tan jeans, a pale yellow blouse, thick white tube socks, and Adidas jogging shoes. Benny chose blue jeans, a white shirt, tube socks, and similar shoes, and they changed out of their badly rumpled clothes in the public rest rooms of a service station at the north end of Palm Canyon Drive. Unwilling to waste time stopping for breakfast, partly because they were afraid of being spotted, they grabbed Egg McMuffins and coffee at McDonald's, and ate as they drove.

Rachael had infected Benny with her premonition of oncoming death and her sudden—almost clairvoyant— sense that time was running out, which had first struck her at the motel, just after they had made love for the second time. Benny had attempted to reassure her, calm her, but instead he had grown more uneasy by the minute. They were like two animals independently and instinctively perceiving the advance of a terrible storm.

Wishing they could have gone back for her red Mercedes, which would have made better time than the rental Ford, Rachael slumped in the passenger's seat and nibbled at her take-out breakfast without enthusiasm, while Benny drove north on State Route 111, then west on Interstate 10. Although he squeezed as much speed out of the Ford as anyone could have, handling it with that startling combination of recklessness and ease that was so out of character for a real-estate salesman, they would not reach Eric's cabin, above Lake Arrowhead, until almost one o'clock in the afternoon.

She hoped to God that would be soon enough.

And she tried not to think about what Eric might be like when—and if—they found him.

⋄ 18 ⋄

ZOMBIE BLUES

The dark rage passed, and Eric Leben regained his senses—such as they were—in the debris-strewn bedroom of the cabin, where he had smashed nearly everything he could get his hands on. A hard, sharp pain pounded through his head, and a duller pain throbbed in all of his muscles. His joints felt swollen and stiff. His eyes were grainy, watery, hot. His teeth ached, and his mouth tasted of ashes.

Following each fit of mindless fury, Eric found himself, as now, in a gray mood, in a gray world, where colors were washed out, where sounds were muted, where the edges of objects were fuzzy, and where every light, regardless of the strength of its source, was murky and too thin to sufficiently illuminate anything. It was as if the fury had drained him, and as if he had been forced to power down until he could replenish his reserves of energy. He moved sluggishly, somewhat clumsily, and he had difficulty thinking clearly.

When he had finished healing, the periods of coma and the gray spells would surely cease. However, that knowledge did not lift his spirits, for his muddy thought processes made it difficult for him to think ahead to a better future. His condition was eerie, unpleasant, even frightening; he felt that he was not in control of his destiny and that, in fact, he was trapped within his own body, chained to this now-imperfect, half-dead flesh.

He staggered into the bathroom, slowly showered, brushed his teeth. He kept a complete wardrobe at the cabin, just as he did at the house in Palm Springs, so he would never need to pack a suitcase when visiting either place, and now he changed into khaki pants, a red plaid shirt, wool socks, and a pair of woodsman's boots. In his strange gray haze, that morning routine required more time than it should have: He had trouble adjusting the shower controls to get the right temperature; he kept dropping the toothbrush into the sink; he cursed his stiff fingers as they fumbled with the buttons on his shirt; when he tried to roll up his long sleeves, the material resisted him as if it possessed a will of its own; and he succeeded in lacing the boots only with monumental effort.

Eric was further distracted by the shadowfires.

Several times, at the periphery of his vision, ordinary shadows burst into flames. Just short-circuiting electrical impulses in his badly damaged—but healing—brain. Illusions born in sputtering cerebral synapses between neurons. Nothing more. However, when he turned to look directly at the fires, they never faded or winked out as mere mirages might have done, but grew even brighter.

Although they produced no smoke or heat, consumed no fuel, and had no real substance, he stared at those nonexistent flames with greater fear each time they appeared, partly because within them—or perhaps beyond them—he saw something mysterious, frightening; darkly shrouded and monstrous figures that beckoned through the leaping brightness. Although he knew the phantoms were only figments of his overwrought imagination, although he had no idea what they might represent to him or why he should be afraid of them, he *was* afraid. And at times, mesmerized by shadowfires, he heard himself whimpering as if he were a terrorized child.

Food. Although his genetically altered body was capable of miraculous regeneration and rapid recuperation, it still required proper nutrition—vitamins, minerals, carbohydrates, proteins—the building blocks with which to repair its damaged tissues. And for the first time since arising in the morgue, he was hungry.

He shuffled unsteadily into the kitchen, shambled to the big refrigerator.

He thought he saw something crawling out of the slots in a wall plug just at the edge of vision. Something long, thin. Insectile. Menacing. But he knew it was not real. He had seen things like it before. It was another symptom of his brain damage. He just had to ignore it, not let it frighten him, even though he heard its chitinous feet tap-tap-tapping on the floor. Tap-tap-tapping. He refused to look. *Go away.* He held on to the refrigerator. Tapping. He gritted his teeth. *Go away.* The sound faded. When he looked toward the wall plug, there was no strange insect, nothing out of the ordinary.

But now his uncle Barry, long dead, was sitting at the kitchen table, grinning at him. As a child, he had frequently been left with Uncle Barry Hampstead, who had abused him, and he had been too afraid to tell anyone. Hampstead had threatened to hurt him, to cut off his penis, if he told anyone, and those threats had been so vivid and hideous that Eric had not doubted them for a minute. Now Uncle Barry sat at the table, one hand in his lap, grinning, and said, "Come here, little sweetheart; let's have some fun," and Eric could *hear* the voice as clearly as he'd heard it thirty-five years ago, though he knew that neither the man nor the voice was real, and he was as terrified of Barry Hampstead as he had been long ago, though he knew he was now far beyond his hated uncle's reach.

He closed his eyes and willed the illusion to go away. He must have stood there, shaking, for a minute or more, not wanting to open his eyes until he was certain the apparition would be gone. But then he began to think that Barry *was* there and was slipping closer to him while his eyes were closed and was going to grab him by the privates any second now, grab him and squeeze—

His eyes snapped open.

The phantom Barry Hampstead was gone.

Breathing easier, Eric got a package of Farmer John sausage-and-biscuit sandwiches from the freezer compartment and heated them on a tray in the oven, concentrating intently on the task to avoid burning himself. Fumblingly, patiently, he brewed a pot of Maxwell House. Sitting at the table, shoulders hunched, head held low, he washed the food down with cup after cup of the hot black coffee.

He had an insatiable appetite for a while, and the very act of eating made him feel more truly alive than anything he'd done since he'd been reborn. Biting, chewing, tasting, swallowing—by those simple actions, he was brought further back among the living than at any point since he'd stepped in the way of the garbage truck on Main Street. For a while, his spirits began to rise.

Then he slowly became aware that the taste of the sausage was neither as strong nor as pleasing as when he had been fully alive and able to appreciate it; and though he put his nose close to the hot, greasy meat and drew deep breaths, he was unable to smell its spicy aroma. He stared at his cool, ash-gray, clammy hands, which held the biscuit-wrapped sausage, and the wad of steaming pork looked more alive than his own flesh.

Suddenly the situation seemed uproariously funny to Eric: a dead man sitting at breakfast, chomping stolidly on Farmer John sausages, pouring hot Maxwell House down his cold gullet, desperately pretending to be one of the living, as if death could be reversed by pretense, as if life could be regained merely by the performance of enough mundane activities—showering, brushing his teeth, eating, drinking, crapping—and by the consumption of enough homely products. He *must* be alive, because they wouldn't have Farmer John sausages and Maxwell House in either heaven or hell. Would they? He must be alive, because he had used his Mr. Coffee machine and his General Electric oven, and over in the corner his Westinghouse refrigerator was humming softly, and although those manufacturers' wares were widely distributed, surely none of them would be found on the far shores of the river Styx, so he *must* be alive.

Black humor certainly, very black indeed, but he laughed out loud, laughed and laughed—until he heard his laughter. It sounded hard, coarse, cold, not really laughter but a poor imitation, rough and harsh, as if he were choking, or as if he had swallowed stones that now rattled and clattered against one another in his throat. Dismayed by the sound, he shuddered and began to weep. He dropped the sausage-stuffed biscuit, swept the food and dishes to the floor, and collapsed forward, folding his arms upon the table and resting his head in his arms. Great gasping sobs of grief escaped him, and for a while he was immersed in a deep pool of self-pity.

The mice, the mice, remember the mice bashing against the walls of their cages . . .

He still did not know the meaning of that thought, could not recall any mice, though he felt that he was closer to understanding than ever before. A memory of mice, white mice, hovered tantalizingly just beyond his grasp.

His gray mood darkened.

His dulled senses grew even duller.

After a while, he realized he was sinking into another coma, one of those periods of suspended animation during which his heart slowed dramatically and his respiration fell to a fraction of the normal rate, giving his body an opportunity to continue with repairs and accumulate new reserves of energy. He slipped from his chair to the kitchen floor and curled fetally beside the refrigerator.

◗ ◗

Benny turned off Interstate 10 at Redlands and followed State Route 30 to 330. Lake Arrowhead lay only twenty-eight miles away.

The two-lane blacktop cut a twisty trail into the San Bernardino Mountains. The pavement was hoved and rough in some spots, slightly potholed in others, and frequently the shoulder was only a few inches wide, with a steep drop beyond the flimsy guardrails, leaving little leeway for mistakes. They were forced to slow considerably, though Benny piloted the Ford much faster than Rachael could have done.

Last night Rachael had spilled her secrets to Benny—the details of Wildcard and of Eric's obsessions—and she had expected him to divulge his in return, but he had said nothing that would explain the way he had dealt with Vincent Baresco, the uncanny way he could handle a car, or his knowledge of guns. Though her curiosity was great, she did not press him. She sensed that his secrets were of a far more personal nature than hers and that he had spent a long time building barriers around them, barriers that could not easily be torn down. She knew he would tell her everything when he felt the time was right.

They traveled only a mile on Route 330 and were still twenty miles from Running Springs when he apparently decided that, in fact, the time had come. As the road wound higher into the sharply angled mountains, more trees rose up on all sides—birches and gnarled oaks at first, then pines of many varieties, tamarack, even a few spruce—and soon the pavement was more often than not cloaked in the velvety shadows of those overhanging boughs. Even in the air-conditioned car, you could feel that the desert heat was being left behind, and it was as if the escape from those oppressive temperatures buoyed Benny and encouraged him to talk. In a darkish tunnel of pine shadows, he began to speak in a soft yet distinct voice.

"When I was eighteen, I joined the Marines, volunteered to fight in Vietnam. I wasn't antiwar like so many were, but I wasn't prowar either. I was just for my country, right or wrong. As it turned out, I had certain aptitudes, natural abilities, that made me a candidate for the Corps' elite cadre: Marine Reconnaissance, which is sort of the equivalent of the Army Rangers or Navy Seals. I was spotted early, approached about recon training, volunteered, and eventually they honed me into as deadly a soldier as any in the world. Put any weapon in my hands, I knew how to use it. Leave me empty-handed, and I could still kill you so quick and easy you wouldn't know I was coming at you until you felt your own neck snap. I went to Nam in a recon unit, guaranteed to see plenty of action, which is what I wanted—plenty of action— and for a few months I was totally gung ho, delighted to be in the thick of it."

Benny still drove the car with consummate skill, but Rachael noticed that the speed began to drop slowly as his story took him deeper into the jungles of Southeast Asia.

He squinted as the sun found its way through holes in the tree shadows and as spangles of light cascaded across the windshield. "But if you spend several months knee-deep in blood, watching your buddies die, sidestepping death yourself again and again, seeing civilians caught repeatedly in the cross fire, villages burned, little children maimed . . . well, you're bound to start doubting. And I began to doubt."

"Benny, my God, I'm sorry. I never suspected you'd been through anything like that, such horror—"

"No point feeling sorry for me. I came back alive and got on with my life. That's better than what happened to a lot of others."

Oh, God, Rachael thought, what if you hadn't come back? I would have never met you, never loved you, never known what I'd missed.

"Anyway," he said softly, "doubts set in, and for the rest of that year, I was in turmoil. I was fighting to preserve the elected government of South Vietnam, yet that government seemed hopelessly corrupt. I was fighting to preserve the Vietnamese culture from obliteration under communism, yet that very same culture was being obliterated by the tens of thousands of U.S. troops who were diligently Americanizing it."

"We wanted freedom and peace for the Vietnamese," Rachael said. "At least that's how I understood it." She was not yet thirty, seven years younger than Benny; but those were seven crucial years, and it had not been *her* war. "There's nothing so wrong with fighting for freedom and peace."

"Yeah," he said, his voice haunted now, "but we seemed to be intent on creating that peace by killing everyone and leveling the whole damn country, leaving no one to enjoy whatever freedom might follow. I had to wonder . . . Was my country misguided? Downright wrong? Even possibly . . . evil? Or was I just too young and too naive, in spite of my Marine training, to understand?" He was silent for a moment, pulling the car through a sharp right-hand turn, then left just as sharply when the mountainside angled again. "By the time my tour of duty ended, I'd answered none of those questions to my satisfaction . . . and so I volunteered for another tour."

"You stayed in Nam when you could have gone home?" she asked, startled. "Even though you had such terrible doubts?"

"I had to work it out," he said. "I just had to. I mean, I'd killed people, a lot of people, in what I thought was a just cause, and I had to know whether I'd been right or wrong. I couldn't walk away, put it out of my mind, get on with my life, and just *forget* about it. Hell, no. I had to work it out, decide if I was a good man or a killer, and then figure what accommodation I could reach with life, with my own conscience. And there was no better place to work it out, to analyze the problem, than right there in the middle of it. Besides, to understand why I stayed on for a second tour, you've got to understand me, the me that existed then: very young, idealistic, with patriotism as much a part of me as the color of my eyes. I loved my country, *believed* in my country, totally believed, and I couldn't just shed that belief like . . . well, like a snake sheds skin."

They passed a road sign that said they were sixteen miles from Running Springs and twenty-three miles from Lake Arrowhead.

Rachael said, "So you stayed in Nam another whole year?"

He sighed wearily. "As it turned out . . . two years."

◊   ◊

In his cabin high above Lake Arrowhead, for a time that he could not measure, Eric Leben drifted in a peculiar twilight state, neither awake nor asleep, neither alive nor dead, while his genetically altered cells increased production of enzymes, proteins, and other substances that would contribute to the healing process. Brief dark dreams and unassociated nightmare images flickered through his mind, like hideous shadows leaping in the bloody light of tallow candles.

When at last he rose from his trancelike condition, full of energy again, he was acutely aware that he had to arm himself and be prepared for action. His mind was still not entirely clear, his memory threadbare in places, so he did not know exactly who might be coming after him, but instinct told him that he was being stalked.

Sure as hell, someone'll find this place through Sarah Kiel, he told himself.

That thought jolted him because he could not remember who Sarah Kiel was. He stood with one hand on a kitchen counter, swaying, straining to recall the face and identity that went with that name.

Sarah Kiel . . .

Suddenly he remembered, and he cursed himself for having brought the damn girl here. The cabin was supposed to be his secret retreat. He should never have told anyone. One of his problems was that he needed young women in order to feel young himself, and he always tried to impress them. Sarah *had* been impressed by the five-room cabin, outfitted as it was with all conveniences, the acres of private woods, and the spectacular view of the lake far below. They'd had good sex outside, on a blanket, under the boughs of an enormous pine, and he had felt wonderfully young. But now Sarah knew about his secret retreat, and through her others—the stalkers whose identities he could not quite fix upon—might learn of the place and come after him.

With new urgency, Eric pushed away from the counter and headed toward the door that opened from the kitchen into the garage. He moved less stiffly than before, with more energy, and his eyes were less bothered by bright light, and no phantom uncles or insects crept out of the corners to frighten him; the period of coma had apparently done him some good. But when he put his hand on the doorknob, he stopped, jolted by another thought:

Sarah can't tell anyone about this place because Sarah is dead, I killed her only a few hours ago . . .

A wave of horror washed over Eric, and he held fast to the doorknob as if to anchor himself and prevent the wave from sweeping him away into permanent darkness, madness. Suddenly he recalled going to the house in Palm Springs, remembered beating the girl, the naked girl, mercilessly hammering her with his fists. Images of her bruised and bleeding face, twisted in terror, flickered through his damaged memory like slides through a broken stereopticon. But had he actually killed her? No, no, surely not. He enjoyed playing rough with women, yes, he could admit that, enjoyed hitting them, liked nothing more than watching them cower before him, but he would never *kill* anyone, never had and never would, no, surely not, no, he was a law-abiding citizen, a social and economic winner, not a thug or psychopath. Yet he was abruptly assaulted by another unclear but fearful memory of nailing Sarah to the wall in Rachael's house in Placentia, nailing her naked above the bed as a warning to Rachael, and he shuddered, then realized it had not been Sarah but someone else nailed up on that wall, someone whose name he did not even know, a stranger who had vaguely resembled Rachael, but that was ridiculous, he had not killed *two* women, had not even killed one, but now he also recalled a garbage dumpster, a filthy alleyway, and yet *another* woman, a third woman, a pretty Latino, her throat slashed by a scalpel, and he had shoved her corpse into the dumpster . . .

No. My God, what have I made of myself? he wondered, nausea twisting his belly. I'm both researcher and subject, creator and creation, and that has to've been a mistake, a terrible mistake. Could I have become . . . my own Frankenstein monster?

For one dreadful moment, his thought processes cleared, and truth shone through to him as brightly as the morning sun piercing a freshly washed window.

He shook his head violently, pretending that he wanted to be rid of the last traces of the mist that had been clouding his mind, though in fact he was trying desperately to rid himself of his unwelcome and unbearable clarity. His badly injured brain and precarious physical condition made the rejection of the truth an easy matter. The violent shaking of his head was enough to make him dizzy, blur his vision, and bring the shrouding mists back to his memory, hindering his thought processes, leaving him confused and somewhat disoriented.

The dead women were false memories, yes, of course, yes, they could not be real, because he was incapable of cold-blooded murder. They were as unreal as his uncle Barry and the strange insects that he sometimes thought he saw.

Remember the mice, the mice, the frenzied, biting, angry mice . . .

What mice? What do angry mice have to do with it? Forget the damn mice.

The important thing was that he could not possibly have murdered even one person, let alone three. Not him. Not Eric Leben. In the murkiness of his half-lit and turbulent memory, these nightmare images were surely nothing but illusions, just like the shadowfires that sprang from nowhere. They were merely the result of short-circuiting electrical impulses in his shattered brain tissue, and they would not stop plaguing him until that tissue was entirely healed. Meanwhile, he dared not dwell on them, for he would begin to doubt himself and his perceptions, and in his fragile mental condition, he did not have the energy for self-doubt.

Trembling, sweating, he pulled open the door, stepped into the garage, and switched on the light. His black Mercedes 560 SEL was parked where he had left it last night.

When he looked at the Mercedes, he was suddenly stricken by a memory of another car, an older and less elegant one, in the trunk of which he had stashed a dead woman—

No. False memories again. Illusions. Delusions.

He carefully placed one splayed hand against the wall, leaned for a moment, gathering strength and trying to clear his head. When at last he looked up, he could not recall why he was in the garage.

Gradually, however, he was once again filled with the instinctive sense that he was being stalked, that someone was coming to get him, and that he must arm himself. His muddied mind would not produce a clear picture of the people who might be pursuing him, but he *knew* he was in danger. He pushed away from the wall, moved past the car, and went to the workbench and tool rack at the front of the garage.

He wished that he'd had the foresight to keep a gun at the cabin. Now he had to settle for a wood ax, which he took down from the clips by which it was mounted on the wall, breaking a spider's web anchored to the handle. He had used the ax to split logs for the fireplace and to chop kindling. It was quite sharp, an excellent weapon.

Though he was incapable of cold-blooded murder, he knew he could kill in self-defense if necessary. No fault in protecting himself. Self-defense was far different from murder. It was justifiable.

He hefted the ax, testing its weight. Justifiable.

He took a practice swing with the weapon. It cut through the air with a whoosh. Justifiable.

◊　　　◊

Approximately nine miles from Running Springs and sixteen miles from Lake Arrowhead, Benny pulled off the road and parked on a scenic lay-by, which featured two picnic tables, a trash barrel, and lots of shade from several huge bristlecone pines. He switched off the engine and rolled down his window. The mountain air was forty degrees cooler than the air in the desert from which they had come; it was still warm but not stifling, and Rachael found the mild breeze refreshing as it washed through the car, scented by wildflowers and pine sap.

She did not ask why he was pulling off the road, for his reasons were obvious: It was vitally important to him that she understand the conclusions he had reached in Vietnam and that she have no illusions about the kind of man that the war had made of him, and he did not trust himself to convey all of those things adequately while also negotiating the twisty mountain lane.

He told her about his second year of combat. It had begun in confusion and despair, with the awful realization that he was not involved in a *clean* war the way World War II had been clean, with well-delineated moral choices. Month by month, his recon unit's missions took him deeper into the war zone. Frequently they crossed the line of battle, striking into enemy territory on clandestine missions. Their purpose was not only to engage and destroy the enemy, but also to engage civilians in a peaceful capacity in hope of winning hearts and minds. Through those varied contacts, he saw the special savagery of the enemy, and he finally reached the conclusion that this unclean war forced participants to choose between degrees of immorality: On one hand, it was immoral to stay and fight, to be a part of death dealing and destruction; on the other hand, it was an even greater moral wrong to walk away, for the political mass murder that would follow a collapse of South Vietnam and Cambodia was certain to be many times worse than the casualties of continued warfare.

In a voice that made Rachael think of the dark confessionals in which she had knelt as a youth, Benny said, "In a sense, I realized that, bad as we were for Vietnam, after us there would be only worse. After us, a bloodbath. Millions executed or worked to death in slave-labor camps. After us . . . the deluge."

He did not look at her but stared through the windshield at the forested slopes of the San Bernardino Mountains.

She waited.

At last he said, "No heroes. I wasn't yet even quite twenty-one years old, so it was a tough realization for me—that I was no hero, that I was essentially just the lesser of two evils. You're supposed to be an idealist at twenty-one, an optimist and an idealist, but I saw that maybe a lot of life was shaped by those kinds of choices, by choosing between evils and hoping always to choose the least of them."

Benny took a deep breath of the mountain air coming through the open window, expelled it forcefully, as though he felt sullied just by talking about the war and as though the clean air of the mountains would, if drawn in deeply enough, expunge old stains from his soul.

Rachael said nothing, partly because she did not want to break the spell before he told her everything. But she was also rendered speechless by the discovery that he had been a professional soldier, for that revelation forced her to reevaluate him completely.

She'd thought of him as a wonderfully uncomplicated man, as an ordinary real-estate broker; his very plainness had been attractive. God knew, she'd had more than enough color and flamboyance with Eric. The image of simplicity which Benny projected was soothing; it implied equanimity, reliability, dependability. He was like a deep, cool, and placid stream, slow-moving, soothing. Until now, Benny's interest in trains and old novels and forties music had seemed merely to confirm that his life had been free of serious trauma, for it did not seem possible that a life-battered and complicated man could take such unalloyed pleasure from those simple things. When he was occupied with those pastimes, he was wrapped in childlike wonder and innocence of such purity that it was hard to believe he'd ever known disillusionment or profound anguish.

"My buddies died," he said. "Not all of them but too damn many, blown away in firefights, cut down by snipers, hit by antipersonnel mines, and some got sent home crippled and maimed, faces disfigured, bodies *and* minds scarred forever. It was a high price to pay if we weren't fighting for a noble cause, if we were just fighting for the lesser of two evils, a *damn* high price. But it seemed to me the only alternative—just walking away—was an out only if you shut your eyes to the fact that there are degrees of evil, some worse than others."

"So you volunteered for a third tour of duty," Rachael said.

"Yes. Stayed, survived. Not happy, not proud. Just doing what had to be done. A lot of us made that commitment, which wasn't easy. And then . . . that was the year we pulled our troops out, which I'll never forgive or forget, because it wasn't just an abandonment of the Vietnamese, it was an abandonment of *me*. I understood the terms, and still I'd been willing to make the sacrifice. Then my country, in which I'd believed so deeply, forced me to walk away, to just let the greater evil win, as if I was supposed to find it easy to deny the complexity of the moral issues after I'd finally grasped the tangled nature of them, as if it had all been a fuckin' *game* or something!"

She had never before heard anger like this in his voice, anger as hard as steel and ice-cold, never imagined he had the capacity for it. It was a fully controlled, quiet rage—but profound and a little frightening.

He said, "It was a bad shock for a twenty-one-year-old kid to learn that life wasn't going to give him a chance to be a real pure hero, but it was even worse to learn that his own country could force him to do the *wrong* thing. After we left, the Cong and Khmer Rouge slaughtered three or four million in Cambodia and Vietnam, and another half million died trying to escape to the sea in pathetic, flimsy little boats. And . . . and in a way I can't quite convey, I feel those deaths are on my hands, on all our hands, and I feel the weight of them, sometimes so heavy I don't think I can hold up under it."

"You're being too hard on yourself."

"No. Never too hard."

"One man can't carry the world on his shoulders," she said.

But Benny would not allow that weight to be lifted from him, not even a fraction of it. "That's why I'm past-focused, I guess. I've learned that the worlds I have to live in—the present world and the world to come—aren't clean, never will be, and give us no choices between black and white. But there's always at least the illusion that things were a lot different in the past."

Rachael had always admired his sense of responsibility and his unwavering honesty, but now she saw that those qualities ran far deeper in him than she had realized—perhaps too deep. Even virtues like responsibility and honesty could become obsessions. But, oh, what lovely obsessions compared with those of other men she had known.

At last he looked at her, met her gaze, and his eyes were full of a sorrow—almost a melancholy—that she had never seen in them before. But other emotions were evident in his eyes as well, a special warmth and tenderness, great affection, love.

He said, "Last night and this morning . . . after we made love . . . Well, for the first time since before the war, I saw an important choice that was strictly black and white, no grays whatsoever, and in that choice there's a sort of . . . a sort of salvation that I thought I'd never find."

"What choice?" she asked.

"Whether to spend my life with you—or not," he said. "To spend it with you is the right choice, entirely right, no ambiguities. And to let you slip away is wrong, all wrong; I've no doubt about that."

For weeks, maybe months, Rachael had known she was in love with Benny. But she had reined in her emotions, had not spoken of the depth of her feelings for him, and had not permitted herself to think of a long-term commitment. Her childhood and adolescence had been colored by loneliness and shaped by the terrible perception that she was unloved, and those bleak years had engendered in her a craving for affection. That craving, that *need* to be wanted and loved, was what had made her such easy prey for Eric Leben and had led her into a bad marriage. Eric's obsession with youth in general and with her youth in particular had seemed like love to Rachael, for she had desperately wanted it to be love. She had spent the next seven years learning and accepting the grim and hurtful truth—that love had nothing to do with it. Now she was cautious, wary of being hurt again.

"I love you, Rachael."

Heart pounding, wanting to believe that she could be loved by a man as good and sweet as Benny, but afraid to believe it, she tried to look away from his eyes because the longer she stared into them the closer she came to losing the control and cool detachment with which she armored herself. But she could not look away. She tried not to say anything that would make her vulnerable, but with a curious mixture of dismay, delight, and wild exhilaration, she said, "Is this what I think it is?"

"What do you think it is?"

"A proposal."

"Hardly the time or place for a proposal, is it?" he said.

"Hardly."

"Yet . . . that's what it is. I wish the circumstances were more romantic."

"Well . . ."

"Champagne, candlelight, violins."

She smiled.

"But," he said, "when Baresco was holding that revolver on us, and when we were being chased down Palm Canyon Drive last night, the thing that scared me most wasn't that I might be killed . . . but that I might be killed *before I'd let you know how I felt about you.* So I'm letting you know. I want to be with you always, Rachael, always."

More easily than she would have believed possible, the words came to her own lips. "I want to spend my life with you, too, Benny."

He put a hand to her face.

She leaned forward and kissed him lightly.

"I love you," he said.

"God, I love you."

"If we get through this alive, you'll marry me?"

"Yes," she said, seized by a sudden chill. "But damn it, Benny, why'd you have to bring the *if* part into it?"

"Forget I said it."

But she could not forget. Earlier in the day, in the motel room in Palm Springs, just after they had made love the second time, she'd experienced a presentiment of death that had shaken her and had filled her with the need to *move,* as if a deadly weight would fall on them if they stayed in the same place any longer. That uncanny feeling returned. The mountain scenery, which had been fresh and alluring, acquired a somber and threatening aspect that chilled her even though she knew it was entirely a subjective change. The trees seemed to stretch into mutant shapes, their limbs bonier, their shadows darker.

"Let's go," she said.

He nodded, apparently understanding her thoughts and perceiving the same change of mood that she felt.

He started the car, pulled onto the road. When they had rounded the next bend, they saw another sign: LAKE ARROWHEAD—15 MILES.

◑   ◑

Eric looked over the other tools in the garage, seeking another instrument for his arsenal. He saw nothing useful.

He returned to the house. In the kitchen, he put the ax on the table and pulled open a few drawers until he located a set of knives. He chose two—a butcher's knife and a smaller, pointier blade.

With an ax and two knives, he was prepared for both arm's-length combat and close-in fighting. He still wished he had a gun, but at least he was no longer defenseless. If someone came looking for him, he would be able to take care of himself. He would do them serious damage before they brought him down, a prospect that gave him some satisfaction and that, somewhat to his surprise, brought a sudden grin to his face.

The mice, the mice, the biting, frenzied mice . . .

Damn. He shook his head.

The mice, mice, mice, maniacal, clawing, spitting . . .

That crazy thought, like a fragment of a demented nursery rhyme, spun through his mind again, frightening him, and when he tried to focus on it, tried to understand it, his thoughts grew muddy once more, and he simply could not grasp the meaning of the mice.

The mice, mice, bloody-eyed, bashing against cage walls . . .

When he continued to strain for the elusive memory of the mice, a throbbing white pain filled his head from crown to temples and burned across the bridge of his nose, but when he stopped trying to remember and attempted, instead, to put the mice out of his mind, the pain grew even worse, a sledgehammer striking rhythmically behind his eyes. He had to grit his teeth to endure it, broke out in a sweat, and with the sweat came anger duller than the pain but growing even as the pain grew, unfocused anger at first but not for long. He said, "Rachael, Rachael," and clenched the butcher's knife. "Rachael . . ."

◊ 19 ◊

SHARP AND
THE STONE

On arriving at the hospital in Palm Springs, Anson
Sharp had done easily what Jerry Peake had been
unable to do with mighty striving. In ten minutes, he
turned Nurse Alma Dunn's stonefaced implacability to
dust, and he shattered Dr. Werfell's authoritarian calm,
reducing both of them to nervous, uncertain, respectful,
cooperative citizens. Theirs was grudging cooperation,
but it was cooperation nonetheless, and Peake was
deeply impressed. Though Sarah Kiel was still under
the influence of the sedatives that she had taken in
the middle of the night, Werfell agreed to wake her
by whatever means necessary.

As always, Peake watched Sharp closely, trying to
learn how the deputy director achieved his effects,
much as a young magician might study a master
prestidigitator's every move upon the stage. For one
thing, Sharp used his formidable size to intimidate;
he stood close, towering over his adversaries, staring
down ominously, huge shoulders drawn up, full of
pent-up violence, a volatile man. Yet the threat never
became overt, and in fact Sharp frequently smiled.
Of course, the smile was a weapon, too, for it was

too wide, too full of teeth, utterly humorless, and strange.

More important than Sharp's size was his use of every trick available to a highly placed government agent. Before leaving the Geneplan labs in Riverside, he had employed his Defense Security Agency authority to make several telephone calls to various federal regulatory agencies in Washington, from whose computer files he had obtained what information he could on Desert General Hospital and Dr. Hans Werfell, information that could be used to strong-arm them.

Desert General's record was virtually spotless. The very highest standards for staff physicians, nurses, and technicians were strictly enforced; nine years had passed since a malpractice suit had been filed against the hospital, and no suit had ever been successful; the patient-recovery rate for every illness and surgical procedure was higher than the normal average. In twenty years, the only stain on Desert General had been the Case of the Purloined Pills. That was what Peake named the affair when Sharp quickly briefed him on arrival, before confronting Dunn and Werfell; it was a name Peake did not share with Sharp, since Sharp was not a reader of mysteries as Peake was and did not have Peake's sense of adventure. Anyway, just last year, three nurses at Desert General had been caught altering purchase and dispensation records in the pharmacy, and upon investigation it was discovered they had been stealing drugs for years. Out of spite, the three had falsely implicated six of their superiors, including Nurse Dunn, though the police had eventually cleared Dunn and the others. Desert General was put on the Drug Enforcement Agency's "watch list" of medical institutions, and Alma Dunn, though cleared, was shaken by the experience and still felt her reputation endangered.

Sharp took advantage of that weak spot. In a discreet session with Alma Dunn in the nurses' lounge, with only Peake as a witness, Sharp subtly threatened the woman with a very public reopening of the original investigation, this time at the federal level, and not only solicited her cooperation but brought her almost to tears,

a feat that Peake—who likened Alma Dunn to Agatha
Christie's indomitable Miss Jane Marple—had thought
impossible.

At first, it appeared as if Dr. Werfell would be
more difficult to crack. His record as a physician was
unblemished. He was highly regarded in the medical
community, possessed an AMA Physician of the Year
Award, contributed six hours a week of his time to a
free clinic for the disadvantaged, and from every angle
appeared to be a saint. Well . . . from every angle but
one: He had been charged with income-tax evasion five
years ago and had lost in court on a technicality. He
had failed to comply *precisely* with IRS standards of
record keeping, and though his failure was unintentional,
a simple ignorance of the law, ignorance of the law was
not an acceptable defense.

Cornering Werfell in a two-bed room currently unoccupied by patients, Sharp used the threat of a new
IRS investigation to bring the doctor to his knees in
about five minutes flat. Werfell seemed certain that
his records would be found acceptable now and that
he would be cleared, but he also knew how expensive
and time-consuming it was to defend himself against an
IRS probe, and he knew that his reputation would be tar-
nished even when he was cleared. He looked to Peake for
sympathy a few times, knowing he would get none from
Sharp, but Peake did his best to imitate Anson Sharp's
air of granite resolution and indifference to others. Being
an intelligent man, Werfell quickly determined that the
prudent course would be to do as Sharp wished in order
to avoid another tax-court nightmare, even if it meant
bending his principles in the matter of Sarah Kiel.

"No reason to fault yourself or lose any sleep over
a misguided concern about professional ethics, Doctor,"
Sharp said, clapping one beefy hand on the physician's
shoulder in a gesture of reassurance, suddenly friendly
and empathetic now that Werfell had broken. "The
welfare of our country comes before anything else.
No one would dispute that or think you'd made the
wrong decision."

Dr. Werfell did not exactly recoil from Sharp's touch, but he looked sickened by it. His expression did not change when he looked from Sharp to Jerry Peake.

Peake winced.

Werfell led them out of the untenanted room, down the hospital corridor, past the nurses' station—where Alma Dunn watched them warily while pretending not to look— to the private room where Sarah Kiel remained sedated. As they went, Peake noticed that Werfell, who had previously seemed to resemble Dashiell Hammett and who had looked tremendously imposing, was now somewhat shrunken, diminished. His face was gray, and he seemed older than he had been just a short while ago.

Although Peake admired Anson Sharp's ability to command and to get things done, he did not see how he could adopt his boss's methods as his own. Peake wanted not only to be a successful agent but to be a legend, and you could be a legend only if you played fair and *still* got things done. Being infamous was not at all the same as being a legend, and in fact the two could not coexist. If he had learned nothing else from five thousand mystery novels, Peake had at least learned that much.

Sarah Kiel's room was silent except for her slow and slightly wheezy breathing, dark but for a single softly glowing lamp beside her bed and the few thin beams of bright desert sun that burned through at the edges of the heavy drapes drawn over the lone window.

The three men gathered around the bed, Dr. Werfell and Sharp on one side, Peake on the other.

"Sarah," Werfell said quietly. "Sarah?" When she didn't respond, the physician repeated her name and gently shook her shoulder.

She snorted, murmured, but did not wake.

Werfell lifted one of the girl's eyelids, studied her pupil, then held her wrist and timed her pulse. "She won't wake naturally for . . . oh, perhaps another hour."

"Then do what's necessary to wake her *now*," Anson Sharp said impatiently. "We've already discussed this."

"I'll administer an injection to counteract," Werfell said, heading toward the closed door.

"Stay here," Sharp said. He indicated the call button on the cord that was tied loosely to one of the bed rails. "Have a nurse bring what you need."

"This is questionable treatment," Werfell said. "I won't ask any nurse to be involved in it." He went out, and the door sighed slowly shut behind him.

Looking down at the sleeping girl, Sharp said, "Scrumptious."

Peake blinked in surprise.

"Tasty," Sharp said, without raising his eyes from the girl.

Peake looked down at the unconscious teenager and tried to see something scrumptious and tasty about her, but it wasn't easy. Her blond hair was tangled and oily because she was perspiring in her drugged sleep, her limp and matted tresses were unappealingly sweat-pasted to forehead, cheeks, and neck. Her right eye was blackened and swollen shut, with several lines of dried and crusted blood radiating from it where the skin had been cracked and torn. Her right cheek was covered by a bruise from the corner of her swollen eye all the way to her jaw, and her upper lip was split and puffy. Sheets covered her almost to the neck, except for her thin right arm, which had to be exposed because one broken finger was in a cast; two fingernails had been cracked off at the cuticle, and the hand looked less like a hand than like a bird's long-toed, bony claw.

"Fifteen when she first moved in with Leben," Sharp said softly. "Not much past sixteen now."

Turning his attention from the sleeping girl to his boss, Jerry Peake studied Sharp as Sharp studied Sarah Kiel, and he was not merely struck by an incredible insight but *whacked* by it so hard he almost reeled backward. Anson Sharp, deputy director of the DSA, was both a pedophile and a sadist.

Perverse hungers were apparent in the man's hard green eyes and predatory expression. Clearly, he thought Sarah was scrumptious and tasty not because she looked so great right now but because she was only sixteen and badly battered. His rapturous gaze moved lovingly over her blackened eye and bruises, which obviously had as great an erotic impact upon him as breasts and buttocks might have upon a normal man. He was a tightly controlled sadist, yes, and a pedophile who kept his sick libido in check, a pervert who had redirected his mutant needs into wholly acceptable channels, into the aggressiveness and ambition that had swiftly carried him almost to the top of the agency, but a sadist and a pedophile nonetheless.

Peake was as astonished as he was appalled. And his astonishment arose not only from this terrible insight into Sharp's character but from the very fact that he'd had such an insight in the first place. Although he wanted to be a legend, Jerry Peake knew that, even for twenty-seven, he was naive and—especially for a DSA man—woefully prone to look only at the surfaces of people and events rather than down into more profound levels. Sometimes, in spite of his training and his important job, he felt as if he were still a boy, or at least as if the boy in him were still too much a part of his character. Now, staring at Anson Sharp as Sharp hungered for Sarah Kiel, absolutely *walloped* by this insight, Jerry Peake was suddenly exhilarated. He wondered if it was possible to finally begin to grow up even as late as twenty-seven.

Anson Sharp was staring at the girl's torn and broken hand, his green eyes radiant, a vague smile playing at the corners of his mouth.

With a thump and swish that startled Peake, the door to the room opened, and Dr. Werfell returned. Sharp blinked and shook himself as if coming out of a mild trance, stepped back, and watched as Werfell raised the bed, bared Sarah's left arm, and administered an injection to counteract the effect of the two sedatives she had taken.

In a couple of minutes, the girl was awake, relatively aware, but confused. She could not remember where she was, how she had gotten there, or why she was so battered and in pain. She kept asking who Werfell, Sharp, and Peake were, and Werfell patiently answered all her questions, but mostly he monitored her pulse and listened to her heart and peered into her eyes with a lighted instrument.

Anson Sharp grew impatient with the girl's slow ascension from her drugged haze. "Did you give her a large enough dose to counteract the sedative or did you hedge it, Doctor?"

"This takes time," Werfell said coldly.

"We don't *have* time," Sharp said.

A moment later, Sarah Kiel stopped asking questions, gasped in shock at the sudden return of her memory, and said, "Eric!"

Peake would not have imagined that her face could go paler than it was already, but it did. She began to shiver.

Sharp returned swiftly to the bed. "That'll be all, Doctor."

Werfell frowned. "What do you mean?"

"I mean she's alert now, and we can question her, and you can get out and leave us to it. Clear?"

Dr. Werfell insisted he should stay with his patient in case she had a delayed reaction to the injection. Sharp became more adamant, invoking his federal authority. Werfell relented but moved toward the window to open the drapes first. Sharp told him to leave them closed, and Werfell went to the light switch for the overhead fluorescents, but Sharp told him to leave them off. "The bright light will hurt the poor girl's eyes," Sharp said, though his sudden concern for Sarah was transparently insincere.

Peake had the uncomfortable feeling that Sharp intended to be hard on the girl, frighten her half to death, whether or not that approach was necessary. Even if she told them everything they wanted to know, the deputy director was going to terrorize her for the sheer fun of it. He probably viewed mental and emotional abuse as being at least partially satisfying and socially acceptable alternatives to the things he really wanted to do: beat her and fuck her. The bastard wanted to keep the room as dark as possible because shadows would contribute to the mood of menace that he intended to create.

When Werfell left the room, Sharp went to the girl's bed. He put down the railing on one side and sat on the edge of the mattress. He took her uninjured left hand, held it in both his hands, gave it a reassuring squeeze, smiled down at her, and as he spoke he began to slide one of his huge hands up and down her slender arm, even all the way up under the short sleeve of her hospital gown, slowly up and down, which was not at all reassuring but provocative.

Peake stepped back into a corner of the room, where shadows sheltered him, partly because he knew he would not be expected to ask questions of the girl, but also because he did not want Sharp to see his face. Although he had achieved the first startling insight of his life and was gripped by the heady feeling that he was not going to be the same man in a year that he was now, he had not yet changed so much that he could control his expressions or conceal his disgust.

"I can't talk about it," Sarah Kiel told Sharp, watching him warily and shrinking back from him as far as she could. "Mrs. Leben told me not to tell anyone anything."

Still holding her good hand in his left, he raised his right hand, with which he had been stroking her arm, and he gently rubbed his thick knuckles over her smooth, unblemished left cheek. It almost seemed like a gesture of sympathy or affection, but it was not.

He said, "Mrs. Leben is a wanted criminal, Sarah. There's a warrant for her arrest. I had it issued myself. She's wanted for serious violations of the Defense Security Act. She may have stolen defense secrets, may even intend to pass them to the Soviets. Surely you've no desire to protect someone like that. Hmmmmm?"

"She was nice to me," Sarah said shakily.

Peake saw that the girl was trying to ease away from the hand that stroked her face but was plainly afraid of giving offense to Sharp. Evidently she was not yet certain that he was threatening her. She'd get the idea soon.

She continued: "Mrs. Leben's paying my hospital bills, gave me some money, called my folks. She . . . she was s-so nice, and she told me not to talk about this, so I won't break my promise to her."

"How interesting," Sharp said, putting his hand under her chin and lifting her head to make her look at him with her one good eye. "Interesting that even a little whore like you has some principles."

Shocked, she said, "I'm no whore. I never—"

"Oh, yes," Sharp said, gripping her chin now and preventing her from turning her head away. "Maybe you're too thickheaded to see the truth about yourself, or too drugged up, but that's what you are, a little whore, a slut in training, a piglet who's going to grow up to be a fine sweet pig."

"You can't talk to me like this."

"Honey, I talk to whores any way I want."

"You're a cop, some kind of cop, you're a public *servant*," she said, "you can't treat me—"

"Shut up, honey," Sharp said. The light from the only lamp fell across his face at an angle, weirdly exaggerating some features while leaving others entirely in shadow, giving his face a deformed look, a demonic aspect. He grinned, and the effect was even more unnerving. "You shut your dirty little mouth and open it only when you're ready to tell me what I want to know."

The girl gave out a thin, pathetic cry of pain, and tears burst from her eyes. Peake saw that Sharp was squeezing her left hand very hard and grinding the fingers together in his big mitt.

For a while, the girl talked to avoid the torture. She told them about Leben's visit last night, about the way his head was staved in, about how gray and cool his skin had felt.

But when Sharp wanted to know if she had any idea where Eric Leben had gone after leaving the house, she clammed up again, and he said, "Ah, you do have an idea," and he began to grind her hand again.

Peake felt sick, and he wanted to do something to help the girl, but there was nothing he could do.

Sharp eased up on her hand, and she said, "Please, that was the thing . . . the thing Mrs. Leben most wanted me not to tell anyone."

"Now, honey," Sharp said, "it's stupid for a little whore like you to pretend to have scruples. I don't believe you have any, and you *know* you don't have any, so cut the act. Save us some time and save yourself a lot of trouble." He started to grind her hand again, and his other hand slipped down to her throat and then to her breasts, which he touched through the thin material of her hospital gown.

In the shadowed corner, Peake was almost too shocked to breathe, and he wanted to be *out* of there. He certainly did not want to watch Sarah Kiel be abused and humiliated; however, he could not look away or close his eyes, because Sharp's unexpected behavior was the most morbidly, horrifyingly fascinating thing Peake had ever seen.

He was nowhere near coming to terms with his previous shattering insight, and already he was experiencing yet another major revelation. He'd always thought of policemen—which included DSA agents—as Good Guys with capital Gs, White Hats, Men on White Horses, valiant Knights of the Law, but that image of purity was suddenly unsustainable if a man like Sharp could be a highly regarded member in good standing of that noble fraternity. Oh, sure, Peake knew there were some bad cops, bad agents, but somehow he had always thought the bad ones were caught early in their careers and that they never had a chance of advancing to high positions, that they self-destructed, that slime like that got what was coming to them and got it pretty quickly, too. He believed only virtue was rewarded. Besides, he had always thought he'd be able to smell corruption in another cop, that it would be evident from the moment he laid eyes on the guy. And he had never imagined that a flat-out *pervert* could hide his sickness and have a successful career in law enforcement. Maybe most men were disabused of such naive ideas long before they were twenty-seven, but it was only now, watching the deputy director behave like a thug, like a regular damn barbarian, that Jerry Peake began to see that the world was painted more in shades of gray than in black and white, and this revelation was so powerful that he could no more have averted his eyes from Sharp's sick performance than he could have looked away from Jesus returning on a chariot of fire through an angel-bedecked sky.

Sharp continued to grind the girl's hand in his, which made her cry harder, and he had a hand on her breasts and was pushing her back hard against the bed, telling her to quiet down, so she was trying to please him now, choking back her tears, but still Sharp squeezed her hand, and Peake was on the verge of making a move, to hell with his career, to hell with his future in the DSA, he couldn't just stand by and watch this brutality, he even took a step toward the bed—

And that was when the door opened wide and The Stone entered the room as if borne on the shaft of light that speared in from the hospital corridor behind him. That was how Jerry Peake thought of the man from the moment he saw him: The Stone.

"What's goin' on here?" The Stone asked in a voice that was quiet, gentle, deep but not real deep, yet commanding.

The guy was not quite six feet tall, maybe five eleven, even five ten, which left him several inches shorter than Anson Sharp, and he was about a hundred and seventy pounds, a good fifty pounds lighter than Sharp. Yet when he stepped through the door, he seemed like the biggest man in the room, and he *still* seemed like the biggest even when Sharp let go of the girl and stood up from the edge of the bed and said, "Who the hell are you?"

The Stone switched on the overhead fluorescents and stepped farther into the room, letting the door swing shut behind him. Peake pegged the guy as about forty, though his face looked older because it was full of wisdom. He had close-cut dark hair, sun-weathered skin, and solid features that looked as if they had been jackhammered out of granite. His intense blue eyes were the same shade as those of the girl in the bed but clearer, direct, piercing.

When he turned those eyes briefly toward Jerry Peake, Peake wanted to crawl under a bed and hide. The Stone was compact and powerful, and though he was really smaller than Sharp, he appeared infinitely stronger, more formidable, as if he actually weighed every ounce as much as Sharp but had compressed his tissues into an unnatural density.

"Please leave the room and wait for me in the hall," said The Stone quietly.

Astonished, Sharp took a couple of steps toward him, loomed over him, and said, "I asked you who the hell you are."

The Stone's hands and wrists were much too large for the rest of him: long, thick fingers; big knuckles; every tendon and vein and sinew stood out sharply, as if they were hands carved in marble by a sculptor with an exaggerated appreciation for detail. Peake sensed that they were not quite the hands that The Stone had been born with, that they had grown larger and stronger in response to day after day of long, hard, manual labor. The Stone looked as if he thrived on the kind of heavy work that was done in a foundry or quarry or, considering his sun-darkened skin, a farm. But not one of those big, easy, modern farms with a thousand machines and an abundant supply of cheap field hands. No, if he had a farm, he had started it with little money, with bad rocky land, and he had endured lousy weather and sundry catastrophes to bring fruit from the reluctant earth, building a successful enterprise by the expenditure of much sweat, blood, time, hopes, and dreams, because the strength of all those successfully waged struggles was in his face and hands.

"I'm her father, Felsen Kiel," The Stone told Sharp.

In a small voice devoid of fear and filled with wonder, Sarah Kiel said, "Daddy . . ."

The Stone started past Sharp, toward his daughter, who had sat up in bed and held out a hand toward him.

Sharp stepped in his way, leaned close to him, loomed over him, and said, "You can see her when we've finished the interrogation."

The Stone looked up at Sharp with a placid expression that was the essence of equanimity and imperturbability, and Peake was not only gladdened but *thrilled* to see that Sharp was not going to intimidate this man. "Interrogate? What right have you to interrogate?"

Sharp withdrew his wallet from his jacket, opened it to his DSA credentials. "I'm a federal agent, and I am in the middle of an urgent investigation concerning a matter of national security. Your daughter has information that I've got to obtain as soon as possible, and she is being less than cooperative."

"If you'll step into the hall," The Stone said quietly, "I'll speak with her. I'm sure she isn't obstructin' you on purpose. She's a troubled girl, yes, and she's allowed herself to be misguided, but she's never been bad at heart or spiteful. I'll speak to her, find out what you need to know, then convey the information to you."

"No," Sharp said. *"You'll* go into the hall and wait."

"Please move out of my way," The Stone said.

"Listen, mister," Sharp said, moving right up against The Stone, glaring down at him, "if you want trouble from me, you'll get it, more than you can deal with. You obstruct a federal agent, and you're just about giving him a license to come down on you as hard as he wants."

Having read the name on the DSA credentials, The Stone said, "Mr. Sharp, last night I was awakened by a call from a Mrs. Leben, who said my daughter needed me. That's a message I've been waitin' a long time to hear. It's the growin' season, a busy time—"

The guy *was* a farmer, by God, which gave Peake new confidence in his powers of observation. In spit-polished city shoes, polyester pants, and starched white shirt, The Stone had the uncomfortable look specific to a simple country man who has been forced by circumstances to exchange his work clothes for unfamiliar duds.

"—a very busy season. But I got dressed the moment I hung up the phone, drove the pickup a hundred miles to Kansas City in the heart of the night, got the dawn flight out to Los Angeles, then the connector flight here to Palm Springs, a taxi—"

"Your travel journal doesn't interest me one damn bit," Sharp said, still blocking The Stone.

"Mr. Sharp, I am plain bone-weary, which is the fact I'm tryin' to impress upon you, and I am most eager to see my girl, and from the looks of her she's been cryin', which upsets me mightily. Now, though I'm not an angry man by nature, or a trouble-makin' man, I don't know quite what I might do if you keep treatin' me high-handed and try to stop me from seein' what my girl's cryin' about."

Sharp's face tightened with anger. He stepped back far enough to give himself room to plant one big hand on The Stone's chest.

Peake was not sure whether Sharp intended to guide the man out of the room and into the corridor or give him one hell of a shove back against the wall. He never found out which it was because The Stone put his own hand on Sharp's wrist and bore down and, without seeming to make any effort whatsoever, he removed Sharp's hand from his chest. In fact, he must have put as much painful pressure on Sharp's wrist as Sharp had applied to Sarah's fingers, for the deputy director went pale, the redness of anger draining right out of him, and a queer look passed through his eyes.

Letting go of Sharp's hand, The Stone said, "I know you're a federal agent, and I have the greatest respect for the law. I know you can see this as obstruction, which would give you a good excuse to knock me on my can and clap me in handcuffs. But I'm of the opinion that it wouldn't do you or your agency the least bit of good if you roughed me up, 'specially since I've told you I'll encourage my daughter to cooperate. What do you think?"

Peake wanted to applaud. He didn't.

Sharp stood there, breathing heavily, trembling, and gradually his rage-clouded eyes cleared, and he shook himself the way a bull sometimes will shake itself back to its senses after unsuccessfully charging a matador's cape. "Okay. I just want to get my information *fast*. I don't care how. Maybe you'll get it faster than I can."

"Thank you, Mr. Sharp. Give me half an hour—"

"Five minutes!" Sharp said.

"Well, sir," The Stone said quietly, "you've got to give me time to say hello to my daughter, time to hug her. I haven't seen her in almost eighteen months. And I need time to get the whole story from her, to find out what sort of trouble she's in. That's got to come first, 'fore I start throwin' questions at her."

"Half an hour's too damn long," Sharp said. "We're in pursuit of a man, a dangerous man, and we—"

"If I was to call an attorney to advise my daughter, which is her right as a citizen, it'd take him hours to get here—"

"Half an hour," Sharp told The Stone, "and not one damn minute more. I'll be in the hall."

Previously, Peake had discovered that the deputy director was a sadist and a pedophile, which was an important thing to know. Now he had made another discovery about Sharp: The son of a bitch was, at heart, a coward; he might shoot you in the back or sneak up on you and slit your throat, yes, those things seemed within his character, but in a face-to-face confrontation, he would chicken out if the stakes got high enough. And that was an even *more* important thing to know.

Peake stood for a moment, unable to move, as Sharp went to the door. He could not take his eyes off The Stone.

"Peake!" Sharp said as he pulled the door open.

Finally Peake followed, but he kept glancing back at Felsen Kiel, The Stone. Now *there,* by God, was a legend.

◊ 20 ◊

COPS ON SICK LEAVE

Detective Reese Hagerstrom went to bed at four o'clock Tuesday morning, after returning from Mrs. Leben's house in Placentia, and he woke at ten-thirty, unrested because the night had been full of terrible dreams. Glassy-eyed dead bodies in trash dumpsters. Dead women nailed to walls. Many of the nightmares had involved Janet, the wife Reese had lost. In the dreams, she was always clutching the door of the blue Chevy van, the infamous van, and crying, "They've got Esther, they've got Esther!" In every dream, one of the guys in the van shot her exactly as he had shot her in real life, point-blank, and the large-caliber slug pulverized her lovely face, blew it away . . .

Reese got out of bed and took a very hot shower. He wished that he could unhinge the top of his head and sluice out the hideous images that lingered from the nightmares.

Agnes, his sister, had taped a note on the refrigerator in the kitchen. She had taken Esther to the dentist for a scheduled checkup.

Standing by the sink, looking out the window at the big coral tree in the rear yard, Reese drank hot black coffee and ate a slightly stale doughnut. If Agnes could see the breakfast he made for himself, she would be upset. But his dreams had left him queasy, and he had no appetite for anything heavier. Even the doughnut was hard to swallow.

"Black coffee and greasy doughnuts," Agnes would say if she knew. "One'll give you ulcers, other'll clog your arteries with cholesterol. Two slow methods of suicide. You want to commit suicide, I can tell you a hundred quicker and less painful ways to go about it."

He thanked God for Agnes, in spite of her tendency, as his big sister, to nag him about everything from his eating habits to his taste in neckties. Without her, he might not have held himself together after Janet's death.

Agnes was unfortunately big-boned, stocky, plain-looking, with a deformed left hand, destined for spinsterhood, but she had a kind heart and a mothering instinct second to none. After Janet died, Agnes arrived with a suitcase and her favorite cookbook, announcing that she would take care of Reese and little Esther "just for the summer," until they were able to cope on their own. As a fifth-grade teacher in Anaheim, she had the summer off and could devote long hours to the patient rebuilding of the shattered Hagerstrom household. She had been with them five years now, and without her, they'd be lost.

Reese even liked her good-natured nagging. When she encouraged him to eat well-balanced meals, he felt cared for and loved.

As he poured another cup of black coffee, he decided to bring Agnes a dozen roses and a box of chocolates when he came home today. He was not, by nature, given to frequent expressions of his feelings, so he tried to compensate now and then by surprising those he cared for with gifts. The smallest surprises thrilled Agnes, even coming from a brother. Big-boned, stocky, plain-faced women were not used to getting gifts when there was no occasion requiring them.

Life was not only unfair but sometimes decidedly cruel. That was not a new thought to Reese. It was not even inspired by Janet's untimely and brutal death—or by the fact that Agnes's warm, loving, generous nature was trapped forever inside a body that most men, too focused on appearances, could never love. As a policeman, frequently confronted by the worst in humankind, he had learned a long time ago that cruelty was the way of the world—and that the only defense against it was the love of one's family and a few close friends.

His closest friend, Julio Verdad, arrived as Reese was pouring a third cup of black coffee. Reese got another cup from the cabinet and filled it for Julio, and they sat at the kitchen table.

Julio looked as if he'd had little sleep, and in fact Reese was probably the only person capable of detecting the subtle signs of overwork in the lieutenant. As usual, Julio was well dressed: smartly tailored dark blue suit, crisp white shirt, perfectly knotted maroon-and-blue tie with gold chain, maroon pocket handkerchief, and oxblood Bally loafers. He was as neat and precise and alert as always, but vague sooty smudges were visible under his eyes, and his soft voice was surely if immeasurably softer than usual.

"Up all night?" Reese asked.

"I slept."

"How long? An hour or two? That's what I thought. You worry me," Reese said. "You'll wear yourself down to bone someday."

"This is a special case."

"They're all special cases to you."

"I feel a special obligation to the victim, Ernestina."

"This is the *thousandth* victim you've felt a special obligation toward," Reese noted.

Julio shrugged and sipped his coffee. "Sharp wasn't bluffing."

"About what?"

"About pulling this out of our hands. The names of the victims—Ernestina Hernandez and Rebecca Klienstad—are still in the files, but *only* the names. Plus a memorandum indicating that federal authorities requested the case be remanded to their jurisdiction for 'reasons of national security.' This morning, when I pushed Folbeck about letting you and me assist the feds, he came down hard. Said, 'Holy fuckin' Christ, Julio, stay out of it. That's an order.' His very words."

Folbeck was chief of detectives, a devout Mormon who could hold his own with the most foulmouthed men in the department but who *never* took the Lord's name in vain. That was where he drew the line. In spite of his vivid and frequent use of four-letter words, Nicholas Folbeck was capable of angrily lecturing any detective heard to mutter a blasphemy. In fact, he'd once told Reese, "Hagerstrom, please don't say 'goddamn' or 'holy Christ' or anything like that in my presence ever again. I purely hate that shit, and I won't fuckin' tolerate it." If Nick Folbeck's warning to Julio had included blasphemy as well as mere trash talk, the pressure on the department to stay out of this case had come from higher authorities than Anson Sharp.

Reese said, "What about the file on the body-snatching case, Eric Leben's corpse?"

"Same thing," Julio said. "Removed from our jurisdiction."

Business talk had taken Reese's mind off last night's bloody dreams of Janet, and his appetite had returned a little. He got another doughnut from the breadbox. He offered one to Julio, but Julio declined. Reese said, "What else have you been up to?"

"For one thing . . . I went to the library when it opened and read everything I could find on Dr. Eric Leben."

"Rich, a scientific genius, a business genius, ruthless, cold, too stupid to know he had a great wife—we already know about him."

"He was also obsessed," Julio said.

"I guess geniuses usually are, with one thing or another."

"What obsessed him was immortality."

Reese frowned. "Say what?"

"As a graduate student, and in the years immediately following his acquisition of a doctorate, when he was one of the brightest young geneticists doing recombinant

DNA research anywhere in the world, he wrote articles for a lot of journals and published research papers dealing with various aspects of the extension of the human life span. A *flood* of articles; the man is driven."

"Was driven. Remember that garbage truck," Reese said.

"Even the driest, most technical of those pieces have a . . . well, a *fire* in them, a passion that grips you," Julio said. He pulled a sheet of paper from one of his inside jacket pockets, unfolded it. "This is a line from an article that appeared in a popular science magazine, more colorful than the technical journal stuff: 'It may be possible, ultimately, for man to reshape himself genetically and thereby deny the claim of the grave, to live longer than Methuselah—and even to be both Jesus and Lazarus in one, raising *himself* up from the mortuary slab even as death lays him down upon it."

Reese blinked. "Funny, huh? His body's stolen from the morgue, which is sort of being 'raised up,' though not the way he meant it."

Julio's eyes were strange. "Maybe not funny. Maybe not stolen."

Reese felt a strangeness coming into his own eyes. He said, "You don't mean . . . no, of course not."

"He was a genius with unlimited resources, perhaps the brightest man ever to work in recombinant DNA research, and he was obsessed with staying young and avoiding death. So when he just seems to get up and walk away from a mortuary . . . is it so impossible to imagine that he did, in fact, get up and walk away?"

Reese felt his chest tightening, and he was surprised to feel a thrill of fear pass through him. "But is such a thing possible, after the injuries he suffered?"

"A few years ago, definitely impossible. But we're living in an age of miracles, or at least in an age of infinite possibilities."

"But how?"

"That's part of what we'll have to find out. I called UCI and got in touch with Dr. Easton Solberg, whose work on aging is mentioned in Leben's articles. Turns out Leben knew Solberg, looked up to him as a mentor, and for a while they were fairly close. Solberg has great praise for Leben, says he isn't the least surprised that Leben made a fortune out of DNA research, but Solberg also says there was a dark side to Eric Leben. And he's willing to talk about it."

"What dark side?"

"He wouldn't say on the phone. But we have an appointment with him at UCI at one o'clock."

As Julio pushed his chair back and got up, Reese said, "How can we keep digging into this and stay out of trouble with Nick Folbeck?"

"Sick leave," Julio said. "As long as I'm on sick leave, I'm not officially investigating anything. Call it personal curiosity."

"That won't hold up if we're caught at it. Cops aren't supposed to *have* personal curiosity in a situation like this."

"No, but if I'm on sick leave, Folbeck's not going to be worrying about what I'm doing. It's less likely that anyone'll be looking over my shoulder. In fact, I sort of implied that I wanted nothing to do with anything this hot. Told Folbeck that, given the heat on this, it might be best for me to get away for a few days, in case the media pick up on it and want me to answer questions. He agreed."

Reese got to his feet. "I better call in sick, too."

"I already did it for you," Julio said.

"Oh. Okay, then, let's go."

"I mean, I thought it would be all right. But if you don't want to get involved in this—"

"Julio, I'm in."

"Only if you're sure."

"I'm *in,*" Reese said exasperatedly.

And he thought but did not say: You saved my Esther, my little girl, went right after those guys in the Chevy van and got her out of there alive, you were like a man possessed, they must've thought it was a demon on their tail, you put your own life on the line and saved Esther, and I loved you before that because you were my partner and a good one, but after that I *loved* you, you crazy little bastard, and as long as I live I'm going to be there when you need me, no matter what.

In spite of his natural difficulty expressing his most profound feelings, Reese wanted to say all of that to Julio, but he kept silent because Julio did not want effusive gratitude and would be embarrassed by it. All Julio wanted was the commitment of a friend and partner. Undying gratitude would, if openly expressed, impose a barrier between them by obviously placing Julio in a superior position, and ever afterward they would be awkward with each other.

In their daily working relationship, Julio always had been in the superior position, of course, deciding how to proceed at nearly every step of a homicide investigation, but his control was never blatant or obvious, which made all the difference. Reese would not have cared if Julio's dominance had been obvious; he did not mind deferring to Julio because in some ways Julio was the quicker and smarter of the two.

But Julio, having been born and raised in Mexico, having come to the States and made good, had a reverence and a passion for democracy, not only for democracy in the political arena but for democracy in all things, even in one-to-one relationships. He could assume the mantle of leadership and dominance if it were conveyed by mutual unspoken consent; but if his role were made overt, he would not be able to fulfill it, and the partnership would suffer.

"I'm in," Reese repeated, rinsing their coffee cups in the sink. "We're just two cops on sick leave. So let's go recuperate together."

◊ 21 ◊

ARROWHEAD

The sporting-goods store was near the lake. It was built in the form of a large log cabin, and a rustic wooden sign advertised BAIT, TACKLE, BOAT RENTALS, SPORTING GOODS. A Coors sign was in one window, a Miller Lite sign in another. Three cars, two pickup trucks, and one Jeep stood in the sunny part of the parking lot, the early-afternoon sun glinting off their chrome and silvering their windows.

"Guns," Ben said when he saw the place. "They might sell guns."

"We have guns," Rachael said.

Ben drove to the back of the lot, off the macadamed area, onto gravel that crunched under the tires, then through a thick carpet of pine needles, finally parking in the concealing shade of one of the massive evergreens that encircled the property. He saw a slice of the lake beyond the trees, a few boats on the sun-dappled water, and a far shore rising up into steep wooded slopes.

"Your thirty-two isn't exactly a peashooter, but it's not particularly formidable, either," Ben told her as he switched off the engine. "The .357 I took off Baresco is better, next thing to a cannon, in fact, but a shotgun would be perfect."

"Shotgun? Sounds like overkill."

"I always prefer to go for overkill when I'm tracking down a walking dead man," Ben said, trying to make a joke of it but failing. Rachael's already haunted eyes were touched by a new bleak tint, and she shivered.

"Hey," he said, "it'll be all right."

They got out of the rental car and stood for a moment, breathing in the clean, sweet mountain air. The day was warm and undisturbed by even the mildest breeze. The trees stood motionless and silent, as if their boughs had turned to stone. No cars passed on the road, and no other people were in sight. No birds flew or sang. The stillness was deep, perfect, preternatural.

Ben sensed something ominous in the stillness. It almost seemed to be an omen, a warning to turn back from the high vastness of the mountains and retreat to more civilized places, where there was noise and movement and other people to turn to for help in an emergency.

Apparently stricken by the same uneasy feeling that gripped Ben, Rachael said, "Maybe this is nuts. Maybe we should just get out of here, go away somewhere."

"And wait for Eric to recover from his injuries?"

"Maybe he won't recover enough to function well."

"But if he does, he'll come looking for you."

She sighed, nodded.

They crossed the parking lot and went into the store, hoping to buy a shotgun and some ammunition.

◊　　◊

Something strange was happening to Eric, stranger even than his return from the dead. It started as another headache, one of the many intense migraines that had come and gone since his resurrection, and he did not immediately realize there was a difference about this one, a weirdness. He just squinted his eyes to block out some of the light that irritated him, and refused to succumb to the unrelenting and debilitating throbbing that filled his skull.

He pulled an armchair in front of the living-room window and took up a vigil, looking down through the sloping forest, along the dirt road that led up from the more heavily populated foothills nearer the lake. If enemies came for him, they would follow the lane at least part of the way up the slope before sneaking into the woods. As soon as he saw where they left the road, he would slip out of the cabin by the back door, move around through the trees, creep in behind the intruders, and take them by surprise.

He had hoped that the pounding in his head would subside a bit when he sat down and leaned back in the big comfortable chair. But it was getting much worse than anything he had experienced previously. He felt almost as if his skull were . . . soft as clay . . . and as if it were being hammered into a new shape by every fierce throb. He clenched his jaws tighter, determined to weather this new adversity.

Perhaps the headache was made worse by the concentration required to study the tree-shadowed road for advancing enemies. If it became unbearable, he would have to lie down, though he was loath to leave his post. He sensed danger approaching.

He kept the ax and the two knives on the floor beside the chair. Each time he glanced down at those sharp blades, he felt not only reassured but strangely exultant. When he put his fingertips to the handle of the ax, a dark and almost erotic thrill coursed through him.

Let them come, he thought. I'll show them Eric Leben is still a man to be reckoned with. Let them come.

Though he still had difficulty understanding who might be seeking him, he somehow knew that his fear was not unreasonable. Then names popped into his mind: Baresco, Seitz, Geffels, Knowls, Lewis. Yes, of course, his partners in Geneplan. They would know what he'd done. They would decide that he had to be found quickly and terminated in order to protect the secret of Wildcard. But they were not the only men he had to fear. There were others . . . shadowy figures he could not recall, men with more power than the partners in Geneplan.

For a moment he felt that he was about to break through a wall of mist into a clear place. He was on the verge of achieving a clarity of thought and a fullness of memory that he had not known since rising from the gurney in the morgue. He held his breath and leaned forward in his chair with tremulous anticipation. He almost had it, all of it: the identity of the other pursuers, the meaning of the mice, the meaning of the hideous image of the crucified woman that kept recurring to him . . .

Then the unremitting pain in his head knocked him back from the brink of enlightenment, into the mist again. Muddy currents invaded the clearing stream of his thoughts, and in a moment all was clouded as before. He let out a thin cry of frustration.

Outside, in the forest, movement caught his attention. Squinting his hot watery eyes, Eric slid forward to the chair's edge, leaned toward the large window, peered intently at the tree-covered slope and the shadow-dappled dirt lane. No one there. The movement was simply the work of a sudden breeze that had finally broken the summer stillness. Bushes stirred, and the evergreen boughs lifted slightly, drooped, lifted, drooped, as if the trees were fanning themselves.

He was about to ease farther back in the chair when a scintillant blast of pain, shooting across his forehead, virtually *threw* him back. For a moment he was in such horrendous agony that he could not move or cry out or breathe. When at last breath could be drawn, he screamed, though by then it was a scream of anger rather than pain, for the pain went as abruptly as it had come.

Afraid that the bright explosion of pain had signified a sudden turn for the worse, perhaps even a coming apart of his broken skull, Eric raised one shaky hand to his head. First he touched his damaged right ear, which had nearly been torn off yesterday morning but which was now firmly attached, lumpish and unusually gristly to the touch but no longer drooping and raw.

How could he heal so fast? The process was supposed to take a few weeks, not a few hours.

He slowly slipped his fingers upward and gingerly

explored the deep depression along the right side of his skull, where he had made contact with the garbage truck. The depression was still there. But not as deep as he remembered it. And the concavity was solid. It had been slightly mushy before. Like bruised and rotting fruit. But no longer. He felt no tenderness in the flesh, either. Emboldened, he pressed his fingers harder into the wound, massaged, probed from one end of the indentation to the other, and everywhere he encountered healthy flesh and a firm shell of bone. The cracked and splintered skull had already knit up in less than a day, and the holes had filled in with new bone, which was flat-out impossible, damn it, impossible, but that was what had happened. The wound was healed, and his brain tissue was once more protected by a casing of unbroken bone.

He sat stupefied, unable to comprehend. He remembered that his genes had been edited to enhance the healing process and to promote cell rejuvenation, but damned if he remembered that it was supposed to happen this fast. Grievous wounds closing in mere hours? Flesh, arteries, and veins reconstituted at an almost visible rate? Extensive bone re-formation completed in less than a day? Christ, not even the most malignant cancer cells in their most furious stages of unchecked reproduction could match that pace!

For a moment he was exhilarated, certain that his experiment had proved a far greater success than he had hoped. Then he realized that his thoughts were still confused, that his memory was still tattered, even though his brain tissue must have healed as thoroughly as his skull had done. Did that mean that his intellect and clarity of mind would never be fully restored, even if his tissues were repaired? That prospect frightened him, especially as he again saw his uncle Barry Hampstead, long dead, standing over in the corner, beside a crackling pillar of shadowfire.

Perhaps, though he had come back from the land of the dead, he would always remain, in part, a dead man, regardless of his miraculous new genetic structure.

No. He did not want to believe that, for it would mean

that all his labors, plans, and risks were for nothing.

In the corner, Uncle Barry grinned and said, "Come kiss me, Eric. Come show me that you love me."

Perhaps death was more than the cessation of physical and mental activity. Perhaps some other quality was lost . . . a quality of spirit that could not be reanimated as successfully as flesh and blood and brain activity.

Almost of its own volition, his questing hand moved tremblingly from the side of his head to his brow, where the recent explosion of pain had been centered. He felt something odd. Something *wrong*. His forehead was no longer a smooth plate of bone. It was lumpy, knotted. Strange excrescences had arisen in an apparently random pattern.

He heard a mewling sound of pure terror, and at first he did not realize that he had made the noise himself.

The bone over each eye was far thicker than it should have been.

And a smooth knot of bone, almost an inch high, had appeared at his right temple.

How? My God, how?

As he explored the upper portion of his face in the manner of a blind man seeking an impression of a stranger's appearance, crystals of icy dread formed in him.

A narrow gnarled ridge of bone had appeared down the center of his forehead, extending to the bridge of his nose.

He felt thick, pulsing arteries along his hairline, where there should have been no such vessels.

He could not stop mewling, and hot tears sprang to his eyes.

Even in his clouded mind, the terrifying truth of the situation was evident. Technically, his genetically modified body had been killed by his brutal encounter with the garbage truck, but life of a kind had been maintained on a cellular level, and his edited genes, functioning on a mere trickle of life force, had sent urgent signals through his cooling tissues to command the amazingly rapid production of all substances needed for regeneration and rejuvenation. And now that repairs had been made, his altered genes were not switching off the frantic growth. Something was wrong. The genetic switches were staying open. His body was frenetically adding bone and flesh and blood, and though the new tissues were probably perfectly healthy, the process had become something like a cancer, though the rate of growth far outstripped that of even the most virulent cancer cells.

His body was re-forming itself.

But into what?

His heart was hammering, and he had broken into a cold sweat.

He pushed up from the armchair. He had to get to a mirror. He had to see his face.

He did not want to see it, was repelled by the thought of what he would find, was scared of discovering a grotesquely alien reflection in the mirror, but at the same time he urgently had to know what he was becoming.

◊   ◊

In the sporting-goods store by the lake, Ben chose a Remington semi-automatic 12-gauge shotgun with a five-round magazine. Properly handled, it could be a devastating weapon—and he knew how to handle it. He picked up two boxes of shells for the shotgun, plus one box of ammunition for the Smith & Wesson .357 Combat Magnum that he had taken off Baresco, and another box for Rachael's .32-caliber pistol.

They looked as if they were preparing for war.

Although no permit or waiting period was required when purchasing a shotgun—as was the case with a handgun—Ben had to fill out a form, divulging his name, address, and Social Security number, then provide the clerk with proof of identity, preferably a California driver's license with a laminated photograph. While Ben stood at the yellow Formica counter with Rachael, completing the form, the clerk—"Call me Sam," he'd said, when he had shown them the shop's gun selection—excused himself and went to the north end of the room to assist a group of fishermen who had questions about several fly rods.

The second clerk was with another customer at the south end of the long room, carefully explaining the differences among types of sleeping bags.

Behind the counter, on a wall shelf, beside a large display of cellophane-wrapped packages of beef jerky, stood a radio tuned to a Los Angeles AM station. While Ben and Rachael had selected a shotgun and ammunition, only pop music and commercials had issued from the radio. But now the twelve-thirty news report was under way, and suddenly Ben heard his own name, and Rachael's, coming over the airwaves.

" . . . *Shadway and Rachael Leben on a federal warrant. Mrs. Leben is the wife of the wealthy entrepreneur Eric Leben, who was killed in a traffic accident yesterday. According to a Justice Department spokesman, Shadway and Mrs. Leben are wanted in connection with the theft of highly sensitive, top-secret research files from several Geneplan Corporation projects funded by the Department of Defense, as well as for suspicion of murder in the case of two Palm Springs police officers killed last night in a brutal machine-gun attack.*"

Rachael heard it too. "That's crazy!"

Putting one hand on her arm to quiet her, Ben glanced nervously at the two clerks, who were still busy elsewhere in the store, talking to other customers. The last thing Ben wanted was to draw their attention to the news report. The clerk named Sam had already seen Ben's driver's license before pulling a firearms information form from the file. He knew Ben's name, and if he heard it on the radio, he was almost certain to react to it.

Protestations of innocence would be of no use. Sam would call the cops. He might even have a gun behind the counter, under the cash register, and might try to use it to keep Ben and Rachael there until the police arrived, and Ben did not want to have to take a gun away from him and maybe hurt him in the process.

"*Jarrod McClain, director of the Defense Security Agency, who is coordinating the investigation and the manhunt for Shadway and Mrs. Leben, issued a statement to the press in Washington within the past hour, calling the case 'a matter of grave concern that can reasonably be described as a national security crisis.' "*

Sam, over in the fishing-gear department, laughed at something a customer said—and started back toward the cash register. One of the fishermen was coming with him. They were talking animatedly, so if the news report was registering with them, it was getting through, at best, on only a subconscious level. But if they stopped talking before the report concluded . . .

"Though asserting that Shadway and Mrs. Leben have seriously damaged their country's security, neither McClain nor the Justice Department spokesman would specify the nature of the research being done by Geneplan for the Pentagon."

The two approaching men were twenty feet away, still discussing the merits of various brands of fly rods and spinning reels.

Rachael was staring at them apprehensively, and Ben bumped lightly against her to distract her, lest her expression alert them to the significance of the news on the radio.

" . . . recombinant DNA as Geneplan's sole business . . ."

Sam rounded the end of the sales counter. The customer's course paralleled that of the clerk, and they continued talking across the yellow Formica as they approached Rachael and Ben.

"Photographs and descriptions of Benjamin Shadway and Rachael Leben have gone out to all police agencies in California and most of the Southwest, along with a federal advisory that the fugitives are armed and dangerous."

Sam and the fisherman reached the cash register, where Ben turned his attention back to the government form.

The newscaster had moved on to another story.

Ben was startled and delighted to hear Rachael launch smoothly into a line of bubbly patter, engaging the fisherman's attention. The guy was tall, burly, in his fifties, wearing a black T-shirt that exposed his beefy arms, both of which featured elaborate blue-and-red tattoos. Rachael professed to be simply fascinated by tattoos, and the angler, like most men, was flattered and pleased by the gushy attention of a beautiful young woman. Anyone listening to Rachael's charming and slightly witless chatter—for she assumed the attitude of a California beach girl airhead—would never have suspected that she had just listened to a radio reporter describe her as a fugitive wanted for murder.

The same slightly pompous-sounding reporter was currently talking about a terrorist bombing in the Mideast, and Sam, the clerk, clicked a knob on the radio, cutting him off in midsentence. "I'm plain sick of hearing about those damn A-rabs," he said to Ben.

"Who isn't?" Ben said, completing the last line of the form.

"Far as I'm concerned," Sam said, "if they give us any more grief, we should just nuke 'em and be done with it."

"Nuke 'em," Ben agreed. "Back to the Stone Age."

The radio was part of the tape deck, and Sam switched that on, popped in a cassette. "Have to be farther back than the Stone Age. They're *already* living in the damn Stone Age."

"Nuke 'em back to the Age of Dinosaurs," Ben said as a song by the Oak Ridge Boys issued from the cassette player.

Rachael was making astonished and squeamish sounds as the fisherman told her how the tattoo needles embedded the ink way down beneath all three layers of skin.

"Age of the Dinosaurs," Sam agreed. "Let 'em try their terrorist crap on a tyrannosaurus, huh?"

Ben laughed and handed over the completed form.

The purchases had already been charged to Ben's Visa card, so all Sam had to do was staple the charge slip and the cash-register tape to one copy of the firearms information form and put the paperwork in the bag that held the four boxes of ammunition. "Come see us again."

"I'll sure do that," Ben said.

Rachael said good-bye to the tattooed fisherman, and Ben said hello *and* good-bye to him, and they both said good-bye to Sam. Ben carried the box containing the shotgun, and Rachael carried the plastic sack that contained the boxes of ammunition, and they moved nonchalantly across the room toward the front door, past stacks of aluminum bait buckets with perforated Styrofoam liners, past furled minnow-seining nets and small landing nets that looked like tennis rackets with badly stretched strings, past ice chests and thermos bottles and colorful fishing hats.

Behind them, in a voice that he believed to be softer than it actually was, the tattooed fisherman said to Sam: "Quite a woman."

You don't know the half of it, Ben thought as he pushed open the door for Rachael and followed her outside.

Less than ten feet away, a San Bernardino County sheriff's deputy was getting out of a patrol car.

◗   ◗

Fluorescent light bounced off the green and white ceramic tile, bright enough to reveal every hideous detail, too bright.

The bathroom mirror, framed in brass, was unmarred by spots or yellow streaks of age, and the reflections it presented were crisp and sharp and clear in every detail, too clear.

Eric Leben was not surprised by what he saw, for while sitting in the living-room armchair, he had already hesitantly used his hands to explore the startling changes in the upper portions of his face. But visual confirmation of what his disbelieving hands had told him was shocking, frightening, depressing—and more fascinating than anything else he'd seen in his entire life.

A year ago, he had subjected himself to the imperfect Wildcard program of genetic editing and augmentation. Since then, he had caught no colds, no flu, had been plagued by no mouth ulcers or headaches, not even acid indigestion. Week by week, he had gathered evidence supporting the contention that the treatment had wrought a desirable change in him without negative side effects.

Side effects.

He almost laughed. Almost.

Staring in horror at the mirror, as if it were a window onto hell, he raised one trembling hand to his forehead and touched, again, the narrow rippled ridge of bone that had risen from the bridge of his nose to his hairline.

The catastrophic injuries he had suffered yesterday had triggered his new healing abilities in a way and to a degree that invasive cold and flu viruses had not. Thrown into overdrive, his cells had begun to produce interferon, a wide spectrum of infection-fighting antibodies, and especially growth hormones and proteins, at an astonishing rate. For some reason, those substances were continuing to flood his system after the healing was complete, after the need for them was past. His body was no longer merely replacing damaged tissue but was adding new tissue at an alarming rate, tissue without apparent function.

"No," he said softly, "no," trying to deny what he saw before him. But it was true, and he felt its truth under his fingertips as he explored farther along the top of his head. The strange bony ridge was most prominent on his forehead, but it was on top of his head, as well, beneath his hair, and he even thought he could feel it growing as he traced its course toward the back of his skull.

His body was transforming itself either at random or to some purpose that he could not grasp, and there was no way of knowing when it would finally stop. It might never stop. He might go on growing, changing, reconstituting himself in myriad new images, endlessly. He was metamorphosing into a freak . . . or just possibly, ultimately, into something so utterly alien that it could no longer be called human.

The bony ridge tapered away at the back of his skull. He moved his hand forward again to the thickened shelf of bone above his eyes. It made him look vaguely like a Neanderthal, though Neanderthal man had not had a bony crest up the center of his head. Or a knob of bone at one temple. Nor had Neanderthals—or any other ancestors of humanity—ever featured the huge, swollen blood vessels where they shone darkly and pulsed disgustingly in his brow.

Even in his current degenerative mental condition, with every thought fuzzy at the edges and with his memory clouded, Eric grasped the full and horrible meaning of this development. He would never be able to reenter society in any acceptable capacity. Beyond a doubt, he was his own Frankenstein monster, and he had made—was continuously making—a hopeless and eternal outcast of himself.

His future was so bleak as to give new meaning to the word. He might be captured and survive in a laboratory somewhere, subjected to the stares and probes of countless fascinated scientists, who would surely devise endless tests that would seem like valid and justifiable experiments to them but would be pure and simple torture to him. Or he might flee into the wilderness and somehow make a pathetic life there, giving birth to legends of a new monster, until someday a hunter stumbled across him by accident and brought him down. But no matter which of many terrible fates awaited him, there would be two grim constants: unrelenting fear, not so much fear of what others would do to him, but fear of what his own body was doing to him; and loneliness, a profound and singular loneliness that no other man had ever known or ever would know, for he would be the only one of his kind on the face of the earth.

Yet his despair and terror were at least slightly ameliorated by curiosity, the same powerful curiosity that had made him a great scientist. Studying his hideous reflection, staring at this genetic catastrophe in the making, he was riveted, aware that he was seeing things no man had ever seen. Better yet: things that man had not been *meant* to see. That was an exhilarating feeling. It was what a man like him lived for. Every scientist, to some degree, seeks a glimpse of the great dark mysteries underlying life and hopes to understand what he sees if he is ever given that glimpse. This was more than a glimpse. This was a long, slow look into the enigma of human growth and development, as long a look as he cared to make it, its duration determined only by the extent of his courage.

The thought of suicide flickered only briefly through his mind and then was gone, for the opportunity presented to him was even more important than the certain physical, mental, and emotional anguish that he would endure henceforth. His future would be a strange landscape, shadowed by fear, lit by the lightning of pain, yet he was compelled to journey through it toward an unseen horizon. *He had to find out what he would become.*

Besides, his fear of death had by no means diminished due to these incredible developments. If anything, because he now seemed nearer the grave than at any time in his life, his necrophobia had an even tighter grip on him. No matter what form and quality of life lay ahead of him, he must go on; though his metamorphosis was deeply depressing and bloodcurdling, the alternative to life held even greater terror for him.

As he stared into the mirror, his headache returned.

He thought he saw something new in his eyes.

He leaned closer to the mirror.

Something about his eyes was definitely odd, different, but he could not quite identify the change.

The headache became rapidly more severe. The fluorescent lights bothered him, so he squinted to close out some of the white glare.

He looked away from his own eyes and let his gaze travel over the rest of his reflection. Suddenly he thought he perceived changes occurring along his right temple as well as in the zygomatic bone and zygomatic arch around and under his right eye.

Fear surged through him, purer than any fear he had known thus far, and his heart raced.

His headache now blazed throughout his skull and even down into a substantial portion of his face.

Abruptly he turned away from the mirror. It was difficult though possible to look upon the monstrous changes after they had occurred. But watching the flesh and bone transform itself before his eyes was a far more demanding task, and he possessed neither the fortitude nor the stomach for it.

Crazily he thought of Lon Chaney, Jr., in that old movie, *The Wolfman,* Chaney so appalled by the sight of his lupine metamorphosis that he was overcome by terror of—and pity for—himself. Eric looked at his own large hands, half expecting to see hair sprouting on them. That expectation made him laugh, though as before, his laugh was a harsh and cold and broken sound, utterly humorless, and it quickly turned into a series of wrenching sobs.

His entire head and face were filled with pain now— even his lips stung—and as he lurched out of the bathroom, bumping first into the sink, then colliding with the doorjamb, he made a thin high-pitched keening sound that was, in one note, a symphony of fear and suffering.

◗   ◗

The San Bernardino County sheriff's deputy wore dark sunglasses that concealed his eyes and, therefore, his intentions. However, as the policeman got out of the patrol car, Ben saw no telltale tension in his body, no indications that he recognized them as the infamous betrayers of Truth, Justice, and the American Way, of whom the radio newsman had recently spoken.

Ben took Rachael's arm, and they kept moving.

Within the past few hours, their descriptions and photographs had been wired to all police agencies in California and the Southwest, but that did not mean they were every lawman's first priority.

The deputy seemed to be staring at them.

But not all cops were sufficiently conscientious to study the latest bulletins before hitting the road, and those who had gone on duty early this morning, as this man might have done, would have left before Ben's and Rachael's photographs had been posted.

"Excuse me," the deputy said.

Ben stopped. Through the hand he had on Rachael's arm, he felt her stiffen. He tried to stay loose, smile. "Yes, sir?"

"That your Chevy pickup?"

Ben blinked. "Uh . . . no. Not mine."

"Got a taillight busted out," the deputy said, taking off his sunglasses, revealing eyes free of suspicion.

"We're driving that Ford," Ben said.

"You know who owns the truck?"

"Nope. Probably one of the other customers in there."

"Well, you folks have a nice day, enjoy our beautiful mountains," the deputy said, moving past them and into the sporting-goods store.

Ben tried not to run straight to the car, and he sensed that Rachael was resisting a similar urge. Their measured stroll was almost too nonchalant.

The eerie stillness, so complete when they had arrived, was gone, and the day was full of movement. Out on the water, an outboard motor buzzed like a swarm of hornets. A breeze had sprung up, coming in off the blue lake, rustling the trees, stirring the grass and weeds and wildflowers. A few cars passed on the state route, rock and roll blaring through the open windows of one of them.

They reached the rental Ford in the cool shadows of the pines.

Rachael pulled her door shut, winced at the loud *chunk* it made, as if the sound would draw the deputy back. Her green eyes were wide with apprehension. "Let's get out of here."

"You got it," he said, starting the engine.

"We can find another place, more private, where you can unpack the shotgun and load it."

They pulled out onto the two-lane blacktop that encircled the lake, heading north. Ben kept checking the rearview mirror. No one was following them; his fear that their pursuers were right on their tail was irrational, paranoid. He kept checking the mirror anyway.

The lake lay on their left and below them, glimmering, and the mountains rose on their right. In some areas, houses stood on large plots of forested land: Some were magnificent, almost country-style mansions, and others were neatly kept but humble summer cottages.

In other places, the land was either government-owned or too steep to provide building sites, and the wilderness encroached in a weedy and brambled tangle of trees. A lot of dry brush had built up, too, and signs warned of the fire danger, an annual summer-autumn threat throughout southern California. The road snaked and rolled, climbed and fell, through alternating patches of shade and golden sunlight.

After a couple of minutes, Rachael said, "They can't really believe we stole defense secrets."

"No," Ben agreed.

"I mean, I didn't even know Geneplan *had* defense contracts."

"That's not what they're worried about. It's a cover story."

"Then why *are* they so eager to get their hands on us?"

"Because we know that Eric has . . . come back."

"And you think the government knows, too?" she asked.

"You said the Wildcard project was a closely held secret. The only people who knew were Eric, his partners in Geneplan, and you."

"That's right."

"But if Geneplan had its hand in the Pentagon's pocket on other projects, then you can bet the Pentagon knew everything worth knowing about the owners of Geneplan and what they were up to. You can't accept lucrative top-secret research work and at the same time hold on to your privacy."

"That makes sense," she said. "But Eric might not have realized it. Eric believed he could have the best of everyone, all the time."

A road sign warned of a dip in the pavement. Ben braked, and the Ford jolted over a rough patch, springs squeaking, frame rattling.

When they came through to smoother blacktop, he said, "So the Pentagon knew enough about Wildcard to realize what Eric had done to himself when his body disappeared from the morgue. And now they want to contain the story, keep the secret, because they see it as a weapon or, at least, as a source of tremendous power."

"Power?"

"If perfected, the Wildcard process might mean immortality to those who undergo treatment. So the people who control Wildcard will decide who lives forever and who doesn't. Can you imagine any better weapon, any better tool with which to establish political control of the whole damn world?"

Rachael was silent awhile. Then she said softly, "Jesus, I've been so focused on the personal aspects of this, so intent on what it means to *me*, that I haven't looked at it from a broader perspective."

"So they have to get hold of us," Ben said.

"They don't want us blowing the secret till Wildcard's perfected. If it were blown first, they couldn't continue research unhampered."

"Exactly. Since you're going to inherit the largest block of stock in Geneplan, the government might figure you can be persuaded to cooperate for the good of your country and for your own gain."

She shook her head. "I couldn't be persuaded. Not about this. For one thing, if there's any hope at all of dramatically extending the human life span and promoting healing through genetic engineering, then the research should be done publicly, and the benefits should be available to everyone. It's immoral to handle it any other way."

"I figured that's how you'd feel," he said, pulling the Ford through a sharp right-hand turn, then sharply to the left again.

"Besides, I couldn't be persuaded to continue research along the same avenue the Wildcard group has been following, because I'm sure it's the wrong route."

"I knew you'd say that," Ben said approvingly.

"Admittedly, I know very little about genetics, but I can see there's just too much danger involved in the approach they're taking. Remember the mice I told you about. And remember . . . the blood in the trunk of the car at the house in Villa Park."

He remembered, which was one reason he had wanted the shotgun.

She said, "If I took control of Geneplan, I might want to fund continued longevity research, but I'd insist on scrapping Wildcard and starting fresh from a new direction."

"I knew you'd say that, too," Ben told her, "and I figure the government also has a pretty good idea what you'd say. So I don't have much hope that they just want a chance to persuade you. If they know anything about you—and as Eric's wife, you've got to be in their files—then they know you couldn't be bribed or threatened into doing something you thought was really wrong, couldn't be corrupted. So they probably won't even bother trying."

"It's my Catholic upbringing," she said with a touch of irony. "A very stern, strict, religious family, you know."

He didn't know. This was the first she had ever spoken of it.

Softly she said, "And very early, I was sent to a boarding school for girls, administrated by nuns. I grew to hate it . . . the endless Masses . . . the humiliation of the confessional, revealing my pathetic little sins. But I guess it shaped me for the better, huh? Might not be so all-fired incorruptible if I hadn't spent all those years in the hands of the good sisters."

He sensed that these revelations were but a twig on an immense and perhaps ugly tree of grim experience.

He glanced away from the road for a second, wanting to see her expression. But he was foiled by the constantly, rapidly changing mosaic of tree shadows and sunlight that came through the windshield and dappled her countenance. There was an illusion of fire, and her face was only half revealed to him, half hidden beyond the shifting and shimmering curtain of those phantom flames.

Sighing, she said, "Okay, so if the government knows it can't persuade me, why's it issuing warrants on a bunch of trumped-up charges and putting so much manpower into the search for me?"

"They want to kill you," Ben said bluntly.

"*What?*"

"They'd rather get you out of the picture and deal with Eric's partners, Knowls and Seitz and the others, because they already know those men are corruptible."

She was shocked, and he was not surprised by her shock. She was not unworldly or terribly naive. But she was, by choice, a present-focused person who had given little thought to the complexities of the changing world around her, except when that world impinged upon her primary desire to wring as much pleasure as possible from the moment. She accepted a variety of myths as a matter of convenience, as a way of simplifying her life, and one myth was that her government would always have her best interests at heart, whether the issue was war, a reform of the justice system, increased taxation, or anything else. She was apolitical and saw no reason to be concerned about who might win—or usurp—the power flowing from the ballot box, for it was easy to believe in the benign intentions of those who so ardently desired to serve the public.

She gaped in astonishment at him. He did not even have to see that expression through the flickering light and shadow to know it held tenancy of her face, for he sensed it in the change in her breathing and in the greater tension that suddenly gripped her and caused her to sit up straighter.

"Kill me? No, no, Benny. The U.S. government just executing civilians as if this were some banana republic? No, surely not."

"Not necessarily the whole government, Rachael. The House, Senate, president, and cabinet secretaries haven't held meetings to discuss the obstacle you pose, haven't conspired by the hundreds to terminate you. But someone in the Pentagon or the DSA or the CIA has determined that you're standing in the way of the national interest, that you pose a threat to the welfare of millions of citizens. When they weigh the welfare of millions against one or two little murders, the choice is clear to them, as it always is to collectivist thinkers. One or two little murders—tens of *thousands* of murders—are always justifiable when the welfare of the masses is at stake. At least, that's how they see it, even if they do pretend to believe in the sanctity of the individual. So they can order one or two little murders and even feel righteous about it."

"Dear God," she said with feeling. "What have I dragged you into, Benny?"

"You didn't drag me into anything," he said. "I forced my way in. You couldn't keep me out of it. And I've no regrets."

She seemed unable to speak.

Ahead, on the left, a branch road led down to the lake. A sign announced: LAKE APPROACH—BOAT LAUNCHING FACILITIES.

Ben turned off the state route and followed the narrower gravel road down through a crowd of immense trees. In a quarter of a mile, he drove out of the trees, into a sixty-foot-wide, three-hundred-foot-long open area by the shore. Sequins of sunlight decorated the lake in some places, and serpentine streams of sunlight wriggled across the shifting surface in other places, and here and there brilliant shafts bounced off the waves and dazzled the eye.

More than a dozen cars, pickups, and campers were parked at the far end of the clearing, several with empty boat trailers behind them. A big recreational pickup— black with red and gray stripes, bedecked with gobs of sun-heated chrome—was backed up near the water's edge, and three men were launching a twenty-four-foot twin-engine Water King from their trailer. Several people were eating lunch at picnic tables near the shore, and an Irish setter was sniffing under a table in search of scraps, and two young boys were tossing a football back and forth, and eight or ten fishermen were tending their poles along the bank.

They all looked as if they were enjoying themselves. If any of them realized the world beyond this pleasant haven was turning dark and going mad, he was keeping it to himself.

Benny drove to the parking area but tucked the Ford in

by the edge of the forest, as far from the other vehicles as he could get. He switched off the engine and rolled down his window. He put his seat back as far as it would go in order to give himself room to work, took the shotgun box on his lap, opened it, withdrew the gun, and threw the empty box into the back seat.

"Keep a watch out," he told Rachael. "You see anybody coming, let me know. I'll get out and meet him. Don't want anybody to see the shotgun and be spooked. It's sure as hell not hunting season."

"Benny, what're we going to do?"

"Just what we planned to do," he said, using one of the car keys to slit the shrink-wrapped plastic in which the shotgun was encased. "Follow the directions Sarah Kiel gave you, find Eric's cabin, and see if he's there."

"But the warrants for our arrest . . . people wanting to kill us . . . doesn't that change everything?"

"Not much." He discarded the shredded plastic and looked the gun over. It came fully assembled, a nice piece of work, and it felt good and reliable in his hands. "Originally we wanted to get to Eric and finish him before he healed entirely and came looking to finish *you*. Now maybe what we'll have to do is capture him instead of kill him—"

"Take him alive?" Rachael said, alarmed by that suggestion.

"Well, he's not exactly alive, is he? But I think we're going to have to take him in whatever condition he's in, tie him up, drive him someplace like . . . well, someplace like the offices of the *Los Angeles Times*. Then we can hold a real shocker of a press conference."

"Oh, Benny, no, no, we can't." She shook her head adamantly. "That's crazy. He's going to be violent, extremely violent. I told you about the mice. You saw the blood in the trunk of the car, for God's sake. The destruction everywhere he's been, the knives in the wall of the Palm Springs house, the beating he gave Sarah. We can't risk getting close to him. He won't respect the gun, if that's what you're thinking. He won't have any fear of it at all. You get close enough to try to capture him, and he'll take your head off in spite of the gun. He might even have a gun of his own. No, no, if we see him, we've got to finish him right away, shoot him without any hesitation, shoot him again and again, do so much damage to him that he won't be able to *come back* again."

A panicky note had entered her voice, and she had spoken faster and faster as she strove to convince Ben. Her skin was powder-white, and her lips had acquired a bluish tint. She was shivering.

Even considering their precarious situation and the admittedly hideous nature of their quarry, her fear seemed too great to Ben, and he wondered how much her reaction to Eric's resurrection was heightened by the ultrareligious childhood that had formed her. Without fully understanding her own feelings, perhaps she was afraid of Eric not merely because she knew his potential for violence, and not merely because he was a walking dead man, but because he had dared to seize the power of God by defeating death and thereby had become not simply a zombie but some hellborn creature returned from the realm of the damned.

Forgetting the shotgun for a moment, taking both her hands in his, he said, "Rachael, honey, I can handle him; I've handled worse than him, much worse—"

"Don't be so confident! That's what'll get you killed."

"I'm trained for war, well trained to take care of myself—"

"Please!"

"And I've kept in top shape all these years because Nam taught me that the world can turn dark and mean overnight and that you can't count on anything but yourself and your closest friends. That was a nasty lesson about the modern world that I didn't want to admit I'd learned, which is why I've spent so much time immersed in the past. But the very fact that I've kept in shape and kept practicing my fighting skills is proof of the lesson. Tip-top shape, Rachael. And I'm well armed." He hushed her when she tried to object. "We have no choice, Rachael. That's what it comes down to. No other choice. If we just kill him, blast the sucker with twenty or thirty rounds from the shotgun, kill him so bad he stays dead for good this time—then we have no proof of what he did to himself. We just have a corpse. Who could prove he'd been reanimated? It'd look as if we stole his body from the morgue, pumped it full of buckshot, and concocted this crazy story, maybe concocted it to cover the very crimes the government is accusing us of."

"Lab tests of his cell structure would prove something," Rachael said. "Examination of his genetic material—"

"That would take weeks. Before then, the government would've found a way to claim the body, eliminate us, and doctor the test results to show nothing out of the ordinary."

She started to speak, hesitated, and stopped because she was obviously beginning to realize that he was right. She looked more forlorn than any woman he had ever seen.

He said, "Our only hope of getting the government off our backs is to get proof of Wildcard and break the story to the press. The only reason they want to kill us is to keep the secret, so when the secret is blown, we'll be safe. Since we didn't get the Wildcard file from Eric's office safe, Eric himself is the only proof we have a chance of putting our hands on. And we need him alive. They need to see him breathing, functioning, in spite of his staved-in head. They need to *see* the change in him that you suspect there'll be—the irrational rages, the sullen quality of the living dead."

She swallowed hard. She nodded. "All right. Okay. But I'm so scared."

"You can be strong; you have it in you."

"I know I do. I know. But . . ."

He leaned forward and gave her a kiss.

Her lips were icy.

◑   ◑

Eric groaned and opened his eyes.

Evidently he had descended once more into a short period of suspended animation, a minor but deep coma, for he slowly regained consciousness on the floor of the living room, sprawled among at least a hundred sheets of typing paper. His splitting headache was gone, although a peculiar burning sensation extended from the top of his skull downward to his chin, all across his face, and in most of his muscles and joints as well, in shoulders and arms and legs. It was not an unpleasant burning, and not pleasant either, just a neutral sensation unlike anything he had felt before.

I'm like a candy man, made of chocolate, sitting on a sun-washed table, melting, melting, but melting from the *inside*.

For a while he just lay there, wondering where the weird thought had come from. He was disoriented, dizzy. His mind was a swamp in which unconnected thoughts burst like stinking bubbles on the watery surface. Gradually the water cleared a bit and the soupy mud of the swamp grew somewhat firmer.

Pushing up to a sitting position, he looked at the papers strewn around him and could not remember what they were. He picked up a few and tried to read them. The blurry letters would not at first resolve into words; then the words would not form coherent sentences. When at last he could read a bit, he could understand only a fraction of what he read, but he could grasp enough to realize that this was the third paper copy of the Wildcard file.

In addition to the project data stored in the Geneplan computers, there had been one hard-copy file in Riverside, one in his office safe at the headquarters in Newport Beach, and a third here. The cabin was his secret retreat, known only to him, and it had seemed prudent to keep a fully updated file in the hidden basement safe, as insurance against the day when Seitz and Knowls— the money men behind his work—tried to take the corporation away from him through clever financial maneuvering. That anticipated treachery was unlikely because they needed him, needed his genius, and would most likely still need him when Wildcard was perfected. But he was not a man who took chances. (Other than the one big chance, when he had injected himself with the devil's brew that was turning his body into pliable clay.) He had not wanted to risk being booted out of Geneplan and finding himself cut off from data crucial to the production of the immortality serum.

Evidently, after stumbling out of the bathroom, he had gone down to the basement, had opened the safe, and had brought the file up here for perusal. What had he been seeking? An explanation for what was happening to him? A way to undo the changes that had occurred—that were *still* occurring—in him?

That was pointless. These monstrous developments had been unanticipated. Nothing in the file would refer to the possibility of runaway growth or point the way to salvation. He must have been seized by delirium, for only in such a state would he have bothered to pursue a magic cure in this pile of Xeroxes.

He knelt in the scattered papers for a minute or two, preoccupied by the strange though painless burning sensation that filled his body, trying to understand its source and meaning. In some places—along his spine, across the top of his head, at the base of his throat, in his testicles—the heat was accompanied by an eerie tingle. He almost felt as if a billion fire ants had made their home within him and were moving by the millions through his veins and arteries and through a maze of tunnels they had burrowed in his flesh and bone.

Finally he got to his feet, and a fierce anger rose in him for no specific reason, and with no particular target. He kicked out furiously, stirring up a briefly airborne, noisy cloud of papers.

A frightening rage seethed under the surface of the mindswamp, and he was just perceptive enough to realize that it was in some way quite different from the previous rages to which he had succumbed. This one was . . . even more primal, less focused, less of a *human* rage, more like the irrationally churning fury of an animal. He felt as if some deeply buried racial memory were asserting itself, something crawling up out of the genetic pit, up from ten million years ago, up from the faraway time when men were only apes, or from a time even farther removed than that, from an unthinkably ancient age when men were as yet only amphibian creatures crawling painfully onto a volcanic shore and breathing air for the first time. It was a cold rage instead of hot like the ones before it, as cold as the heart of the Arctic, a billion years of coldness . . . reptilian. Yes, that was the feel of it, an icy reptilian rage, and when he began to grasp its nature, he recoiled from further consideration of it and desperately hoped that he would be able to keep it under control.

The mirror.

He was certain that changes had taken place in him while he had been unconscious on the living-room floor, and he knew he should go into the bathroom and look at himself in the mirror. But suddenly he was shaken anew by fear of what he was becoming, and he could not find the courage to take even one step in that direction.

Instead, he decided to employ the Braille approach by which he had previously discovered the first alterations in his face. Feeling the differences before seeing them would prepare him somewhat for the shock of his appearance. Hesitantly he raised his hands to explore his face but did not get that far because he saw that his *hands* were changing, and he was arrested by the sight of them.

They were not radically different hands from what they had been, but they were unquestionably not his hands anymore, not the hands he had used all his life. The fingers were longer and thinner, perhaps a whole inch longer, with fleshier pads at the tips. The nails were different, too: thicker, harder, yellowish, more pointed than ordinary fingernails. They were nascent claws, damned if they weren't, and if the metamorphosis continued, they would probably develop into even more pointed, hooked, and razor-sharp talons. His knuckles were changing, too— larger, bonier, almost like arthritic knuckles.

He expected to find his hands stiff and less usable than they had been, but to his surprise the altered knuckles worked easily, fluidly, and proved superior to the knuckles out of which they had grown. He worked his hands experimentally and discovered that he was incredibly dexterous; his elongated fingers possessed a new suppleness and startling flexibility.

And he sensed that the changes were continuing unchecked, though not fast enough for him to actually see the bones growing and the flesh remaking itself. But by tomorrow his hands would surely be far more radically changed than they were now.

This was electrifyingly different from the apparent random, tumorlike excrescences of bone and tissue that had formed across his forehead. These hands were not just the result of an excess of growth hormones and proteins. This growth had purpose, direction. In fact, he suddenly noticed that on both hands, between thumb and forefinger, below the first knuckle of each digit, translucent webs had begun to fill in the empty space.

Reptilian. Like the cold rage that he knew would (if he let it) erupt in a frenzy of destruction. Reptilian.

He lowered his hands, afraid to look at them anymore.

He no longer had the courage to explore the contours of his face, not even by touch. The mere prospect of looking into a mirror filled him with dread.

His heart was hammering, and with each thunderous beat, it seemed to pound spikes of fear and loneliness into him.

For a moment he was utterly lost, confused, directionless. He turned left, then right, took a step in one direction, then in another, the Wildcard papers crunching like dead leaves under his feet. Not sure what to do or where to go, he stopped and stood with shoulders slumped, head hung low under a weight of despair—

—until suddenly the weird burning in his flesh and the eerie tingle along his spine were supplemented with a new sensation: hunger. His stomach growled, and his knees grew weak, and he started to shake with hunger. He began to work his mouth and to swallow continuously, involuntarily, hard swallows that almost hurt, as if his body were *demanding* to be fed. He headed toward the kitchen, his shakes getting worse with every step, his knees growing weaker. The sweat of need poured from him in streams, in rivers. A hunger unlike anything he had ever known before. Rabid hunger. Painful. Tearing at him. His vision clouded, and his thoughts funneled down toward one subject: food. The macabre changes taking place in him would require a great deal more fuel than usual, energy for tearing down old tissues, building blocks with which to construct new tissues—yes, of course—his metabolism was running wild, like a great furnace out of control, a raging fire, it had broken down and assimilated the Farmer John sausage-and-biscuit sandwiches that he had eaten earlier, and it needed more, much more, so by the time he opened the cupboard doors and began pulling cans of soup and stew from the shelves, he was wheezing and gasping, muttering wordlessly, grunting like a savage or a wild beast, sickened and repelled by his loss of control but too hungry to worry about it, frightened but hungry, despairing but so hungry, hungry, hungry . . .

◊   ◊

Following the directions Sarah Kiel had given Rachael, Ben turned off the state route onto a narrow, poorly maintained macadam lane that climbed a steep slope. The lane led deeper into the forest, where the deciduous trees gave way entirely to evergreens, many of which were ancient and huge. They drove half a mile, passing widely separated driveways that served houses and summer cottages. A couple of structures were fully visible, though most could barely be seen between the trees or were entirely hidden by foliage and forest shadows.

The farther they went, the less the sun intruded upon the forest floor, and Rachael's mood darkened at the same rate as the landscape. She held the thirty-two pistol in her lap and peered anxiously ahead.

The pavement ended, but the road continued with a gravel surface for more than another quarter of a mile. They passed just two more driveways, plus two Dodge Chargers and a small motor home parked in a lay-by near one driveway, before coming to a closed gate. Made of steel pipe, painted sky blue, and padlocked, the gate was unattached to any fence and served only to limit vehicular access to the road beyond, which further declined in quality from gravel to dirt.

Wired securely to the center of the barrier, a black-and-red sign warned:

NO TRESPASSING
PRIVATE PROPERTY

"Just like Sarah told you," Ben said.

Beyond the gate lay Eric Leben's property, his secret retreat. The cabin was not visible, for it was another quarter of a mile up the mountainside, entirely screened by trees from this angle.

"It's still not too late to turn back," Rachael said.

"Yes, it is," Ben said.

She bit her lip and nodded grimly. She carefully switched off the double safeties on her pistol.

◊   ◊

Eric used the electric opener to take the lid off a large can of Progresso minestrone, realized he needed a pot in which to heat it, but was shaking too badly to wait any longer, so he just drank the cold soup out of the can, threw the can aside, wiping absentmindedly at the broth that dripped off his chin. He kept no fresh food in the cabin, only a few frozen things, mostly canned goods, so he opened a family-size Dinty Moore beef stew, and he ate that cold, too, all of it, so fast he kept choking on it.

He chewed the beef with something akin to manic glee, taking a strangely intense pleasure from the tearing and rending of the meat between his teeth. It was a pleasure unlike any he had experienced before—primal, savage—and it both delighted and frightened him.

Although the stew was fully cooked, requiring only reheating, and although it was laden with spices and preservatives, Eric could smell the traces of blood remaining in the beef. Though the blood content was minuscule and thoroughly cooked, Eric perceived it not merely as a vague scent but as a strong, nearly overpowering odor, a thrilling and thoroughly delicious organic *incense*, which caused him to shudder with excitement. He breathed deeply and was dizzied by the blood fragrance, and on his tongue it was ambrosian.

When he finished the cold beef stew, which took only a couple of minutes, he opened a can of chili and ate that even more quickly, then another can of soup, chicken noodle this time, and finally he began to take the sharp edge off his hunger. He unscrewed the lid from a jar of peanut butter, scooped some out with his fingers, and ate it. He did not like it as well as he liked the meat, but he knew it was good for him, rich in the nutrients that his racing metabolism required. He consumed more, cleaned out most of the jar, then threw it aside and stood for a moment, gasping for breath, exhausted from eating.

The queer, painless fire continued to burn in him, but the hunger had substantially abated.

Out of the corner of his eye, he saw his uncle Barry Hampstead sitting in a chair at the small kitchen table, grinning at him. This time, instead of ignoring the phantom, Eric turned toward it, took a couple of steps closer, and said, "What do you want here, you son of a bitch?" His voice was gravelly, not at all like it had once been. "What're you grinning at, you goddamn pervert? You get the hell out of here."

Uncle Barry actually began to fade away, although that was not surprising: He was only an illusion born of degenerated brain cells.

Unreal flames, feeding on shadows, danced in the darkness beyond the cellar door, which Eric had evidently left open when he had come back upstairs with the Wildcard file. He watched the shadowfires. As before, he felt some mystery beckoning, and he was afraid. However, emboldened by his success in chasing away Barry Hampstead's shade, he started toward the flickering red and silver flames, figuring either to dispel them or to see, at last, what lay within them.

Then he remembered the armchair in the living room, the window, the lookout he had been keeping. He had been distracted from that important task by a chain of events: the unusually brutal headache, the changes he had felt in his face, the macabre reflection in the mirror, the Wildcard file, his sudden crippling hunger, Uncle Barry's apparition, and now the false fires beyond the cellar door. He could not concentrate on one thing for any length of time, and he cried out in frustration at this latest evidence of mental dysfunction.

He moved back across the kitchen, kicking aside an empty Dinty Moore beef stew can and a couple of soup cans, heading for the living room and his abandoned guardpost.

◊   ◊

Reeeeee, reeeeee, reeeeee . . . The one-note songs of the cicadas, monotonous to the human ear but most likely rich in meaning to other insects, echoed shrilly yet hollowly through the high forest.

Standing beside the rental car, keeping a wary eye on the woods around them, Ben distributed four extra shotgun shells and eight extra rounds for the Combat Magnum in the pockets of his jeans.

Rachael emptied out her purse and filled it with three boxes of ammunition, one for each of their guns. That was surely an excessive supply—but Ben did not suggest that she take any less.

He carried the shotgun under one arm. Given the slightest provocation, he could swing it up and fire in a fraction of a second.

Rachael carried the thirty-two pistol and the Combat Magnum, one in each hand. She wanted Ben to carry both the Remington and the .357, but he could not handle both efficiently, and he preferred the shotgun.

They moved off into the brush just far enough to slip around the padlocked gate, returning to the dirt track on the other side.

Ahead, the road rose under a canopy of pine limbs, flanked by rock-lined drainage ditches bristling with dead dry weeds that had sprung up during the rainy season and withered during the arid spring and summer. About two hundred yards above them, the lane took a sharp turn to the right and disappeared. According to Sarah Kiel, the lane ran straight and true beyond the bend, directly to the cabin, which was approximately another two hundred yards from that point.

"Do you think it's safe to approach right out on the road like this?" Rachael whispered, even though they were still so far from the cabin that their normal speaking voices could not possibly have carried to Eric.

Ben found himself whispering, too. "It'll be okay at least until we reach the bend. As long as we can't see him, he can't see us."

She still looked worried.

He said, "*If* he's even up there."

"He's up there," she said.

"Maybe."

"He's up there," she insisted, pointing to vague tire tracks in the thin layer of dust that covered the hard-packed dirt road.

Ben nodded. He had seen the same thing.

"Waiting," Rachael said.

"Not necessarily."

"Waiting."

"He could be recuperating."

"No."

"Incapacitated."

"No. He's ready for us."

She was probably right about that as well. He sensed the same thing she did: oncoming trouble.

Curiously, though they stood in the shadows of the trees, the nearly invisible scar along her jawline, where Eric had once cut her with a broken glass, was visible, more visible than it usually was in ordinary light. In fact, to Ben, it seemed to glow softly, as if the scar responded to the nearness of the one who had inflicted it, much the way that a man's arthritic joints might alert him to an oncoming storm. Imagination, of course. The scar was no more prominent now than it had been an hour ago. The illusion of prominence was just an indication of how much he feared losing her.

In the car, on the drive up from the lake, he had tried his best to persuade her to remain behind and let

him handle Eric alone. She was opposed to that idea—
possibly because she feared losing Ben as much as he
feared losing her.

They started up the lane.

Ben looked nervously left and right as they went,
uncomfortably aware that the heavily forested mountainside, gloomy even at midday, provided countless hiding
places—ambush points—very close to them on both
sides.

The air was heavily laced with the odor of evergreen
sap, the crisp and appealing fragrance of dry pine needles,
and the musty scent of some rotting deadwood.

Reeeeee, reeeeee, reeeeee . . .

◊   ◊

He had returned to the armchair with a pair of
binoculars that he had remembered were in the bedroom
closet. Only minutes after settling down at the window,
before his dysfunctioning thought processes could take
off on yet another tangent, he saw movement two
hundred yards below, at the sharp bend in the road.
He played with the focus knob, pulling the scene in
clearer, and in spite of the depth of the shadows at that
point along the lane, he saw the two people in perfect
detail: Rachael and the bastard she had been sleeping
with, Shadway.

He had not known whom he expected—other than
Seitz, Knowls, and the men of Geneplan—but he had
certainly not expected Rachael and Shadway. He was
stunned and could not imagine how she had learned
of this place, though he knew that the answer would
be obvious to him if his mind had been functioning
normally.

They were crouched along the bank that flanked the
road down there, fairly well concealed. But they had to
reveal a little of themselves in order to get a good look
at the cabin, and what little they revealed was enough
for Eric to identify them in the magnified field of the
binoculars.

The sight of Rachael enraged him, for she had rejected
him, the only woman in his adult life to reject him—the

bitch, the ungrateful stinking *bitch!*—and she turned her back on his money, too. Even worse: in the miasmal swamp of his deranged mind, *she* was responsible for his death, had virtually killed him by angering him to distraction and then letting him rush out onto Main Street, into the path of the truck. He could believe she had actually planned his death in order to inherit the very fortune on which she'd claimed to have no designs. Yes, of course, why not? And now there she was with her lover, with the man she had been fucking behind his back, and she had clearly come to finish the job that the garbage truck had started.

They pulled back beyond the bend, but a few seconds later he saw movement in the brush, to the left of the road, and he caught a glimpse of them moving off into the trees. They were going to make a cautious indirect approach.

Eric dropped the binoculars and shoved up from the armchair, stood swaying, in the grip of a rage so great that he almost felt crushed by it. Steel bands tightened across his chest, and for a moment he could not draw his breath. Then the bands snapped, and he sucked in great lungsful of air. He said, "Oh, Rachael, Rachael," in a voice that sounded as if it were echoing up from hell. He liked the sound of it, so he said her name again: "Rachael, Rachael . . ."

From the floor beside the chair, he plucked up the ax.

He realized that he could not handle the ax and both knives, so he chose the butcher's knife and left the other blade behind.

He would go out the back way. Circle around. Slip up on them through the woods. He had the cunning to do it. He felt as if he had been born to stalk and kill.

Hurrying across the living room toward the kitchen, Eric saw an image of himself in his mind's eye: He was ramming the knife deep into her guts, then ripping it upward, tearing open her flat young belly. He made a shrill sound of eagerness and almost fell over the empty soup and stew cans in his haste to reach the back door. He would cut her, cut her, cut. And when she dropped to the ground with the knife in her belly, he would go at her with the ax, use the blunt edge of it first, smashing her bones to splinters, breaking her arms and legs, and then he would turn the wondrous shiny instrument over in his hands—his strange and powerful new hands!—and use the sharp edge.

By the time he reached the rear door and yanked it open and went out of the house, he was in the grip of that reptilian fury that he had feared only a short while ago, a cold and calculating fury, called forth out of genetic memories of inhuman ancestors. Having at last surrendered to that primeval rage, he was surprised to discover that it felt *good*.

◊ 22 ◊

WAITING
FOR THE STONE

Jerry Peake should have been asleep on his feet, for he had been up all night. But seeing Anson Sharp humiliated had revitalized him better than eight hours in the sheets could have. He felt marvelous.

He stood with Sharp in the corridor outside Sarah Kiel's hospital room, waiting for Felsen Kiel to come and tell them what they needed to know. Peake required considerable restraint to keep from laughing at his boss's vindictive grousing about the farmer from Kansas.

"If he wasn't a know-nothing shit-kicker, I'd come down so hard on him that his teeth would still be vibrating next Christmas," Sharp said. "But what's the point, huh? He's just a thick-headed Kansas plowboy who doesn't know any better. No point talking to a brick wall, Peake. No point getting angry with a brick wall."

"Right," Peake said.

Pacing back and forth in front of Sarah's closed door, glowering at the nurses who passed in the corridor, Sharp said, "You know, those farm families way out there on the plains, they get strange 'cause they breed too much among themselves, cousin to cousin, that sort of thing, which makes them more stupid generation by generation.

But not only stupid, Peake. That inbreeding makes them stubborn as mules."

"Mr. Kiel sure does seem stubborn," Peake said.

"Just a dim-witted shit-kicker, so what's the point of wasting energy breaking his butt? He wouldn't learn his lesson anyway."

Peake could not risk an answer. He required almost superhuman determination to keep a grin off his face.

Six or eight times during the next half hour, Sharp said, "Besides, it's faster to let *him* get the information out of the girl. She's a dim bulb herself, a drugged-up little whore who's probably had syphilis and clap so often her brain's like oatmeal. I figured it'd take us hours to get anything out of her. But when that shit-kicker came into the room, and I heard the girl say 'Daddy' in that happy-shaky little voice, I knew he'd get out of her what we needed a lot faster than we could get it. Let him do our job for us, I thought."

Jerry Peake marveled at the deputy director's boldness in trying to reshape Peake's perception of what had actually happened in Sarah's room. Then again, maybe Sharp was beginning to believe that he had not backed down and had cleverly manipulated The Stone, getting the best of him. He was fruitcake enough to buy his own lies.

Once, Sharp put a hand on Peake's shoulder, not in a comradely manner but to be sure of his subordinate's attention. "Listen, Peake, don't you get the wrong idea about the way I came on with that little whore. The foul language I used, the threats, the little bit of hurt I caused her when I squeezed her hand . . . the way I touched her . . . didn't mean a thing. Just a technique, you know. A good method for getting quick answers. If this wasn't a national security crisis, I'd never have tried that stuff. But sometimes, in special situations like this, we have to do things for our country that maybe neither we nor our country would ordinarily approve of. We understand each other?"

"Yes, sir. Of course." Surprised by his own ability to fake naïveté and admiration, and to do it convincingly,

Peake said, "I'm amazed you'd worry that I'd misunderstand. I'd never have thought of such an approach myself. But the moment you went to work on her . . . well, I knew what you were doing, and I admired your interrogation skills. I see this case as an opportunity, sir. I mean, the chance to work with you, which I figured would be a very valuable learning experience, which it has been—even more valuable than I'd hoped."

For a moment Sharp's marble-hard green eyes fixed on Peake with evident suspicion. Then the deputy director decided to take him at his word, for he relaxed a bit and said, "Good. I'm glad you feel that way, Peake. This is a nasty business sometimes. It can even make you feel dirty now and then, what you have to do, but it's for the country, and that's what we always have to keep in mind."

"Yes, sir. I always keep that in mind."

Sharp nodded and began to pace and grumble again.

But Peake knew that Sharp had enjoyed intimidating and hurting Sarah Kiel and had *immensely* enjoyed touching her. He knew that Sharp was a sadist and a pedophile, for he had seen those dark aspects of his boss surge clearly to the surface in that hospital room. No matter what lies Sharp told him, Jerry Peake was never going to forget what he had seen. Knowing these things about the deputy director gave Peake an enormous advantage—though, as yet, he had absolutely no idea how to benefit from what he had learned.

He had also learned that Sharp was, at heart, a coward. In spite of his bullying ways and impressive physical appearance, the deputy director would back down in a crunch, even against a smaller man like The Stone, as long as the smaller man stood up to him with conviction. Sharp had no compunctions about violence and would resort to it when he thought he was fully protected by his government position or when his adversary was sufficiently weak and unthreatening, but he would back off if he believed he faced the slightest chance of being hurt himself. Possessing that knowledge, Peake had another big advantage, but he did not yet see a way to use that one, either.

Nevertheless, he was confident he would eventually know how to apply the things he had learned. Making well-considered, fair, and effective use of such insights was precisely what a legend did best.

Unaware of having given Peake two good knives, Sharp paced back and forth with the impatience of a Caesar.

The Stone had demanded half an hour alone with his daughter. When thirty minutes had passed, Sharp began to look at his wristwatch more frequently.

After thirty-five minutes, he walked heavily to the door, put a hand against it, started to push inside, hesitated, and turned away. "Hell, give him another few minutes. Can't be easy getting anything coherent out of that spaced-out little whore."

Peake murmured agreement.

The looks that Sharp cast at the closed door became increasingly murderous. Finally, forty minutes after they had left the room at The Stone's insistence, Sharp tried to cover his fear of confrontation with the farmer by saying, "I have to make a few important calls. I'll be at the public phones in the lobby."

"Yes, sir."

Sharp started away, then looked back. "When the shit-kicker comes out of there, he's just going to have to wait for me no matter how long I take, and I don't give a damn how much that upsets him."

"Yes, sir."

"It'll do him good to cool his heels awhile," Sharp said, and he stalked off, head held high, rolling his big shoulders, looking like a very important man, evidently convinced that his dignity was intact.

Jerry Peake leaned against the wall of the corridor and watched the nurses go by, smiling at the pretty ones and engaging them in brief flirtatious conversation when they were not too busy.

Sharp stayed away for twenty minutes, giving The Stone a full hour with Sarah, but when he came back from making his important—probably nonexistent— phone calls, The Stone had still not appeared. Even a coward could explode if pushed too far, and Sharp was furious.

"That lousy dirt-humping hayseed. He can't come in here, reeking of pigshit, and screw up *my* investigation."

He turned away from Peake and started toward Sarah's room.

Before Sharp took two steps, The Stone came out.

Peake had wondered whether Felsen Kiel would look as imposing on second encounter as he had appeared when stepping dramatically into Sarah's room and interrupting Anson Sharp in an act of molestation. To Peake's great satisfaction, The Stone was even more imposing than on the previous occasion. That strong, seamed, weathered face. Those oversized hands, work-gnarled knuckles. An air of unshakable self-possession and serenity. Peake watched with a sort of awe as the man crossed the hallway, as if he were a slab of granite come to life.

"Gentlemen, I'm sorry to keep you waitin'. But, as I'm sure you understand, my daughter and I had a lot of catchin' up to do."

"And as *you* must understand, this is an urgent national security matter," Sharp said, though more quietly than he had spoken earlier.

Unperturbed, The Stone said, "My daughter says you want to know if maybe she has some idea where a fella named Leben is hidin' out."

"That's right," Sharp said tightly.

"She said somethin' about him bein' a livin' dead man, which I can't quite get clear with her, but maybe that was just the drugs talkin' through her. You think?"

"Just the drugs," Sharp said.

"Well, she knows of a certain place he might be," The Stone said. "The fella owns a cabin above Lake Arrowhead, she says. It's a sort of secret retreat for him." He took a folded paper from his shirt pocket. "I've written down these directions." He handed the paper to Peake. To Peake, not to Anson Sharp.

Peake glanced at The Stone's precise, clear hand-writing, then passed the paper to Sharp.

"You know," The Stone said, "my Sarah was a good girl up until three years ago, a fine daughter in every way. Then she fell under the spell of a sick person who got her onto drugs, put twisted thoughts in her head. She was only thirteen then, impressionable, vulnerable, easy pickin'."

"Mr. Kiel, we don't have time—"

The Stone pretended not to hear Sharp, even though he was looking directly at him. "My wife and I tried our best to find out who it was that had her spellbound, figured it had to be an older boy at school, but we could never identify him. Then one day, after a year durin' which hell moved right into our home, Sarah up and disappeared, ran off to California to 'live the good life.' That's what she wrote in the note to us, said she wanted to live the good life and that we were unsophisticated country people who didn't know anythin' about the world, said we were full of funny ideas. Like honesty, sobriety, and self-respect, I suppose. These days, lots of folks think those are funny ideas."

"Mr. Kiel—"

"Anyway," The Stone continued, "not long after that, I finally learned who it was corrupted her. A teacher. Can you credit that? A *teacher*, who's supposed to be a figure of respect. New young history teacher. I demanded the school board investigate him. Most of the other teachers rallied round him to fight any investigation 'cause these days a lot of 'em seem to think we exist just to keep our mouths shut and pay their salaries no matter what garbage they want to pump into our children's heads. Two-thirds of the teachers—"

"Mr. Kiel," Sharp said more forcefully, "none of this is of any interest to us, and we—"

"Oh, it'll be of interest when you hear the whole story," The Stone said. "I can assure you."

Peake knew The Stone was not the kind of man who rambled, knew all of this had some purpose, and he was eager to see where it was going to wind up.

"As I was sayin'," The Stone continued, "two-thirds of the teachers and half the town were agin me, like *I* was the troublemaker. But in the end they turned up worse stuff about that history teacher, worse than givin' and sellin' drugs to some of his students, and by the time it was over, they were glad to be shed of him. Then, the day after he was canned, he showed up at the farm, wantin' to go man to man. He was a good-sized fella, but he was on somethin' even then, what you call pot-marijuana or maybe even stronger poison, and it wasn't so hard to handle him. I'm sorry to say I broke both his arms, which is worse than I intended."

Jesus, Peake thought.

"But even that wasn't the end of it, 'cause it turned out he had an uncle was president of the biggest bank in our county, the very same bank has my farm loans. Now, any man who allows personal grudges to interfere with his business judgment is an idiot, but this banker fella was an idiot 'cause he tried to pull a fast one to teach me a lesson, tried to reinterpret one of the clauses in my biggest loan, hopin' to call it due and put me at risk of my land. The wife and I been fightin' back for a year, filed a lawsuit and everythin', and just last week the bank had to back down and settle our suit out of court for enough to pay off half my loans."

The Stone was finished, and Peake understood the point, but Sharp said impatiently, "So? I still don't see what it has to do with me."

"Oh, I think you do," The Stone said quietly, and the eyes he turned on Sharp were so intense that the deputy director winced.

Sharp looked down at the directions on the piece of paper, read them, cleared his throat, looked up. "This is all we want. I don't believe we'll need to talk further with either you or your daughter."

"I'm certainly relieved to hear that," The Stone said. "We'll be goin' back to Kansas tomorrow, and I wouldn't want to think this will be followin' us there."

Then The Stone smiled. At Peake, not at Sharp.

The deputy director turned sharply away and stalked down the hall. Peake returned The Stone's smile, then followed his boss.

♦ 23 ♦

THE DARK
OF THE WOODS

Reeeeee, reeeeee, reeeeee, reeeeee ... At first the steam-whistle cries of the cicadas pleased Rachael because they were reminiscent of grade-school field trips to public parks, holiday picnics, and the hiking she had done while in college. However, she quickly grew irritated by the piercing noise. Neither the brush nor the heavy pine boughs softened the racket. Every molecule of the cool dry air seemed to reverberate with that grating sound, and soon her teeth and bones were reverberating with it, too.

Her reaction was, in part, a result of Benny's sudden conviction that he had heard something in the nearby brush that was not part of the ordinary background noises of a forest. She silently cursed the insects and willed them to shut up so she could hear any unnatural sounds— such as twigs snapping and underbrush rustling from the passage of something more substantial than the wind.

The Combat Magnum was in her purse, and she was holding only the thirty-two pistol. She had discovered she needed one hand to push aside tall weeds and to grab convenient branches to pull herself over steeper or more treacherous stretches of ground. She considered getting the .357 out of the bag, but the sound of the zipper would pinpoint their location to anyone who might be seeking them.

Anyone. That was a cowardly evasion. Surely, only one person might be seeking them out here. Eric.

She and Benny had been moving directly south across the face of the mountainside, catching brief glimpses of the cabin on the slope a couple of hundred yards above, being careful to interpose trees and brush and rock formations between themselves and the large picture windows that made her think of enormous, square eye sockets. When they had been about thirty yards past the cabin, they had turned east, which was upslope, and the way proved sufficiently steep that they had progressed at only half the speed they had been making previously. Benny's intention had been to circle the cabin and come in behind it. Then, when they had ascended only about a hundred yards—which put them still a hundred yards below and thirty south of the structure—Benny heard something, stopped, eased up against the protective cover of a spruce trunk that had a five-foot diameter, cocked his head, and raised the shotgun.

Reeeeee, reeeeee, reeeeee . . .

In addition to the ceaseless cicada chorus—which had not fallen silent because of their presence and, therefore, would not fall silent to reveal anyone else's presence, either—there was the annoyance of a noisy wind. The breeze that had sprung up when they had come out of the sporting-goods store down by the lake, less than three-quarters of an hour ago, had evidently grown stronger. Not much of it reached as far as the sheltered forest floor, barely a soft breath. But the upper reaches of the massive trees stirred restlessly, and a hollow mournful moaning settled down from above as the wind wove through the interstices of the highest branches.

Rachael stayed close to Benny and pressed against the trunk of the spruce. The rough bark prickled even through her blouse.

She felt as if they remained frozen there, listening alertly and peering intently into the woods, for at least a quarter of an hour, though she knew it must have been less than a minute. Then, warily, Benny started uphill again, angling slightly to the right to follow a shallow dry wash that was mostly free of brush. She stayed close behind him. Sparse brown grass, crisp as paper, lightly stroked their legs. They had to take care to avoid stepping on some loose stones deposited by last spring's runoff of melting snow, but they made somewhat better progress than they had outside the wash.

The flanking walls of brush presented the only drawback to the easier new route. The growth was thick, some dry and brown, some dark green, and it pressed in at both sides of the shallow wash, with only a few widely separated gaps through which Benny and Rachael could look into the woods beyond. She half expected Eric to leap through the bushes and set upon them. She was encouraged only by the brambles tangled through a lot of the brush and by the wicked thorns she saw on some of the bushes themselves, which might give a would-be attacker second thoughts about striking from that direction.

On the other hand, having already returned from the dead, would Eric be concerned about such minor obstacles as thorns?

They went only ten or fifteen yards, before Benny froze again, half crouching to present a smaller target, and raised the shotgun.

This time, Rachael heard it, too: a clatter of dislodged pebbles.

Reeeeee, reeeeee . . .

A soft scrape as of shoe leather on stone.

She looked left and right, then up the slope, then down, but she saw no movement associated with the noise.

A whisper of something moving through brush more purposeful than mere wind.

Nothing more.

Ten seconds passed uneventfully.

Twenty.

As Benny scanned the bushes around them, he no longer retained any vestige of that deceptive I'm-just-an-ordinary-everyday-real-estate-salesman look. His pleasant but unexceptional face was now an arresting sight: The intensity of his concentration brought a new sharpness to his brow, cheekbones, and jaws; an instinctive sense of danger and an animal determination to survive were evident in his squint, in the flaring of his nostrils, and in the way his lips pulled back in a humorless, feral grin. He was spring-tense, acutely aware of every nuance of the forest, and just by looking at him, Rachael could tell that he had hair-trigger reflexes. This was the work he had been trained for—hunting and being hunted. His claim to being largely a past-focused man seemed like pretense or self-delusion, for there was no doubt whatsoever that he possessed an uncanny ability to focus entirely and powerfully on the present, which he was doing now.

The cicadas.

The wind in the attic of the forest.

The occasional trilling of a distant bird.

Nothing else.

Thirty seconds.

In these woods, at least, they were supposed to be the hunters, but suddenly they seemed to be the prey, and this reversal of roles frustrated Rachael as much as it frightened her. The need to remain silent was nerve-shredding, for she wanted to curse out loud, shout at Eric, challenge him. She wanted to *scream*.

Forty seconds.

Cautiously Benny and Rachael began moving uphill again.

They circled the large cabin until they came to the edge of the forest at the rear of it, and every step of the way they were stalked—or believed themselves to be stalked. Six more times, even after they left the dry wash and turned north through the woods, they stopped in response to unnatural sounds. Sometimes the snap of a twig or a not-quite-identifiable scraping noise would be so close to them that it seemed as if their nemesis must be only a few feet away and easily seen, yet they saw nothing.

Finally, forty feet in back of the cabin, just inside the tree line where they were still partially concealed by purple shadows, they crouched behind upthrusting blocks of granite that poked out of the earth like worn and slightly rotted teeth. Benny whispered, "Must be a lot of animals in these woods. That must've been what we heard."

"What kind of animals?" she whispered.

In a voice so low that Rachael could barely hear it, Benny said, "Squirrels, foxes. This high up . . . maybe a wolf or two. Can't have been Eric. No way. He's not had the survival or combat training that'd make it possible to be that quiet or to stay hidden so well and so long. If it was Eric, we'd have spotted him. Besides, if it'd been Eric, and if he's as deranged as you think he might be, then he'd have tried to jump us somewhere along the way."

"Animals," she said doubtfully.

"Animals."

With her back against the granite teeth, she looked at the woods through which they had come, studying every pocket of darkness and every peculiar shape.

Animals. Not a single, purposeful stalker. Just the sounds of several animals whose paths they had crossed. Animals.

Then why did she still feel as if something were back there in the woods, watching her, hungering for her?

"Animals," Benny said. Satisfied with that explanation, he turned from the woods, got up from a squat to a crouch, and peered over the lichen-speckled granite formation, examining the rear of Eric's mountain retreat.

Rachael was not convinced that the only source of danger was the cabin, so she rose, leaned one hip and shoulder against the rock, and took a position that allowed her to shift her attention back and forth from the rustic building in front of them to the forest behind.

At the rear of the mountain house, which stood on a wide shelf of land between slopes, a forty-foot-wide area had been cleared to serve as a backyard, and the summer sun fell across the greater part of it. Rye grass had been planted but had grown only in patches, for the soil was stony. Besides, Eric apparently had not installed a sprinkler system, which meant even the patchy grass would be green only for a short while between the melting of the winter snow and the parching summer. Having died a couple of weeks ago, in fact, the grass was now mown to a short, brown, prickly stubble. But flower beds—evidently irrigated by a passive-drip system—ringed the wide stained-wood porch that extended the length of the house; a profusion of yellow, orange, fire-red, wine-red, pink, white, and blue blossoms trembled and swayed and dipped in the gusty breeze—zinnias, geraniums, daisies, baby chrysanthemums, and more.

The cabin was of notched-log-and-mortar construction, but it was not a cheap, unsophisticated structure. The workmanship looked first-rate; Eric must have spent a bundle on the place. It stood upon an elevated foundation of invisibly mortared stones, and it boasted large casement-style French windows, two of which were partway open to facilitate ventilation. A black slate roof discouraged dry-wood moths and the playful squirrels attracted to shake-shingle roofs, and there was even a satellite dish up there to assure good TV reception.

The back door was open even wider than the two casement windows, and, taken with the bright bobbing flowers, that should have given the place a welcoming look. Instead, to Rachael, the open door resembled the gaping lid of a trap, flung wide to disarm the sniffing prey that sought the scented bait.

Of course, they would go in anyway. That was why they had come here: to go in, to find Eric. But she didn't have to like it.

After studying the cabin, Benny whispered, "Can't sneak up on the place; there's no cover. Next-best thing is a fast approach, straight in at a run, and hunker down along the porch railing."

"Okay."

"Probably the smartest thing is for you to wait here, let me go first, and see if maybe he's got a gun and starts taking potshots at me. If there's no gunfire, you can come after me."

"Stay here alone?"

"I'll never be far away."

"Even ten feet is too far."

"And we'll be separated only for a minute."

"That's exactly sixty times longer than I could stand being alone here," she said, looking back into the woods, where every deep pool of shadow and every unidentifiable form appeared to have crept closer while her attention was diverted. "No way, José. We go together."

"I figured you'd say that."

A tempest of warm wind whirled across the yard, stirring up dust, whipping the flowers, and lashing far enough into the perimeter of the forest to buffet Rachael's face.

Benny edged to the end of the granite formation, the shotgun held in both hands, peered around the corner, taking one last look at each of the rear windows to be sure no one was looking out of them.

The cicadas had stopped singing.

What did their sudden silence mean?

Before she could call that new development to Benny's attention, he flung himself forward, out of the concealment of the woods. He bolted across the patchy, dead brown lawn.

Propelled by the electrifying feeling that something murderous was bounding through the shadowed forest behind her—was reaching for her hair, was going to seize her, was going to drag her away into the dark of the woods—Rachael plunged after Benny, past the rocks, out of the trees, into the sun. She reached the back porch even as he was hunkering down beside the steps.

Breathless, she stopped beside him and looked back toward the forest. Nothing was pursuing her. She could hardly believe it.

Fast and light on his feet, Benny sprang up the porch steps, to the wall beside the open door, where he put his back to the logs and listened for movement inside the house. Evidently he heard nothing, for he pulled open the screen door and went inside, staying low, the shotgun aimed in front of him.

Rachael went after him, into a kitchen that was larger and better equipped than she expected. On the table, a plate held the remnants of an unfinished breakfast of sausages and biscuits. Soup cans and an empty jar of peanut butter littered the floor.

The cellar door was open. Benny cautiously, quietly pushed it shut, closing off the sight of steps descending into the gloom beyond.

Without being told what to do, Rachael hooked a kitchen chair with one hand, brought it to the door, tilted it under the knob, and wedged it into place, creating an effective barricade. They could not go into the cellar until they had searched the main living quarters of the cabin; for if Eric was in one of the ground-floor rooms, he might slip into the kitchen as soon as they went down the steps, might close the door and lock them in the dark basement. Conversely, if he was in the windowless basement already, he might creep upstairs while they were searching for him and sneak in behind them, a possibility they had just precluded by wedging that door shut.

She saw that Benny was pleased by the perception she'd shown when she'd put that chair under the knob. They made a good team.

She braced another door, which probably opened onto the garage, used a chair on that one, too. If Eric was in there, he could escape by rolling up the big outer door, of course, but they would hear it no matter where they were in the cabin and would have him pinpointed.

They stood in the kitchen for a moment, listening. Rachael could hear only the gusty breeze humming in the fine-mesh screen of the open kitchen window, sighing through the deep eaves under the overhanging slate roof.

Staying low and moving fast, Benny rushed through the doorway between the kitchen and the living room, looking left and right as he crossed the threshold. He signaled to Rachael that the way was clear, and she went after him.

In the ultramodern living room, the cabin's front door was open, though not as wide as the back door had been. A couple of hundred loose sheets of paper, two small ring-bound notebooks with black vinyl covers, and several manila file folders were scattered across the floor, some rumpled and torn.

Also on the floor, beside an armchair near the big front window, lay a medium-size knife with a serrated blade and a point tip. A couple of sunbeams, having pierced the forest outside, struck through the window, and one touched the steel blade, making its polished surface gleam, rippling lambently along its cutting edge.

Benny stared worriedly at the knife, then turned toward one of the three doors that, in addition to the kitchen archway, opened off the living room.

Rachael was about to pick up some of the papers to see what they were, but when Benny moved, she followed.

Two of the doors were closed tight, but the one Benny had chosen was ajar an inch. He pushed it open all the way with the barrel of the shotgun and went through with his customary caution.

Guarding the rear, Rachael remained in the living room, where she could see the open front door, the two closed doors, the kitchen arch, but where she also had a view of the room into which Benny had gone. It was a bedroom, wrecked in the same way that the bedroom in the Villa Park mansion and the kitchen in the Palm Springs house had been wrecked, proof that Eric had been here and that he had been seized by another demented rage.

In the bedroom, Benny gingerly rolled aside one of the large mirrored doors on a closet, looked warily inside, apparently found nothing of interest. He moved across the bedroom to the adjoining bath, where he passed out of Rachael's sight.

She glanced nervously at the front door, at the porch beyond, at the kitchen archway, at each of the other two closed doors.

Outside, the gusty breeze moaned softly under the overhanging roof and made a low, eager whining noise. The rustle of wind-stirred trees carried through the open front door.

Inside the cabin, the deep silence grew even deeper. Curiously enough, that stillness had the same effect on Rachael as a crescendo in a symphony: while it built, she became tenser, more convinced that events were hurtling toward an explosive climax.

Eric, damn it, where are you? Where are you, Eric?

Benny seemed to have been gone an ominously long time. She was on the verge of calling to him in panic, but finally he reappeared, unharmed, shaking his head to indicate that he had found no sign of Eric and nothing else of interest.

They discovered that the two closed doors opened onto two more bedrooms that shared a second bath between them, although Eric had furnished neither chamber with beds. Benny explored both rooms, closets, and the connecting bath, while Rachael stood in the living room by one doorway and then by the other, watching. She could see that the first room was a study with several bookshelves laden with thick volumes, a desk, and a computer; the second was empty, unused.

When it became clear that Benny was not going to find Eric in that part of the cabin, either, Rachael bent down, plucked up a few sheets of paper—Xerox copies, she noted—from the floor, and quickly scanned them. By the time Benny returned, she knew what she had found, and her heart was racing. "It's the Wildcard file," she said sotto voce. "He must've kept another copy here."

She started to gather up more of the scattered pages, but Benny stopped her. "We've got to find Eric first," he whispered.

Nodding agreement, she reluctantly dropped the papers.

Benny went to the front door, eased open the creaky screen door with the least amount of noise he could manage, and satisfied himself that the plank-floored porch was deserted. Then Rachael followed him into the kitchen again.

She slipped the tilted chair out from under the knob of the basement door, pulled the door open, and backed quickly out of the way as Benny covered it with the shotgun.

Eric did not come roaring out of the darkness.

With tiny beads of sweat shimmering on his forehead, Benny went to the threshold, found the switch on the wall of the stairwell, and flicked on the lights below.

Rachael was also sweating. As was surely the case with Benny, her perspiration was not occasioned by the warm summer air.

It was still not advisable for Rachael to accompany Benny into the windowless chamber below. Eric might be outside, watching the house, and he might slip inside at the opportune moment; then, as they returned to the kitchen, they might be ambushed from above when they were in the middle of the stairs and most vulnerable. So she remained at the threshold, where she could look down the cellar steps and also have a clear view of the entire kitchen, including the archway to the living room and the open door to the rear porch.

Benny descended the plank stairs more quietly than seemed humanly possible, although some noise was unavoidable: a few creaks, a couple of scraping noises. At the bottom, he hesitated, then turned left, out of sight. For a moment Rachael saw his shadow on the wall down there, made large and twisted into an odd shape by the angle of the light, but as he moved farther into the cellar, the shadow dwindled and finally went with him.

She glanced at the archway. She could see a portion of the living room, which remained deserted and still.

In the opposite direction, at the porch door, a huge yellow butterfly clung to the screen, slowly working its wings.

A clatter sounded from below, nothing dramatic, as if Benny had bumped against something.

She looked down the steps. No Benny, no shadow.

The archway. Nothing.

The back door. Just the butterfly.

More noise below, quieter this time.

"Benny?" she said softly.

He did not answer her. Probably didn't hear her. She had spoken at barely more than a whisper, after all.

The archway, the back door . . .

The stairs: still no sign of Benny.

"Benny," she repeated, then saw a shadow below. For a moment her heart twisted because the shadow looked so strange, but Benny appeared and started up toward her, and she sighed with relief.

"Nothing down there but an open wall safe tucked behind the water heater," he said when he reached the kitchen. "It's empty, so maybe that's where he kept the files that're spread over the living room."

Rachael wanted to put down her gun and throw her arms around him and hug him tight and kiss him all over his face just because he had come back from the cellar alive. She wanted him to know how happy she was to see him, but the garage still had to be explored.

By unspoken agreement, she removed the tilted chair from under the knob and opened the door, and Benny covered it with the shotgun. Again, there was no sign of Eric.

Benny stood on the threshold, fumbled for the switch, found it, but the lights in the garage were dim. Even with a small window high in one wall, the place remained shadowy. He tried another switch, which operated the big electric door. It rolled up with much humming-rumbling-creaking, and bright brassy sunlight flooded inside.

"That's better," Benny said, stepping into the garage.

She followed him and saw the black Mercedes 560 SEL, additional proof that Eric had been there.

The rising door had stirred up some dust, motes of which drifted lazily through the in-slanting sunlight. Overhead in the rafters, spiders had been busy spinning ersatz silk.

Rachael and Benny circled the car warily, looked through the windows (saw the keys dangling in the ignition), and even peered underneath. But Eric was not to be found.

An elaborate workbench extended across the entire back of the garage. Above it was a peg board tool

rack, and each tool hung in a painted outline of itself.
Rachael noticed that no wood ax hung in the ax-shaped
outline, but she did not even give the missing instrument
a second thought because she was only looking for places
where Eric could hide; she was not, after all, doing an
inventory.

The garage provided no sheltered spaces large enough
for a man to conceal himself, and when Benny spoke
again, he no longer bothered to whisper. "I'm beginning
to think maybe he's been here and gone."

"But that's his Mercedes."

"This is a two-car garage, so maybe he keeps a vehicle
up here all the time, a Jeep or four-wheel-drive pickup
good for scooting around these mountain roads. Maybe
he knew there was a chance the feds would learn what
he'd done to himself and would be after him, with an APB
on the car, so he split in the Jeep or whatever it was."

Rachael stared at the black Mercedes, which stood
like a great sleeping beast. She looked up at the webs
in the rafters. She stared at the sun-splashed dirt road that
led away from the garage. The stillness of the mountain
redoubt seemed less ominous than it had since their
arrival; not peaceful and serene by any means, certainly not welcoming, either, but it was somewhat less
threatening.

"Where would he go?" she asked.

Benny shrugged. "I don't know. But if I do a thorough
search of the cabin, maybe I'll find something that'll point
me in the right direction."

"Do we have time for a search? I mean, when we left
Sarah Kiel at the hospital last night, I didn't know the feds
might be on this same trail. I told her not to talk about what
had happened and not to tell anyone about this place. At
worst, I thought maybe Eric's business partners would
start sniffing around, trying to get something out of her,
and I figured she'd be able to handle them. But she won't
be able to stall the government. And if she believes we're
traitors, she'll even think she's doing the right thing when
she tells them about this place. So they'll be here sooner
or later."

"I agree," Benny said, staring thoughtfully at the Mercedes.

"Then we've no time to worry about where Eric went. Besides, that's a copy of the Wildcard file in there on the living-room floor. All we have to do is pick it up and get out of here, and we'll have all the proof we need."

He shook his head. "Having the file is important, maybe even crucial, but I'm not so sure it's enough."

She paced agitatedly, the thirty-two pistol held with the muzzle pointed at the ceiling rather than down, for an accidentally triggered shot would ricochet off the concrete floor. "Listen, the whole story's right there in black and white. We just give it to the press—"

"For one thing," Benny said, "the file is, I assume, a lot of highly technical stuff—lab results, formulae—and no reporter's going to understand it. He'll have to take it to a first-rate geneticist for review, for *translation*."

"So?"

"So maybe the geneticist will be incompetent or just conservative in his assumption of what's possible in his field, and in either case he might disbelieve the whole thing; he might tell the reporter it's a fraud, a hoax."

"We can deal with that kind of setback. We can keep looking until we find a geneticist who—"

Interrupting, Benny said, "Worse: Maybe the reporter will take it to a geneticist who does his own research for the government, for the Pentagon. And isn't it logical that federal agents have contacted a lot of scientists specializing in recombinant DNA research, warning them that media types might be bringing them certain stolen files of a highly classified nature, seeking analysis of the contents?"

"The feds can't know that's my intention."

"But if they've got a file on you—and they do— then they know you well enough to suspect that'd be your plan."

"All right, yes," she admitted unhappily.

"So any Pentagon-supported scientist is going to be real eager to please the government and keep his own fat research grants, and he's sure as hell going to alert them the moment such a file comes into his hands. Certainly he's not going to risk *losing* his grants or being prosecuted for compromising defense secrets, so at best he'll tell the reporter to take his damn file and get lost, and he'll keep his mouth shut. At best. Most likely he'll give the reporter to the feds, and the reporter will give *us* to the feds. The file will be destroyed, and very likely we'll be destroyed, too."

Rachael didn't want to believe what he said, but she knew there was truth in it.

Out in the woods, the cicadas were singing again.

"So what do we do now?" she asked.

Evidently Benny had been thinking hard about that question as they had gone through room after room of the cabin without finding Eric, for his answer was well prepared. "With both Eric and the file in our possession, we're in a lot stronger position. We wouldn't have just a bunch of cryptic research papers that only a handful of people could understand; we'd also have a walking dead man, his skull staved in, and by God, *that's* dramatic enough to guarantee that virtually any newspaper or television network will run an all-stops-pulled story before getting expert opinions on the file itself. Then there'll be no reason for the government or anyone else trying to shut us up. Once Eric's seen on TV news, his picture'll show up on the covers of *Time* and *Newsweek*, and the *National Enquirer* will have enough material for a decade, and David Letterman will be making zombie jokes every night, so silencing us won't achieve anything."

He took a deep breath, and she had a hunch that he was going to propose something she would not like in the least.

When he continued, he confirmed her hunch. "All right, like I said, I need to search this place thoroughly to see if I can come up with any clue that'll tell us where Eric's gone. But the authorities may show up here soon. Now that we've got a copy of the Wildcard file, we can't risk having it taken away from us, so you've got to leave with the file while I—"

"You mean, split up?" she said. "Oh, no."

"It's the only way, Rachael. We—"

"No."

The thought of leaving him alone here was chilling.

The thought of being alone herself was almost too much to bear, and she realized with terrible poignancy how tight the bonds between them had become in just the past twenty-four hours.

She loved him. God, how she loved him.

He fixed her with his gentle, reassuring brown eyes. In a voice neither patronizing nor abrasively commanding but nevertheless full of authority and reason, a voice which brooked no debate—probably the tone he had learned to use in Vietnam, in crises, with soldiers of inferior rank— he said, "You'll take the Wildcard file out of here, get copies made, send some off to friends in widely separated places, and secrete a few others where you can get your hands on them with short notice. Then we won't have to worry about losing our only copy or having it taken away from us. We'll have real good insurance. Meanwhile, I'll thoroughly search the cabin here, see what I can turn up. If I find something that points us toward Eric, I'll meet up with you at a prearranged place, and we'll go after him together. If I don't get a lead on him, we'll meet up and hide out together, until we can decide what to do next."

She did not want to split up and leave him alone here. Eric might still be around. Or the feds might show up. Either way Benny might be killed. But his arguments for splitting up were convincing; damn it, he was right.

Nevertheless, she said, "If I go alone and take the car, how will you get out of here?"

He glanced at his wristwatch not because he needed to know the time (she thought) but to impress upon her that time was running out. "You'll leave the rental Ford for me," he said. "That's got to be ditched soon, anyway, because the cops might be onto it. You'll take this Mercedes, and I'll take the Ford just far enough to swap it for something else."

"They'll be on the lookout for the Mercedes, too."

"Oh, sure. But the APB will specify a black 560 SEL with this particular license number, driven by a man fitting Eric's description. You'll be driving, not Eric, and we'll switch license plates with one of those cars parked along the gravel road farther down the mountain, which ought to take care of things."

"I'm not so sure."

"I am."

Hugging herself as if this were a day in November rather than a day in June, Rachael said, "But where would we meet up later?"

"Las Vegas," he said.

The answer startled her. "Why there?"

"Southern California's too hot for us. I'm not confident we can hide out here. But if we hop over to Vegas, I have a place."

"What place?"

"I own a motel on Tropicana Boulevard, west of the Strip."

"You're a Vegas wheeler-dealer? Old-fashioned, conservative Benny Shadway is a Vegas wheeler-dealer?"

"My real-estate development company's been in and out of Vegas property several times, but I'm hardly a wheeler-dealer. It's small stuff by Vegas standards. In this case, it's an older motel with just twenty-eight rooms and a pool. And it's not in the best repair. In fact, it's closed up at the moment. I finished the purchase two weeks ago, and we're going to tear it down next month, put up a new place: sixty units, a restaurant. There's still electrical service. The manager's suite is pretty shabby, but it has a working bathroom, furniture, telephone—so we can hide out there if we have to, make plans. Or just wait for Eric to show up someplace very public and cause a sensation that the feds can't put a lid on. Anyway, if we can't get a lead on him, hiding out is all we *can* do."

"I'm to drive to Vegas?" she asked.

"That'd be best. Depending on how badly the feds want us—and considering what's at stake, I think they want us real bad—they'll probably have men at the major airports. You can take the state route past Silverwood Lake, then pick up Interstate Fifteen, be in Vegas this evening. I'll follow in a couple of hours."

"But if the cops show up—"

"Alone, without you to worry about, I can slip away from them."

"You think they're going to be incompetent?" she asked sourly.

"No. I just know I'm *more* competent."

"Because you were trained for this. But that was more than one and a half decades ago."

He smiled thinly. "Seems like yesterday, that war."

And he had kept in shape. She could not dispute that. What was it he'd said—that Nam had taught him to be prepared because the world had a way of turning dark and mean when you least expected it?

"Rachael?" he asked, looking at his watch again.

She realized that their best chance of surviving, of having a future together, was for her to do what he wanted.

"All right," she said. "All right. We'll split. But it scares me, Benny. I guess I don't have the guts for this kind of thing, the right stuff. I'm sorry, but it really scares me."

He came to her, kissed her. "Being scared isn't anything to be ashamed of. Only madmen have no fear."

◊ 24 ◊

A SPECIAL FEAR
OF HELL

Dr. Easton Solberg had been more than fifteen minutes late for his one o'clock meeting with Julio Verdad and Reese Hagerstrom. They had stood outside his locked office, and he had finally come hurrying along the wide hall, clutching an armload of books and manila folders, looking harried, more like a twenty-year-old student late to class than a sixty-year-old professor overdue for an appointment.

He was wearing a rumpled brown suit one size too large for him, a blue shirt, and a green-and-orange-striped tie that looked, to Julio, as if it had been sold exclusively in novelty shops as a joke gift. Even by a generous appraisal, Solberg was not an attractive man, not even plain. He was short and stocky. His moonish face featured a small flat nose that would have been called pug on some men but that was simply porcine on him, small close-set gray eyes that looked watery and myopic behind his smudged glasses, a mouth that was strangely wide considering the scale on which the rest of his visage was constructed, and a receding chin.

In the hall outside his office, apologizing effusively, he had insisted on shaking hands with the two detectives, in spite of the load in his arms; therefore, he kept dropping books, which Julio and Reese stooped to pick up.

Solberg's office was chaos. Books and scientific journals filled every shelf, spilled onto the floor, rose in teetering stacks in the corners, were piled every which way on top of furniture. On his big desk, file folders, index cards, and yellow legal-size tablets were heaped in apparent disorder. The professor shifted mounds of papers off two chairs to give Julio and Reese places to sit.

"Look at that lovely view!" Solberg said, stopping suddenly and gaping at the windows as he rounded his desk, as if noticing for the first time what lay beyond the walls of his office.

The Irvine campus of the University of California was blessed with many trees, rolling green lawns, and flower beds, for it sprawled over a large tract of prime Orange County land. Below Dr. Solberg's second-floor office, a walkway curved across manicured grass, past impatiens blazing with thousands of bright blossoms—coral, red, pink, purple—and vanished under the branches of jacarandas and eucalyptus.

"Gentlemen, we are among the most fortunate people on earth: to be here, in this beautiful land, under these temperate skies, in a nation of plenty and tolerance." He stepped to the window and opened his stubby arms, as if to embrace all of southern California. "And the trees, especially the trees. There are some wonderful specimens on this campus. I love trees, I really do. That's my hobby: trees, the study of trees, the cultivation of unusual specimens. It makes for a welcome change from human biology and genetics. Trees are so majestic, so *noble*. Trees give and give to us—fruit, nuts, beauty, shade, lumber, oxygen—and take nothing in return. If I believed in reincarnation, I'd pray to return as a tree." He glanced at Julio and Reese. "What about you? Don't you think it'd be grand to come back as a tree, living the long majestic life of an oak or giant spruce, giving of yourself the way orange and apple trees give, growing great strong limbs in which children could climb?" He blinked, surprised by his own monologue. "But of course you're not here to talk about trees and reincarnation, are you? You'll have to forgive me . . . but, well, that *view*, don't you know? Just captured me for a moment."

In spite of his unfortunate porcine face, disheveled appearance, apparent disorganization, and evident tendency to be late, Dr. Easton Solberg had at least three things to recommend him: keen intelligence, enthusiasm for life, and optimism. In a world of doomsayers, where half the intelligentsia waited almost wistfully for Armageddon, Julio found Solberg refreshing. He liked the professor almost at once.

As Solberg went behind his desk, sat in a large leather chair, and half disappeared from view beyond his paperwork, Julio said, "On the phone you said there was a dark side to Eric Leben that you could discuss only in person—"

"And in strictest confidence," Solberg said. "The information, if pertinent to your case, must go in a file somewhere, of course, but if it's not pertinent, I expect discretion."

"I assure you of that," Julio said. "But as I told you earlier, this is an extremely important investigation involving at least two murders and the possible leak of top-secret defense documents."

"Do you mean Eric's death might not have been accidental?"

"No," Julio said. "That was definitely an accident. But there are other deaths . . . the details of which I'm not at liberty to discuss. And more people may die before this case is closed. So Detective Hagerstrom and I hope you'll give us full and immediate cooperation."

"Oh, of course, of course," Easton Solberg said, waving one pudgy hand to dismiss the very idea that he might be uncooperative. "And although I don't know for a certainty that Eric's emotional problems are related to your case, I expect—and fear—that they may be. As I said . . . he had a dark side."

However, before Solberg got around to telling them of Leben's dark side, he spent a quarter of an hour praising the dead geneticist, apparently unable to speak ill of the man until he had first spoken highly of him. Eric was a genius. Eric was a hard worker. Eric was generous in support of colleagues. Eric had a fine sense of humor, an appreciation for art, good taste in most things, and he liked dogs.

Julio was beginning to think they ought to form a committee and solicit contributions to build a statue of Leben for display under a fittingly imposing rotunda in a major public building. He glanced at Reese and saw his partner was plainly amused by the bubbly Solberg.

Finally the professor said, "But he was a troubled man, I'm sorry to say. Deeply, deeply troubled. He had been my student for a while, though I quickly realized the student was going to outdistance the teacher. When we were no longer student-teacher but colleagues, we remained friendly. We weren't friends, just friendly, because Eric did not allow any relationship to become close enough to qualify as friendship. So, close as we were professionally, it was years before I learned about his . . . obsession with young girls."

"How young?" Reese asked.

Solberg hesitated. "I feel as if I'm . . . betraying him."

"We may already know much of what you've got to tell us," Julio said. "You'll probably only be confirming what we know."

"Really? Well . . . I knew of one girl who was fourteen. At the time, Eric was thirty-one."

"This was before Geneplan?"

"Yes. Eric was at UCLA then. Not rich yet, but we could all see he would one day leave academia and take the real world by storm."

"A respected professor wouldn't go around bragging about bedding fourteen-year-old girls," Julio said. "How'd you find out?"

"It happened on a weekend," Dr. Solberg said, "when his lawyer was out of town and he needed someone to post bail. He trusted no one but me to keep quiet about the ugly details of the arrest. I sort of resented that, too. He knew I'd feel a moral obligation to endorse any censure movement against a colleague involved in such sordid business, but he also knew I'd feel obligated to keep any confidences he imparted, and he counted on the second obligation being stronger than the first. Maybe, to my discredit, it was."

Easton Solberg gradually settled deeper in his chair while he talked, as if trying to hide behind the mounds of papers on his desk, embarrassed by the sleazy tale he had to tell. That Saturday, eleven years ago, after receiving Leben's call, Dr. Solberg had gone to a police precinct house in Hollywood, where he had found an Eric Leben far different from the man he knew: nervous, uncertain of himself, ashamed, lost. The previous night, Eric had been arrested in a vice-squad raid at a hot-bed motel where Hollywood streetwalkers, many of them young runaways with drug problems, took their johns. He was caught with a fourteen-year-old girl and charged with statutory rape, a mandatory count even when an underage girl admittedly solicits sex for pay.

Initially Leben told Easton Solberg that the girl had looked considerably older than fourteen, that he'd had no way of knowing she was a juvenile. Later, however, perhaps disarmed by Solberg's kindness and concern, Leben broke down and talked at length of his obsession with young girls. Solberg had not really wanted to know any of it, but he could not refuse Eric a sympathetic ear. He sensed that Eric—who was a distant and self-possessed loner, unlikely ever to have unburdened himself to anyone—desperately needed to confide his intimate feelings and fears to someone at that bleak, low point in his life. So Easton Solberg listened, filled with both disgust and pity.

"His was not just a lust for young girls," Solberg told Julio and Reese. "It was an obsession, a compulsion, a terrible gnawing *need*."

Only thirty-one then, Leben was nevertheless deeply frightened of growing old and dying. Already longevity research was the center of his career. But he did not approach the problem of aging *only* in a scientific spirit; privately, in his personal life, he dealt with it in an emotional and irrational manner. For one thing, he felt that he somehow absorbed the vital energies of youth from the girls he bedded. Although he knew that notion was ridiculous, almost superstitious, he was still compelled to pursue those girls. He was not really a child molester in the classic sense, did not force himself on mere children. He only went after those girls who were willing to cooperate, usually teenage runaways reduced to prostitution.

"And sometimes," Easton Solberg said with soft dismay, "he liked to . . . slap them around. Not really beat them but rough them up. When he explained it to me, I had the feeling that he was explaining it to himself for the first time. These girls were so young that they were full of the special arrogance of youth, that arrogance born of the certainty they'd live forever; and Eric felt that, by hurting them, he was knocking the arrogance out of them, teaching them the fear of death. He was, as he put it, 'stealing their innocence, the energy of their youthful innocence,' and he felt that somehow this made him younger, that the stolen innocence and youth became his own."

"A psychic vampire," Julio said uneasily.

"Yes!" Solberg said. "Exactly. A psychic vampire who could stay young forever by draining away the youth of these girls. Yet at the same time, he knew it was a fantasy, knew the girls could not keep him young, but knowing and acknowledging it did nothing to loosen the grip of the fantasy. And though he knew he was sick—even mocked himself, called himself a degenerate—he couldn't break free of his obsession."

"What happened to the charge of statutory rape?" Reese asked. "I'm not aware he was tried or convicted. He had no police record."

"The girl was remanded to juvenile authorities," Solberg said, "and put in a minimum-security facility. She slipped away, skipped town. She'd been carrying no identification, and the name she gave them proved false, so they had no way of tracking her. Without the girl, they had no case against Eric, and the charges were dropped."

"You urged him to seek psychiatric help?" Julio asked.

"Yes. But he wouldn't. He was an extremely intelligent man, introspective, and he had already analyzed himself. He knew—or at least believed that he knew—the cause of his mental condition."

Julio leaned forward in his chair. "And the cause as he saw it?"

Solberg cleared his throat, started to speak, shook his head as if to say that he needed a moment to decide how to proceed. He was obviously embarrassed by the conversation and was equally disturbed by his betrayal of Eric Leben's confidence even though Leben was now dead. The heaps of papers on the desk no longer provided adequate cover behind which to hide, so Solberg got up and went to the window because it afforded the opportunity to turn his back on Julio and Reese, thus concealing his face.

Solberg's dismay and self-reproach over revealing confidential information about a dead man—of whom he had been little more than an acquaintance—might have seemed excessive to some, yet Julio admired Solberg for it. In an age when few believed in moral absolutes, many would betray a friend without a qualm, and a moral dilemma of this nature would be beyond their understanding. Solberg's old-fashioned moral anguish seemed excessive only by current, decadent standards.

"Eric told me that, as a child, he was sexually molested by an uncle," Solberg said to the window glass. "Hampstead was the man's name. The abuse started when Eric was four and continued till he was nine. He was terrified of this uncle but too ashamed to tell anyone what was happening. Ashamed because his family was so religious. That's important, as you'll see. The Leben family was devoutly, ardently religious. Nazarenes. Very strict. No music. No dancing. That cold, narrow religion that makes life a bleakness. Of course, Eric felt like a sinner because of what he'd done with his uncle, even though he was forced into it, and he was afraid to tell his parents."

"It's a common pattern," Julio said, "even in families that aren't religious. The child blames himself for the adult's crime."

Solberg said, "His terror of Barry Hampstead—that was the first name, yes—grew greater month by month, week by week. And finally, when Eric was nine, he stabbed Hampstead to death."

"Nine?" Reese said, appalled. "Good heavens."

"Hampstead was asleep on the sofa," Solberg continued, "and Eric killed him with a butcher's knife."

Julio considered the effects of that trauma on a nine-year-old boy who was already emotionally disturbed from the ordeal of long-term physical abuse. In his mind's eye, he saw the knife clutched in the child's small hand, rising and falling, blood flying off the shining blade, and the boy's eyes fixed in horror upon his grisly handiwork, repelled by what he was doing, yet compelled to finish it.

Julio shivered.

"Though everyone then learned what had been going on," Solberg said, "Eric's parents somehow, in their twisted way, saw him as both a fornicator and a murderer, and they began a fevered and very psychologically damaging campaign to save his soul from hell, praying over him day and night, disciplining him, forcing him to read and reread passages of the Bible aloud until his throat cracked and his voice faded to a hoarse whisper. Even after he got out of that dark and hateful house and got through college by working part-time jobs and winning scholarships, even after he'd piled up a mountain of academic achievements and had become a respected man of science, Eric continued to half believe in hell and in his own certain damnation. Maybe he even more than *half* believed."

Suddenly Julio saw what was coming, and a chill as cold as any he had ever felt sneaked up the small of his back. He glanced at his partner and saw, in Reese's face, a look of horror that mirrored Julio's feelings.

Still staring out at the verdant campus, which was as thoroughly sun-splashed as before but which seemed to have grown darker, Easton Solberg said, "You already know of Eric's deep and abiding commitment to longevity research and his dream of immortality achieved through genetic engineering. But now perhaps you see why he was so obsessed with achieving that unrealistic—some would call it irrational and impossible—goal. In spite of all his education, in spite of his ability to reason, he was illogical about this one thing: in his heart he believed that he would go to hell when he died, not merely because he had sinned with his uncle but because he had killed his uncle as well, and was both a fornicator and a murderer. He told me once that he was afraid he'd meet his uncle again in hell and that eternity would be, for him, total submission to Barry Hampstead's lust."

"Dear God," Julio said shakily, and he unconsciously made the sign of the cross, something he had not done outside of church since he was a child.

Turning away from the window and facing the detectives at last, the professor said, "So for Eric Leben, immortality on earth was a goal sought not only out of a love of life but out of a special fear of hell. I imagine you can see how, with such motivation, he was destined to be a driven man, obsessed."

"Inevitably," Julio said.

"Driven to young girls, driven to seek ways to extend the human life span, driven to cheat the devil," Solberg said. "Year by year it became worse. We drifted apart after that weekend when he made his confessions, probably because he regretted that he'd told me his secrets. I doubt he even told his wife about his uncle and his childhood when he married her a few years later. I was probably the only one. But in spite of the growing distance between us, I heard from poor Eric often enough to know his fear of death and damnation became worse as he grew older. In fact, after forty, he was downright frantic. I'm sorry he died yesterday; he was a brilliant man, and he had the power to contribute so much to humanity. On the other hand, his was not a happy life. And perhaps his death was even a blessing in disguise because . . ."

"Yes?" Julio said.

Solberg sighed and wiped one hand over his moonish face, which had sagged somewhat with weariness. "Well, sometimes I worried about what Eric might do if he ever achieved a breakthrough in the kind of research he was pursuing. If he thought he had a means of editing his genetic structure to dramatically extend his life span, he might have been just foolish enough to experiment on himself with an unproven process. He would know the terrible risks of tampering with his own genetic makeup, but compared to his unrelenting dread of death and the afterlife, those risks might seem minor. And God knows what might have happened to him if he had used himself as a guinea pig."

What would you say if you knew that his body disappeared from the morgue last night? Julio wondered.

◊ 25 ◊

ALONE

They did not attempt to put the Xerox of the Wildcard file in order, but scooped up all the loose papers from the cabin's living-room floor and dropped them in a plastic Hefty garbage bag that Benny got from a box in one of the kitchen drawers. He twisted the top of the bag and secured it with a plastic-coated wire tie, then placed it on the rear floor of the Mercedes, behind the driver's seat.

They drove down the dirt road to the gate, on the other side of which they had parked the Ford. As they had hoped, on the same ring with the car keys, they found a key that fit the padlock on the gate.

Benny brought the Ford inside, and as he edged past her, Rachael drove the Mercedes out through the gate and parked just beyond.

She waited nervously with the 560 SEL, her thirty-two in one hand and her gaze sweeping the surrounding forest.

Benny went down the road on foot, out of sight, to the three vehicles that were parked on the lay-by near one of the driveway entrances they had passed earlier on their way up the mountainside. He carried with him the two license plates from the Mercedes—plus a screwdriver and a pair of pliers. When he returned, he had the plates from one of the Dodge Chargers, which he attached to the Mercedes.

He got in the car with her and said, "When you get to Vegas, go to a public phone, look up the number for a guy named Whitney Gavis."

"Who's he?"

"An old friend. And he works for me. He's watching over that rundown motel I told you about—the Golden Sand Inn. In fact, he found the property and turned me on to its potential. He's got keys. He can let you in. Tell him you need to stay in the manager's suite and that I'll be joining you tonight. Tell him as much as you want to tell him; he can keep his mouth shut, and if he's going to be dragged into it, he should know how serious this is."

"What if he's heard about us on the radio or TV?"

"Won't matter to Whitney. He won't believe we're killers or Russian agents. He's got a good head on him, an excellent bullshit detector, and nobody has a better sense of loyalty than Whit. You can trust him."

"If you say so."

"There's a two-car garage behind the motel office. Make sure you put the Mercedes in there, out of sight, soon as you arrive."

"I don't like this."

"I'm not crazy about it, either," Benny said. "But it's the right plan. We've already discussed it." He leaned over and put one hand against her face, then kissed her.

The kiss was sweet, and when it ended she said, "As soon as you've searched the cabin, you'll leave? Whether or not you've found any clue to where Eric might've gone?"

"Yes. I want to get out before the feds show up."

"And if you find a clue to where he's gone, you won't go after him alone?"

"What did I promise you?"

"I want to hear you say it again."

"I'll come for you first," Benny said. "I won't tackle Eric alone. We'll handle him together."

She looked into his eyes and was not sure if he was telling the truth or lying. But even if he was lying, she could do nothing about it because time was running out. They could delay no longer.

"I love you," he said.

"I love you, Benny. And if you get yourself killed, I'm never going to forgive you."

He smiled. "You're some woman, Rachael. You could rouse a heartbeat in a rock, and you're all the motivation I need to come back alive. Don't you worry about that. Now, lock the doors when I get out—okay?"

He kissed her again, lightly this time. He got out of the car, slammed the door, waited until he saw the power-lock buttons sinking into their mountings, then waved her on.

She drove down the gravel lane, glancing repeatedly in the rearview mirror to keep Benny in sight as long as possible, but eventually the road turned, and he disappeared beyond the trees.

◗ ◗

Ben drove the rental Ford up the dirt lane, parked in front of the cabin. A few big white clouds had appeared in the sky, and the shadow of one of them rippled across the log structure.

Holding the twelve-gauge in one hand and the Combat Magnum in the other—Rachael had taken only the thirty-two—he climbed the steps to the porch, wondering if Eric was watching him.

Ben had told Rachael that Eric had left, gone to some other hiding place. Perhaps that was true. Indeed, the odds were high that it was true. But a chance remained, however slim, that the dead man was still here, perhaps observing from some lookout in the forest.

Reeeeee, reeeeee . . .

He tucked the revolver into his belt, at his back, and entered the cabin cautiously by the front door, the shotgun ready. He went through the rooms again, looking for something that might tell him where Eric had established another hidey-hole comparable to the cabin.

He had not lied to Rachael; it really was necessary to conduct such a search, but he did not require an hour to do it, as he'd claimed. If he did not find anything useful in fifteen minutes, he would leave the cabin and prowl the perimeter of the lawn for some sign of a place where Eric had entered the woods—trampled brush, footprints in soft soil. If he found what he was looking for, he would pursue his quarry into the forest.

He had not told Rachael about that part of his plan because, if he had, she would never have gone to Vegas. But he could not enter those woods and track down his man with Rachael at his side. He had realized as much on the way up through the forest, on their first approach to the cabin. She was not as sure of herself in the wilds as Ben was, not as quick. If she went with him, he would worry about her, be distracted by her, which would give the advantage to Eric if the dead man was, in fact, out there somewhere.

Earlier, he had told Rachael that the odd sounds they had heard in the woods were caused by animals. Maybe. But when they had found the cabin abandoned, he had let those forest noises sound again in his memory, and he had begun to feel that he had been too quick to dismiss the possibility that Eric had been stalking them through the shadows, trees, and brush.

◊   ◊

All the way down the narrow lane, from gravel to black-top, until she reached the state route that rounded Lake Arrowhead, Rachael was more than half convinced that Eric was going to rush the car from the surrounding woods and fling himself at the door. With superhuman strength born of a demonic rage, he might even be able to put a fist through the closed window. But he did not appear.

On the state route, circling the lake, she worried less about Eric and more about police and federal agents.

Every vehicle she encountered looked, at first sight, like a patrol car.

Las Vegas seemed a thousand miles away.

And she felt as if she had deserted Benny.

◊   ◊

When Peake and Sharp had arrived at the Palm Springs airport, directly from their meeting with The Stone, they had discovered that the helicopter, a Bell Jet Ranger, had developed engine trouble. The deputy director, full of pent-up anger that he had been unable to vent on The Stone, nearly took off the chopper pilot's head, as if the poor man not only flew the craft but was also responsible for its design, construction, and maintenance.

Peake winked at the pilot behind Sharp's back.

No other helicopter had been for hire, and the two choppers belonging to the county sheriff's substation had been engaged and unavailable for quick reassignment. Reluctantly Sharp had decided they had no choice but to drive from Palm Springs to Lake Arrowhead. The dark green government sedan came with a red emergency beacon that was usually kept in the trunk but which could be mounted to the roof beading with a thumbscrew clamp in less than a minute. They had a siren, too. They had used both the flashing beacon and the siren to clear traffic out of their way, hurtling north on Highway 111, then virtually *flying* west on I-10 toward the Redland exit. They had topped ninety miles an hour nearly all the way, the Chevy's engine roaring, the frame shimmying under them. Jerry Peake, behind the wheel, had worried about a blowout because if a tire blew at that speed they were dead men.

Sharp seemed unconcerned about a blowout, but he complained about the lack of air-conditioning and about the warm wind blowing into his face through the open windows. It was as if, certain of his destiny, he were incapable of imagining himself dying now, here, in a rolling car; as if he believed he was entitled to every comfort regardless of the circumstances—like a crown prince. In fact, Peake realized that was probably *exactly* how Sharp looked at it.

Now they were in the San Bernardino Mountains, on State Route 330, a few miles from Running Springs, forced by the twisting road to travel at safer speeds. Sharp was silent, brooding, as he had been ever since they had turned off I-10 at the Redland exit. His anger had subsided. He was calculating now, scheming. Peake could almost hear the clicking, whirring, ticking, and humming of the Machiavellian mechanism that was Anson Sharp's mind.

Finally, as alternating bursts of sunlight and forest shadows slapped the windshield and filled the car with flickering ghostly movement, Sharp said, "Peake, you may be wondering why only the two of us have come here, why I haven't alerted the police or brought more backup of my own."

"Yes, sir. I was wondering," Peake said.

Sharp studied him for a while. "Jerry, are you ambitious?"

Watch your ass, Jerry! Peake thought as soon as Sharp called him by his first name, for Sharp was not a man who would ever be chummy with a subordinate.

He said, "Well, sir, I want to do well, be a good agent, if that's what you mean."

"I mean more than that. Do you hope for promotion, greater authority, the chance to be in charge of investigations?"

Peake suspected that Sharp would be suspicious of a junior agent with too much ambition, so he did not mention his dream of becoming a Defense Security Agency legend. Instead, he said disingenuously, "Well, I've always sort of dreamed of one day working my way up to assistant chief of the California office, where I could have some input on operations. But I've got a lot to learn first."

"That's all?" Sharp asked. "You strike me as a bright, capable young man. I'd expect you to've set your sights on something higher."

"Well, sir, thank you, but there are quite a few bright, capable guys in the agency about my age, and if I could make assistant chief of the district office with *that* competition, I'd be happy."

Sharp was silent for a minute, but Peake knew the conversation was not over. They had to slow to make a sharp rightward curve, and around the bend a raccoon was crossing the road, so Peake eased down on the brake and slowed even further, letting the animal scurry out of the way. At last the deputy director said, "Jerry, I've been watching you closely, and I like what I see. You have what it takes to go far in the company. If you've a desire to go to Washington, I'm convinced you'd be an asset in various posts at headquarters."

Jerry Peake was suddenly scared. Sharp's flattery was excessive, and his implied patronage too generous. The deputy director wanted something from Peake, and in return he wanted Peake to buy something from him, something with a high price tag, maybe a lot higher than Peake was willing to pay. But if he refused to accept the deal Sharp was leading to, he'd make a lifelong enemy of the deputy director.

Sharp said, "This is not public knowledge, Jerry, and I'd ask you to keep it to yourself, but within two years the director is going to retire and recommend that I take his place at the head of the agency."

Peake believed that Sharp was sincere, but he also had the queer feeling that Jarrod McClain, director of the DSA, would be surprised to hear about his own pending retirement.

Sharp continued: "When that happens, I'll be getting rid of many of the men Jarrod has installed in high positions. I don't mean to be disrespectful of the director, but he's too much of the old school, and the men he's promoted are less company agents than bureaucrats. I'll be bringing in younger and more aggressive men— like you."

"Sir, I don't know what to say," Peake told him, which was as true as it was evasive.

As intently as Peake watched the road ahead, Sharp watched Peake. "But the men I'll have around me must be totally reliable, totally committed to my vision for the agency. They must be willing to take any risks, make any sacrifices, give whatever is required to further the cause of the agency and, of course, the welfare of the country. At times, rarely but predictably, they'll be in situations where they must bend the law a little or even break it altogether for the good of country and agency. When you're up against the scum we've got to deal with—terrorists, Soviet agents—you can't always play strictly within the rules, not if you want to win, and our government has created the agency to *win*, Jerry. You're young, but I'm sure you've been around long enough to know what I'm talking about. I'm sure you've bent the law a few times yourself."

"Well, sir, yes, a little, maybe," Peake said carefully, beginning to sweat under the collar of his white shirt.

They passed a sign: LAKE ARROWHEAD—10 MILES.

"All right, Jerry, I'm going to level with you and hope you're the solid, reliable man I think you are. I haven't brought a lot of backup with us because the word's come down from Washington that Mrs. Leben and Benjamin Shadway have to go. And if we're going to take care of them, we need to keep the party small, quiet, discreet."

"Take care of them?"

"They're to be terminated, Jerry. If we find them at the cabin with Eric Leben, we try our best to take Leben prisoner so he can be studied under lab conditions, but Shadway and the woman have to be terminated, with prejudice. That would be difficult if not impossible with a lot of police present; we'd have to delay the terminations until we had Shadway and Mrs. Leben in our sole custody, then stage a fake escape attempt or something. And with too many of our own men present, there'd be a greater chance of the terminations leaking out to the media. In a way, it's sort of a blessing that you and I are getting a chance to handle this alone, because we'll be able to stage it just right before the police and media types are brought in."

Terminate? The agency had no license to terminate civilians. This was mad. But Peake said, "Why terminate Shadway and Mrs. Leben?"

"I'm afraid that's classified, Jerry."

"But the warrant that cites them for suspected espionage and for the police murders in Palm Springs ... well, that's just a cover story, right? Just a way to get the local cops to help us in the search."

"Yes," Sharp said, "but there's a great deal about this case you don't know, Jerry. Information that's tightly held and that I can't share with you, not even though I'm asking you to assist me in what may appear, to you, to be a highly illegal and possibly even immoral undertaking. But as deputy director, I assure you, Shadway and Mrs. Leben *are* a mortal danger to this country, so dangerous that we dare not let them speak with the media or with local authorities."

Bullshit, Peake thought, but he said nothing, just drove onward under felt-green and blue-green trees that arched over the road.

Sharp said, "The decision to terminate is not mine alone. It comes from Washington, Jerry. And not just from Jarrod McClain. Much higher than that, Jerry. Much higher. The very highest."

Bullshit, Peake thought. Do you really expect me to believe the president ordered the cold-blooded killing of two hapless civilians who've gotten in over their heads by no real fault of their own?

Then he realized that, before the insights he had achieved at the hospital in Palm Springs a short while ago, he might well have been naive enough to believe every word of what Sharp was telling him. The new Jerry Peake, enlightened both by the way Sharp had treated Sarah Kiel and by the way he'd reacted to The Stone, was not quite so gullible as the old Jerry Peake, but Sharp had no way of knowing that.

"From the highest authority, Jerry."

Somehow, Peake knew that Anson Sharp had his own reasons for wanting Shadway and Rachael Leben dead, that Washington knew nothing about Sharp's plans. He could not cite the reason for his certainty in this matter, but he had no doubt. Call it a hunch. Legends—and would-be legends—had to trust their hunches.

"They're armed, Jerry—and dangerous, I assure you. Though they aren't guilty of the crimes we've specified on the warrant, they are guilty of other crimes of which I can't speak because you don't have a high enough security clearance. But you can rest assured that we won't exactly be gunning down a pair of upstanding citizens."

Peake was amazed by the tremendously increased sensitivity of his crap detector. Only yesterday, when he had been in awe of every superior agent, he might not have perceived the pure, unadulterated stink of Sharp's smooth line, but now the stench was overwhelming.

"But sir," Peake said, "if they surrender, give up their guns? We still terminate . . . with prejudice?"

"Yes."

"We're judge, jury, and executioner?"

A note of impatience entered Sharp's voice. "Jerry, damn it all, do you think I *like* this? I killed in the war, in Vietnam, when my country told me killing was necessary, and I didn't like that much, not even when it was a certifiable enemy, so I'm not exactly jumping with joy over the prospect of killing Shadway and Mrs. Leben, who on the surface would appear to deserve killing a whole hell of a lot less than the Vietcong did. However, I am privy to top-secret information that's convinced me they're a terrible threat to my country, and I am in receipt of orders *from the highest authority* to terminate them. If you want to know the truth, it makes me a little sick. Nobody likes to face the fact that sometimes an immoral act is the only right thing to be done, that the world is a place of moral grays, not just black and white. I don't like it, but I know my duty."

Oh, you like it well enough, Peake thought. You like it so much that the mere prospect of blowing them away has you so excited you're ready to piss in your pants.

"Jerry? Do you know your duty, too? Can I count on you?"

◊   ◊

In the living room of the cabin, Ben found something that he and Rachael had not noticed before: a pair of binoculars on the far side of the armchair near the window. Putting them to his eyes and looking out the window, he could clearly see the bend in the dirt road where he and Rachael had crouched to study the cabin. Had Eric been in the chair, watching them with the binoculars?

In less than fifteen minutes, Ben finished searching the living room and the three bedrooms. It was at the window of the last of these chambers that he saw the broken brush at the far edge of the lawn, at a point well removed from that place where he and Rachael had come out of the forest on their initial approach to the cabin. That was, he suspected, where Eric had gone into the woods just after spotting them with the binoculars. Increasingly, it appeared that the noises they heard in the forest had been the sounds of Eric stalking them.

Very likely Leben was still out there, watching.

The time had come to go after him.

Benny left the bedroom, crossed the living room. In the kitchen, as he pushed open the rear screen door, he saw the ax out of the corner of his eye: It was leaning against the side of the refrigerator.

Ax?

Turning away from the door, frowning, puzzled, he looked down at the sharp blade. He was certain it had not been there when he and Rachael had entered the cabin through the same door.

Something cold crawled through the hollow of his spine.

After he and Rachael had made the first circuit of the house, they had wound up in the garage, where they had discussed what they must do next. Then they had come back inside and had gone straight through the kitchen to the living room to gather up the Wildcard file. That done, they had returned to the garage, gotten into the Mercedes, and driven down to the gate. Neither time had they passed *this* side of the refrigerator. Had the ax been here then?

The icy entity inside Ben's spine had crept all the way up to the base of his skull.

Ben saw two explanations for the ax—only two. First, perhaps Eric had been in the kitchen while they'd been in the adjacent garage planning their next move. He could have been holding the weapon, waiting for them to return to the house, intending to catch them by surprise. They had been only feet away from Eric without realizing it, only moments away from the quick, biting agony of the ax. Then, for some reason, as Eric listened to them discuss strategy, he had decided against attacking, opted for some other course of action, and had put down the ax.

Or . . .

Or Eric had not been in the cabin then, had only entered later, after he saw them drive away in the Mercedes. He had discarded the ax, thinking they were gone for good, then had fled without it when he heard Benny returning in the Ford.

One or the other.

Which? The need to answer that question seemed urgent and all-important. Which?

If Eric had been here earlier, when Rachael and Ben were in the garage, why hadn't he attacked? What had changed his mind?

The cabin was almost as empty of sound as a vacuum. Listening, Ben tried to determine if the silence was one of expectation, shared by him and one other lurking presence, or a silence of solitude.

Solitude, he soon decided. The dead, hollow, empty stillness that you experienced only when you were utterly and unquestionably alone. Eric was not in the house.

Ben looked through the screen door at the woods that lay beyond the brown lawn. The forest appeared still, as well, and he had the unsettling feeling that Eric was not out there, either, that he would have the woods to himself if he searched for his prey among the trees.

"Eric?" he said softly but aloud, expecting and receiving no answer. "Where the hell have you gone, Eric?"

He lowered the shotgun, no longer bothering to hold it at the ready because he knew in his bones that he would not encounter Eric on this mountain.

More silence.

Heavy, oppressive, profound silence.

He sensed that he was teetering precariously on the edge of a horrible revelation. He had made a mistake. A deadly mistake. One that he could not correct. But what was it? What mistake? Where had he gone wrong? He looked hard at the discarded ax, desperately seeking understanding.

Then his breath caught in his throat.

"My God," he whispered. "Rachael."

◊   ◊

LAKE ARROWHEAD—3 MILES.

Peake got behind a slow-moving camper in a no-passing zone, but Sharp did not seem bothered by the delay because he was busy seeking Peake's agreement to the double murder of Shadway and Mrs. Leben.

"Of course, Jerry, if you have the slightest qualms at all about participating, then you leave it to me. Naturally, I expect you to back me up in a pinch—that's part of your job, after all—but if we can disarm Shadway and the woman without trouble, then I'll handle the terminations myself."

I'll still be an accessory to murder, Peake thought.

But he said, "Well, sir, I don't want to let you down."

"I'm glad to hear you say that, Jerry. I would be disappointed if you didn't have the right stuff. I mean, I was so sure of your commitment and courage when I decided to bring you along on this assignment. And I can't stress strongly enough how grateful your country and the agency will be for your wholehearted cooperation."

You psycho creep, you lying sack of shit, Peake thought.

But he said, "Sir, I don't want to do anything that would be opposed to the best interests of my country—

or that would leave a black mark of any kind on my agency record."

Sharp smiled, reading total capitulation in that statement.

◊   ◊

Ben moved slowly around the kitchen, peering closely at the floor, where traces of broth from the discarded soup and stew cans glistened on the tile. He and Rachael had taken care to step over and around the spills when they had gone through the kitchen, and Ben had not previously noticed any of Eric's footprints in the mess, which was something he was certain he would have seen.

Now he found what had not been there earlier: almost a full footprint in a patch of thick gravy from the Dinty Moore can, and a heelprint in a gob of peanut butter. A man's boots, large ones, by the look of the tread.

Two more prints shone dully on the tile near the refrigerator, where Eric had tracked the gravy and peanut butter when he had gone over there to put down the ax and, of course, to hide. To hide. Jesus. When Ben and Rachael had entered the kitchen from the garage and had stepped into the living room to gather up the scattered pages of the Wildcard file, Eric had been crouched at the far side of the refrigerator, hiding.

Heart racing, Ben turned away from the prints and hurried to the door that connected with the garage.

◊   ◊

LAKE ARROWHEAD.

They had arrived.

The slow-moving camper pulled into the parking lot of a sporting-goods store, getting out of their way, and Peake accelerated.

Having consulted the directions that The Stone had written on a slip of paper, Sharp said, "You're headed the right way. Just follow the state route north around the lake. In four miles or so, look for a branch road on the right, with a cluster of ten mailboxes, one of them with a big red-and-white iron rooster on top of it."

As Peake drove, he saw Sharp lift a black attaché case onto his lap and open it. Inside were two thirty-eight pistols. He put one on the seat between them.

Peake said, "What's that?"

"Your gun for this operation."

"I've got my service revolver."

"It's not hunting season. Can't have a lot of noisy gunfire, Jerry. That might bring neighbors poking around or even alert some sheriff's deputy who just happens to be in the area." Sharp withdrew a silencer from the attaché case and began to screw it onto his own pistol. "You can't use a silencer on a revolver, and we sure don't want anybody interrupting us until it's over and we've had plenty of time to adjust the bodies to fit our scenario."

What the hell am I going to do? Peake wondered as he piloted the sedan north along the lake, looking for a red-and-white iron rooster.

◊   ◊

On another road, State Route 138, Rachael had left Lake Arrowhead behind. She was approaching Silverwood Lake, where the scenery of the high San Bernardinos was even more breathtaking—though she had no eye for scenery in her current state of mind.

From Silverwood, 138 led out of the mountains and almost due west until it connected with Interstate 15. There, she intended to stop for gasoline, then follow 15 north and east, all the way across the desert to Las Vegas. That was a drive of more than two hundred miles over some of the most starkly beautiful and utterly desolate land on the continent, and even under the best of circumstances, it could be a lonely journey.

Benny, she thought, I wish you were here.

She passed a lightning-blasted tree that reached toward the sky with dead black limbs.

The white clouds that had recently appeared were getting thicker. A few of them were not white.

◊   ◊

In the empty garage, Ben saw a two-inch-by-four-inch patch of boot-tread pattern imprinted on the concrete floor in some oily fluid that glistened in the beams of intruding sunlight. He knelt and put his nose to the spot. He was certain that the vague smell of beef gravy was not an imaginary scent.

The tread mark must have been here when he and Rachael returned to the car with the Wildcard pages, but he had not noticed it.

He got up and moved farther into the garage, studying the floor closely, and in only a few seconds he saw a small moist brown glob about half the size of a pea. He touched his finger to it, brought the finger to his nose. Peanut butter. Carried here on the sole or heel of one of Eric Leben's boots while Ben and Rachael were in the living room, busily stuffing the Wildcard file into the garbage bag.

Returning here with Rachael and the file, Ben had been in a hurry because it had seemed to him that the most important thing was to get her out of the cabin and off the mountain before either Eric or the authorities showed up. So he had not looked down and had not noticed the tread mark or the peanut butter. And, of course, he'd seen no reason to search for signs of Eric in places he had searched only minutes earlier. He could not have anticipated this cleverness from a man with devastating brain injuries—a walking dead man who, if he followed at all in the pattern of the lab mice, should be somewhat disoriented, deranged, mentally and emotionally unstable. Therefore, Ben could not blame himself; no, he had done the right thing when he had sent Rachael off in the Mercedes, thinking he was sending her away all by herself, never realizing that she was not alone in the car. How could he have realized? It was the *only* thing he could have done. It was not at all his fault, this unforeseeable development was not his fault, not his fault—but he cursed himself vehemently.

Waiting in the kitchen with the ax, listening to them plan their next moves as they stood in the garage, Eric must have realized that he had a chance of getting Rachael alone, and evidently that prospect appealed to him so much that he was willing to forgo a whack at Ben. He'd hidden beside the refrigerator until they were in the living room, then crept into the garage, took the keys from the ignition, quietly opened the trunk, returned the keys to the ignition, climbed into the trunk, and pulled the lid shut behind himself.

If Rachael had a flat tire and opened the trunk . . .

Or if, on some quiet stretch of desert highway, Eric decided to kick the back seat of the car off its mountings and climb through from the trunk . . .

His heart pounding so hard that it shook him, Ben raced out of the garage toward the rental Ford in front of the cabin.

◊   ◊

Jerry Peake spotted the red-and-white iron rooster mounted atop one mailbox of ten. He turned into a narrow branch road that led up a steep slope past widely separated driveways and past houses mostly hidden in the forest that encroached from both sides.

Sharp had finished screwing silencers on both thirty-eights. Now he took two fully loaded spare magazines from the attaché case, kept one for himself, and put the other beside the pistol that he had provided for Peake. "I'm glad you're with me on this one, Jerry."

Peake had not actually said that he was with Sharp on this one, and in fact he could not see any way he could participate in cold-blooded murder and still live with himself. For sure, his dream of being a legend would be shattered.

On the other hand, if he crossed Sharp, he would destroy his career in the DSA.

"The macadam should turn to gravel," Sharp said, consulting the directions The Stone had given him.

In spite of all his recent insights, in spite of the advantages those insights should have given him, Jerry Peake did not know what to do. He did not see a way out that would leave him with both his self-respect and his career. As he drove up the slope, deeper into the dark of the woods, a panic began to build in him, and for the first time in many hours he felt inadequate.

"Gravel," Anson Sharp noted as they left the pavement.

Suddenly Peake saw that his predicament was even worse than he had realized because Sharp was likely to kill him, too. If Peake tried to stop Sharp from killing Shadway and the Leben woman, then Sharp would simply shoot Peake first and set it up to look as if the two fugitives had done it. That would even give Sharp an excuse to kill Shadway and Mrs. Leben: "They wasted poor damn Peake, so there was nothing else I could do." Sharp might even come out of it a hero. On the other hand, Peake couldn't just step out of the way and let the deputy director cut them down, for that would not satisfy Sharp; if Peake did not participate in the killing with enthusiasm, Sharp would never really trust him and would most likely shoot him *after* Shadway and Mrs. Leben were dead, then claim one of them had done it. Jesus. To Peake (whose mind was working faster than it had ever worked in his life), it looked as if he had only two choices: join in the killing and thereby gain Sharp's total trust—or kill Sharp before Sharp could kill anyone else. But no, wait, that was no solution, either—

"Not much farther," Sharp said, leaning forward in his seat, peering intently through the windshield. "Slow it to a crawl."

—no solution at all, because if he shot Sharp, no one would ever believe that Sharp had intended to kill Shadway and Mrs. Leben—after all, what was the bastard's *motive?*—and Peake would wind up on trial for blowing away his superior. The courts were never ever easy on cop killers, even if the cop killer was another cop, so sure as hell he'd go to prison, where all those seven-foot-tall, no-neck criminal types would just *delight* in raping a former government agent. Which left—what?—one horrible

choice and only one, which was to join in the killing, descend to Sharp's level, forget about being a
legend and settle for being a goddamn Gestapo thug.
This was crazy, being trapped in a situation with no
right answers, only wrong answers, crazy and unfair,
damn it, and Peake felt as if the top of his head were
going to blow off from the strain of seeking a better
answer.

"That's the gate she described," Sharp said. "And it's
open! Park this side of it."

Jerry Peake stopped the car, switched off the engine.

Instead of the expected quietude of the forest, another
sound came through the open windows the moment the
sedan fell silent: a racing engine, another car, echoing
through the trees.

"Someone's coming," Sharp said, grabbing his
silencer-equipped pistol and throwing open his door
just as a blue Ford roared into view on the road above
them, bearing down at high speed.

◗   ◗

While the service-station attendant filled the Mercedes
with Arco unleaded, Rachael got candy and a can of
Coke from the vending machines. She leaned against the
trunk, alternately sipping Coke and munching on a Mr.
Goodbar, hoping that a big dose of refined sugar would
lift her spirits and make the long drive ahead seem less
lonely.

"Going to Vegas?" the attendant asked.

"That's right."

"I 'spected so. I'm good at guessing where folks is
headed. You got that Vegas look. Now listen, first thing
you play when you get there is roulette. Number twenty-
four, 'cause I have this hunch about it, just looking at
you. Okay?"

"Okay. Twenty-four."

He held her Coke while she got the cash from her
wallet to pay him. "You win a fortune, I'll expect half,
of course. But if you lose, it'll be the devil's work, not
mine."

He bent down and looked in her window just as she was about to drive away. "You be careful out there on the desert. It can be mean."

"I know," she said.

She drove onto I-15 and headed north-northeast toward distant Barstow, feeling very much alone.

❖ 26 ❖

A MAN GONE BAD

   Ben swung the Ford around the bend and started to
accelerate but saw the dark green sedan just beyond the
open gate. He braked, and the Ford fishtailed on the dirt
lane. The steering wheel jerked in his hands. But he did
not lose control of the car, kept it out of the ditches on
both sides, and slid to a halt in a roiling cloud of dust
about fifty yards above the gate.
   Below, two men in dark suits had already gotten out
of the sedan. One of them was hanging back, although
the other—and bigger—man was rushing straight up the
hill, closing fast, like a too-eager marathon runner who
had forgotten to change into his running shorts and shoes.
The yellowish dust gave the illusion of marbled solidity as
it whirled through veined patterns of shade and sunshine.
But in spite of the dust and in spite of the thirty yards that
separated Ben from the oncoming man, he could see the
gun in the guy's hand. He could also see the silencer,
which startled him.
   No police or federal agents used silencers. And Eric's
business partners had opened up with a submachine gun
in the heart of Palm Springs, so it was unlikely they would
suddenly turn discreet.

Then, only a fraction of a second after Ben saw the silencer, he got a good look at the grinning face of the oncoming man, and he was simultaneously astonished, confused, and afraid. Anson Sharp. It had been sixteen years since he had seen Anson Sharp in Nam, back in '72. Yet he had no doubt about the man's identity. Time had changed Sharp, but not much. During the spring and summer of '72, Ben had expected the big bastard to shoot him in the back or hire some Saigon hoodlum to do it—Sharp had been capable of anything—but Ben had been very careful, had not given Sharp the slightest opportunity. Now here was Sharp again, as if he'd stepped through a time warp.

What the hell had brought him here now, more than a decade and a half later? Ben had the crazy notion that Sharp had been looking for him all this time, anxious to settle the score, and just happened to track him down now, in the midst of all these other troubles. But of course that was unlikely—impossible—so somehow Sharp must be involved with the Wildcard mess.

Less than twenty yards away, Sharp took a shooter's spreadlegged stance on the road below and opened fire with the pistol. With a *whap* and a wet crackle of gummy safety glass, a slug punched through the windshield one foot to the right of Ben's face.

Throwing the car into reverse, he twisted around in his seat to see the road behind. Steering with one hand, he drove backward up the dirt lane as fast as he dared. He heard another bullet ricochet off the car, and it sounded very close. Then he was around the turn and out of Sharp's sight.

He reversed all the way to the cabin before he stopped. There he shifted the Ford into neutral, left the engine running, and engaged the handbrake, which was the only thing holding the car on the slope. He got out and quickly put the shotgun and the Combat Magnum on the dirt to one side. Leaning back in through the open door, he gripped the release lever for the handbrake and looked down the hill.

Two hundred yards below, the Chevy sedan came around the bend, moving fast, and started up toward him. They slowed when they saw him, but they did not stop, and he dared to wait a couple of seconds longer before he popped the handbrake and stepped back.

Succumbing to gravity, the Ford rolled down the lane, which was so narrow that the Chevy could not pull entirely out of the way. The Ford encountered a small bump, jolted over it, and veered toward one drainage ditch. For a moment Ben thought the car was going to run harmlessly off to the side, but it stuttered over other ruts that turned it back on course.

The driver of the Chevy stopped, began to reverse, but the Ford was picking up a lot of speed and was bearing down too fast to be avoided. The Ford hit another bump and angled somewhat toward the left again, so at the last second the Chevy swung hard to the right in an evasive maneuver, almost dropping into the ditch. Nevertheless, the two vehicles collided with a clang and crunch of metal, though the impact wasn't as direct or as devastating as Ben had hoped. The right front fender of the Ford hit the right front fender of the Chevy, then the Ford slid sideways to the left, as if it might come around a hundred and eighty degrees until it was sitting alongside the Chevy, both of them facing uphill. But when it had made only a quarter turn, the Ford's rear wheels slammed into the ditch, and it halted with a shudder, perpendicular to the road, effectively blocking it.

The stricken Chevy rolled erratically backward for maybe thirty feet, narrowly missing the other ditch, then came to a halt. Both front doors were flung open. Anson Sharp got out of one, and the driver got out of the other, and neither of them appeared to have been hurt, which was pretty much what Ben had expected when the Ford had not hit them head-on.

Ben grabbed the shotgun and the Combat Magnum, turned, and ran around the side of the cabin. He sprinted across the sun-browned backyard to the toothlike granite formations from which he and Rachael had observed the place earlier. He paused for a moment to scan the woods ahead, looking for the quickest cover, then moved off into the trees, toward the same brush-flanked dry wash that he and Rachael had used before.

Behind him, in the distance, Sharp was calling his name.

◊　　　◊

Still caught in the spiderweb of his moral dilemma, Jerry Peake hung back a little from Sharp and watched his boss warily.

The deputy director had lost his head the moment he had seen Shadway in the blue Ford. He had gone charging up the road, shooting from a disadvantageous position, when he had little or no chance of hitting his target. Besides, he could see that the woman was not in the car with Shadway, and if they did kill the man before asking questions, they might not be able to find out where she had gone. It was shockingly sloppy procedure, and Peake was appalled.

Now Sharp stalked the perimeter of the rear yard, breathing like an angry bull, in such a peculiar state of excitement and rage that he seemed oblivious of the danger of presenting such a high profile. At several places along the edge of the woods, he took a step or two into the knee-high weeds, peering down through the serried ranks of trees.

From three sides of the yard, the forested land fell away in a jumble of rocky slopes and narrow defiles that offered countless shadowed hiding places. They had lost Shadway for the moment. That much was obvious to Peake. They should call for backup now, because otherwise their man was going to slip entirely away from them through the wilderness.

But Sharp was determined to kill Shadway. He was not going to listen to reason.

Peake just watched and waited and said nothing.

Looking down into the woods, Sharp shouted: "United States government, Shadway. Defense Security Agency. You hear me? DSA. We want to talk to you, Shadway."

An invocation of authority was not going to work, not now, not after Sharp had started shooting the moment he had seen Ben Shadway.

Peake wondered if the deputy director was undergoing a breakdown, which would explain his behavior with Sarah Kiel and his determination to kill Shadway and his ill-advised, irresponsible, blazing-gun charge up the road a couple of minutes ago.

Stomping along the edge of the woods, wading a few steps into the underbrush again, Sharp called out: "Shadway! Hey, it's me, Shadway. Anson Sharp. Do you remember me, Shadway? Do you remember?"

Jerry Peake took one step back and blinked as if someone had just slapped him in the face: Sharp and Shadway knew each other, for God's sake; *knew* each other, not merely in the abstract as the hunter and the hunted know each other, but personally. And it was clear— from Sharp's taunting manner, crimson face, bulging eyes, and stentorian breathing—that they were bitter adversaries. This was a grudge match of some kind, which eliminated any small doubt Peake might have had about the possibility that anyone above Sharp in the DSA had ordered Shadway and Mrs. Leben killed. Sharp had decided to terminate these fugitives, Sharp and no one else. Peake's instincts had been on the money. But it did not solve anything to know he had been right when he'd smelled deception in Sharp's story. Right or not, he was still left with the choice of either cooperating with the deputy director or pulling a gun on him, and neither course would leave him with both his career and his self-respect intact.

Sharp plunged deeper into the woods, started down a slope into the gloom beneath interlacing boughs of pine and spruce. He looked back, shouted at Peake to join in the chase, took several more steps into the brush, glanced back again and called out more insistently when he saw that Peake had not moved.

Reluctantly Peake followed. Some of the tall grass was so dry and brittle that it prickled through his socks. Burrs and bits of milkweed fluff adhered to his trousers.

When he leaned against the trunk of a tree, his hand came away sticky with resin. Vines tried to trip him up. Brambles snagged his suit. His leather-soled shoes slipped treacherously on the stones, on patches of dry pine needles, on moss, on everything. Climbing over a fallen tree, he put his foot down in a teeming nest of ants; although he hurriedly moved out of their way and wiped them off his shoe, a few scaled his leg, and finally he had to pause, roll up his trousers, and brush the damn things off his badly bitten calf.

"We're not dressed for this," he told Sharp when he caught up with him.

"Quiet," Sharp said, easing under a low-hanging pine branch heavy with thorn-tipped cones.

Peake's feet almost skidded out from under him, and he grabbed desperately at a branch. Barely managing to stay on his feet, he said, "We're going to break our necks."

"Quiet!" Sharp whispered furiously. Over his shoulder, he looked back angrily at Peake. His face was unnerving: eyes wide and wild, skin flushed, nostrils flared, teeth bared, jaw muscles taut, the arteries throbbing in his temples. That savage expression confirmed Peake's suspicion that since spotting Shadway the deputy director had been out of control, driven by an almost maniacal hatred and by sheer blood lust.

They pushed through a narrow gap in a wall of dense and bristly brush decorated with poisonous-looking orange berries. They stumbled into a shallow dry wash—and saw Shadway. The fugitive was fifteen yards farther along the channel, following it down through the forest. He was moving low and fast, carrying a shotgun.

Peake crouched and sidled against the wall of the channel to make as difficult a target of himself as possible.

But Sharp stood in full view, as if he thought he was Superman, bellowed Shadway's name, pulled off several shots with the silencer-equipped pistol. With a silencer, you traded range and accuracy for the quiet you gained, so considering the distance between Sharp and Shadway, virtually every shot was wasted. Either Sharp did not know the effective range of his weapon—which seemed unlikely—or he was so completely a captive of his hatred that he was no longer capable of rational action. The first shot tore bark off a tree at the edge of the dry wash, two yards to Shadway's left, and with a high thin whine, the second slug ricocheted off a boulder. Then Shadway disappeared where the runoff channel curved to the right, but Sharp fired three more shots, in spite of being unable to see his target.

Even the finest silencer quickly deteriorates with use, and the soft *whump* of Sharp's pistol grew noticeably louder with each round he expended. The fifth and final shot sounded like a wooden mallet striking a hard but rubbery surface, not thunderous by any means but loud enough to echo for a moment through the woods.

When the echo faded, Sharp listened intently for a few seconds, then bounded back across the dry wash toward the same gap in the brush through which they had entered the channel. "Come on, Peake. We'll get the bastard now."

Following, Peake said, "But we can't chase him down in these woods. He's better dressed for it than we are."

"We're getting out of the woods, damn it," Sharp said, and indeed they were headed back the way they had come, up toward the yard behind the cabin. "All I wanted to do was make sure we got him moving, so he wouldn't just lie in here and wait us out. He's moving now, by God, and what he'll do is head straight down the mountain toward the lake road. He'll try to steal some transportation down there, and with any luck at all we'll nail the son of a bitch as he's trying to hot-wire some fisherman's car. Now *come on*."

Sharp still had that savage, frenetic, half-sane look, but Peake realized that the deputy director was not, after all, as overwhelmed and as totally controlled by hatred as he had at first appeared. He was in a rage, yes, and not entirely rational, but he had not lost all of his cunning. He was still a dangerous man.

◊   ◊

Ben was running for his own life, but he was in a panic about Rachael as well. She was heading to Nevada in the Mercedes, unaware that Eric was curled up in the trunk. Somehow Ben had to catch up with her, though minute by minute she was getting a greater lead on him, rapidly decreasing his hope of closing the gap. At the very least he had to find a telephone and get hold of Whitney Gavis, his man in Vegas, so when Rachael got there and called Whitney for the motel keys, he would be able to alert her to Eric's presence. Of course, Eric might break out of that trunk or be released from it long before Rachael arrived in Vegas, but that hideous possibility did not even bear contemplation.

Rachael alone on the darkening desert highway . . . a strange noise in the trunk . . . her cold dead husband suddenly kicking his way out of confinement, knocking the back seat off its hinge pins . . . clambering into the passenger compartment . . .

That monstrous picture shook Ben so badly that he dared not dwell on it. If he gave it too much thought, it would start to seem like an inevitable scenario, and he would be unable to go on.

So he resolutely refused to think the unthinkable, and he left the dry wash for a deer trail that offered a relatively easy descent for thirty yards before turning between two fir trees in a direction he did not wish to pursue. Thereafter, progress became considerably more difficult, the ground more treacherous: a wild blackberry patch, wickedly thorned, forced him to detour fifty yards out of his way; a long slope of rotten shale crumbled under his feet, obliging him to descend at an angle to avoid pitching headfirst to the bottom as the surface shifted beneath him; deadfalls of old trees and brush forced him either to go around or to climb over at the risk of a sprained ankle or broken leg. More than once, he wished that he were wearing a pair of woodsman's boots instead of Adidas running shoes, though his jeans and long-sleeve shirt provided some protection from burrs and scratchy branches. Regardless of the difficulty, he forged ahead because he knew that eventually he would reach the lower slopes where the houses below Eric Leben's cabin stood on less wild property; there he would find the going easier. Besides, he had no choice but to go on because he did not know if Anson Sharp was still on his tail.

Anson Sharp.

It was hard to believe.

During his second year in Nam, Ben had been a lieutenant in command of his own recon squad—serving under his platoon captain, Olin Ashborn—planning and executing a series of highly successful forays into enemy-held territory. His sergeant, George Mendoza, had been killed by machine-gun fire during a mission to free four U.S. prisoners of war being held at a temporary camp before transfer to Hanoi. Anson Sharp was the sergeant assigned to replace Mendoza.

From the moment he had met Sharp, Ben had not cared for him. It was just one of those instinctive reactions, for initially he had not seen anything seriously wrong with Sharp. The man was not a great sergeant, not Mendoza's equal, but he was competent, and he did not do either drugs or alcohol, which put him a notch above a lot of other soldiers in that miserable war. Perhaps he relished his authority a bit too much and came down too hard on the men under him. Perhaps his talk about women was colored by a disquieting disrespect for them, but at first it had seemed like the usual boring and only half-serious misogyny that you sometimes heard from a certain number of men in any large group; Ben had seen nothing evil about it—until later. And perhaps Sharp had been too quick to advise against contact when the enemy was sighted and too quick to encourage withdrawal once the enemy was engaged, but at first he could not have been accurately labeled a coward. Yet Ben had been wary of him and had felt somewhat guilty about it because he had no substantial reasons for distrusting his new sergeant.

One of the things he had disliked was Sharp's apparent lack of conviction in all things. Sharp seemed to have no opinions about politics, religion, capital punishment, abortion, or any of the other issues that interested his contemporaries. Sharp also had no strong feelings about the war, either pro or con. He didn't care who won, and he regarded the quasidemocratic South and the totalitarian North as moral equals—if he thought about it at all in moral terms. He had joined the Marines to avoid being drafted into the Army, and he felt none of that leatherneck pride or commitment that made the corps a home to most of the other men in it. He intended to have a military career, though what drew him to the service was not duty or pride but the hope of promotion to a position of real power, early retirement in just twenty years, and a generous pension; he could talk for hours about military pensions and benefits.

He had no special passion for music, art, books, sports, hunting, fishing, or anything else—except for himself. He himself was his own—and only—passion. Though not a hypochondriac, he was certainly obsessed with the state of his health and would talk at length about his digestion, his constipation or lack of it, and the appearance of his morning stool. Another man might simply say, "I have a splitting headache," but Anson Sharp, plagued by a similar condition, would expend two hundred words describing the degree and nature of the agony in excruciating detail and would use a finger to trace the precise line of the pain across his brow. He spent a lot of time combing his hair, always managed to be clean-shaven even under battle conditions, had a narcissistic attraction to mirrors and other reflective surfaces, and made a virtual crusade of obtaining as many creature comforts as a soldier could manage in a war zone.

It was difficult to like a man who liked nothing but himself.

But if Anson Sharp had been neither a good nor an evil man when he had gone to Nam—just bland and self-centered—the war had worked upon the unformed clay of his personality and had gradually sculpted a monster. When Ben became aware of detailed and convincing rumors of Sharp's involvement in the black market, an investigation had turned up proof of an astonishing criminal career. Sharp had been involved in the hijacking of goods in transit to post exchanges and canteens, and he had negotiated the sale of those stolen supplies to buyers in the Saigon underworld. Additional information indicated that, while not a user or direct seller of drugs, Sharp facilitated the commerce in illegal substances between the Vietnamese Mafia and U.S. soldiers. Most shocking of all, Ben's sleuthing led to the discovery that Sharp used some profits from criminal activity to keep a pied-à-terre in Saigon's roughest nightclub district; there, with the assistance of an exceedingly vicious Vietnamese thug who served as a combination houseboy and dungeon master, Sharp maintained an eleven-year-old girl—Mai Van Trang— as a virtual slave, sexually abusing her whenever he had the opportunity, otherwise leaving her to the mercy of the thug.

The inevitable court-martial had not proceeded as predictably as Ben hoped. He wanted to put Sharp away for twenty years in a military prison. But before the case came to trial, potential witnesses began to die or disappear at an alarming pace. Two Army noncoms— pushers who'd agreed to testify against Sharp in return for lenient treatment—were found dead in Saigon alleyways, throats cut. A lieutenant was fragged in his sleep, blown to bits. The weasel-faced houseboy and poor Mai Van Trang disappeared, and Ben was sure that the former was alive somewhere and that the latter was just as certainly dead and buried in an unmarked grave, not a difficult disposal problem in a nation torn by war and undermined by unmarked graves. In custody awaiting trial, Sharp could effectively plead innocence to involvement in this series of convenient deaths and vanishings, though it was surely his influence with the Vietnamese underworld that provided for such favorable developments. By the start of the court-martial, all of the witnesses against Sharp were gone, and the case was essentially reduced to Ben's word—and that of his investigators—against Sharp's smug protestations of innocence. There wasn't sufficient concrete evidence to ensure his imprisonment but far too much circumstantial evidence to get him off the hook entirely. Consequently he was stripped of his sergeant's stripes, demoted to private, and dishonorably discharged.

Even that comparatively light sentence had been a blow to Sharp, whose deep and abiding self-love had not permitted him to entertain the prospect of any punishment whatsoever. His personal comfort and well-being were his central—perhaps only—concern, and he seemed to take it for granted that, as a favored child of the universe, he would always be assured of unrelieved good fortune. Before shipping out of Vietnam in disgrace, Sharp had used all of his remaining contacts to arrange a short surprise visit to Ben, too short to do any harm, but just long enough to convey a threat: "Listen, asshole, when you get stateside again, just remember I'll be there, waiting for you. I'll know when you're coming home, and I'll have a greeting ready for you."

Ben had not taken the threat seriously. For one thing, well before the court-martial, Sharp's hesitancy on the battlefield had grown worse, so bad on some occasions that he had come perilously close to disobeying orders rather than risk his precious skin. If he had not been brought to court for theft, black-marketeering, drug dealing, and statutory rape, he very likely would have been arraigned on charges of desertion or other offenses related to his increasing cowardice. He might talk of stateside vengeance, but he would not have the guts for it. And for another thing, Ben was not worried about what would happen to him when he went home because, by then, for better or worse, he had committed himself to the war until the end of it; and that commitment gave him every reason to believe he would go home in a box, in no condition to give a damn whether or not Anson Sharp was waiting for him.

Now, descending through the shadowy forest and at last reaching the first of the half-cleared properties where houses were tucked in among the trees, Ben wondered how Anson Sharp, stripped of rank and dishonorably discharged, could have been accepted into training as a DSA agent. A man gone bad, like Sharp, usually continued skidding downward once his slide began. By now he should have been on his second or third term in prison for civilian crimes. At best, you could have expected to encounter him as a seedy grifter scratching out a dishonest living, so pathetically small-time that he did not draw the notice of the authorities. Even if he had cleaned up his act, he could not have wiped a dishonorable discharge off his record. And with that discredit, he would have been summarily rejected by *any* law-enforcement agency, especially by an organization with standards as high as those of the Defense Security Agency.

So how the hell did he swing it? Ben wondered.

He chewed on that question as he climbed over a split-rail fence and cautiously skirted a two-story brick and weathered-pine chalet, dashing from tree to tree and bush to bush, staying out of sight as much as possible. If someone looked out a window and saw a man with a shotgun in one hand and a big revolver tucked into the waistband at his back, a call to the county sheriff would be inevitable.

Assuming that Sharp wasn't lying when he had identified himself as a Defense Security Agency operative— and there seemed no point in lying about it—the next thing Ben had to wonder about was how far Sharp had risen in the DSA. After all, it seemed far too coincidental for Sharp to have been assigned, by mere chance, to an investigation involving Ben. More likely Sharp had arranged his assignment when he had read the Leben file and discovered that Ben, his old and perhaps mostly forgotten nemesis, had a relationship with Rachael. He'd seen a long-delayed chance for revenge and had seized it. But surely an ordinary agent could not choose assignments, which meant Sharp must be in a sufficiently high position to set his own work schedule. Worse than that: Sharp was of such formidable rank that he could open fire on Ben without provocation and expect to be able to cover up a murder committed in the plain sight of one of his fellow DSA operatives.

With the threat of Anson Sharp layered on top of all the other threats that he and Rachael faced, Ben began to feel as if he were caught up in a war again. In war, incoming fire usually started up when you least expected it, and from the most unlikely source and direction. Which was exactly what Anson Sharp's appearance was: surprise fire from the most unlikely source.

At the third mountainside house, Ben nearly walked in among four young boys who were engaged in their own stealthy game of war, alerted at the last minute when one of them sprang from cover and opened fire on another with a cap-loaded machine gun. For the first time in his life, Ben experienced a vivid flashback to the war, one of those mental traumas that the media ascribed to every veteran. He fell and rolled behind several low-growing dogwoods, where he lay listening to his pounding heart, stifling a scream for half a minute until the flashback passed.

None of the boys had seen him, and when he set out again, he crawled and belly-crawled from one point of cover to another. From the leafy dogwood to a clump of wild azaleas. From the azaleas to a low limestone formation, where the desiccated corpse of a ground squirrel lay as if in warning. Then over a small hill, through rough weeds that scratched his face, under another split-rail fence.

Five minutes later, almost forty minutes after setting out from the cabin, he bulled his way down a brush-covered slope and into a dry drainage ditch alongside the state route that circled the lake.

Forty minutes, for God's sake.

How far into the lonely desert had Rachael gotten in forty minutes?

Don't think about that. Just keep moving.

He crouched in the tall weeds for a moment, catching his breath, then stood up and looked both ways. No one was in sight. No traffic was coming or going on the two-lane blacktop.

Considering that he had no intention of throwing away either the shotgun or the Combat Magnum, which made him frightfully conspicuous, he was lucky to find himself here on a Tuesday and at this hour. The state route would not have been as lightly used at any other time. During the early morning, the road would be busy with boaters, fishermen, and campers on their way to the lake, and later many of them would be returning. But in the middle of the afternoon—it was 2:55—they were comfortably settled for the day. He was also fortunate it was not a weekend, for then the road would have been heavily traveled regardless of the hour.

Deciding that he would be able to hear oncoming traffic before it drew into sight—and would, therefore, have time to conceal himself—he climbed out of the ditch and headed north on the pavement, hoping to find a car to steal.

◊ 27 ◊

ON THE ROAD AGAIN

By 2:55, Rachael was through the El Cajon Pass, still ten miles south of Victorville and almost forty-five miles from Barstow.

This was the last stretch of the interstate on which indications of civilization could be seen with any frequency. Even here, except for Victorville itself and the isolated houses and businesses strung between it and Hesperia and Apple Valley, there was mostly just a vast emptiness of white sand, striated rock, seared desert scrub, Joshua trees and other cactuses. During the hundred and sixty miles between Barstow and Las Vegas, there would be virtually only two outposts— Calico, the ghost town (with a cluster of attendant restaurants, service stations, and a motel or two), and Baker, which was the gateway to Death Valley National Monument and which was little more than a pit stop that flashed by in a few seconds, gone so quickly that it almost seemed like a mirage. Halloran Springs, Cal Neva, and Stateline were out there, too, but none of them really qualified as a town, and in one case the population was fewer than fifty souls. Here, where the great Mojave Desert began, humankind had tested the

wasteland's dominion, but after Barstow its rule remained
undisputed.

If Rachael had not been so worried about Benny, she
would have enjoyed the endless vistas, the power and
responsiveness of the big Mercedes, and the sense of
escape and release that always buoyed her during a
trip across the Mojave. But she could not stop thinking
about him, and she wished she had not left him alone,
even though he had made a good argument for his plan
and had given her little choice. She considered turning
around and going back, but he might have left by the
time she reached the cabin. She might even drive straight
into the arms of the police if she returned to Arrowhead,
so she kept the Mercedes moving at a steady sixty miles
an hour toward Barstow.

Five miles south of Victorville, she was startled by
a strange hollow thumping that seemed to come from
underneath the car: four or five sharp knocks, then
silence. She swore under her breath at the prospect of
a breakdown. Letting the speed fall to fifty and then
slowly to forty, she listened closely to the Mercedes for
more than half a mile.

The hum of the tires on the pavement.

The purr of the engine.

The soft whisper of the air-conditioning.

No knocking.

When the unsettling sound did not recur, she accelerated to sixty again and continued to listen expectantly,
figuring that the unknown trouble was something that
occurred only at higher speeds. But when, after another
mile, there was no noise, she decided she must have
run over potholes in the pavement. She had not seen
any potholes, and she could not recall that the car had
been jolted simultaneously with the thumping sound,
but she could think of no other explanation. The
Mercedes's suspension system and heavy-duty shocks
were superb, which would have minimized the jolt of a
few minor bumps, and perhaps the strange sound itself
had distracted her from whatever little vibration there
had been.

For a few miles, Rachael remained edgy, not exactly waiting for the entire drive train to drop out with a great crash or for the engine to explode, but half expecting some trouble that would delay her. However, when the car continued to perform with its usual quiet reliability, she relaxed, and her thoughts drifted back to Benny.

◊   ◊

The green Chevy sedan had been damaged in the collision with the blue Ford—bent grille, smashed headlight, crumpled fender—but its function had not been impaired. Peake had driven down the dirt road to gravel to macadam to the state route that circled the lake, with Sharp sitting in the passenger seat, scanning the woods around them, the silencer-equipped pistol in his lap. Sharp had been confident (he said) that Shadway had gone in another direction, well away from the lake, but he had been vigilant nonetheless.

Peake had expected a shotgun blast to hit the side window and take him out at any moment. But he got down to the state route alive.

They had cruised back and forth on the main road until they had found a line of six cars and pickups parked along the berm. Those vehicles probably belonged to anglers who had gone down through the woods to the nearby lake, to a favorite but hard-to-reach fishing hole. Sharp had decided that Shadway would come off the mountain to the south of the cars and, perhaps recalling having passed them on his way to the cabin turnoff, would come north on the state route—maybe using one of the drainage ditches for cover or even staying in the forest parallel to the road—with the intention of hot-wiring new wheels for himself. Peake had slipped the sedan behind the last vehicle in the line of six, a dirty and battered Dodge station wagon, pulling over just a bit farther than the cars in front, so Shadway would not be able to see the Chevy clearly when he walked in from the south.

Now Peake and Sharp slumped low in the front seat, sitting just high enough to see through the windshield and through the windows of the station wagon in front

of them. They were ready to move fast at the first sign
of anyone messing with one of the cars. Or at least Sharp
was ready. Peake was still in a quandary.

The trees rustled in the gusty breeze.

A wicked-looking dragonfly swooped past the windshield on softly thrumming, iridescent wings.

The dashboard clock ticked faintly, and Peake had the
weird but perhaps explicable feeling that they were sitting
on a time bomb.

"He'll show up in the next five minutes," Sharp said.

I hope not, Peake thought.

"We'll waste the bastard, all right," Sharp said.

Not me, Peake thought.

"He'll be expecting us to keep cruising the road,
back and forth, looking for him. He won't expect us
to anticipate him and be lying in wait here. He'll walk
right into us."

God, I hope not, Peake thought. I hope he heads south
instead of north. Or maybe goes over the top of the
mountain and down the other side and never comes
near this road. Or God, please, how about just letting
him cross this road and go down to the lake and walk
across the water and off onto the other shore?

Peake said, "Looks to me as if he's got more firepower
than we do. I mean, I saw a shotgun. That's something
to think about."

"He won't use it on us," Sharp said.

"Why not?"

"Because he's a prissy-assed moralist, that's why. A
sensitive type. Worries about his goddamn soul too much.
His type can justify killing only in the middle of a war—
and only a war he believes in—or in some other situation
where he has absolutely no other choice but to kill in
order to save himself."

"Yeah, well, but if we start shooting at him, he won't
have any choice except to shoot back. Right?"

"You just don't understand him. In a situation like
this—which *isn't* a damn war—if there's any place to
run, if he's not backed into a tight corner, then he'll
always choose to run instead of fighting. It's the morally

superior choice, you see, and he likes to think of himself as a morally superior guy. Out here in these woods, he's got plenty of places to run. So if we shoot and hit him, it's over. But if we miss, he won't shoot back—not that pussy-faced hypocrite—he'll run, and we'll have another chance to track him down and take another whack at him, and he'll keep giving us chances until, sooner or later, he either shakes loose of us for good or we blow him away. Just for God's sake don't ever back him into a corner; always leave him an out. When he's running, we have a chance of shooting him in the back, which is the wisest thing we could do, because the guy was in Marine Recon, and he was good, better than most, the best—I have to give him that much—the best. And he seems to've stayed in condition. So if he had to do it, he could take your head off with his bare hands."

Peake was unable to decide which of these new revelations was most appalling: that, to settle a grudge of Sharp's, they were going to kill not only an innocent man but a man with an unusually complex and faithfully observed moral code; or that they were going to shoot him in the back if they had the chance; or that their target would put his own life at extreme risk rather than casually waste them, though they were prepared to casually waste *him*; or that, if given no other choice, the guy had the ability to utterly destroy them without working up a sweat. Peake had last been to bed yesterday afternoon, almost twenty-two hours ago, and he badly needed sleep, but his grainy eyes were open wide and his mind was alert as he contemplated the wealth of bad news that he had just received.

Sharp leaned forward suddenly, as if he'd spotted Shadway coming up from the south, but it must have been nothing, for he leaned back in his seat again and let out his pent-up breath.

He's as scared as he is angry, Peake thought.

Peake steeled himself to ask a question that would most likely anger or at least irritate Sharp. "You know him, sir?"

"Yeah," Sharp said sourly, unwilling to elaborate.

"From where?"

"Another place."

"When?"

"Way back," Sharp said in a tone of voice that made it clear there were to be no more questions.

From the beginning of this investigation yesterday evening, Peake had been surprised that someone as high as the deputy director would plunge right into the fieldwork, shoulder to shoulder with junior agents, instead of coordinating things from an office. This was an important case. But Peake had been involved in other important cases, and he had never seen any of the agency's titled officers actually getting their hands dirty. Now he understood: Sharp had chosen to wade into the muddy center of this one because he had discovered that his old enemy, Shadway, was involved, and because only in the field would he have an opportunity to kill Shadway and stage the shooting to look legitimate.

"Way back," Sharp said, more to himself this time than to Jerry Peake. "Way back."

◗　　◗

The roomy interior of the Mercedes-Benz trunk was warm because it was heated by the sun. But Eric Leben, curled on his side in the darkness, felt another and greater warmth: the peculiar and almost pleasant fire that burned in his blood, flesh, and bones, a fire that seemed to be melting him down into . . . something other than a man.

The inner and outer heat, the darkness, the motion of the car, and the hypnotic humming of the tires had lulled him into a trancelike state. For a time he had forgotten who he was, where he was, and why he had put himself in this place. Thoughts eddied lazily through his mind, like opalescent films of oil drifting, rippling, intertwining, and forming slow-motion whirlpools on the surface of a lake. At times his thoughts were light and pleasant: the sweet body curves and skin textures of Rachael, Sarah, and other women with whom he had made love; the favorite teddy bear he had slept with as a child; fragments of movies he had seen; lines of favorite songs. But sometimes the mental images grew dark and frightening: Uncle Barry grinning and beckoning; an unknown dead woman in a dumpster; another woman nailed to a wall—naked, dead, staring; the hooded figure of Death looming out of shadows; a deformed face in a mirror; strange and monstrous hands somehow attached to his own wrists . . .

Once, the car stopped, and the cessation of movement caused him to float up from the trance. He quickly reoriented himself, and that icy reptilian rage flooded back into him. He eagerly flexed and unflexed his strong, elongated, sharp-nailed hands in anticipation of choking the life out of Rachael—she who had denied him, she who had rejected him, she who had sent him into the path of death. He almost burst out of the trunk, then heard a man's voice, hesitated. Judging by the bits of inane conversation he was able to overhear, and because of the noise of a gas-pump nozzle being inserted into the fuel tank, Eric realized that Rachael had stopped at a service station, where there were sure to be a few— and perhaps a lot of—people. He had to wait for a better opportunity.

Earlier, back at the cabin, when he had opened the trunk, he had immediately noted that the rear wall was a solid metal panel, making it impossible for him to simply kick the car's rear seat off its pins and clamber through into the passenger compartment. Furthermore, the latch mechanism was unreachable from within the trunk because of a metal cover plate fastened in place by several Phillips-head screws. Fortunately, Rachael and Shadway had been so busy gathering up the copy of the Wildcard file that Eric had been able to snatch a Phillips screwdriver off the tool rack, remove the latch plate, climb into the trunk, and close the lid. Even in the dark, he could find the bared latch, slip the blade of the screwdriver into the mechanism, and pop it open with no difficulty.

If he heard no voices the next time they stopped, he could be out of the trunk in a couple of seconds, fast enough to get his hands on her before she realized what was happening.

At the service station, as he waited silently and patiently within the trunk, he brought his hands to his face and thought he detected additional changes from those he had seen and felt at the cabin. Likewise, when he explored his neck, shoulders, and most of his body, he did not seem to be formed quite as he should have been.

He thought he felt a patch of . . . scales.

Revulsion made his teeth chatter.

He quickly stopped examining himself.

He wanted to know what he was becoming.

Yet he didn't want to know.

He needed to know.

And he couldn't bear knowing.

Dimly he suspected that, having intentionally edited a small portion of his own genetic material, he had created an imbalance in unknown—perhaps unknowable—life chemistries and life forces. The imbalance had not been severe until, upon his death, his altered cells had begun to perform as they had never been meant to perform, healing at a rate and to an extent that was unnatural. That activity—the overwhelming flood of growth hormones and proteins it produced—in some manner released the bonds of genetic stability, threw off the biological governor that ensured a slow, slow, measured pace for evolution. Now he was evolving at an alarming rate. More accurately, perhaps, he was *de*volving, his body seeking to re-create ancient forms still stored within the tens of millions of years of racial experience in his genes. He knew that he was fluctuating mentally between the familiar modern intellect of Eric Leben and the alien consciousnesses of several primitive states of the human race, and he was afraid of devolving both mentally and physically to some bizarre form so remote from human experience that he would cease to exist as Eric Leben, his personality dissolved forever in a prehistoric simian or reptilian consciousness.

She had done this to him—had killed him, thereby triggering the runaway response of his genetically altered cells. He wanted vengeance, wanted it so much he ached, wanted to rip the bitch open and slash her steaming guts, wanted to pull out her eyes and break open her head, wanted to claw off that pretty face, that smug and hateful face, chew off her tongue, then put his mouth down against her spurting arteries and drink, drink . . .

He shuddered again, but this time it was a shudder of primal need, a quiver of inhuman pleasure and excitement.

After the fuel tank was filled, Rachael returned to the highway, and Eric was lulled into his trancelike state once more. This time his thoughts were stranger, dreamier than those that had occupied him previously. He saw himself loping across a mist-shrouded landscape, barely half erect; distant mountains smoked on the horizon, and the sky was a purer and darker blue than he had ever seen it before, yet it was familiar, just as the glossy vegetation was different from anything he had ever encountered as Eric Leben but was nevertheless known to some other being buried deep within him. Then, in his half-dreams, he was no longer even partially erect, not the same creature at all, slithering now on his belly over warm wet earth, drawing himself up onto a spongy rotting log, clawing at it with long-toed feet, shredding the bark and mushy wood to reveal a huge nest of squirming maggots, into which he hungrily thrust his face . . .

Transported by a dark savage thrill, he drummed his feet against the sidewall of the trunk, an action that briefly roused him from the tenebrous images and thoughts that filled his mind. He realized that his drumming feet would alert Rachael, and he stopped after—he hoped—only a few hard kicks.

The car slowed, and he fumbled in the dark for the screwdriver in case he had to pop the latch and get out fast. But then the car accelerated again— Rachael had not understood what she had heard—and he fell back into the ooze of primordial memories and desires.

Now, mentally drifting in some far place, he continued to change physically. The dark trunk was like a womb in which an unimaginable mutant child formed and re-formed and re-formed again. It was both something old

and something new in the world. Its time had passed—
and yet its time was still coming.

◑   ◑

Ben figured they would expect him to remember the
line of parked cars along the western shoulder of the
state route and would be waiting for him to steal one.
Furthermore, they would probably count on him making
his way north on the road itself, using the ditch along
the eastern berm for cover when he heard traffic coming.
Or they might think he'd stay on the eastern slope, on
the highland side of the road, cautiously following the
blacktop north but using the trees and brush for cover.
However, he did not think they would expect him to
cross the road, enter the woods on the western side of
it—the lake side—and then head north under the cover
of *those* trees, eventually coming up on the parked cars
from behind.

He figured correctly. When he had gone north some
distance with the highway on his right and the lake on
his left, he cut up the slope to the state route, cautiously
crawled up the final embankment, peered over the top,
and looked south toward the parked cars. He saw two men
slumped in the front seat of the dark green Chevy sedan.
They were tucked behind a Dodge station wagon, so he
would not have been able to see them if he'd approached
from the south instead of circling behind. They were
looking the other way, watching geometrically framed
slices of the two-lane highway through the windows of
the cars parked in front of theirs.

Easing down from the top of the embankment, Ben
lay on the slope for a minute, flat on his back. His
mattress was composed of old pine needles, withered rye grass, and unfamiliar plants with variegated
caladiumlike leaves that bruised under him and pressed
their cool juice into the cloth of his shirt and jeans.
He was so dirty and stained from the frantic descent
of the mountainside below Eric's cabin that he had no
concern about what additional mess these plants might
make of him.

The Combat Magnum, tucked under his waistline, pressed painfully against the small of his back, so he shifted slightly onto one side to relieve that pressure. Uncomfortable though it was, the Magnum was also reassuring.

As he considered the two men waiting for him on the road above, he was tempted to head farther north until he found untended cars elsewhere. He might be able to steal a vehicle from another place and leave the area before they decided he was gone.

On the other hand, he might walk a mile or two or three without discovering other cars parked beyond the view of their owners.

And it was unlikely that Sharp and his fellow agent would wait here very long. If Ben did not show up soon, they would wonder if they had misjudged him. They would start cruising, perhaps stopping now and then to get out and scan the woods on both sides of the road, and though he was better at these games than they were, he could not be sure that they would not surprise him somewhere along the way.

Right now, he had the advantage of surprise, for he knew where they were, while they had no idea where he was. He decided to make good use of that advantage.

First, he looked around for a smooth fist-sized rock, located one, and tested its weight in his hand. It felt right—substantial. He unbuttoned his shirt part of the way, slipped the rock inside against his belly, and rebuttoned.

With the semiautomatic Remington twelve-gauge in his right hand, he stealthily traversed the embankment, moving south until he felt that he was just below the rear end of their Chevrolet. Edging up to the top of the slope again, he found that he had estimated the distance perfectly: The rear bumper of their sedan was inches from his face.

Sharp's window was open—standard government cars seldom boasted air-conditioning—and Ben knew he had to make the final approach in absolute silence. If Sharp heard anything suspicious and looked out his window, or if he even glanced at his side-view mirror, he would see Ben scurrying behind the Chevy.

A convenient noise, just loud enough to provide cover, would be welcome, and Ben wished the wind would pick up a bit. A good strong gust, shaking the trees, would mask his—

Better yet, the sound of a car engine rose, approaching from the north, from behind the sedan. Ben waited tensely, and a gray Pontiac Firebird appeared from that direction. As the Firebird drew nearer, the sound of rock music grew louder: a couple of kids on a pleasure ride, windows open, cassette player blaring, Bruce Springsteen singing enthusiastically about love and cars and foundry workers. Perfect.

Just as the supercharged Firebird was passing the Chevy, when the noise of engine and Springsteen were loudest, and when Sharp's attention was almost certainly turned in a direction exactly opposite that of his side-view mirror, Ben scrambled quickly over the top of the embankment and crept behind the sedan. He stayed low, under their back window, so he would not be seen in the rearview mirror if the other DSA agent checked the road behind.

As the Firebird and Springsteen faded, Ben duck-walked to the left rear corner of the Chevy, took a deep breath, leaped to his feet, and pumped a round from the shotgun into the back tire on that side. The blast shattered the still mountain air with such power that it scared Ben even though he knew it was coming, and both men inside cried out in alarm. One of them shouted, "Stay down!" The car sagged toward the driver's side. His hands stinging from the recoil of the first shot, Ben fired again, strictly to scare them this time, putting the load low over the top of the car, just low enough so some of the shot skipped across the roof, which to those inside must have sounded like pellets impacting in the interior. Both men were down on the front seat, trying to stay out of the line of fire, a position which also made it impossible for them either to see Ben or to shoot at him.

He fired another round into the dirt shoulder as he ran, paused to blow out the front tire on the driver's side, causing the car to sag further in that direction. He pumped one more load into the same tire solely for dramatic effect—the thunderous crash of the shotgun had unnerved even him, so it must have paralyzed Sharp and the other guy—then glanced at the windshield to be sure both of his adversaries were still below the line of fire. He saw no sign of them, and he put his sixth and final shot through the glass, confident that he would not seriously hurt either man but would scare them badly enough to ensure that they would continue to hug the car seat for another half minute or so.

Even as the shotgun pellets were lodging in the back seat of the Chevy and the safety glass was still falling out into the front seat, Ben took three running steps, dropped flat to the ground, and pulled himself under the Dodge station wagon. When they got the courage to lift their heads, they would figure he had run into the woods on one side of the road or the other, where he was reloading and waiting to make another pass at them when they showed themselves. They would never expect to find him lying prostrate on the ground beneath the very next car in line.

His lungs tried to draw breath in great noisy gulps, but he forced himself to breathe slowly, easily, rhythmically, *quietly*.

He wanted to rub his hands and arms, which stung from firing the shotgun so rapidly and from such unusual positions. But he rubbed nothing, just endured, knowing the stinging and numbness would subside unattended.

After a while, he heard them talking back there, and then he heard a door open.

"Damn it, Peake, come on!" Sharp said.

Footsteps.

Ben turned his head to the right, looking out from beneath the station wagon. He saw Sharp's black Freeman wing tips appear beside the car. Ben owned a pair just like them. These were scuffed, and several spiky burrs clung to the laces.

On the left, no shoes appeared.

"*Now*, Peake!" Sharp said in a hoarse whisper that was as good as a shout.

Another door opened back there, followed by hesitant footsteps, and then shoes came into view at the left side of the station wagon as well. Peake's cheaper black oxfords were in even worse shape than Anson Sharp's shoes: mud was smeared over the tops of them and caked along the soles and heels, and there were twice as many burrs clinging to his laces.

The two men stood on opposite sides of the station wagon, neither of them speaking, just listening and looking.

Ben had the crazy idea that they would hear his pounding heart, for to him it sounded like a timpani.

"Might be ahead, between two of these cars, waiting to sandbag us," Peake whispered.

"He's gone back into the woods," Sharp said in a voice as soft as Peake's, but with scorn. "Probably watching us from cover right now, trying not to laugh."

The smooth, fist-sized rock that Ben had tucked inside his shirt was pressing into his belly, but he did not shift his position for fear the slightest sound would give him away.

Finally Sharp and Peake moved together, paralleling each other, stepping out of sight. They were probably looking warily into all the cars and between them.

But they were not likely to get down on their knees and look underneath, because it was insane of Ben to hide there, flat on his belly, nearly helpless, with no quick way out, where he could be shot as easily as the proverbial fish in the barrel. If his risk paid off, he would throw them off his trail, send them sniffing in the wrong direction, and have a chance to boost one of these cars. However, if they thought he was dumb enough—or clever enough—to hide under the station wagon, he was a dead man.

Ben prayed that the owner of the wagon would not return at this inopportune moment and drive the heap away, leaving him exposed.

Sharp and Peake reached the front of the line of vehicles and, having found no enemy, returned, still walking on opposite sides of the cars. They spoke a bit louder now.

"You said he'd never shoot at us," Peake remarked sourly.

"He didn't."

"He shot at me, sure enough," Peake said, his voice rising.

"He shot at the car."

"What's the difference? We were *in* the car."

They stopped beside the station wagon once more.

Ben looked left and right at their shoes, hoping he would not have to sneeze, cough, or fart.

Sharp said, "He shot at the tires. You see? No point disabling our transportation if he was going to kill us."

"He shot out the windshield," Peake said.

"Yeah, but we were staying down, out of the way, and he knew he wouldn't hit us. I tell you, he's a damn pussy, a prissy moralist, sees himself as the guy in the white hat. He'd shoot at us only if he had no choice, and he'd never shoot at us *first*. We'll have to start the action. Listen, Peake, if he'd wanted to kill us, he could have poked the barrel of that piece through either one of our side windows, could've taken us both out in two seconds flat. Think about it."

They were both silent.

Peake was probably thinking about it.

Ben wondered what Sharp was thinking. He hoped Sharp wasn't thinking about Edgar Allan Poe's *The Purloined Letter*. He did not suppose there was much danger of that because he did not think Sharp had ever in his life read anything other than skin magazines.

"He's down in those woods," Sharp said at last, turning his back on the station wagon, showing Ben his heels. "Down toward the lake. He can see us now, I'll bet. Letting us make the next move."

"We have to get another car," Peake said.

"First you've got to go down in these woods, have a look around, see if you can flush him out."

"Me?"

"You," Sharp said.

"Sir, I'm not really dressed for that sort of thing. My shoes—"

"There's less underbrush here than there was up near Leben's cabin," Sharp said. "You'll manage."

Peake hesitated but finally said, "What'll you be doing while I'm poking around down there?"

"From here," Sharp said, "I can look almost straight down through the trees, into the brush. If you get near him down there on his own level, he might be able to move away from you under the cover of rocks and bushes, without you getting a glimpse of him. But see, from up above here, I'm almost sure to see him moving. And when I do, I'll go straight for the bastard."

Ben heard a peculiar noise, like a lid being unscrewed from a mayonnaise jar. For a moment he could not imagine what it was, then realized Sharp was taking the silencer off his pistol.

Sharp confirmed that suspicion. "Maybe the shotgun still gives him the advantage—"

"Maybe?" Peake said with amazement.

"—but there's two of us, two guns, and without silencers we'll get better range. Go on, Peake. Go down there and smoke him out for me."

Peake seemed on the point of rebellion, but he went.

Ben waited.

A couple of cars passed on the road.

Ben remained very still, watching Anson Sharp's shoes. After a while, Sharp moved one step away from the car, which was as far as he could go in that direction, for one step put him at the very brink of the embankment that sloped down into the woods.

When the next car rumbled along, Ben used the cover of its engine noise to slip out from under the Dodge wagon on the driver's side, where he crouched against the front door, below window level. Now the station wagon was between him and Sharp.

Holding the shotgun in one hand, he opened a few buttons on his shirt. He withdrew the rock that he had found in the forest.

On the other side of the Dodge, Sharp moved.

Ben froze, listened.

Evidently Sharp had only been sidestepping along the edge of the embankment to keep Peake in sight below.

Ben knew he had to act swiftly. If another car came by, he would present quite a spectacle to anyone in it: a guy in filthy clothes, holding a rock in one hand and a shotgun in the other, with a revolver tucked into his waistband. With one tap of the horn, any passing driver could warn Sharp of the wild man at his back.

Rising up from a crouch, Ben looked across the station wagon, directly at the back of Sharp's head. If Sharp turned around now, one of them would have to shoot the other.

Ben waited tensely until he was certain that Sharp's attention was directed down toward the northwest portion of the woods. Then he pitched the round fist-sized rock as hard as he could, across the top of the car, very high, very wide of Sharp's head, so the wind of its passage would not draw the man's attention. He hoped Sharp would not see the rock in flight, hoped it would not hit a tree too soon but would fall far into the forest before impacting.

He was doing a lot of earnest hoping and praying lately.

Without waiting to see what happened, he dropped down beside the car again and heard his missile shredding pine boughs or brush and finally impacting with a resonant thunk.

"Peake!" Sharp called out. "Back of you, back of you. Over that way. Movement over there in those bushes, by the drainage cut."

Ben heard a scrape and clatter and rustle that might have been Anson Sharp bolting off the top of the embankment and down into the forest. Suspecting that it was too good to be true, he rose warily.

Amazingly, Sharp was gone.

With the state route to himself, Ben hurried along the line of parked cars, trying doors. He found an unlocked four-year-old Chevette. It was a hideous bile-yellow heap with clashing green upholstery, but he was in no position to worry about style.

He got in, eased the door shut. He took the .357 Combat Magnum out of his waistband and put it on the seat, where he could reach it in a hurry. Using the stock of the shotgun, he hammered the ignition switch until he broke the key plate off the steering column.

He wondered if the noise carried beyond the car and down through the woods to Sharp and Peake.

Putting the Remington aside, he hastily pulled the ignition wires into view, crossed the two bare ends, and tramped on the accelerator. The engine sputtered, caught, raced.

Although Sharp probably had not heard the hammering, he surely heard the car starting, knew what it meant, and was without a doubt frantically climbing the embankment that he had just descended.

Ben disengaged the handbrake. He threw the Chevette in gear and pulled onto the road. He headed south because that was the way the car was facing, and he had no time to turn it around.

The hard, flat crack of a pistol sounded behind him.

He winced, pulled his head down on his shoulders, glanced in the rearview mirror, and saw Sharp lurching between the sedan and the Dodge station wagon out into the middle of the road, where he could line up a shot better.

"Too late, sucker," Ben said, ramming the accelerator all the way to the floor.

The Chevette coughed as if it were a tubercular, spavined old dray horse being asked to run the Kentucky Derby.

A bullet clipped the rear bumper or maybe a fender, and the high-pitched *skeeeeeen* sounded like the Chevette's startled bleat of pain.

The car stopped coughing and shuddering, surged forward at last, spewing a cloud of blue smoke in its wake.

In the rearview mirror, Anson Sharp dwindled beyond the smoke as if he were a demon tumbling back into Hades. He might have fired again, but Ben did not hear the shot over the scream of the Chevette's straining engine.

The road topped a hill and sloped down, turned to the right, sloped some more, and Ben slowed a bit. He remembered the sheriff's deputy at the sporting-goods store. The lawman might still be in the area. Ben figured he had used up so much good luck in his escape from Sharp that he would be tempting fate if he exceeded the speed limit in his eagerness to get away from Arrowhead. After all, he was in filthy clothes, driving a stolen car, carrying a shotgun and a Combat Magnum, so if he was stopped for speeding, he could hardly expect to be let off with just a fine.

He was on the road again. That was the most important thing now—staying on the road until he had caught up with Rachael either out on I-15 or in Vegas.

Rachael was going to be all right.

He was sure that she would be all right.

White clouds had moved in low under the blue summer sky. They were growing thicker. The edges of some of them were gunmetal-gray.

On both sides of the road, the forest settled deeper into darkness.

◆ 28 ◆

DESERT HEAT

Rachael reached Barstow at 3:40 Tuesday afternoon. She thought about pulling off I-15 to grab a sandwich; she had eaten only an Egg McMuffin this morning and two small candy bars purchased at the Arco service station before she'd gotten on the interstate. Besides, the morning's coffee and the recent can of Coke were working through her; she began to feel a vague need to use a rest room, but she decided to keep moving. Barstow was large enough to have a police department plus a California Highway Patrol substation. Though there was little chance that she would encounter police of any kind and be identified as the infamous traitor of whom the radio reporter had spoken, her hunger and bladder pressure were both too mild to justify the risk.

On the road between Barstow and Vegas, she would be relatively safe, for CHiPs were rarely assigned to that long stretch of lonely highway. In fact, the threat of being stopped for speeding was so small (and so well and widely understood) that the traffic moved at an average speed of seventy to eighty miles an hour.

She pushed the Mercedes up to seventy, and other cars passed her, so she was confident that she would not be pulled over by a patrol car even in the unlikely event that one appeared.

She recalled a roadside rest stop with public facilities about thirty miles ahead. She could wait to use that bathroom. As for food, she was not going to risk malnutrition merely by postponing dinner until she got to Vegas.

Since coming through the El Cajon Pass, she had noticed that the number and size of the clouds were increasing, and the farther she drove into the Mojave, the more somber the heavens became. Previously the clouds had been all white, then white with pale gray beards, and now they were primarily gray with slate-dark streaks. The desert enjoyed little precipitation, but during the summer the skies could sometimes open as if in reenactment of the biblical story of Noah, sending forth a deluge that the barren earth was unprepared to absorb. For the majority of its course, the interstate was built above the runoff line, but here and there road signs warned FLASH FLOODS. She was not particularly worried about being caught in a flood. However, she was concerned that a hard rain would slow her down considerably, and she was eager to make Vegas by six-fifteen or six-thirty.

She would not feel half safe until she was settled in Benny's shuttered motel. And she would not feel entirely safe until he was with her, the drapes drawn, the world locked out.

Minutes after leaving Barstow, she passed the exit for Calico. Once the service stations and motels and restaurants at that turnoff were behind her, virtually unpeopled emptiness lay ahead for the next sixty miles, until the tiny town of Baker. The interstate and the traffic upon it were the only proof that this was an inhabited planet rather than a sterile, lifeless hunk of rock orbiting silently in a sea of cold space.

As this was a Tuesday, traffic was light, more trucks than cars. Thursday through Monday, tens of thousands of people were on their way to and from Vegas. Frequently,

Fridays and Sundays, the traffic was so heavy that it looked startlingly anachronistic in this wasteland—as if all the commuters from a great city had been simultaneously transported back in time to a barren era prior to the Mesozoic epoch. But now, on several occasions, Rachael's was the only vehicle in sight on her side of the divided highway.

She drove over a skeletal landscape of scalped hills and bony plains, where white and gray and umber rock poked up like exposed ribs—like clavicles and scapulae, radii and ulnae, here an ilium, there a femur, here two fibulae, and over there a cluster of tarsals and metatarsals—as if the land were a burial ground for giants of another age, the graves reopened by centuries of wind. The many-armed Joshua trees—like monuments to Shiva—and the other cactuses of the higher desert were not to be found in these lower and hotter regions. The vegetation was limited to some worthless scrub, here and there a patch of dry brown bunchgrass. Mostly the Mojave was sand, rock, alkaline plains, and solidified lava beds. In the distance, to the north, were the Calico mountains, and still farther north the Granite Mountains rose purple and majestic at the horizon, and far to the southeast were the Cady Mountains: all appeared to be stark, hard-edged monoliths of bare and forbidding stone.

At 4:10, she reached the roadside rest area that she had recalled when deciding not to stop in Barstow. She slowed, left the highway, and drove into a large empty parking lot. She stopped in front of a low concrete-block building that housed men's and women's rest rooms. To the right of the rest rooms, a piece of ground was shaded by sturdy metal latticework on four eight-foot metal poles, and under that sun-foiling shelter were three picnic tables. The scrub and bunchgrass were cleared away from the surrounding area, leaving clean bare sand, and blue garbage cans with hinged lids bore polite requests in white block letters—PLEASE DO NOT LITTER.

She got out of the Mercedes, taking only the keys and her purse, leaving the thirty-two and the boxes of ammunition hidden under the driver's seat, where she had put them when she stopped for gas at the entrance to I-15. She closed the door, locked it more from habit than out of necessity.

For a moment she looked up at the sky, which was ninety percent concealed behind steel-gray clouds, as if it were girdling itself in armor. The day remained very hot, between ninety and one hundred degrees, although two hours ago, before the cloud cover settled in, the temperature had surely been ten or even twenty degrees higher.

Out on the interstate, two enormous eighteen-wheelers roared by, heading east, ripping apart the desert's quiet fabric but laying down an even more seamless cloth of silence in their wake.

Walking to the door of the women's rest room, she passed a sign that warned travelers to watch out for rattlesnakes. She supposed they liked to slither in from the desert and stretch full-length on the sunbaked concrete sidewalks.

The rest room was hot, ventilated only by jalousie windows set high in the walls, but at least it had been cleaned recently. The place smelled of pine-scented disinfectant. She also detected the limey odor of concrete that had cooked too long in the fierce desert sun.

◑   ◑

Eric ascended slowly from an intense and vivid dream—or perhaps an unthinkably ancient racial memory—in which he was something other than a man. He was crawling inside a rough-walled burrow, not his own but that of some other creature, creeping downward, following a musky scent with the sure knowledge that succulent eggs of some kind could be found and devoured in the gloom below. A pair of glowing amber eyes in the inkiness was the first indication he had of resistance to his plans. A warm-blooded furry beast, well armed with teeth and claws, rushed at him to protect its subterranean nest, and he was suddenly engaged in a fierce battle that was simultaneously terrifying and exhilarating. Cold, reptilian fury filled him, making him forget the hunger that had driven him in search of eggs. In the darkness, he and his adversary bit, tore, and lashed at each other. Eric hissed— the other squealed and spat—and he inflicted more ruinous wounds than he received, until the burrow filled with the exciting stink of blood and feces and urine . . .

Regaining human consciousness, Eric realized that the car was no longer moving. He had no idea how long it had been stopped—maybe only a minute or two, maybe hours. Struggling against the hypnotic pull of the dreamworld that he'd just left, wanting to retreat back into that thrillingly violent and reassuringly simple place of primal needs and pleasures, he bit down on his lower lip to clear his head and was startled—but, on consideration, not surprised—to find that his teeth seemed sharper than they had been previously. He listened for a moment, but he heard no voices or other noises outside. He wondered if they had gone all the way to Vegas and if the car was now parked in the motel garage where Shadway had told Rachael to put it.

The cold, inhuman rage that he had felt in his dream was in him still, although redirected now from an amber-eyed, burrow-dwelling little mammal to Rachael. His hatred of her was overwhelming, and his need to get his hands on her—tear out her throat, rip open her guts— was building toward a frenzy.

He fumbled in the pitch-black trunk for the screwdriver. Though there was no more light than before, he did not seem quite as blind as he had been. If he was not actually *seeing* the vague dimensions of his Stygian cell, then he was evidently apprehending them with some newfound sixth sense, for he possessed at least a threshold awareness of the position and features of each metal wall. He also perceived the screwdriver lying against the wall near his knees, and when he reached down to test the validity of that perception, he put his hand on the ribbed Lucite handle of the tool.

He popped the trunk lid.

Light speared in. For a moment his eyes stung, then adjusted.

He pushed the lid up.

He was surprised to see the desert.

He climbed out of the trunk.

◊   ◊

Rachael washed her hands at the sink—there was hot water but no soap—and dried them in the blast of the hot-air blower that was provided in lieu of paper towels.

Outside, as the heavy door closed behind her, she saw that no rattlesnakes had taken up residence on the walkway. She went only three steps before she also saw that the trunk of the Mercedes was open wide.

She stopped, frowning. Even if the trunk had not been locked, the lid could not have slipped its catch spontaneously.

Suddenly she knew: *Eric*.

Even as his name flashed through her mind, he appeared at the corner of the building, fifteen feet away from her. He stopped and stared as if the sight of her riveted him as much as she was frozen by the sight of him.

It was Eric, yet it was not Eric.

She stared at him, horrified and disbelieving, not immediately able to comprehend his bizarre metamorphosis, yet sensing that the manipulation of his genetic structure had somehow resulted in these monstrous changes. His body appeared deformed; however, because of his clothing, it was hard to tell precisely what had happened to him. Something was different about his knee joints and his hips. And he was hunchbacked: his red plaid shirt was straining at the seams to contain the mound that had risen from shoulder to shoulder. His arms had grown two or three inches, which would have been obvious even if his knobby and strangely jointed wrists had not thrust out beyond his shirt cuffs. His hands looked fearfully powerful, deformed by human standards, yet with a suggestion of suppleness and dexterity; they were mottled yellow-brown-gray; the hugely knuckled and elongated fingers terminated in claws; in places, his skin seemed to have been supplanted by pebbly scales.

His strangely altered face was the worst thing about him. Every aspect of his once-handsome countenance was changed, yet just enough of his familiar features remained to leave him recognizable. Bones had re-formed, becoming broader and flatter in some places, narrower and more rounded in others, heavier over and under his now-sunken eyes and through his jawline, which was prognathous. A hideous serrated bony ridge had formed up the center of his lumpish brow and—diminishing—trailed across the top of his scalp.

"Rachael," he said.

His voice was low, vibratory, and hoarse. She thought there was a mournful, even melancholy, note in it.

On his thickened forehead were twin conical protrusions that appeared to be half formed, although they seemed destined to be horns the size of Rachael's thumb when they were finished growing. Horns would have made no sense at all to her if the patches of scaly flesh on his hands had not been matched by patches on his face and by wattles of dark leathery skin under his jaw and along his neck in the manner of certain reptiles; a few lizards had horns, and perhaps at some point in mankind's distant beginnings, evolution had included an amphibian stage boasting such protuberances (though that seemed unlikely). Other elements of his tortured visage were human, while still others were apelike. She dimly began to perceive that tens of millions of years of genetic heritage had been unleashed within him, that every stage of evolution was fighting for control of him at the same time; long-abandoned forms—a multitude of possibilities—were struggling to reassert themselves as if his tissues were just so much putty.

"Rachael," he repeated but still did not move. "I want . . . I want . . ." He could not seem to find the words to finish the thought, or perhaps he simply did not know what it was he wanted.

She could not move, either, partly because she was paralyzed by terror but partly because she desperately wanted to understand what had happened to him. If in fact he was being pulled in opposing directions by the many racial memories within his genes, if he was devolving toward a subhuman state while his modern form and intellect strove to retain dominance of its tissues, then it seemed every change in him should be functional, with a purpose obviously connected to one prehuman form or another. However, that did not appear to be the case. In his face, pulsing arteries and gnarled veins and bony excrescences and random concavities seemed to exist without reason, with no connection to any known creature on the evolutionary ladder. The same was true of the hump on his back. She suspected that, in addition to the reassertion of various forms from human biological heritage, *mutated* genes were causing purposeless changes in him or, perhaps, were pushing him toward some alien life-form utterly different from the human species.

"Rachael . . ."

His teeth were sharp.

"Rachael . . ."

The gray-blue irises of his eyes were no longer perfectly round but were tending toward a vertical-oval shape like those in the eyes of serpents. Not all the way there, yet. Apparently still in the middle of metamorphosis. But no longer quite the eyes of a man.

"Rachael . . ."

His nose seemed to have collapsed part of the way into his face, and the nostrils were more exposed than before.

"Rachael . . . please . . . please . . ." He held one monstrous hand toward her in a pathetic gesture, and in his raspy voice was a note of misery and another of self-pity. But there was an even more obvious and more affecting note of love and longing that seemed to surprise him every bit as much as it surprised her. "Please . . . please . . . I want . . ."

"Eric," she said, her own voice almost as strange as his, twisted by fear and weighted down with sadness. "What do you want?"

"I want . . . I . . . I want . . . not to be . . ."

"Yes?"

" . . . afraid . . ."

She did not know what to say.

He took one step toward her.

She immediately backed up.

He took another step, and she saw that he was having a little trouble with his feet, as if they had changed within his boots and were no longer comfortable in that confinement.

Again she retreated to match his advance.

Squeezing the words out as if it were agony to form and expel them, he said, "I want . . . you . . ."

"Eric," she said softly, pityingly.

" . . . you . . . you . . ."

He took three quick, lurching steps; she scampered four backward.

In that voice fit for a man trapped in hell, he said, "Don't . . . don't reject me . . . don't . . . Rachael, don't . . ."

"Eric, I can't help you."

"Don't reject me."

"You're beyond help, Eric."

"Don't reject me . . . *again*."

She had no weapons, just her car keys in one hand and her purse in the other, and she cursed herself for leaving the pistol in the Mercedes. She backed farther away from him.

With a savage cry of rage that made Rachael go cold in the late-June heat, Eric came at her in a head-long rush.

She threw her purse at his head, turned, and sprinted into the desert behind the comfort station. The soft sand shifted under her feet, and a couple of times she almost twisted an ankle, almost fell, and the sparse scrub brush whipped at her legs and almost tripped her, but she did not fall, kept going, ran fast as the wind, tucked her head down, drew her elbows in to her sides, ran, ran for her life.

◗　◗

When confronting Rachael on the walk beside the rest rooms, Eric's initial reaction had surprised him. Seeing her beautiful face, her titian hair, and her lovely body beside which he had once lain, Eric was unexpectedly overcome with remorse for the way he had treated her and was filled with an unbearable sense of loss. The primal fury that had been churning in him abruptly subsided, and more human emotions held sway, though tenuously. Tears stung his eyes. He found it difficult to speak, not only because changes within his throat made speech more difficult, but because he was choked up with regret and grief and a sudden crippling loneliness.

But she rejected him again, confirming the worst suspicions he had of her and jolting him out of his anguish and self-pity. Like a wave of dark water filled with churning ice, the cold rage of an ancient consciousness surged into him again. The desire to stroke her hair, to gently touch her smooth skin, to take her in his arms—that vanished instantly and was replaced by something stronger than desire, by a profound need to kill her. He wanted to gut her, bury his mouth in her still-warm flesh, and finally proclaim his triumph by urinating on her lifeless remains. He threw himself at her, still wanting her but for different purposes.

She ran, and he pursued.

Instinct, racial memory of countless other pursuits— memories not only in the recesses of his mind but flowing in his blood—gave him an advantage. He would bring her down. It was only a matter of time.

She was fast, this arrogant animal, but they were always fast when propelled by terror and the survival instinct, fast for a while but not forever. And in their fear, the hunted were never as cunning as the hunter. Experience assured him of that.

He wished that he had taken off the boots, for they restricted him now. But his own adrenaline level was so high that he had blocked out the pain in his cramped toes and twisted heels; temporarily the discomfort did not register.

The prey fled south, though nothing in that direction offered the smallest hope of sanctuary. Between them and the faraway mountains, the inhospitable land was home only to things that crawled and crept and slithered, things that bit and stung and sometimes ate their own young to stay alive.

◊   ◊

Having run only a few hundred yards, Rachael was already gasping for breath. Her legs felt leaden.

She was not out of shape; it was just that the desert heat was so fierce it virtually had substance, and running through it seemed almost as bad as trying to run through water. For the most part, the heat did not come down from above, because all but a sliver or two of sky was clouded over. Instead, the heat came *up*, rising from the scorching sand that had been baking in the now-hidden sun, storing that terrific heat since dawn, until the clouds had arrived within the last hour or so. The day was still warm, ninety degrees, but the air rising off the sand must have been well over a hundred. She felt as if she were running across a furnace grate.

She glanced back.

Eric was about twenty yards behind her.

She looked straight ahead and pushed harder, really pumping her legs, putting everything she had into it, crashing through that wall of heat, only to find endless other walls beyond it, sucking in hot air until her mouth went dry and her tongue cleaved to the roof of her mouth and her throat began to crack and her lungs began to burn. A natural hedge line of stunted mesquite lay ahead, extending twenty or thirty yards to the left, an equal distance to the right. She didn't want to detour around it, because she was afraid she'd lose ground to Eric. The mesquite was only knee high, and as far as she could see it was neither too solid nor too deep, so she plunged through the hedge, whereupon it proved to be deeper than it looked, fifteen or twenty feet across, and also somewhat more tightly grown than it appeared. The spiky, oily plant poked at her legs and snagged her jeans and delayed her with such tenacity that it seemed to be sentient and in league with Eric. Her racing heart began to pound harder, too hard, slamming against her breastbone. Then she was through the hedge, with hundreds of bits of mesquite bark and leaves stuck on her jeans and socks. She increased her pace again, gushing sweat, blinking salty streams of the same effluvient from her eyes before it could blur her vision too much, tasting it at the corners of her mouth. If she kept pouring at this rate, she'd dehydrate dangerously. Already she saw whirls of color at the periphery of her vision, felt a flutter of nausea in her stomach, and sensed incipient dizziness that might abruptly overwhelm her. But she kept pumping her legs, streaking across the barren land, because there was absolutely nothing else she could do.

She glanced back again.

Eric was closer. Only fifteen yards now.

At great cost, Rachael reached into herself and found a little more strength, a little more energy, an additional measure of stamina.

The ground, no longer treacherously soft, hardened into a wide flat sheet of exposed rock. The rock had been abraded by centuries of blowing sand that had carved hundreds of fine, elaborate whorls in its surface—the fingerprints of the wind. It provided good traction, and she picked up speed again. Soon, however, her reserves would be used up, and dehydration would set in—though she dared not think about that. Positive thinking was the key, so she thought positively for fifty more strides, confident of widening the gap between them.

The third time she glanced back, she loosed an involuntary cry of despair.

Eric was closer. Ten yards.

That was when she tripped and fell.

The rock ended, and sand replaced it. Because she had not been looking down and had not seen that the ground was going to change, she twisted her left ankle. She tried to stay up, tried to keep going, but the twist had destroyed her rhythm. The same ankle twisted again the very next time she put that foot down. She shouted—"No!"—and pitched to the left, rolled across a few weeds, stones, and clumps of crisp bunchgrass.

She wound up at the brink of a big arroyo—a naturally carved water channel through the desert, which was a roaring river during a flash flood but dry most of the time, dry now—about fifty feet across, thirty deep, with walls that sloped but only slightly. Even as she stopped rolling at the arroyo, she took in the situation, saw what she must do, did it: She threw herself over the brink, rolling again, down the steep wall this time, desperately hoping to avoid sharp rocks and rattlesnakes.

It was a bruising descent, and she hit bottom with enough force to knock half the wind out of her. Nevertheless, she scrambled to her feet, looked up, and saw Eric—or the thing that Eric had become—staring down at her from the top of the arroyo wall. He was just thirty or thirty-five feet above her, but thirty vertical feet seemed like more distance than thirty horizontally measured feet; it was as if she were standing in a city street, with him peering down from the roof of a three-story building. Her boldness and his hesitation had gained her some time. If he had rolled down right behind her, he very likely would have caught her by now.

She had won a brief reprieve, and she had to make the best of it. Turning right, she ran along the flat bed of the arroyo, favoring her twisted ankle. She did not know where the arroyo would lead her. But she stayed on the move and kept her eyes open for something that she could easily turn to her advantage, something that would save her, something . . .

Something.

Anything.

What she needed was a miracle.

She expected Eric to plunge down the wall of the gulch when she began to run, but he did not. Instead, he stayed up there at the edge of the channel, running alongside the brink, looking down at her, matching her progress step for step.

She supposed he was looking for an advantage of his own.

◊ 29 ◊

REMADE MEN

With the help of the Riverside County Sheriff's Department, which provided a patrol car and a deputy to drive it, Sharp and Peake were back in Palm Springs by four-thirty Tuesday afternoon. They took two rooms in a motel along Palm Canyon Drive.

Sharp called Nelson Gosser, the agent who had been left on duty at Eric Leben's Palm Springs house. Gosser bought bathrobes for Peake and Sharp, took their clothes to a one-hour laundry and dry cleaner, and brought them two buckets of Kentucky Fried Chicken with coleslaw, fries, and biscuits.

While Sharp and Peake had been at Lake Arrowhead, Rachael Leben's red Mercedes 560 SL had been found, with one flat tire, behind an empty house a few blocks west of Palm Canyon Drive. Also, the blue Ford that Shadway had been driving in Arrowhead was traced to an airport rental agency. Of course, neither car offered any hope of a lead.

Sharp called the airport and spoke with the pilot of the Bell JetRanger. Repairs on the chopper were nearly completed. It would be fully fueled and at the deputy director's disposal within an hour.

Avoiding the french fries because he believed that eating them was begging for heart disease, ignoring the coleslaw because it had turned sour last April, he peeled the crisp and greasy breading off the fried chicken and ate just the meat, no fatty skin, while he made a number of other calls to subordinates at the Geneplan labs in Riverside and at several places in Orange County. More than sixty agents were on the case. He could not speak to all of them, but by contacting six, he got a detailed picture of where the various aspects of the investigation were going.

Where they were going was nowhere.

Lots of questions, no answers. Where was Eric Leben? Where was Ben Shadway? Why hadn't Rachael Leben been with Shadway at the cabin above Lake Arrowhead? Where had she gone? Where was she now? Was there any danger of Shadway and Mrs. Leben putting their hands on the kind of proof that could blow Wildcard wide open?

Considering all of those urgent unanswered questions and the humiliating failure of the expedition to Arrowhead, most other men would have had little appetite, but with gusto Anson Sharp worked through the last of the chicken and biscuits. And considering that he had put his entire future at risk by virtually subordinating the agency's goals in this case to his own personal vendetta against Ben Shadway, it seemed unlikely that he would be able to lie down and enjoy the deep and untroubled sleep of an innocent child. But as he turned back the covers on the queen-sized motel bed, he had no fear of insomnia. He was always able to sleep the moment he rested his head on the pillow, regardless of the circumstances.

He was, after all, a man whose only passion was himself, whose only commitment was to himself, whose only interests lay in those things which impinged directly upon him. Therefore, taking care of himself—eating well, sleeping, staying fit, and maintaining a good appearance—was of paramount importance. Besides, truly believing himself to be superior to other men and favored by fate, he could not be devastated by any setback, for he was certain that bad luck and disappointment were transitory conditions, insignificant anomalies in his otherwise smooth and ever-ascending path to greatness and acclaim.

Before slipping into bed, Sharp sent Nelson Gosser to deliver some instructions to Peake. Then he directed the motel switchboard to hold all calls, pulled the drapes shut, took off his robe, fluffed his pillow, and stretched out on the mattress.

Staring at the dark ceiling, he thought of Shadway and laughed.

Poor Shadway must be wondering how in the hell a man could be court-martialed and dismissed from the Marine Corps with a dishonorable discharge and still become a DSA agent. That was the primary problem with good old pure-hearted Ben: He labored under the misconception that some behavior was moral and some immoral, that good deeds were rewarded and that, ultimately at least, bad deeds brought misery down upon the heads of those committing them.

But Anson Sharp knew there was no justice in the abstract, that you had to fear retribution from others only if you *allowed* them to retaliate, and that altruism and fair play were not automatically rewarded. He knew that morality and immorality were meaningless concepts; your choices in life were not between good and evil but between those things that would benefit you and those things that would not. And only a fool would do anything that did not benefit him or that benefited someone else more than it did him. Looking out for number one was all that counted, and any decision or action that benefited number one was good, regardless of its effect on others.

With his actions limited only by that extremely accommodating philosophy, he'd found it relatively easy to erase the dishonorable discharge from his record. His respect for computers and knowledge of their capabilities were also invaluable.

In Vietnam, Sharp had been able to steal large quantities of PX and USO-canteen supplies with astonishing success because one of his coconspirators—Corporal

Eugene Dalmet—was a computer operator in the division quartermaster's office. With the computer, he and Gene Dalmet were able to accurately track all supplies within the system and choose the perfect place and time at which to intercept them. Later, Dalmet often managed to erase all record of a stolen shipment from the computer; then, through computer-generated orders, he was able to direct unwitting supply clerks to destroy the paper files relating to that shipment—so no one could prove the theft had ever occurred because no one could prove there had been anything to steal in the first place. In this brave new world of bureaucrats and high technology, it seemed that nothing was actually real unless there were paperwork and extensive computer data to support its existence. The scheme worked wonderfully until Ben Shadway started nosing around.

Shipped back to the States in disgrace, Sharp was not despairing because he took with him the uplifting knowledge of the computer's wondrous talent for remaking records and rewriting history. He was sure he could use it to remake his reputation as well.

For six months he took courses in computer programming, worked at it day and night, to the exclusion of all else, until he was not only a first-rate operator-programmer but a hacker of singular skill and cleverness. And those were the days when the word *hacker* had not yet been invented.

He landed a job with Oxelbine Placement, an executive-employment agency large enough to require a computer programmer but small and low-profile enough to be unconcerned about the damage to its image that might result from hiring a man with a dishonorable discharge. All Oxelbine cared about was that he had no civilian criminal record and was highly qualified for his work in a day when the computer craze had not yet hit the public, leaving businesses hungry for people with advanced data-processing skills.

Oxelbine had a direct link with the main computer at TRW, the largest credit-investigating firm. The TRW files were the primary source for local and national credit-rating agencies. Oxelbine paid TRW for information about executives who applied to it for placement and, whenever possible, reduced costs by selling to TRW information that TRW did not process. In addition to his work for Oxelbine, Sharp secretly probed at TRW's computer, seeking the scheme of its data-encoding system. He used a tedious trial-and-error approach that would be familiar to any hacker a decade later, though in those days the process was slower because the computers were slower. In time, however, he learned how to access any credit files at TRW and, more important, discovered how to add and delete data. The process was easier then than it would be later because, in those days, the need for computer security had not yet been widely recognized. Accessing his own dossier, he changed his Marine discharge from dishonorable to honorable, even gave himself a few service commendations, promoted himself from sergeant to lieutenant, and cleaned up a number of less important negatives on his credit record. Then he instructed TRW's computer to order a destruction of the company's existing hard-copy file on him and to replace it with a file based on the new computer record.

No longer stigmatized by the dishonorable-discharge notation on his credit record, he was able to obtain a new job with a major defense contractor, General Dynamics. The position was clerical and did not require security clearance, so he avoided coming under the scrutiny of the FBI and the GAO, both of which had linkages with an array of Defense Department computers that would have turned up his true military history. Using the Hughes computer's links with those same Defense Department systems, Sharp was eventually able to access his service records at the Marine Corps Office of Personnel (MCOP) and change them as he had changed his file at TRW. Thereafter, it was a simple matter to have the MCOP computer issue an order for the destruction of the hard copy of Sharp's Marine records and replacement with the "updated, corrected, and amended" file.

The FBI maintained its own records of men involved in criminal activity while in military service. It used these

for cross-checking suspects in civilian criminal cases—
and when required to conduct an investigation of a federal
job applicant who was in need of a security clearance.
Having compromised the MCOP computer, Sharp directed it to send a copy of his new records to the FBI, along
with a notation that his previous file contained "serious
inaccuracies of libelous nature, requiring its immediate
destruction." In those days, before anyone had heard of
hackers or realized the vulnerability of electronic data,
people believed what computers told them; even bureau
agents, trained to be suspicious, believed computers.
Sharp was relatively confident that his deception would
succeed.

A few months later, he applied to the Defense Security Agency for a position in its training program, and
waited to see if his campaign to remake his reputation
had succeeded. It had. He was accepted into the DSA after
passing an FBI investigation of his past and character.
Thereafter, with the dedication of a true powermonger
and the cunning of a natural-born Machiavelli, he had
begun a lightning-fast ascent through the DSA. It didn't
hurt that he was able to use *that* computer to improve
his agency records by inserting forged commendations
and exceptional service notations from senior officers
after they were killed in the line of duty or died of
natural causes and were unable to dispute those postdated
tributes.

Sharp had decided that he could be tripped up only
by a handful of men who'd served with him in Vietnam
and had participated in his court-martial. Therefore, after
joining the DSA, he began keeping track of those who
posed a threat. Three had been killed in Nam after Sharp
was shipped home. Another died years later in Jimmy
Carter's ill-conceived attempt to rescue the Iranian hos-
tages. Another died of natural causes. Another was shot
in the head in Teaneck, New Jersey, where he'd opened
an all-night convenience store after retiring from the
Marines and where he'd had the misfortune to be
clerking when a Benzedrine-crazed teenager tried to
commit armed robbery. Three other men—each capable

of revealing Sharp's true past and destroying him—returned to Washington after the war and began careers in the State Department, FBI, and Justice Department. With great care—but without delay, lest they discover Sharp at the DSA—he planned the murder of all three and executed those plans without a hitch.

Four others who knew the truth about him were still alive—including Shadway—but none of them was involved in government or seemed likely to discover him at the DSA. Of course, if he ascended to the director's chair, his name would more often appear in the news, and enemies like Shadway might be more likely to hear of him and try to bring him down. He had known for some time that those four must die sooner or later. When Shadway had gotten mixed up in the Leben case, Sharp had seen it as yet one more gift of fate, additional proof that he, Sharp, was destined to rise as far as he wished to go.

Given his own history, Sharp was not surprised to learn of Eric Leben's self-experimentation. Others professed amazement or shock at Leben's arrogance in attempting to break the laws of God and nature by cheating death. But long ago Sharp had learned that absolutes like Truth—or Right or Wrong or Justice or even Death—were no longer so absolute in this high-tech age. Sharp had remade his reputation by the manipulation of electrons, and Eric Leben had attempted to remake himself from a corpse into a living man by the manipulation of his own genes, and to Sharp it was all part of the same wondrous enchiridion to be found in the sorcerer's bag of twentieth-century science.

Now, sprawled comfortably in his motel bed, Anson Sharp enjoyed the sleep of the amoral, which is far deeper and more restful than the sleep of the just, the righteous, and the innocent.

◗   ◗

Sleep eluded Jerry Peake for a while. He had not been to bed in twenty-four hours, had chased up and down mountains, had achieved two or three shattering insights, and had been exhausted when they got back to Palm Springs a short while ago, too exhausted to eat any of the Kentucky Fried Chicken that Nelson Gosser supplied. He was still exhausted, but he could not sleep.

For one thing, Gosser had brought a message from Sharp to the effect that Peake was to catch two hours of shut-eye and be ready for action by seven-thirty this evening, which gave him half an hour to shower and dress after he woke. Two hours! He needed ten. It hardly seemed worth lying down if he had to get up again so soon.

Besides, he was no nearer to finding a way out of the nasty moral dilemma that had plagued him all day: serve as an accomplice to murder at Sharp's demand and thereby further his career at the cost of his soul; or pull a gun on Sharp if that became necessary, thus ruining his career but saving his soul. The latter course seemed an obvious choice, except that if he pulled a gun on Sharp he might be shot and killed. Sharp was cleverer and quicker than Peake, and Peake knew it. He had hoped that his failure to shoot at Shadway would have put him in such disfavor with the deputy director that he would be booted off the case, dropped with disgust, which would not have been good for his career but would sure have solved this dilemma. But Sharp's talons were deep in Jerry Peake now, and Peake reluctantly acknowledged that there would be no easy way out.

What most bothered him was the certainty that a smarter man than he would already have found a way to use this situation to his great advantage. Having never known his mother, having been unloved by his sullen widowed father, having been unpopular in school because he was shy and introverted, Jerry Peake had long dreamed of remaking himself from a loser into a winner, from a nobody into a legend, and now his chance had come to start the climb, but he did not know what to do with the opportunity.

He tossed. He turned.

He planned and schemed and plotted against Sharp and for his own success, but his plans and schemes and plots repeatedly fell apart under the weight of their own poor conception and naïveté. He wanted so badly to be George Smiley or Sherlock Holmes or James Bond, but what he *felt* like was Sylvester the Cat witlessly plotting to capture and eat the infinitely clever Tweetie Bird.

His sleep was filled with nightmares of falling off ladders and off roofs and out of trees while pursuing a macabre canary that had Anson Sharp's face.

◊ ◊

Ben had wasted time ditching the stolen Chevette at Silverwood Lake and finding another car to steal. It would be suicidal to keep the Chevette when Sharp had both its description and license number. He finally located a new black Merkur parked at the head of a long footpath that led down to the lake, out of sight of its fisherman owner. The doors were locked, but the windows were open a crack for ventilation. He had found a wire coat hanger in the trunk of the Chevette—along with an incredible collection of other junk—and he had brought it along for just this sort of emergency. He'd used it to reach through the open top of the window and pop the door latch, then had hot-wired the Merkur and headed for Interstate 15.

He did not reach Barstow until four forty-five. He had already arrived at the unnerving conclusion that he would never be able to catch up to Rachael on the road. Because of Sharp, he had lost too much time. When the lowering sky released a few fat drops of rain, he realized that a storm would slow the Merkur down even more than the reliably maneuverable Mercedes, widening the gap between him and Rachael. So he swung off the lightly trafficked interstate, into the heart of Barstow, and used a telephone booth at a Union 76 station to call Whitney Gavis in Las Vegas.

He would tell Whitney about Eric Leben hiding in the trunk of Rachael's car. With any luck at all, Rachael would not stop on the road, would not give Eric an easy opportunity to go after her, so the dead man would wait in his hidey-hole until they were all the way into Vegas. There, forewarned, Whit Gavis could fire about six rounds of heavy buckshot into the trunk as Eric opened it from the inside, and Rachael, never having realized she was in danger, would be safe.

Everything was going to be all right.

Whit would take care of everything.

Ben finished tapping in the number, using his AT&T card for the call, and in a moment Whit's phone began to ring a hundred and sixty miles away.

The storm was still having trouble breaking. Only a few big drops of rain spattered against the glass walls of the booth.

The phone rang, rang.

The previously milky clouds had curdled into immense gray-black thunderheads, which in turn had formed still-darker, knotted, more malignant masses that were moving at great speed toward the southeast.

The phone rang again and again and again.

Be there, damn it, Ben thought.

But Whit was not there, and wishing him home would not make it true. On the twentieth ring, Ben hung up.

For a moment he stood in the telephone booth, despairing, not sure what to do.

Once, he'd been a man of action, with never a doubt in a crisis. But in reaction to various unsettling discoveries about the world he lived in, he had tried to remake himself into a different man—student of the past, train fancier. He had failed in that remake, a failure that recent events had made eminently clear: He could not just stop being the man he had once been. He accepted that now. And he had thought that he had lost none of his edge. But he realized that all those years of pretending to be someone else had dulled him. His failure to look in the Mercedes's trunk before sending Rachael away, his current despair, his confusion, his sudden lack of direction were all proof that too much pretending had its deadly effect.

Lightning sizzled across the swollen black heavens, but even that scalpel of light did not split open the belly of the storm.

He decided there was nothing to be done but hit the road, head for Vegas, hope for the best, though hope seemed futile now. He could stop in Baker, sixty miles ahead, and try Whit's number again.

Maybe his luck would change.

It *had* to change.

He opened the door of the booth and ran to the stolen Merkur.

Again, lightning blasted the charred sky.

A cannonade of thunder volleyed back and forth between the sky and the waiting earth.

The air stank of ozone.

He got in the car, slammed the door, started the engine, and the storm finally broke, throwing a million tons of water down upon the desert in a sudden deluge.

◊ 30 ◊

RATTLESNAKES

Rachael had been following the bottom of the wide arroyo for what seemed miles but was probably only a few hundred yards. The illusion of greater distance resulted partly from the hot pain in her twisted ankle, which was subsiding but only slowly.

She felt trapped in a maze through which she might forever search futilely for a nonexistent exit. Narrower arroyos branched off the primary channel, all on the right-hand side. She considered pursuing another gulch, but each intersected the main run at an angle, so she couldn't see how far they extended. She was afraid of deviating into one, only to encounter a dead end within a short distance.

To her left, three stories above, Eric hurried along the brink of the arroyo, following her limping progress as if he were the mutant master of the maze in a Dungeons and Dragons game. If and when he started down the arroyo wall, she would have to turn and immediately climb the opposite wall, for she now knew she could not hold her own in a chase. Her only chance of survival was to get above him and find some rocks to hurl down on him as he ascended in her wake. She hoped he would not come after her for a few more minutes, because she needed time for the pain in her ankle to subside further before testing it in a climb.

Distant thunder sounded from Barstow in the west: one long peal, another, then a third that was louder than the first two. The sky over this part of the desert was gray and soot-black, as if heaven had caught fire, burned, and was now composed only of ashes and cold black coals. The burnt-out sky had settled lower as well, until it almost seemed to be a lid that was going to come down all the way and clamp tightly over the top of the arroyo. A warm wind whistled mournfully and moaned up there on the surface of the Mojave, and some gusts found their way down into the channel, flinging bits of sand in Rachael's face. The storm already under way in the west had not reached here yet, but it would arrive soon; a pre-storm scent was heavy in the air, and the atmosphere had the electrically charged feeling that preceded a hard rain.

She rounded a bend and was startled by a pile of dry tumbleweeds that had rolled into the gulch from the desert above. Stirred by a downdraft, they moved rapidly toward her with a scratchy sound, almost a hiss, as if they were living creatures. She tried to sidestep those bristly brown balls, stumbled, and fell full-length into the powdery silt that covered the floor of the channel. Falling, she feared for the ankle she had already hurt, but fortunately she did not twist it again.

Even as she fell, she heard more noise behind her. She thought for a moment that the sound was made by the tumbleweeds still rubbing against one another in their packlike progress along the arroyo, but a harder clatter alerted her to the true source of the noise. When she looked back and up, she saw that Eric had started down the wall of the gulch. He'd been waiting for her to fall or to encounter an obstacle; now that she was down, he was swiftly taking advantage of her bad luck. He had descended a third of the incline and was still on his feet, for the slope was not quite as steep here as it had been where Rachael had rolled over the edge. As he came, he dislodged a minor avalanche of dirt and stones, but the wall of the arroyo did not give way entirely. In a minute he would reach the bottom and then, in ten steps, would be on top of her.

Rachael pushed up from the ground, ran toward the other wall of the gulch, intending to climb it, but realized she had dropped her car keys. She might never find her way back to the car; in fact, she'd probably either be brought down by Eric or get lost in the wasteland, but if by some miracle she did reach the Mercedes, she had to have the keys.

Eric was almost halfway down the slope, descending through dust that rose from the slide he had started.

Frantically looking for the keys, she returned to the place where she'd fallen, and at first she couldn't see them. Then she glimpsed the shiny notched edges poking out of the powdery brown silt, almost entirely buried. Evidently she'd fallen atop the keys, pressing them into the soft soil. She snatched them up.

Eric was more than halfway to the arroyo floor.

He was making a strange sound: a thin, shrill cry—half stage whisper, half shriek.

Thunder pounded the sky, somewhat closer now.

Still pouring sweat, gasping for breath, her mouth seared by the hot air, her lungs aching, she ran to the far wall again, shoving the car keys into a pocket of her jeans. This embankment had the same degree of slope as the one Eric was descending, but Rachael discovered that ascending on her feet was not as easy as coming down that way; the angle worked against her as much as it would have worked for her if she'd been going the other direction. After three or four yards, she had to drop forward against the bank, desperately using hands and knees and feet to hold on and thrust herself steadily up the incline.

Eric's eerie whisper-shriek rose behind her, closer.

She dared not look back.

Fifteen feet farther to the top.

Her progress was maddeningly hampered every foot of the way by the softness of the earth face she was climbing. In spots, it tended to crumble under her as she tried to find or make handholds and footholds. She required all the tenacity of a spider to retain what ground she gained, and she was terrified of suddenly slipping back all the way to the bottom.

The top of the arroyo was less than twelve feet away, so she must be about two stories above the floor of it.

"Rachael," the Eric-thing said behind her in a raspy voice like a rat-tail file drawn across her spine.

Don't look down, don't, don't, for God's sake, don't . . .

Vertical erosion channels cut the wall from top to bottom, some only a few inches wide and a few inches deep, others a foot wide and two feet deep. She had to stay away from those; for, where they scored the slope too close to one another, the earth was especially rotten and most prone to collapse under her.

Fortunately, in some places there were bands of striated stone—pink, gray, brown, with veins of what appeared to be white quartz. These were the outer edges of rock strata that the eroding arroyo had only recently begun to uncover, and they provided firmer footholds.

"Rachael . . ."

She grabbed a foot-deep rock ledge that thrust out of the soft earth above her, intending to pull and kick her way onto it, hoping that it would not break off, but before she could test it, something grabbed at the heel of her right shoe. She couldn't help it: she had to look down this time, and there he was, dear God, the Eric-thing, on the arroyo wall beneath her, holding himself in place with one hand, reaching up with the other, trying to get a grip on her shoe, coming up only an inch short of his goal.

With dismaying agility, more like an animal than a human being, he flung himself upward. His hands and knees and feet refastened to the earthen wall with frightening ease. He reached eagerly for her again. He was now close enough to clutch at her calf instead of at the bottom of her shoe.

But she was not exactly moving like a sloth. She was damn fast, too, responding even as he moved toward her. Reflexes goosed by a flood of adrenaline, she let go of the wall with her knees and feet, holding on only to the rock ledge an arm's length above her head, dangling, recklessly letting the untested stone support her entire weight. As he reached for her, she pulled her legs up, then kicked down with both feet, putting all the power of her thighs into it, striking his grasping hand, smashing his long bony, mutant fingers.

He loosed an inhuman wail.

She kicked again.

Instead of slipping back down the wall, as Rachael had hoped he would, Eric held on to it, surged upward another foot, shrieking in triumph, and took a swipe at her.

At the same moment she kicked out again, smashing one foot into his arm, stomping the other squarely into his face.

She heard her jeans tear, then felt a flash of pain and knew that he had hooked claws through the denim even as her kick had landed.

He bellowed in pain, finally lost his hold on the wall, and hung for an instant by the claws in her jeans. Then the claws snapped, and the cloth tore, and he fell away into the arroyo.

Rachael didn't wait long enough to watch him tumble two stories to the bottom of the gulch, but turned at once to the demanding task of heaving herself onto the narrow stone ledge from which she hung precariously. Pulsations of pain, throbbing in time with her wildly pounding heart, coursed through her arms from wrists to shoulders. Her straining muscles twitched and rebelled at her demands. Clenching her teeth, breathing through her nose so hard that she snorted like a horse, she struggled upward, digging at the wall beneath the ledge with her feet to provide what little thrust she could. By sheer perseverance and determination—spiced with a generous measure of motivating terror—she clambered onto the ledge at last.

Exhausted, suffering several pains, she nevertheless refused to pause. She dragged herself up the last eight feet of the arroyo wall, finding handholds in a few final outcroppings of rock and among the erosion-exposed roots of the mesquite bushes that grew at the brink. Then she was at the edge, over the top, pushing through a break in the mesquite, and she rolled onto the surface of the desert.

Lightning stepped down the sky as if providing a staircase for some descending god, and all around Rachael the low desert scrub threw short-lived, giant shadows.

Thunder followed, hard and flat, and she felt it reverberate in the ground against her back.

She dragged herself back to the brink of the arroyo, praying that she would see the Eric-thing still at the bottom, motionless, dead a second time. Maybe he'd fallen on a rock. There *were* a few rocks on the floor of the gulch. It was possible. Maybe he had landed on one of them and had snapped his spine.

She peered over the edge.

He was more than halfway up the wall again.

Lightning flashed, illuminating his deformed face, silvering his inhuman eyes, plating an electric gleam to his too-sharp teeth.

Leaping up, Rachael started kicking at the loose earth along the brink and at the brush that grew there, knocking it down on top of him. He hung from the quartz-veined ledge, keeping his head under it for protection, so the sandy earth and brush cascaded harmlessly over him. She stopped kicking dirt, looked around for some stones, found a few about the size of eggs, and hurled them down at his hands. When the stones connected with his grotesque fingers, he let go of the ledge and moved entirely under it, clinging to the earth in the shadow of that stone shelf, where she could not hit him.

She could wait for him to reappear, then pelt him again. She could keep him pinned there for hours. But nothing would be gained. It would be a tense, wearying, futile enterprise; when she exhausted the supply of stones within her reach and had only dirt to throw, he would ascend with animal quickness, undeterred by that pathetic bombardment, and he would finish her.

A white-hot celestial cauldron tipped, spilling forth a third molten streak of lightning. It made contact with the earth much closer than the two before it, no more than a quarter of a mile away, accompanied by a simultaneous crash worthy of Armageddon, and with a crackle-sizzle that was the voice of Death speaking in the language of electricity.

Below, unfazed by the lightning, emboldened by the cessation of the attack Rachael had been waging, the Eric-thing put one monstrous hand over the edge of the ledge.

She kicked more dirt down on him, lots of it. He withdrew his hand, taking shelter again, but she continued to stomp away at the rotten brink of the embankment. Suddenly an enormous chunk collapsed directly under her feet, and she nearly fell into the arroyo. As the ground began to shift, she threw herself backward just in time to avoid catastrophe, and landed hard on her buttocks.

With so much dirt pouring down over him, he might hesitate longer before making another attempt to pull himself across the overhanging ledge. His caution might give her an extra couple of minutes' lead time. She got up and sprinted off into the forbidding desert.

The overused muscles in her legs were repeatedly stabbed and split by cleaver-sharp pains. Her right ankle remained tender, and her right calf burned where the claws had cut through her jeans.

Her mouth was drier than ever, and her throat was cracking. Her lungs felt seared by her deep shuddering gasps of hot desert air.

She didn't succumb to the agony, couldn't afford to succumb, just kept on running, not as fast as before but as fast as she could.

Ahead, the land became less flat than it had been, began to roll in a series of low hills and hollows. She ran up a hill and down, up another, on and on, trying to put concealing barriers between herself and Eric before he crawled out of the arroyo. Eventually, deciding to stay in one of the hollows, she turned in a direction that she thought was north; though her sense of direction might have become totally fouled up during the chase, she believed she had to go north first, then east, if she hoped to circle around to the Mercedes, which was now at least a mile away, probably much farther.

Lightning . . . *lightning*.

This time, an incredibly long-lived bolt glimmered between the thunderheads and the ground below for at least ten seconds, racing-jigging south to north, like a gigantic needle trying to sew the storm tight to the land forever.

That flash and the empyrean blast that followed were sufficient to bring the rain, at last. It fell hard, pasting Rachael's hair to her skull, stinging her face. It was cool, blessedly cool. She licked her chapped lips, grateful for the moisture.

Several times she looked back, dreading what she would see, but Eric was never there.

She had lost him. And even if she'd left footprints to mark her flight, the rain would swiftly erase them. In his alien incarnation, he might somehow be able to track her by scent, but the rain would provide cover in that regard as well, scrubbing her odor from the land and air. Even if his strange eyes provided better vision than the human eyes they had once been, he would not be able to see far in this heavy rain and gloom.

You've escaped, she told herself as she hurried north. You're going to be safe.

It was probably true.

But she didn't believe it.

◊   ◊

By the time Ben Shadway drove just a few miles east of Barstow, the rain not only filled the world but became the world. Except for the metronomic thump of the windshield wipers, all sounds were those of water in motion, drowning out everything else: a ceaseless drumming on the roof of the Merkur, the snap-snap-snap of droplets hitting the windshield at high speed, the slosh and hiss of wet pavement under the tires. Beyond the comfortable—though abruptly humid—confines of the car, most of the light had bled out of the bruised and wounded storm-dark sky, and little remained to be seen other than the omnipresent rain falling in millions of slanting gray lines. Sometimes the wind caught sheets of water the same way it might catch sheer curtains at an open window, blowing them across the vast desert floor in graceful, undulant patterns, one filmy layer after another, gray on gray. When the lightning flashed—which it did with unnerving frequency—billions of drops turned bright silver, and for a second or two, it appeared as if snow were falling on the Mojave; at other times, the lightning-transformed rain seemed more like glittery, streaming tinsel.

The downpour grew worse until the windshield wipers could not keep the glass clear. Hunching over the steering wheel, Ben squinted into the storm-lashed day. The highway ahead was barely visible. He had switched on the headlights, which did not improve visibility. But the headlights of oncoming cars—though few—were refracted by the film of water on the windshield, stinging his eyes.

He slowed to forty, then thirty. Finally, because the nearest rest area was over twenty miles ahead, he drove onto the narrow shoulder of the highway, stopped, left the engine running, and switched on the Merkur's emergency blinkers. Since he had failed to reach Whitney Gavis, his concern for Rachael was greater than ever, and he was more acutely aware of his inadequacies by the minute, but it would be foolhardy to do anything other than wait for the blinding storm to subside. He would be of no help whatsoever to Rachael if he lost control of the car on the rain-greased pavement, slid into one of the big eighteen-wheelers that constituted most of the sparse traffic, and got himself killed.

After Ben had waited through ten minutes of the hardest rain he had ever seen, as he was beginning to wonder if it would ever let up, he saw that a sluice of fast-moving dirty water had overflowed the drainage channel beside the road. Because the highway was elevated a few feet above the surrounding land, the water could not flow onto the pavement, but it did spill into the desert beyond. As he looked out the side window of the Merkur, he saw a sinuous dark form gliding smoothly across the surface of the racing yellow-brown torrent, then another similar form, then a third and a fourth. For a moment he stared uncomprehendingly before he realized they were rattlesnakes driven out of the ground when their dens flooded. There must have been several nests of rattlers in the immediate area, for in moments two score of them appeared. They made their way across the steadily widening spate to higher and drier ground, where they came together, coiling among one another—weaving, tangling, knotting their long bodies—forming a writhing and fluxuous mass, as if they were not individual creatures but parts of one entity that had become detached in the deluge and was now struggling to re-form itself.

Lightning flashed.

The squirming rattlers, like the mane of an otherwise buried Medusa, appeared to churn with greater fury as the stroboscopic storm light revealed them in stuttering flashes.

The sight sent a chill to the very marrow of Ben's bones. He looked away from the serpents and stared straight ahead through the rain-washed windshield. Minute by minute, his optimism was fading; his despair was growing; his fear for Rachael had attained such depth and intensity that it began to shake him, physically shake him, and he sat shivering in the stolen car, in the blinding rain, upon the somber storm-hammered desert.

◊　　　◊

The cloudburst erased whatever trail Rachael might have left, which was good, but the storm had drawbacks, too. Though the downpour had reduced the temperature only a few degrees, leaving the day still very warm, and although she was not even slightly chilled, she was nevertheless soaked to the skin. Worse, the drenching rain fell in cataracts which, combined with the midday gloom that the gray-black clouds had imposed upon the land, made it difficult to maintain a good sense of direction; even when she risked ascending from one of the hollows onto a hill, to get a fix on her position, the poor visibility left her less than certain that she was heading back toward the rest area and the Mercedes. Worse still, the lightning shattered through the malignant bellies of the thunderheads and crashed to the ground with such frequency that she figured it was only a matter of time until she was struck by one of those bolts and reduced to a charred and smoking corpse.

But worst of all, the loud and unrelenting noise of the rain—the hissing, chuckling, sizzling, crackling, gurgling, dripping, burbling, and hollow steady drumming—blotted out any warning sounds that the Eric-thing might have made in pursuit of her, so she was in greater danger of being set upon by surprise. She repeatedly looked behind her and glanced worriedly at the tops of the gentle slopes on both sides of the shallow little hollow through which she hurried. She slowed every time she approached a turn in the course of the hollow, fearing that he would be just around the bend, would loom out of the rain, strange eyes radiant in the gloom, and would seize her in his hideous hands.

When, without warning, she encountered him at last, he did not see her. She turned one of those bends that she found so frightening, and Eric was only twenty or thirty feet away, on his knees in the middle of the hollow, preoccupied with some task that Rachael could not at first understand. A wind-carved, flute-holed rock formation projected out from the slope in a wedge-shaped wing, and Rachael quickly took cover behind it before he saw her. She almost turned at once to creep back the way she had come, but his peculiar posture and attitude had intrigued her. Suddenly it seemed important to know what he was doing because, by secretly observing him, she might learn something that would guarantee her escape or even something that would give her an advantage over him in a confrontation at some later time. She eased along the rock formation, peering into several convexities and flute holes, until she found a wind-sculpted bore about three inches in diameter, through which she could see Eric.

He was still kneeling on the wet ground, his broad humped back bowed to the driving rain. He appeared to have . . . changed. He did not look quite the same as when he had confronted her outside the public rest rooms. He was still monstrously deformed, though in a vaguely different way from before. A subtle difference but important . . . What was it, exactly? Peering out of the flute hole in the stone, wind whistling softly through the eight- or ten-inch-deep bore and blowing in her face, Rachael strained her eyes to get a better view of him. The rain and murky light hampered her, but she thought he seemed more apelike. Hulking, slump-shouldered, slightly longer in the arms. Perhaps he was also less reptilian than he had been, yet still with those grotesque, bony, long, and wickedly taloned hands.

Surely any change she perceived must be imaginary, for the very structure of his bones and flesh couldn't have altered noticeably in less than a quarter of an hour. Could it? Then again . . . why not? If his genetic integrity had collapsed thoroughly since he had beaten Sarah Kiel last night—when he'd still been human in appearance—if his face and body and limbs had been altered so drastically in the twelve hours between then and now, the pace of his metamorphosis was obviously so frantic that, indeed, a difference might be noticeable in just a quarter of an hour.

The realization was unnerving.

It was followed by a worse realization: Eric was holding a thick, writhing snake—one hand gripping it near the tail, the other hand behind its head—and he was eating it alive. Rachael saw the snake's jaws unhinged and gaping, fangs like twin slivers of ivory in the flickering storm light, as it struggled unsuccessfully to curl its head back and bite the hand of the man-thing that held it. Eric was tearing at the middle of the serpent with his inhumanly sharp teeth, ripping hunks of meat loose and chewing enthusiastically. Because his jaws were heavier and longer than the jaws of any man, their obscenely eager movement—the crushing and grinding of the snake—could be seen even at this distance.

Shocked and nauseated, Rachael wanted to turn away from the spy-hole in the rock. However, she did not vomit, and she did not turn away, because her nausea and disgust were outweighed by her bafflement and her need to understand Eric.

Considering how much he wanted to get his hands on her, why had he abandoned the chase? Had he forgotten her? Had the snake bitten him and had he, in his savage rage, traded bite for bite?

But he was not merely striking back at the snake: he was *eating* it, eagerly consuming one solid mouthful after another. Once, when Eric looked up at the fulminous heavens, Rachael saw his storm-lit countenance twisted in a frightening expression of inhuman ecstasy. He shuddered with apparent delight as he tore at the serpent. His hunger seemed as urgent and insatiable as it was unspeakable.

Rain slashed, wind moaned, thunder crashed, lightning flashed, and she felt as if she were peering through a chink in the walls of hell, watching a demon devour the souls of the damned. Her heart hammered hard enough to compete with the sound of the rain drumming on the ground. She knew she should run, but she was mesmerized by the pure evil of the sight framed in the flute hole.

She saw a second snake—then a third, fourth, fifth— oozing out of the rain-pooled ground around Eric's knees. He was kneeling at the entrance to a den of the deadly creatures, a nest that was apparently flooding with the runoff from the storm. The rattlers wriggled forth and, finding the man-thing in their midst, immediately struck at his thighs and arms, biting him repeatedly. Though Eric neither cried out nor flinched, Rachael was filled with relief, knowing that he would soon collapse from the effects of the venom.

He threw aside the half-eaten snake and seized another. With no diminishment of his perverse hunger, he sank his pointed, razored teeth into the snake's living flesh and tore loose one dripping gobbet after another. Maybe his altered metabolism was capable of dealing with the potent venom of the rattlers—either breaking it down into an array of harmless chemicals, or repairing tissues as rapidly as the venom damaged them.

Chain lightning flashed back and forth across the malevolent sky, and in that incandescent flare, Eric's long sharp teeth gleamed like shards of a broken mirror. His strangely shining eyes cast back a cold reflection of the celestial fire. His wet, tangled hair streamed with short-lived silvery brightness; the rain glistered like molten silver on his face; and all around him the earth sizzled as if the lightning-lined water was actually melted fat bubbling and crackling in a frying pan.

At last, Rachael broke the mesmeric hold that the scene exerted, turned from the flute hole, and ran back the way she had come. She sought another hollow between other low hills, a different route that would lead her to the roadside comfort station and the Mercedes.

Leaving the hilly area and recrossing the sandy plains, she was frequently the tallest thing in sight, much taller than the desert scrub. Once more, she worried about being struck by lightning. In the eerie stroboscopic light, the bleak and barren land appeared to leap and fall and leap again, as if eons of geological activity were being compressed into a few frantic seconds.

She tried to enter an arroyo, where she might be safe from the lightning. But the deep gulch was two-thirds full of muddy, churning water. Flotillas of whirling tumbleweed boats and bobbing mesquite rafts were borne on the water's rolling back.

She was forced to find a route around the network of flooded arroyos. But in time she came to the rest area where she had first encountered Eric. Her purse was still where she had dropped it, and she picked it up. The Mercedes was also exactly where she'd left it.

A few steps from the car, she halted abruptly, for she saw that the trunk lid, previously open, was now closed. She had the dreadful feeling that Eric—or the thing that had once been Eric—had returned ahead of her, had climbed into the trunk again, and had pulled the lid shut behind him.

Shaking, indecisive, afraid, Rachael stood in the drenching rain, reluctant to go closer to the car. The

parking lot, lacking adequate drainage, was being transformed into a shallow lake. She stood in water that came
over the tops of her running shoes.

The thirty-two pistol was under the driver's seat. If
she could reach it before Eric threw open the trunk lid
and came out . . .

Behind her, the staccato plop-plop-plop of water dripping off the picnic-table cover sounded like scurrying rats.
More water sheeted off the comfort-station roof, splashing on the sidewalk. All around, the falling rain slashed
into the pools and puddles with a crackling-cellophane
sound that seemed to grow louder by the second.

She took a step toward the car, another, halted again.

He might not be in the trunk but inside the car itself.
He might have closed the trunk and slipped into the back
seat or even into the front, where he could be lying now—
silent, still, unseen—waiting for her to open the door.
Waiting to sink his teeth into her the way he'd sunk
them into the snakes . . .

Rain streamed off the roof of the Mercedes, rippled
down the windows, blurring her view of the car's shadowy interior.

Scared to approach the car but equally afraid of turning
back, Rachael at last took another step forward.

Lightning flashed. Looming large and ominous in the
stuttering light, the black Mercedes suddenly reminded
her of a hearse.

Out on the highway, a large truck passed, engine
roaring, big tires making a slushy sound on the wet
pavement.

Rachael reached the Mercedes, jerked open the driver's
door, saw no one inside. She fumbled under the seat for
the pistol. Found it. While she still had the courage to
act, she went around to the back of the car, hesitated only
a second, pushed on the latch button, and lifted the trunk
lid, prepared to empty the clip of the thirty-two into the
Eric-thing if it was crouching there.

The trunk was empty. The carpet was soaked, and
a gray puddle of rain spread over the center of the
compartment, so she figured it had remained open to

the elements until an especially strong gust of wind had blown it shut.

She slammed the lid, used her keys to lock it, returned to the driver's door, and got in behind the wheel. She put the pistol on the passenger's seat, where she could grab it quickly.

The car started without hesitation. The windshield wipers flung the rain off the glass.

Outside, the desert beyond the concrete-block comfort station was rendered entirely in shades of slate: grays, blacks, browns, and rust. In that dreary sandscape, the only movement was the driving rain and the windblown tumbleweed.

Eric had not followed her.

Maybe the rattlesnakes had killed him, after all. Surely he could not have survived so many bites from so many snakes. Perhaps his genetically altered body, though capable of repairing massive tissue damage, was not able to counteract the toxic effects of such potent venom.

She drove out of the rest area, back onto the highway, heading east toward Las Vegas, grateful to be alive. The rain was falling too hard to permit safe travel above forty or fifty miles an hour, so she stayed in the extreme right lane, letting the more daring motorists pass her. Mile by mile she tried to convince herself that the worst was past—but she remained unconvinced.

◐   ◐

Ben put the Merkur in gear and pulled onto the highway again.

The storm was moving rapidly eastward, toward Las Vegas. The rolling thunder was more distant than before, a deep rumble rather than a bone-jarring crash. The lightning, which had been striking perilously close on all sides, now flickered farther away, near the eastern horizon. Rain was still falling hard, but it no longer came down in blinding sheets, and driving was possible again.

The dashboard clock confirmed the time on Ben's watch: 5:15. Yet the summer day was darker than it should have been at that hour. The storm-blackened sky had brought an early dusk, and ahead the somber land was fading steadily in the embrace of a false twilight.

At his current speed, he would not reach Las Vegas until about eight-thirty tonight, probably two or three hours after Rachael had gotten there. He would have to stop in Baker, the only outpost in this part of the Mojave, and try to reach Whitney Gavis again. But he had the feeling he was not going to get hold of Whit. A feeling that maybe his and Rachael's luck had run out.

◊ 31 ◊

FEEDING FRENZY

Eric remembered the rattlesnakes only vaguely. Their fangs had left puncture wounds in his hands, arms, and thighs, but those small holes had already healed, and the rain had washed the bloodstains from his sodden clothes. His mutating flesh burned with that peculiar painless fire of ongoing change, which completely masked the lesser sting of venom. Sometimes his knees grew weak, or his stomach churned with nausea, or his vision blurred, or a spell of dizziness seized him, but those symptoms of poisoning grew less noticeable minute by minute. As he moved across the storm-darkened desert, images of the serpents rose in his memory—writhing forms curling like smoke around him, whispering in a language that he could almost understand—but he had difficulty believing that they had been real. A few times, he recalled biting, chewing, and swallowing mouthfuls of rattler meat, gripped by a feeding frenzy. A part of him responded to those bloody memories with excitement and satisfaction. But another part of him—the part that was still Eric Leben—was disgusted and repelled, and he repressed those grim recollections, aware that he would lose his already tenuous grip on sanity if he dwelt on them.

He moved rapidly toward an unknown place, propelled by instinct. Mostly he ran fully erect, more or less like a man, but sometimes he loped and shambled, with his shoulders hunched forward and his body bent in an apelike posture. Occasionally he was overcome with the urge to drop forward on all fours and scuttle across the wet sand on his belly; however, that queer compulsion frightened him, and he successfully resisted it.

Shadowfires burned here and there upon the desert floor, but he was not drawn toward them as he had been before. They were not as mysterious and intriguing as they had been previously, for he now suspected that they were gateways to hell. Previously, when he had seen those phantom flames, he had also seen his long-dead uncle Barry, which probably meant that Uncle Barry had come out of the fire. Eric was sure that Barry Hampstead resided in hell, so he figured the doors were portals to damnation. When Eric had died in Santa Ana yesterday, he had become Satan's property, doomed to spend eternity with Barry Hampstead, but at the penultimate moment he had thrown off the claims of the grave and had rescued his own soul from the pit. Now Satan was opening these doors around him, in hopes he would be impelled by curiosity to investigate one gate or another and, on stepping through, would deliver himself to the sulfurous cell reserved for him. His parents had warned him that he was in danger of going to hell, that his surrender to his uncle's desires—and, later, the murder of his tormentor—had damned his soul. Now he knew they were right. Hell was close. He dared not look into its flames, where something beckoned and smiled.

He raced on through the desert scrub. The storm, like clashing armies, blasted the day with bright bursts and rolling cannonades.

His unknown destination proved to be the comfort station at the roadside rest area where he had first confronted Rachael. Activated by solenoids that had misinterpreted the storm as nightfall, banks of fluorescent lights had blinked on at the front of the structure and over the doors on each side. In the parking lot, a few mercury-vapor arc lamps cast a bluish light on the puddled pavement.

When he saw the squat concrete-block building in the rain-swept murk ahead, Eric's muddy thoughts cleared, and suddenly he remembered everything Rachael had done to him. His encounter with the garbage truck on Main Street was *her* doing. And because the violent shock of death was what had triggered his malignant growth, he blamed his monstrous mutation on her as well. He'd almost gotten his hands on her, had almost torn her to pieces, but she'd slipped away from him when he'd been overcome by hunger, by a desperate need to provide fuel for his out-of-control metabolism. Now, thinking of her, he felt that cold reptilian rage well up in him again, and he loosed a thin bleat of fury that was lost in the noise of the storm.

Rounding the side of the building, he sensed someone near. A thrill coursed through him. He dropped to all fours and crouched against the block wall, in a pool of shadow just beyond the reach of the nearest fluorescent light.

He listened—head cocked, breath held. A jalousie window was open above his head, high in the men's-room wall. Movement inside. A man coughed. Then Eric heard soft, sweet whistling: "All Alone in the Moonlight," from the musical *Cats*. The scrape and click of footsteps on concrete. The door opened outward onto the walk, eight or ten feet from where Eric crouched, and a man appeared.

The guy was in his late twenties, solidly built, rugged-looking, wearing boots, jeans, cowboy shirt, and a tan Stetson. He stood for a moment beneath the sheltering overhang, looking out at the falling rain. Suddenly he became aware of Eric, turned, stopped whistling, and stared in disbelief and horror.

As the other turned toward him, Eric moved so fast he seemed to be a leaping reflection of the lightning that flashed along the eastern horizon. Tall and well-muscled, the cowboy would have been a dangerous adversary in a fight with an ordinary man, but Eric Leben was no longer an ordinary man—or even quite a man at all. And the cowboy's shock at his attacker's appearance was a grave disadvantage, for it paralyzed him. Eric slammed into his prey and drove all five talons of his right hand into the man's belly, very deep. At the same time, seizing his prey's throat with his other hand, he destroyed the windpipe, ripping out the voice box and vocal cords, ensuring instant silence. Blood spurted from severed carotid arteries. Death glazed the cowboy's eyes even before Eric tore open his belly. Steaming guts cascaded onto rain-wet concrete, and the dead man collapsed into his own hot entrails.

Feeling wild and free and powerful, Eric settled down atop the warm corpse. Strangely, killing no longer repulsed or frightened him. He was becoming a primal beast who took a savage delight in slaughter. However, even the part of him that remained civilized— the Eric Leben part—was undeniably exhilarated by the violence, as well as by the enormous power and catlike quickness of his mutant body. He knew he should have been shocked, nauseated, but he was not. All his life, he had needed to dominate others, to crush his adversaries, and now the need found expression in its purest form: cruel, merciless, violent murder.

He was also, for the first time, able to remember clearly the murder of the two young women whose car he had stolen in Santa Ana on Monday evening. He felt no burdensome responsibility for their deaths, no rush of guilt, only a sweet dark satisfaction and a fierce sort of glee. Indeed, the memory of their spilled blood, the memory of the naked woman whom he had nailed to the wall, only contributed to his exhilaration over the murder of the cowboy, and his heart pounded out a rhythm of icy joy.

Then, for a while, lowering himself onto the corpse by the men's-room door, he lost all conscious awareness of himself as a creature of intellect, as a creature with a past and a future. He descended into a dreamy state where the only sensations were the smell and taste of blood. The drumming and gurgling of rain continued to reach him, too, but it seemed now that it was an internal rather than external noise, perhaps the sound of change surging through his arteries, veins, bones, and tissues.

He was jolted out of his trance by a scream. He looked up from the ruined throat of his prey, where he'd buried his muzzle. A woman was standing at the corner of the building, wide-eyed, one arm held defensively across her breasts. Judging by her boots, jeans, and cowboy shirt, she was with the man whom Eric had just killed.

Eric realized that he had been feeding on his prey, and he was neither startled nor appalled by that realization. A lion would not be surprised or dismayed by its own savagery. His racing metabolism generated hunger unlike any he had ever known, and he needed rich nutrients to allay those pangs. In the meat of his prey, he found the food he required, just as the lion found what it needed in the flesh of the gazelle.

The woman tried to scream again but could not make a sound.

Eric rose from the corpse. He licked his blood-slicked lips.

The woman ran into the wind-driven rain. Her Stetson flew off, and her yellow hair streamed behind her, the only brightness in the storm-blackened day.

Eric pursued her. He found indescribable pleasure in the feel of his feet pounding on the hard concrete, then on waterlogged sand. He splashed across the flooded macadam parking lot, gaining on her by the second.

She was heading toward a dull red pickup truck. She glanced back and saw him drawing nearer. She must have realized that she would not reach the pickup in time to start it and drive away, so she turned toward the interstate, evidently hoping to get help from the driver of one of the infrequently passing cars or trucks.

The chase was short. He dragged her down before she had reached the end of the parking lot. They rolled through dirty ankle-deep water. She flailed at him, tried to claw him. He sank his razored talons into her arms, nailing them to her sides, and she let out a terrible cry of pain. Thrashing furiously, they rolled one last time, and then he had her pinned down in the storm runoff, which was chilly in spite of the warm air around them.

For a moment he was surprised to find his blood subsiding, replaced by carnal hunger as he looked down upon the helpless woman. But he merely surrendered to that need as he had surrendered to the urgent need for blood. Beneath him, sensing his intent, the woman tried desperately to throw him off. Her screams of pain gave way to shrill cries of pure terror. Ripping his talons loose of her arm, he shredded her blouse and put his dark, gnarled, inhuman hand upon her bare breasts.

Her screams faded. She stared up at him emptily—voiceless, shaking, paralyzed by dread.

A moment later, having torn open her pants, he eagerly withdrew his manhood from his own jeans. Even in his frenzy to couple with her, he realized that the erect organ in his hand was not human; it was large, strange, hideous. When the woman's gaze fell upon that monstrous staff, she began to weep and whimper. She must have thought that the gates of hell had opened and that demons had come forth. Her horror and abject fear further inflamed his lust.

The storm, which had been subsiding, grew worse for a while, as if in malevolent accompaniment to the brutal act that he was about to perpetrate.

He mounted her.

The rain beat upon them.

The water sloshed around them.

A few minutes later, he killed her.

Lightning blazed, and as its reflection played across the flooded parking lot, the woman's spreading blood looked like opalescent films of oil on the water.

After he had killed her, he fed.

When he was satiated, his primal urges grew less demanding, and the part of him that possessed an intellect gained dominance over the savage beast. Slowly he became aware of the danger of being seen. There was little traffic on the interstate, but if one of the passing cars or trucks pulled into the rest area, he would be spotted. He hurriedly dragged the dead woman across the macadam, around the side of the comfort station, and into the mesquite behind the building. He disposed of the dead man there as well.

He found the keys in the ignition of the pickup. The engine turned over on the second try.

He had taken the cowboy's hat. Now he jammed it on his head, pulling the brim down, hoping it would disguise the strangeness of his face. The pickup's fuel gauge indicated a full tank, so he would not need to stop between here and Vegas. But if a passing motorist glanced over and saw his face . . . He must remain alert, drive well, attract no notice—always resisting the retrograde evolution that steadily pulled him into the mindless perspective of the beast. He had to remember to avert his grotesque face from the vehicles he passed and from those that passed him. If he took those precautions, then the hat—in conjunction with the early dusk brought by the storm—might provide sufficient cover.

He looked into the rearview mirror and saw a pair of unmatched eyes. One was a luminous pale green with a vertical slit-shaped orange iris that gleamed like a hot coal. The other was larger, dark, and . . . multifaceted.

That jarred him as nothing had for a while, and he looked quickly away from the mirror. Multifaceted? That was far too alien to bear consideration. Nothing like that had featured in any stage of human evolution, not even in ancient eras when the first gasping amphibians had crawled out of the sea onto the shore. Here was proof that he was not merely devolving, that his body was not merely struggling to express all the potential in the genetic heritage of humankind; here was proof that his genetic structure had run amok and that it was conveying him toward a form and consciousness that had nothing to do with the human race. He was becoming something *else*, something beyond reptile or ape or Neanderthal or Cro-Magnon man or modern European man, something so strange that he did not have the courage or the curiosity to confront it.

Henceforth, when he glanced in the mirror, he would be certain that it provided a view only of the roadway behind and revealed no slightest aspect of his own altered countenance.

He switched on the headlights and drove away from the rest area onto the highway.

The steering wheel felt odd in his malformed, monstrous hands. Driving, which should have been as familiar to him as walking, seemed like a singularly exotic act—and difficult, too, almost beyond his capabilities. He clutched the wheel and concentrated on the rainy highway ahead.

The whispering tires and metronomic thump of the windshield wipers seemed to pull him on through the storm and the gathering darkness, toward a special destiny. Once, when his full intellect returned to him for a brief moment, he thought of William Butler Yeats and remembered a fitting scrap of the great man's poetry:

And what rough beast, its hour come round at last,
Slouches towards Bethlehem to be born?

$\diamond$ 32 $\diamond$

FLAMINGO PINK

Tuesday afternoon, after their meeting with Dr. Easton Solberg at UCI, Detectives Julio Verdad and Reese Hagerstrom, still on sick leave, had driven to Tustin, where the main offices of Shadway Realty were located in a suite on the ground floor of a three-story Spanish-style building with a blue tile roof. Julio had spotted the stakeout car on the first pass. It was an unmarked muck-green Ford, sitting at the curb half a block from Shadway Realty, where the occupants had a good view of those offices and of the driveway that serviced the parking lot alongside the building. Two men in blue suits were in the Ford: One was reading a newspaper and the other was keeping watch.

"Feds," Julio said as he cruised by the stakeout.

"Sharp's men? DSA?" Reese wondered.

"Must be."

"A little obvious, aren't they?"

"I guess they don't really expect Shadway to turn up here," Julio said. "But they have to go through the motions."

Julio parked half a block behind the stakeout, putting several cars between him and the DSA's Ford, so it was possible to watch the watchers without being seen.

Reese had participated in scores of stakeouts with Julio, and surveillance duty had never been the ordeal it might have been with another partner. Julio was a complex man whose conversation was interesting hour after hour. But when one or both of them did not feel up to conversation, they could sit through long silences in comfort, without awkwardness—one of the surest tests of friendship.

Tuesday afternoon, while they watched the watchers and also watched the offices of Shadway Realty, they talked about Eric Leben, genetic engineering, and the dream of immortality. That dream was by no means Leben's private obsession. A deep longing for immortality, for commutation of the death sentence, had surely filled humankind since the first members of the species had acquired self-awareness and a crude intelligence. The subject had a special poignancy for Reese and Julio because both had witnessed the deaths of much-loved wives and had never fully recovered from their losses.

Reese could sympathize with Leben's dream and even understand the scientist's reasons for subjecting himself to a dangerous genetic experiment. It had gone wrong, yes: the two murders and the hideous crucifixion of the one dead girl were proof that Leben had come back from the grave as something less than human, and he must be stopped. But the deadly result of his experiments—and the folly of them—did not entirely foreclose sympathy. Against the rapacious hunger of the grave, all men and women were united, brothers and sisters.

As the sunny summer day grew dreary under an incoming marine layer of ash-gray clouds, Reese felt a cloak of melancholy settle upon him. He might have been overwhelmed by it if he had not been on the job, but he *was* on the job in spite of also being on sick leave.

They—like the DSA stakeout team—were not expecting Shadway to arrive at his headquarters, but they were hoping to identify one of the real-estate agents operating out of the office. As the afternoon wore on they saw several people entering and leaving the premises, but one tall, thin woman with a Betty Boop cap of black hair was the most noticeable, her angular storklike frame emphasized by a clinging flamingo-pink dress. Not pale pink, not frilly pink, but bold flame-hot pink. She came and went twice, both times chauffeuring middle-aged couples who had arrived at the office in their own cars—evidently clients for whom she was tracking down suitable houses. Her own car, with its personalized license plate—REQUEEN, which most likely stood for Real Estate Queen—was a new canary-yellow Cadillac Seville with wire wheels, as memorable as the woman herself.

"That one," Julio said when she returned to the office with the second couple.

"Hard to lose in traffic," Reese agreed.

At 4:50, she had again come out of the Shadway Realty door and had hurried like a scurrying bird for her car. Julio and Reese had decided that she was probably going home for the day. Leaving the DSA stakeout to its fruitless wait for Benjamin Shadway, they followed the yellow Cadillac down First Street to Newport Avenue and north to Cowan Heights. She lived in a two-story stucco house with a shake-shingle roof and lots of redwood balconies and decking on one of the steeper streets in the Heights.

Julio parked in front as the pink lady's Caddy disappeared behind the closing garage door. He got out of the car to check the contents of the mailbox—a federal crime—in hope of discovering the woman's name. A moment later he got back into the car and said, "Theodora Bertlesman. Apparently goes by the name Teddy, because that was on one of the letters."

They waited a couple of minutes, then went to the house, where Reese rang the bell. Summer wind, warm in spite of the winter-gray sky from which it flowed, breathed through surrounding bougainvillea, red-flowered hibiscus, and fragrant star jasmine. The street was still, peaceful, the sounds of the outside world eliminated by the most effective filter known to man—money.

"Should've gotten into real estate, I think," Reese said. "Why on earth did I ever want to be a cop?"

"You were probably a cop in a previous life," Julio said dryly, "in another century when being a cop was a

better scam than selling real estate. You just fell into the
same pattern this time around, without realizing things
had changed."

"Caught in a karma loop, huh?"

A moment later, the door opened. The stork-tall woman
in the flamingo-pink dress looked down at Julio, then only
slightly up at Reese, and she was less birdlike and more
impressive close up than she had been from a distance.
Earlier, watching her from the car, Reese had not been
able to see the porcelain clarity of her skin, her startling
gray eyes, or the sculpted refinement of her features.
Her Betty Boop hair, which had looked lacquered—
even ceramic—from fifty yards, now proved to be thick
and soft. She was no less tall, no less thin, and no less
flamboyant than she had seemed before, but her chest
was certainly not flat, and her legs were lovely.

"May I help you?" Teddy Bertlesman asked. Her voice
was low and silken. She radiated such an air of quiet self-
assurance that if Julio and Reese had been two dangerous
men instead of two cops, they might not have dared try
anything with her.

Presenting his ID and badge, Julio introduced himself
and said, "This is my partner, Detective Hagerstrom,"
and explained that they wanted to question her about
Ben Shadway. "Maybe my information is out of date,
but I believe you work as a sales agent in his firm."

"Of course, you know perfectly well that I do," she
said without scorn, even with some amusement. "Please
come in."

She led them into a living room as bold in its decor as
she was in her dress but with undeniable style and taste. A
massive white-marble coffee table. Contemporary sofas
upholstered in a rich green fabric. Chairs in peach silk
moiré, with elaborately carved arms and feet. Four-foot-
tall emerald vases holding huge stalks of white-plumed
pampas grass. Very large and dramatic modern art filled
the high walls of the cathedral-ceilinged room, giving
a comfortable human scale to what could have been a
forbidding chamber. A wall of glass presented a panorama
of Orange County. Teddy Bertlesman sat on a green sofa,

the windows behind her, a pale nimbus of light around her head, and Reese and Julio sat on moiré chairs, separated from her by the enormous marble table that seemed like an altar.

Julio said, "Ms. Bertlesman—"

"No, please," she said, slipping off her shoes and drawing her long legs up under herself. "Either call me Teddy or, if you insist on remaining formal, it's *Miss* Bertlesman. I despise that ridiculous *Miz* business; it makes me think of the South before the Civil War— dainty ladies in crinolines, sipping mint juleps under magnolia trees while black mammies tend to them."

"Miss Bertlesman," Julio continued, "we are most eager to speak to Mr. Shadway, and we hope you might have an idea where he is. For instance, it occurs to us that, being a real-estate developer and investor as well as broker, he might own rental properties that are currently vacant, one of which he might now be using—"

"Excuse me, but I don't see how this falls in your jurisdiction. According to your ID, you're Santa Ana policemen. Ben has offices in Tustin, Costa Mesa, Orange, Newport Beach, Laguna Beach, and Laguna Niguel, but none in Santa Ana. And he lives in Orange Park Acres."

Julio assured her that part of the Shadway-Leben case fell into the jurisdiction of the Santa Ana Police Department, and he explained that cross-jurisdictional cooperation was not uncommon, but Teddy Bertlesman was politely skeptical and subtly uncooperative. Reese admired the diplomacy, finesse, and aplomb with which she fielded probing questions and answered without saying anything useful. Her respect for her boss and her determination to protect him became increasingly evident, yet she said nothing that made it possible to accuse her of lying or harboring a wanted man.

At last, recognizing the futility of the authoritarian approach, apparently hoping revelation of his true motives and a blatant bid for sympathy would work where authority had failed, Julio sighed, leaned back in his chair, and said, "Listen, Miss Bertlesman, we've lied to you. We aren't here in any official capacity. Not strictly speaking. In fact, we're both supposed to be on sick leave. Our captain would be furious if he knew we were still on this case, because federal agencies have taken charge and have told us to back off. But for a lot of reasons, we can't do that, not and keep our self-respect."

Teddy Bertlesman frowned—quite prettily, Reese thought—and said, "I don't understand—"

Julio held up one slim hand. "Wait. Just listen for a moment."

In a soft, sincere, and intimate voice far different from his official tone, he told her how Ernestina Hernandez and Becky Klienstad had been brutally murdered—one thrown in a dumpster, the other nailed to a wall. He told her about his own baby brother, Ernesto, who had been killed by rats a long time ago in a faraway place. He explained how that tragedy had contributed to his obsession with unjust death and how the similarity between the names Ernesto and Ernestina was one of the several things that had made the Hernandez girl's murder a special and very personal crusade for him.

"Though I'll admit," Julio said, "if the names weren't similar and if other factors weren't the same, then I'd simply have found different reasons to make a crusade of this. Because I almost *always* make a crusade of a case. It's a bad habit of mine."

"A wonderful habit," Reese said.

Julio shrugged.

Reese was surprised that Julio was so thoroughly aware of his own motivations. Listening to his partner, contemplating the degree of insight and self-awareness at which these statements hinted, Reese acquired an even greater respect for the man.

"The point is," Julio told Teddy Bertlesman, "I believe your boss and Rachael Leben are guilty of nothing, that they may be just pawns in a game they don't even fully understand. I think they're being used, that they might be killed as scapegoats to further the interests of others, perhaps even the interests of the government. They need help, and I guess what I'm trying to tell you is that they've sort of become another crusade of mine. Help me to help them, Teddy."

Julio's performance was astonishing, and from anyone else it might have looked like exactly that—a mere performance. But there was no mistaking his sincerity or the depth of his concern. Though his dark eyes were watchful, and though there was a shrewdness in his face, his commitment to justice and his great warmth were unmistakably genuine.

Teddy Bertlesman was smart enough to see that Julio was not shucking and jiving her, and she was won over. She swung her long legs off the sofa and slid forward to the edge of it in a whispery rustle of pink silk, a sound that seemed to pass like a breeze over Reese, raising the small hairs on the backs of his hands and sending a pleasant shiver through him. "I knew darn well Ben Shadway was no threat to national security," Teddy said. "Those federal agents came sniffing around with that line, and it was all I could do to keep from laughing in their faces. No, in fact, it was all I could do to keep from *spitting* in their faces."

"Where might Ben Shadway have gone, he and Rachael Leben?" Julio asked. "Sooner or later, the feds are going to find them, and I think that for their sake Reese and I had better find them first. Do you have any idea where we should look?"

Rising from the sofa in a brilliant hot-pink whirl, stalking back and forth across the living room on stiltlike legs that ought to have been awkward but were the essence of grace, looking incredibly tall to Reese because he was still sitting on the moiré chair, pausing now and standing provocatively hip-shot in thought, then pacing again, Teddy Bertlesman considered the possibilities and enumerated them: "Well, okay, he owns property— mostly small houses—all over the county. Right now . . . the only ones not rented . . . let me see . . . One, there's a little bungalow in Orange, a place on Pine Street, but I don't figure he'd be there because he's having some work done on it—a new bathroom, improvements to the kitchen. He wouldn't hide where there're going to be workmen coming and going. Two, there's half of a duplex in Yorba Linda . . ."

Reese listened to her, but for the moment he did not care what she said; he left that part to Julio. All Reese had the capacity to care about was the way she looked and moved and sounded; she filled all his senses to capacity, leaving no room for anything else. At a distance she had seemed angular, birdlike, but up close she was a gazelle, lean and swift and not the least angular. Her size was less impressive than her fluidity, which was like that of a professional dancer, and her fluidity was less impressive than her suppleness, and her suppleness was less impressive than her beauty, and her beauty was less impressive than her intelligence and energy and flair.

Even when her pacing took her away from the window wall, she was surrounded by a nimbus of light. To Reese, she seemed to glow.

He had felt nothing like this in five years, since his Janet had been killed by the men in the van who'd tried to snatch little Esther that day in the park. He wondered if Teddy Bertlesman had taken special notice of him, too, or whether he was just another lump of a cop to her. He wondered how he could approach her without making a fool of himself and without giving offense. He wondered if there could ever be anything between a woman like her and a man like him. He wondered if he could live without her. He wondered when he was going to be able to breathe again. He wondered if his feelings showed. He didn't *care* if they showed.

" . . . the motel!" Teddy stopped pacing, looked startled for a moment, then grinned. An amazingly lovely grin. "Yes, of course, that would be the most likely place."

"He owns a motel?" Julio asked.

"A run-down place in Las Vegas," Teddy said. "He just bought it. Formed a new corporation to make the purchase. Might take the feds a while to tumble to the place because it's such a recent acquisition and in another state. Place is empty, out of business, but it was sold with furnishings. Even the manager's apartment was furnished,

I think, so Ben and Rachael could squirrel away there in comfort."

Julio glanced at Reese and said, "What do you think?"

Reese had to look away from Teddy in order to breathe and speak. With a funny little wheeze, he said, "Sounds right."

Pacing again, flamingo-pink silk swirling around her knees, Teddy said, "I *know* it's right. Ben's in that project with Whitney Gavis, and Whitney is maybe the only man on earth Ben really, fully trusts."

"Who's this Gavis?" Julio asked.

"They were in Vietnam together," she said. "They're tight. As tight as brothers. Tighter, maybe. You know, Ben's a real nice guy, one of the best, and anyone'll tell you so. He's gentle, open, so darn honest and honorable that some people just plain don't believe him for a while, until they've gotten to know him better. But it's funny . . . in a way . . . he holds almost everybody at arm's length, never quite reveals himself completely. Except, I think, with Whit Gavis. It's as if things happened to him in the war that made him forever different from other people, that made it impossible for him to be truly close to anyone except those who went through the same thing he went through and came out with their minds in one piece. Like Whit."

"Is he close in the same way with Mrs. Leben?" Julio asked.

"Yes, I think so. I think he loves her," Teddy said, "which makes her about the luckiest woman I know."

Reese sensed jealousy in Teddy's voice, and his heart felt as if it broke loose and plummeted down through his chest.

Apparently Julio heard the same note, for he said, "Forgive me, Teddy, but I'm a cop, and I'm curious by nature, and you sounded as if you wouldn't mind if he'd fallen for you."

She blinked in surprise, then laughed. "Me and Ben? No, no. For one thing, I'm taller than he is, and in heels I positively tower over him. Besides, he's a homebody—

a quiet, peaceful man who reads old mystery novels and collects trains. No, Ben's a great guy, but I'm far too flamboyant for him, and he's too low-key for me."

Reese's heart stopped plummeting.

Teddy said, "Oh, I'm just jealous of Rachael because she's found herself a good man, and I haven't. When you're my size, you know from the start that men aren't going to flock to you—except basketball players, and I hate jocks. Then, when you get to be thirty-two, you can't help feeling a bit sour every time you see someone catch a good one, can't help it even when you're happy for them."

Reese's heart *soared.*

After Julio had asked a few more questions about the motel in Las Vegas and had ascertained its location, he and Reese got up, and Teddy accompanied them to the door. Step by step, Reese wracked his mind for an approach, an opening line. As Julio opened the door, Reese looked back at Teddy and said, "Uh, excuse me, Miss Bertlesman, but I'm a cop, and asking questions is my business, you know, and I was wondering if you're . . ." He didn't know where to go with it. " . . . if you're maybe . . . uh . . . seeing anyone particular." Listening to himself, Reese was amazed and dismayed that Julio could sound so smooth while he, trying to imitate his partner's cool manner, could sound so rough and obvious.

Smiling up at him, she said, "Does this have bearing on the case you're investigating?"

"Well . . . I just thought . . . I mean . . . I wouldn't want you mentioning this conversation to anyone. I mean, it's not just that we could get in trouble with our captain . . . but if you mentioned the motel to anyone, you might jeopardize Mr. Shadway and Mrs. Leben and . . . well . . ."

He wanted to shoot himself, put an end to this humiliation.

She said, "I'm not seeing anyone special, not anyone I'd share secrets with."

Reese cleared his throat. "Well, uh, that's good. All right."

He started to turn toward the door, where Julio was giving him a strange look, and Teddy said, "You are a big one, aren't you?"

Reese faced her again. "Excuse me?"

"You're quite a big guy. Too bad there aren't more your size. A girl like me would almost seem petite to you."

What does she mean by that? he wondered. Anything? Just polite conversation? Is she giving me an opening? If it's an opening, how should I respond to it?

"It would be nice to be thought of as petite," she said.

He tried to speak. Could not.

He felt stupid, awkward, and shy as he'd been at sixteen.

Suddenly he *could* speak, but he blurted out the question as he might have done as a boy of sixteen: "Miss-Bertlesman-would-you-go-out-with-me-sometime?"

She smiled and said, "Yes."

"You would?"

"Yes."

"Saturday night? Dinner? Seven o'clock?"

"Sounds nice."

He stared at her, amazed. "Really?"

She laughed. "Really."

A minute later, in the car, Reese said, "Well, I'll be damned."

"I never realized you were such a smooth operator," Julio said kiddingly, affectionately.

Blushing, Reese said, "By God, life's funny, isn't it? You never know when it might take a whole new turn."

"Slow down," Julio said, starting the engine and driving away from the curb. "It's just a date."

"Yeah. Probably. But . . . I got a feeling it might turn out to be more than just that."

"A smooth operator *and* a romantic fool," Julio said as he steered the car down out of the Heights, toward Newport Avenue.

After some thought, Reese said, "You know what Eric Leben forgot? He was so obsessed with living forever, he forgot to enjoy the life he had. Life may be short, but there's a lot to be said for it. Leben was so busy planning for eternity, he forgot to enjoy the moment."

"Listen," Julio said, "if romance is going to make a philosopher out of you, I may have to get a new partner."

For a few minutes Reese was silent, submerged in memories of well-tanned legs and flamingo-pink silk. When he surfaced again, he realized that Julio was not driving aimlessly. "Where we going?"

"John Wayne Airport."

"Vegas?"

"Is that okay with you?" Julio asked.

"Seems like the only thing we can do."

"Have to pay for tickets out of our own pockets."

"I know."

"You want to stay here, that's all right."

"I'm in," Reese said.

"I can handle it alone."

"I'm in."

"Might get dangerous from here on, and you have Esther to think about," Julio said.

My little Esther and now maybe Theodora "Teddy" Bertlesman, Reese thought. And when you find someone to care about—when you *dare* to care—that's when life gets cruel; that's when they're taken from you; that's when you lose it all. A premonition of death made him shiver.

Nevertheless, he said, "I'm in. Didn't you hear me say I'm in? For God's sake, Julio, I'm *in*."

◊ 33 ◊

VIVA LAS VEGAS

Following the storm across the desert, Ben Shadway reached Baker, California, gateway to Death Valley, at 6:20.

The wind was blowing much harder than it had been back toward Barstow. The driven rain snapped against the windshield with a sound like thousands of impacting bullets. Service-station, restaurant, and motel signs were swinging on their mountings, trying to tear loose and fly away. A stop sign twitched violently back and forth, caught in turbulent currents of air, and seemed about to screw itself out of the ground. At a Shell station, two attendants in yellow rain slickers moved with their heads bowed and shoulders hunched; the tails of their glistening vinyl coats flapped against their legs and whipped out behind them. A score of bristly tumbleweeds, some four or five feet in diameter, bounced-rolled-sailed across tiny Baker's only east-west street, swept in from the desolate landscape to the south.

Ben tried to call Whitney Gavis from a pay phone inside a small convenience store. He couldn't get through to Vegas. Three times, he listened to a recorded message to the effect that service had been temporarily interrupted.

Wind moaned and shrieked against the store's plate-glass windows, and rain drummed furiously on the roof—which was all the explanation he required for AT&T's troubles.

He was scared. He had been badly worried ever since finding the ax propped against the refrigerator in the kitchen of Eric's mountain cabin. But now his fear was escalating by the moment because he began to feel that *everything* was going wrong for him, that luck had turned entirely against him. The encounter with Sharp, the disastrous change in the weather, his inability to reach Whit Gavis when the phones had been working, now the trouble with the lines to Vegas, made it seem as if the universe was, indeed, not accidental but was a machine with dark and frightful purpose, and that the gods in charge of it were conspiring to make certain he would never again see Rachael alive.

In spite of his fear, frustration, and eagerness to hit the road again, he paused long enough to grab a few things to eat in the car. He'd had nothing since breakfast in Palm Springs, and he was famished.

The clerk behind the counter—a blue-jeaned, middle-aged woman with sun-bleached hair, her brown skin toughened by too many years on the desert—sold him three candy bars, a few bags of peanuts, and a six-pack of Pepsi. When Ben asked her about the phones, she said, "I hear tell there's been flash flooding east of here, out near Cal Neva, and worse around Stateline. Undermined a few telephone poles, brought down the lines. Word is, it'll be repaired in a couple of hours."

"I never knew it rained this hard in the desert," he said as she gave him change.

"Don't rain—really rain, I mean—but maybe three times a year. Though when we do get a storm, it sometimes comes down like God is breaking his promise about the fire next time and figures to wipe us out with a great flood like before."

The stolen Merkur was parked half a dozen steps beyond the exit from the store, but Ben was soaked again during the few seconds needed to get to the car.

Inside, he popped open a can of Pepsi, took a long swallow, braced the can between his thighs, peeled the wrapper off a candy bar, started the engine, and drove back toward the interstate.

Regardless of how terrible the weather got, he would have to push toward Vegas at the highest possible speed, seventy or eighty miles an hour, faster if he could manage it, even though the chances were very high that, sooner or later, he would lose control of the car on the rain-greased highway. His inability to reach Whit Gavis had left him with no alternative.

Ascending the entrance ramp to I-15, the car coughed once and shuddered, but then it surged ahead without further hesitation. For a minute, heading east-northeast toward Nevada, Ben listened intently to the engine and glanced repeatedly at the dashboard, expecting to see a warning light blink on. But the engine purred, and the warning lights remained off, and none of the dials or gauges indicated trouble, so he relaxed slightly. He munched on his candy bar and gradually put the Merkur up to seventy, carefully testing its responsiveness on the treacherously wet pavement.

◗   ◗

Anson Sharp was awake and refreshed by 7:10 Tuesday evening. From his motel room in Palm Springs, with the background sound of hard rain on the roof and water gurgling through a downspout near his window, he called subordinates at several places throughout southern California.

From Dirk Cringer, an agent at the case-operation headquarters in Orange County, Sharp learned that Julio Verdad and Reese Hagerstrom had not dropped out of the Leben investigation as they were supposed to have done. Given their well-earned reputation as bulldog cops who were reluctant to quit even hopeless cases, Sharp had ordered both of their personal cars fitted with hidden transmitters last night and had assigned men to follow them electronically, at a distance from which Verdad and Hagerstrom would not spot a tail. That precaution had paid off, for this afternoon they had visited UCI to meet with Dr. Easton Solberg, a former associate of Leben's, and later they had spent a couple of hours on stakeout in front of Shadway Realty's main office in Tustin.

"They spotted our team and set up their own surveillance half a block back," Cringer said, "where they could watch both us and the realty office."

"Must've thought they were real cute," Sharp said, "when all the time we were watching them while they watched us."

"Then they followed one of the real-estate agents home, a woman named Theodora Bertlesman."

"We already interviewed her about Shadway, didn't we?"

"Yeah, everyone who works with him in that office. And this Bertlesman woman wasn't any more cooperative than the rest of them, maybe less."

"How long were Verdad and Hagerstrom at her place?"

"More than twenty minutes."

"Sounds like she might've been more open with them. Have any idea what she told them?"

"No," Cringer said. "She lives on a hillside, so it was hard to get a clear angle on any of the windows with a directional microphone. By the time we could've set it up, Verdad and Hagerstrom were leaving anyway. They went straight from her place to the airport."

"*What?*" Sharp said, surprised. "LAX?"

"No. John Wayne Airport here in Orange County. That's where they are now, waiting for a flight out."

"What flight? To where?"

"Vegas. They bought tickets on the first available flight to Vegas. It leaves at eight o'clock."

"Why Vegas?" Sharp said, more to himself than to Cringer.

"Maybe they finally decided to give up on the case like they were told. Maybe they're going off for a little holiday."

"You don't go off on a holiday without packing suitcases. You said they went straight to the airport, which

I suppose means they didn't make a quick stop home to grab a change of clothes."

"Straight to the airport," Cringer confirmed.

"All right, good," Sharp said, suddenly excited. "Then they're probably trying to get to Shadway and Mrs. Leben before we do, and they've reason to believe the place to look is somewhere in Las Vegas." There was a chance he would get his hands on Shadway, after all. And this time, the bastard would not slip away. "If there're any seats left on that eight o'clock flight, I want you to put two of your men aboard."

"Yes, sir."

"I have men here in Palm Springs, and we'll head to Vegas, too, just as soon as we can. I want to be in place at the airport there and ready to track Verdad and Hagerstrom the moment they arrive."

Sharp hung up and immediately called Jerry Peake's room.

Outside, thunder roared in the north and faded to a soft rumble as it moved south through the Coachella Valley.

Peake sounded groggy when he answered.

"It's almost seven-thirty," Sharp told him. "Be ready to roll in fifteen minutes."

"What's happening?"

"We're going to Vegas after Shadway, and this time luck's on our side."

◗　　◗

One of the many problems of driving a stolen car is that you can't be sure of its mechanical condition. You can't very well ask for a guarantee of reliability and a service history from the owner before you make off with his wheels.

The stolen Merkur failed Ben forty miles east of Baker. It began coughing, wheezing, and shuddering as it had done on the entrance ramp to the interstate a while ago, but this time it did not cease coughing until the engine died. He steered onto the berm and tried to restart the car, but it would not respond. All he was doing was draining the battery, so he sat for a moment, despairing, as the rain fell by the pound and by the hundred-weight upon the car.

But surrender to despair was not his style. After only a few seconds, he formulated a plan and put it into action, inadequate though it might be.

He tucked the .357 Combat Magnum under his belt, against the small of his back, and pulled his shirt out of his jeans to cover the gun. He would not be able to take the shotgun, and he deeply regretted the loss of it.

He switched on the Merkur's emergency flashers and got out into the pouring rain. Fortunately, the lightning had passed away to the east. Standing in the storm-gray twilight gloom beside the disabled car, he shielded his eyes with one hand and looked into the rain, toward the west, where distant headlights were approaching.

I-15 was still lightly traveled. A few determined gamblers were trekking toward their mecca and would probably have been undeterred by Armageddon, though there were more big trucks than anything else. He waved his arms, signaling for help, but two cars and three trucks passed him without slowing. As their tires cut through puddles on the pavement, they sent sheets of water pluming in their wake, some of which cascaded over Ben, adding to his misery.

About two minutes later, another eighteen-wheeler came into view. It was bearing so many lights that it appeared to be decorated for Christmas. To Ben's relief, it began to brake far back and came to a full stop on the berm behind the Merkur.

He ran back to the big rig and peered up at the open window where a craggy-faced man with a handlebar mustache squinted down at him from the warm, dry cab. "Broke down!" Ben shouted above the cacophony of wind and rain.

"Closest mechanic you're going to find is back in Baker," the driver called down to him. "Best cross over to the westbound lanes and try to catch a ride going that way."

"Don't have time to find a mechanic and get her fixed!" Ben shouted. "Got to make Vegas fast as I can." He had prepared the lie while waiting for someone to stop. "My wife's in the hospital there, hurt bad, maybe dying."

"Good Lord," the driver said, "you better come aboard, then."

Ben hurried around to the passenger's door, praying that his benefactor was a highballer who would keep the pedal to the metal in spite of the weather and rocket into Vegas in record time.

◗   ◗

Driving across the rain-lashed Mojave on the last leg of the trip to Las Vegas, with the darkness of the storm slowly giving way to the deeper darkness of night, Rachael felt lonelier than she'd ever felt before—and she was no stranger to loneliness. The rain had not let up for the past couple of hours, largely because she was more than keeping pace with the storm as it moved eastward, driving deeper into the heart of it. The hollow beating of the windshield wipers and the droning of the tires on the wet road were like the shuttles of a loom that wove not cloth but isolation.

Much of her life had been lived in loneliness and in emotional—if not always physical—isolation. By the time Rachael was born, her mother and father had discovered that they could not abide each other, but for religious reasons they had been unwilling to consider divorce. Therefore, Rachael's earliest years passed in a loveless house, where her parents' resentment toward each other was inadequately concealed. Worse, each of them seemed to view her as the other's child—a reason to resent her, too. Neither was more than dutifully affectionate.

As soon as she was old enough, she was sent to Catholic boarding schools where, except for holidays, she remained for the next eleven years. In those institutions, all run by nuns, she made few friends, none close, partly because she had a very low opinion of herself and could not believe that anyone would *want* to be friends with her.

A few days after she graduated from prep school, the summer before she was to enter college, her parents were killed in a plane crash on their way home from a business trip. Rachael had been under the impression that her father had made a small fortune in the garment industry by investing money that her mother had inherited the year of their wedding. But when the will was probated and the estate was settled, Rachael discovered that the family business had been skirting bankruptcy for years and that their upper-class life-style had eaten up every dollar earned. Virtually penniless, she had to cancel her plans to attend Brown University and, instead, went to work as a waitress, living in a boarding-house and saving what she could toward a more modest education in California's tax-supported university system.

A year later, when she finally started school, she made no real friends because she had to keep waitressing and had no time for the extracurricular activities through which college relationships are formed. By the time she received her degree and launched herself upon a program of graduate study, she had known at least eight thousand nights of loneliness.

She was easy prey for Eric when, needing to feed on her youth as a vampire feeds on blood, he had determined to make her his wife. He was twelve years her senior, so he knew far more about charming and winning a young woman than men her own age knew; he made her feel wanted and special for the first time in her life. Considering the difference in their ages, perhaps she also saw in him a father figure capable of giving her not only the love of a husband but the parental love she had never known.

Of course, it had turned out less well than she expected. She learned that Eric didn't love her but loved, instead, the thing that she symbolized to him—vigorous, healthful, energetic youth. Their marriage soon proved to be as loveless as that of her parents.

Then she had found Benny. And for the first time in her life she had not been lonely.

But now Benny was gone, and she didn't know if she would ever see him again.

The Mercedes's windshield wipers beat out a monotonous rhythm, and the tires sang a one-note tune—a song of the void, of despair and loneliness.

She attempted to comfort herself with the thought that at least Eric posed no further threat to her or Ben. Surely he was dead from a score of rattlesnake bites. Even if his genetically altered body could safely metabolize those massive doses of virulent poison, even if Eric could return from the dead a second time, he was obviously degenerating, not merely physically but also mentally. (She had a vivid mental image of him kneeling on the rain-soaked earth, eating a living serpent, as frightening and elemental as the lightning that flashed above him.) If he survived the rattlesnakes, he would very likely remain on the desert, no longer a human being but a *thing*, loping hunchbacked or squirming on its belly through the hillocks of sand, slithering down into the arroyos, feeding greedily on other desert dwellers, a threat to any beast he encountered but no longer a threat to her. And even if some glimmer of human awareness and intelligence remained in him, and if he still felt the need to avenge himself on Rachael, he would find it difficult if not impossible to come out of the desert into civilization and move freely about. If he tried that, he would create a sensation—panic, terror—wherever he went, and would probably be chased down and captured or shot.

Yet . . . she was still afraid of him.

She remembered glancing up at him as he followed her from the top of the arroyo wall, remembered staring down at him later when she had been on top and he had been climbing after her, remembered the way he had looked when she had last seen him engaged in battle with the nest of rattlers. In all those memories there was something about him that . . . well . . . something that seemed almost mythic, that transcended nature, that seemed powerfully supernatural, undying and unstoppable.

She shuddered with a sudden chill that spread outward from the marrow of her bones.

A moment later, topping a rise in the highway, she saw that she was nearing the end of the current leg of her journey. In a broad dark valley directly ahead and below, Las Vegas glimmered like a miraculous vision in the rain. So many millions of lights shone in every hue that the city looked bigger than New York, though it was actually one-twentieth the size. Even from this distance, at least fifteen miles, she could make out the Strip with all its dazzling resort hotels and the downtown casino center that some called Glitter Gulch, for those areas blazed with by far the greatest concentrations of lights, all of which seemed to blink, pulse, and twinkle.

Less than twenty minutes later, she came out of the vast empty reaches of the bleak Mojave onto Las Vegas Boulevard South, where the neon shimmered across the rain-mirrored road in waves of purple, pink, red, green, and gold. Pulling up to the front doors of the Bally's Grand, she almost wept with relief when she saw the bellmen, valet-parking attendants, and a few hotel guests standing under the porte cochere. For hours on the interstate, the passing cars had seemed untenanted in the storm-obscured night, so it was wonderful to see people again, even if they were all strangers.

At first, Rachael hesitated to leave the Mercedes with a valet-parking attendant because the precious Wildcard file was in a garbage bag on the floor behind the driver's seat. But she decided that no one was likely to steal a garbage bag, especially not one full of creased and crumpled papers. Besides, it would be safer with the valet than parked in the public lot. She left the car in his care and took a claim check for it.

She had mostly recovered from the twist she'd given her ankle when running from Eric. The claw punctures in her calf throbbed and burned, although those wounds felt better, too. She entered the hotel with only a slight limp.

For a moment, she was almost thrown into shock by the contrast between the stormy night behind her and the excitement of the casino. It was a glittery world of crystal chandeliers, velvet, brocade, plush carpets, marble, polished brass, and green felt, where the sound of wind and rain could not be heard above the roar of voices exhorting Lady Luck, the ringing of slot machines, and the raucous music of a pop-rock band in the lounge.

Gradually Rachael became uncomfortably aware that her appearance made her an object of curiosity in these surroundings. Of course, not everyone—not even a majority of the clientele—dressed elegantly for a night of drinking, nightclub shows, and gambling. Women in cocktail dresses and men in fine suits were common, but others were dressed more casually: some in polyester leisure suits, some in jeans and sports shirts. However, none of them wore a torn and soiled blouse (as she did), and none of them wore jeans that looked as if they might have just been through a rodeo contest (as she did), and none of them boasted filthy sneakers with blackened laces and one sole half torn off from scrambling up and down arroyo walls (as she did), and none of them was dirty-faced and stringy-haired (as she was). She had to assume that, even in the escapist world of Vegas, people watched some TV news and might recognize her as the infamous traitor and fugitive wanted throughout the Southwest. The last thing she needed was to call attention to herself. Fortunately, gamblers are a single-minded group, more intent upon their wagering than upon the need to breathe, and few of them even glanced up from their games to look at her; none looked twice.

She hurried around the perimeter of the casino to the public telephones, which were in an alcove where the casino noise faded to a soft roar. She called information for Whitney Gavis's number. He answered on the first ring. Rather breathlessly she said, "I'm sorry, you don't know me, my name's Rachael—"

"Ben's Rachael?" he interrupted.

"Yes," she said, surprised.

"I know you, know all about you." He had a voice amazingly like Benny's: calm and measured and reassuring. "And I just heard the news an hour ago, that *ridiculous* damn story about defense secrets. What a crock. Anybody who knows Benny wouldn't believe it for a second. I don't know what's going on, but I figured you guys would be coming my way if you needed to go to ground for a while."

"He's not with me, but he sent me to you," Rachael explained.

"Say no more. Just tell me where you are."

"The Grand."

"It's eight o'clock. I'll be there by eight-ten. Don't go wandering around. They have so much surveillance in those casinos you're bound to be on a monitor somewhere if you go onto the floor, and maybe one of the security men on duty will have seen the evening news. Get my drift?"

"Can I go to the rest room? I'm a mess. I could use a quick washup."

"Sure. Just don't go onto the casino floor. And be back by the phones in ten minutes, 'cause that's where I'll meet you. There're no security cameras by the phones. Sit tight, kid."

"Wait!"

"What is it?" he asked.

"What do you look like? How will I recognize you?"

He said, "Don't worry, kid. I'll recognize you. Benny's shown me your picture so often that every detail of your gorgeous face is burned into my cerebral cortex. Remember, sit tight!"

The line went dead, and she hung up.

◑　　◑

Jerry Peake was not sure he wanted to be a legend anymore. He was not even sure he wanted to be a DSA agent, legendary or otherwise. Too much had been happening too fast. He was unable to assimilate it properly. He felt as if he were trying to walk through one of those big rolling barrels that were sometimes used as the entrance to a carnival funhouse, except they were spinning this barrel about five times faster than even the most sadistic carny operator would dare, and it also seemed to be an endless tube from which he would never emerge. He wondered if he would ever get his feet under him and know stability again.

Anson Sharp's call had roused Peake from a sleep so deep that it almost required a headstone. Even a quick cold shower had not entirely awakened him. A ride through rain-washed streets to the Palm Springs airport, with siren wailing and emergency beacon flashing, had seemed like part of a bad dream. At the airfield, at 8:10, a light transport twin turbo-prop arrived from the Marine Corps Training Center at nearby Twentynine Palms, provided as an interservice courtesy to the Defense Security Agency on an emergency basis, little more than half an hour after Sharp had requested it. They boarded and immediately took off into the storm. The daredevil-steep ascent of the hotshot military pilot, combined with the howling wind and driving rain, finally blew away the lingering traces of sleep. Peake was wide awake, gripping the arms of his seat so hard that his white knuckles looked as if they would split through his skin.

"With any luck," Sharp told Peake and Nelson Gosser (the other man he'd brought along), "we'll land at McCarran International, in Vegas, about ten or fifteen minutes ahead of that flight from Orange County. When Verdad and Hagerstrom come waltzing into the terminal, we'll be ready to put them under tight surveillance."

◊   ◊

At 8:10, the 8:00 P.M. flight to Vegas had not yet taken off from John Wayne Airport in Orange County, but the pilot assured the passengers that departure was imminent. Meanwhile, there were beverages, honey-roasted beer nuts, and mint wafers to make the minutes pass more pleasantly.

"I love these honey-roasted beer nuts," Reese said, "but I just remembered something I don't like at all."

"What's that?" Julio asked.

"Flying."

"It's a short flight."

"A man doesn't expect to have to fly all over the map when he chooses a career in law enforcement."

"Forty-five minutes, fifty at most," Julio said soothingly.

"I'm *in*," Reese said quickly before Julio could start to get the wrong idea about his objections to flying. "I'm in the case for the duration, but I just wish there was a boat to Vegas."

At 8:12, they taxied to the head of the runway and took off.

◐   ◐

Driving east in the red pickup, Eric struggled mile by mile to retain sufficient human consciousness to operate the truck. Sometimes bizarre thoughts and feelings plagued him: a wishful longing to leave the truck and run naked across the dark desert plains, hair flying in the wind, the rain sluicing down his bare flesh; an unsettlingly urgent need to burrow, to squirm into a dark moist place and hide; a hot, fierce, demanding sexual urge, not human in any regard, more like an animal's rutting fever. He also experienced memories, clear images in his mind's eye, that were not his own but from some genetic storage bank of racial recollections: scavenging hungrily in a rotting log for grubs and wriggling insects; mating with some musk-drenched creature in a dank and lightless den . . . If he allowed any of these thoughts, urges, or memories to preoccupy him, he would slip away into that mindless subhuman state he had entered both times when he had killed back at the rest area, and in that condition he'd drive the pickup straight off the road. Therefore, he tried to repress those alluring images and urges, strove to focus his attention on the rainy highway ahead. He was largely successful—though at times his vision briefly clouded, and he began to breathe too fast, and the siren call of other states of consciousness became almost too much to bear.

For long stretches of time, he felt nothing physically unusual happening to him. But on several occasions he was aware of changes taking place, and then it was as if his body were a ball of tangled worms that, having recently lain dormant and still, suddenly began to squirm and writhe frantically. After having seen his inhuman eyes in the rearview mirror back at the rest stop—one green and orange with a slit-shaped iris, the other multifaceted and even stranger—he had not dared to look at himself, for he knew that his sanity was already precarious. However, he could see his hands upon the steering wheel, and he was aware of ongoing alterations in them: For a while, his elongated fingers grew shorter, thicker, and the long hooked nails retracted somewhat, and the web between thumb and the first finger all but vanished; then the process reversed itself, and his hands grew larger again, the knuckles lumpier, the claws even sharper and more wickedly pointed than before. At the moment, his hands were so hideous—dark, mottled, with a backward-curving spur at the base of each monstrous nail, and with one extra joint in each finger—that he kept his gaze on the road ahead and tried not to look down.

His inability to confront his own appearance resulted not merely from fear of what he was becoming. He was afraid, yes, but he also took a sick, demented pleasure in his transformation. At least for the moment, he was immensely strong, lightning-quick, and deadly. Except for his inhuman appearance, he was the personification of that macho dream of absolute power and unstoppable fury that every young boy entertained and that no man ever quite outgrew. He could not allow himself to dwell on this, for his power fantasies could trigger a descent into the animal state.

The peculiar and not unpleasant fire in his flesh, blood, and bones was with him now at all times, without pause, and in fact it grew hotter by the hour. Previously he had thought of himself as a man melting into new forms, but now he almost felt as if he were not melting but aflame, as if fire would leap from his fingertips at any moment. He had given it a name: the changefire.

Fortunately, the debilitating spasms of intense pain that had seized him early in his metamorphosis were no longer a part of the changes. Now and then an ache arose, or a brief stabbing agony, but nothing as intense as before and nothing that lasted longer than a minute or two. Apparently, during the past ten hours, amorphousness had become a genetically programmed condition of his body, as natural to him—and therefore as painless—as respiration, a regular heartbeat, digestion, and excretion.

Periodic attacks of cripplingly severe hunger were the only pains he suffered. However, those pangs could be excruciating, unlike any hunger he had ever known in his previous life. As his body destroyed old cells and manufactured new ones at a frantic pace, it required a lot of fuel to fire the process. He also found himself urinating far more frequently than usual, and each time he pulled off the road to relieve his bladder, his urine reeked ever more strongly of ammonia and other chemicals.

Now, as he drove the pickup over a rise in the highway and suddenly found himself looking down upon the sprawling, scintillant spectacle of Las Vegas, he was hit once more by a hunger that seized his stomach in a viselike grip and twisted hard. He began to sweat and shake uncontrollably.

He steered the pickup onto the berm and stopped. He fumbled for the handbrake, pulled it on.

He had begun to whimper when the first pangs struck him. Now he heard himself growling deep in his throat, and he sensed his self-control rapidly slipping away as his animal needs became more demanding, less resistible.

He was afraid of what he might do. Maybe leave the car and go hunting in the desert. He could get lost out there in those trackless barrens, even within a few miles of Vegas. Worse: all intellect fled, guided by pure instinct, he might go onto the highway and somehow stop a passing car, drag the screaming driver from the vehicle, and rip him to pieces. Others would see, and then there would be no hope of journeying secretly to the shuttered motel in Vegas where Rachael was hiding.

Nothing must stop him from reaching Rachael. The very thought of her brought a blood-red tinge to his vision and elicited an involuntary shriek of rage that rebounded shrilly off the rain-washed windows of the truck. Taking his revenge on her, killing her, was the one desire powerful enough to have given him the strength to resist devolution during the long drive across the desert. The possibility of revenge had kept him sane, had kept him going.

Desperately repressing the primal consciousness that acute hunger had unleashed within him, he turned eagerly to the Styrofoam cooler that was in the open storage compartment behind the pickup's front seat. He had seen it when he had gotten into the truck at the rest area, but he had not thus far explored its contents. He lifted the lid and saw, with some relief, that the cowboy and the girl had been making a sort of picnic of their trip to Vegas. The cooler contained half a dozen sandwiches in tightly sealed Ziploc bags, two apples, and a six-pack of beer.

With his dragon hands, Eric shredded the plastic bags and ate the sandwiches almost as fast as he could stuff them into his mouth. Several times he choked on the food, gagged on gummy wads of bread and meat, and had to concentrate on chewing them more thoroughly.

Four of the sandwiches were filled with thick slices of rare roast beef. The taste and smell of the half-cooked flesh excited him almost unbearably. He wished the beef had been raw and dripping. He wished he could have sunk his teeth into the living animal and could have torn loose throbbing chunks of its flesh.

The other two sandwiches were Swiss cheese and mustard, no meat, and he ate them, too, because he needed all the fuel he could get, but he did not like them, for they lacked the delicious and exhilarating flavor of blood. He remembered the taste of the cowboy's blood. Even better, the intensely coppery flavor of the woman's blood, taken from her throat and from her breast . . . He began to hiss and to twist back and forth in his seat, exhilarated by those memories. Ravenous, he ate the two apples as well, although his enlarged jaws, strangely reshaped tongue, and sharply pointed teeth had not been designed for the consumption of fruit.

He drank all of the beer, choking and spluttering on it as he poured it down. He had no fear of intoxication, for he knew that his racing metabolism would burn off the alcohol before he felt any effect from it.

For a while, having devoured every ounce of food in the cooler, he slumped back in the driver's seat, panting. He stared stupidly at the water-filmed windows, the beast within him temporarily subdued. Dreamy memories of murder and vaguer recollections of coupling with the cowboy's woman drifted like tendrils of smoke across the back of his mind.

Out on the night-clad desert, shadowfires burned.

Doorways to hell? Beckoning him to the damnation that had been his destiny but that he had escaped by beating death?

Or merely hallucinations? Perhaps his tortured subconscious mind, terrified of the changes taking place in the body it inhabited, was trying desperately to externalize the changefire to transfer the heat of metamorphosis out of his flesh and blood and into these vivid illusions.

That was the most intellectual train of thought he had ridden in many hours, and for a moment he felt a heartening resurgence of the cognitive powers that had earned him the reputation of a genius in his field. But only for a moment. Then the memory of blood returned, and a shiver of savage pleasure passed through him, and he made a thick guttural sound in the back of his throat.

A few cars and trucks passed on the highway to his left. Heading east. Heading to Vegas. Vegas . . .

Slowly he recalled that he was also bound for Vegas, for the Golden Sand Inn, for a rendezvous with revenge.

PART THREE

◊ ◊

DARKEST

Night can be sweet as a kiss,
though not a night like this.

—*The Book of Counted Sorrows*

◊ 34 ◊

CONVERGENCE

After washing her face and doing what little she could with her lank and tangled hair, Rachael returned to the vicinity of the public telephones and sat on a red leatherette bench nearby, where she could see everyone who approached from the front of the hotel lobby and from the stairs that led out of the sunken casino. Most people remained down on the bright and noisy gaming level, but the lobby concourse was filled with a steady stream of passersby.

She studied all the men as surreptitiously as possible. She was not trying to spot Whitney Gavis, for she had no idea what he looked like. However, she was worried that someone might recognize her from photographs on television. She felt that enemies were everywhere, all around her, closing in—and while that might be paranoia, it might also be the truth.

If she had ever been wearier and more miserable, she could not remember the time. The few hours of sleep she'd had last night in Palm Springs had not prepared her for today's frantic activity. Her legs ached from all the running and climbing she had done; her arms felt stiff, leaden. A dull pain extended from the back of her neck to the base of her spine. Her eyes were bloodshot, grainy, and sore. Although she had stopped in Baker for a pack of diet sodas and had emptied all six cans during the drive to Vegas, her mouth was dry and sour.

"You look beat, kid," Whitney Gavis said, stepping up to the bench on which she sat, startling her.

She'd seen him approaching from the front of the lobby, but she had turned her attention to other men, certain that he could not be Whitney Gavis. He was about five nine, an inch or two shorter than Benny, perhaps more solidly built than Benny, with heavier shoulders, a broader chest. He was wearing baggy white pants and a soft pastel-blue cotton-knit shirt, a modified *Miami Vice* look without the white jacket. However, the left side of his face was disfigured by a web of red and brown scars, as if he'd been deeply cut or burned—or both. His left ear was lumpy, gnarled. He walked with a stiff and awkward gait, laboriously swinging his left hip in a manner that indicated either that the leg was paralyzed or, more likely, that it was an artificial limb. His left arm had been amputated midway between the elbow and the wrist, and the stump poked out of the short sleeve of his shirt.

Laughing at her surprise, he said, "Evidently Benny didn't warn you: as knight-errant riding to the rescue, I leave something to be desired."

Blinking up at him, she said, "No, no, I'm glad you're here, I'm glad to have a friend no matter . . . I mean, I didn't . . . I'm sure that you . . . Oh, hell, there's no reason to . . ." She started to get up, then realized he might be more comfortable sitting down, then realized *that* was a patronizing thought, and consequently found herself bobbing up and down in embarrassing indecision.

Laughing again, taking her by the arm with his one hand, Whitney said, "Relax, kid. I'm not offended. I've never known anyone who's less concerned about a person's appearance than Benny; he judges you by what you are and what you deliver, not by the way you look or by your physical limitations, so it's just exactly like him to forget to mention my . . . shall we say 'peculiarities'? I refuse to call them handicaps. Anyway, you've every reason to be disconcerted, kid."

"I guess he didn't have time to mention it, even if he'd given it a thought," she said, deciding to remain standing. "We parted in quite a hurry."

She'd been startled because she had known that Benny and Whitney had been in Vietnam together, and on first seeing this man's grievous infirmities, she couldn't understand how he could have been a soldier. Then, of course, she realized he had been a whole man when he had gone to Southeast Asia and that he'd lost his arm and leg in that conflict.

"Ben's all right?" Whitney asked.

"I don't know."

"Where is he?"

"Coming here to join me, I hope. But I don't know for sure."

Suddenly she was stricken by the awful realization that it might just as easily have been her Benny who had returned from the war with his face scarred, one hand gone, one leg blown off, and that thought was devastating. Since Monday night, when Benny had taken the .357 Magnum away from Vince Baresco, Rachael had more or less unconsciously thought of him as endlessly resourceful, indomitable, and virtually invincible. She had been afraid for him at times, and since she had left him alone on the mountain above Lake Arrowhead, she had worried about him constantly. But deep down she had wanted to believe that he was too tough and quick to come to any harm. Now, seeing how Whitney Gavis had returned from the war, and knowing that Benny had served at Whitney's side, Rachael abruptly knew and felt—and finally believed— that Benny was a mortal man, as fragile as any other, tethered to life by a thread as pitifully thin as those by which everyone else was suspended above the void.

"Hey, are you all right?" Whitney asked.

"I . . . I'll be okay," she said shakily. "I'm just exhausted . . . and worried."

"I want to know everything—the *real* story, not the one on the news."

"There's a lot to tell," she said. "But not here."

"No," he said, looking around at the passersby, "not here."

"Benny's going to meet me at the Golden Sand."

"The motel? Yeah, sure, that's a good place to hole up, I guess. Not exactly first-class accommodations."

"I'm in no position to be choosy."

He'd entrusted his car to the valet, too, and he presented both his claim check and Rachael's when they left the hotel.

Beyond the enormous, high-ceilinged porte cochere, wind-harried rain slashed the night. The lightning had abated, but the downpour was not gray and dreary and lightless, at least not in the vicinity of the hotel. Millions of droplets reflected the amber and yellow lights that surrounded the entrance to the Grand, so it looked as if a storm of molten gold were plating the Strip in an armor fit for angels.

Whitney's car, a like-new white Karmann Ghia, was delivered first, but the black Mercedes rolled up behind it. Although she knew that she was calling attention to herself in front of the valets, Rachael insisted on looking carefully in the back seat and in the trunk before she would get behind the wheel and drive away. The plastic garbage bag containing the Wildcard file was where she had left it, though that was not what she was looking for. She was being ridiculous, and she knew it. Eric was dead—or reduced to a subhuman form, creeping around in the desert more than a hundred miles from here. There was no way he could have trailed her to the Grand, no way he could have gotten into the car during the short time it had been parked in the hotel's underground valet garage. Nevertheless, she looked warily in the trunk and was relieved when she found it empty.

She followed Whitney's Karmann Ghia onto Flamingo Boulevard, drove east to Paradise Boulevard, then turned south toward Tropicana and the shelter of the shuttered Golden Sand Inn.

◊   ◊

Even at night and in the cloaking rain, Eric dared not drive along Las Vegas Boulevard South, that garish and baroque street that the locals called the Strip. The night was set ablaze by eight- and ten-story signs of blinking-pulsing-flashing incandescent bulbs, and by hundreds upon hundreds of miles of glowing neon tubes folded upon themselves as if they were the luminous intestines of transparent deep-water fish. The blur of water on the pickup's windows and the cowboy hat, its brim turned down, were not sufficient to disguise his nightmarish face from passing motorists. Therefore, he turned off the Strip well before he reached the hotels, on the first eastbound street he encountered, just past the back of McCarran International Airport. That street boasted no hotels, no carnivalesque banks of lights, and the traffic was sparse. By a circuitous route, he made his way to Tropicana Boulevard.

He had overheard Shadway telling Rachael about the Golden Sand Inn, and he had no difficulty finding it on a relatively undeveloped and somewhat dreary stretch of Tropicana. The single-story, U-shaped building embraced a swimming pool, with the open end exposed to the street. Sun-weathered wood trim in need of paint. Stained, cracked, pockmarked stucco. A tar-and-crushed-rock roof of the type common in the desert, bald and in need of rerocking. A few windows broken and boarded over. Landscaping overrun by weeds. Dead leaves and paper litter drifted against one wall. A large neon sign, broken and unlit, hung between twenty-foot-tall steel posts near the entrance drive, swinging slightly on its pivots as the wind wailed in from the west.

Nothing but empty scrubland lay for two hundred yards on either side of the Golden Sand Inn. Across the boulevard was a new housing development currently under construction: a score of homes in various stages of framing, skeletal shapes in the night and rain. But for the few cars passing on Tropicana, the motel was relatively isolated here on the southeastern edge of the city.

And judging by the total lack of lights, Rachael had not yet arrived. Where was she? He had driven very fast, but he did not believe he could have passed her on the highway.

As he thought about her, his heart began to pound. His vision acquired a crimson tint. The memory of blood made his saliva flow. That familiar cold rage spread out in icy crystals through his entire body, but he clenched his shark-fierce teeth and strove to remain at least functionally rational.

He parked the pickup on the graveled shoulder of the road more than a hundred yards past the Golden Sand, easing the front end into a shallow drainage ditch to give the impression that it had slid off the road and had been abandoned until morning. He switched off the headlights, then the engine. The pounding of the rain was louder now that the competing sound of the engine was gone. He waited until the eastbound and westbound lanes of the boulevard were deserted, then threw open the passenger-side door and got out into the storm.

He sloshed through the drainage ditch, which was full of racing brown water, and made his way across the barren stretch of desert toward the motel. He ran, for if a car came along Tropicana, he had nothing behind which to hide except a few tumbleweeds still rooted in the sandy soil and shaking in the wind.

Exposed to the elements, he again wanted to strip off his clothes and succumb to a deep-seated desire to run free through the wind and night, away from the lights of the city, into wild places. But the greater need for vengeance kept him clothed and focused on his objective.

The motel's small office occupied the northeast corner of the U-shaped structure. Through the big plate-glass windows, he could see only a portion of the unlighted room: the dim shapes of a sofa, one chair, an empty postcard rack, an end table and lamp, and the check-in desk. The manager's apartment, where Shadway had told Rachael to take shelter, was probably reached through the office. Eric tried the door, the knob disappearing in his huge leathery hand; it was locked, as he had expected.

Abruptly he saw a vague reflection of himself in the wet glass, a horned demonic visage bristling with teeth and twisted by strange bony excrescences. He looked quickly away, choking back the whimper that tried to escape him.

He moved into the courtyard, where doors to motel rooms lay on three sides. There were no lights, but he could see a surprising amount of detail, including the dark blue shade of paint on the doors. Whatever he was becoming, it was perhaps a creature with better night vision than a man possessed.

A battered aluminum awning overhung the cracked walkway that served all three wings, forming a shabby promenade. Rain drizzled from the awning, splashed onto the edge of the concrete walk, and puddled in a strip of grass that had been almost entirely choked out by weeds. His boots made thick squelching sounds as he walked through the weeds onto the concrete pool apron.

The swimming pool had been drained, but the storm was beginning to fill it again. Down at the deeper end of the sloped bottom, at least a foot of water had already collected. Beneath the water, an elusive—and perhaps illusory—shadowfire flickered crimson and silver, further distorted by the rippling of the fluid under which it burned.

Something about that shadowfire, more than any other before it, shot sparks of fear through him. Looking down into the black hole of the mostly empty pool, he was overcome by an instinctive urge to run, to put as much distance between himself and this place as possible.

He quickly turned away from the pool.

He stepped under the aluminum awning, where the tinny drumming of the rain made him feel claustrophobic, as if he were sealed inside a can. He went to room 15, near the center of the middle wing of the U, and tried the door. It was locked, too, but the lock looked old and flimsy. He stepped back and began kicking the door. By the third blow, he was so excited by the very act of destruction that he began to keen shrilly and uncontrollably. On the fourth kick, the lock snapped, and the door flew inward with a screech of tortured metal.

He went inside.

He remembered Shadway telling Rachael that electrical service had been maintained, but he did not switch on the lights. For one thing, he did not want to alert Rachael to his presence when, at last, she arrived. Besides, because of his drastically improved night vision, the dimensions of the lightless room and the contours of the furniture were revealed in sufficient detail to allow him to roam the chamber without falling over things.

Quietly he closed the door.

He moved to the window that looked out upon the courtyard, parted the musty, greasy drapes an inch or two, and peered into the lesser gloom of the blustery night. From here, he had a commanding view of the open end of the motel and of the door to the office.

When she came, he would see her.

Once she had settled in, he would go after her.

He shifted his weight impatiently from one foot to the other.

He made a thin, whispery, eager sound.

He longed for the blood.

◊   ◊

Amos Zachariah Tate—the craggy-faced, squint-eyed trucker with the carefully tended handlebar mustache—looked as if he might be the reincarnation of an outlaw who had prowled these same solitary reaches of the Mojave in the days of the Old West, preying upon stagecoaches and pony-express riders. However, his manner was more that of an itinerant preacher from the same age: soft-spoken, most courteous, generous, yet hard-bitten, with firm convictions about the redemption of the soul that was possible through the love of Jesus.

He provided Ben not merely with a free ride to Las Vegas but with a wool blanket to ward off the chill that the truck's air conditioner threw upon his rain-sodden body, coffee from one of two large thermos bottles, a chewy granola bar, and spiritual advice. He was genuinely concerned about Ben's comfort and physical well-being, a natural-born Good Samaritan who was embarrassed by displays of gratitude and who was devoid of self-righteousness, which drained all of the potential offensiveness from his well-meant, low-key pitch for Jesus.

Besides, Amos believed Ben's lie about a desperately injured—perhaps dying—wife in the Sunrise Hospital in Vegas. Although Amos said he did not usually take the laws of the land lightly—even minor laws like speed limits—he made an exception in this case and pushed the big rig up to sixty-five and seventy miles an hour, which was as fast as he felt he dared go in this foul weather.

Huddled under the warm wool blanket, sipping coffee, chewing the sweet granola bar and thinking bitter thoughts of death and loss, Ben was grateful to Amos Tate, but he wished they could make even better speed. If love was the closest that human beings could hope to come to immortality—which was what he'd thought when in bed with Rachael—then he had been given a key to life everlasting when he had found her. Now, at the gates of that paradise, it seemed the key was being snatched out of his hand. When he considered the bleakness of life without her, he wanted to seize control of the truck from Amos, push the driver aside, get behind the wheel, and make the rig *fly* to Vegas.

But all he could do was pull the blanket a little tighter around himself and, with growing trepidation, watch the dark miles go by.

◊   ◊

The manager's apartment at the Golden Sand Inn had been unused for a month or more, and it had a stale smell. Although the odor was not strong, Rachael repeatedly wrinkled her nose in distaste. There was a quality of putrescence in the smell which, over time, would probably leave her nauseated.

The living room was large, the bedroom small, the bathroom minuscule. The tiny kitchen was cramped and dreary but completely equipped. The walls did not look as if they had been painted in a decade. The carpets were threadbare, and the kitchen linoleum was cracked and discolored. The furniture was sagging and scarred and splitting at the seams, and the major kitchen appliances were dented and scraped and yellowing with age.

"Not a layout you're ever going to see in *Architectural Digest*," Whitney Gavis said, bracing himself against the refrigerator with the stump of his left arm and reaching behind with his one good hand to insert the plug in the wall socket. The motor came on at once. "But the stuff works, pretty much, and it's unlikely anyone's going to look for you here."

As they had gone through the apartment, turning on lights, she had begun to tell him the real story behind the warrants for her and Benny's arrest. Now they pulled up chairs at the Formica-topped kitchen table, which was filmed with gray dust and ringed with a score of cigarette scars, and she told him the rest of it as succinctly as she could.

Outside, the moaning wind seemed like a sentient beast, pressing its featureless face to the windows as if it wanted to hear the tale she told or as if it had something of its own to add to the story.

◊   ◊

Standing at the window of room 15, waiting for Rachael to arrive, Eric had felt the changefire growing hotter within him. He began to pour sweat; it streamed off his brow and down his face, gushed from every pore as if trying to match the rate at which the rain ran off the awning of the promenade beyond the window. He felt as if he were standing in a furnace, and every breath he drew seared through his lungs. All around him now, in every corner, the room was filled with the phantom flames of shadowfires, at which he dared not look. His bones felt molten, and his flesh was so hot that he would not have been surprised to see real flames spurt from his fingertips.

"Melting . . ." he said in a voice deep and guttural and thoroughly inhuman. " . . . the . . . melting man."

His face suddenly *shifted.* A terrible crunching-splintering noise filled his ears for a moment, issuing from within his skull, but it turned almost at once into a sickening, spluttering, oozing liquid sound. The process was accelerating insanely. Horrified, terrified—but also with a dark exhilaration and a wild demonic joy—he sensed his face changing shape. For a moment he was aware of a gnarled brow extending so far out over his eyes that it penetrated his peripheral vision, but then it was gone, subsiding, the new bone melting into his nose and mouth and jawline, pulling his nominally human countenance forward into a rudimentary, misshapen snout. His legs began to give way beneath him, so he turned reluctantly from the window, and with a crash he fell to his knees on the floor. Something snapped in his chest. To accommodate the snoutlike restructuring of his visage, his lips split farther back along his cheeks. He dragged himself onto the bed, rolled onto his back, giving himself entirely to the devastating yet not essentially unpleasant process of revolutionary change, and as from a great distance he heard himself making peculiar sounds: a doglike growl, a reptilian hiss, and the wordless but unmistakable exclamations of a man in the throes of sexual orgasm.

For a while, darkness claimed him.

When he came partially to his senses a few minutes later, he found that he had rolled off the bed and was lying beneath the window, where he had recently been keeping a watch for Rachael. Although the changefire had not grown cooler, although he still felt his tissues seeking new forms in every part of his body, he resolutely pushed aside the drapes and reached up toward the window. In the dim light, his hands looked enormous and chitinous, as if they belonged to a crab or lobster that had been gifted with fingers instead of pincers. He grabbed the sill and pulled himself off the floor, stood. He leaned against the glass, his breath coming in great hot gasps that steamed the pane.

Light shone in the windows of the motel office.

Rachael must have arrived.

Instantly he was seething with hatred. The motivating memory-smell of blood filled his nostrils.

But he also had an immense and strangely formed erection. He wanted to mount her, then kill her as he had taken and then slain the cowboy's woman. In his degenerate and mutant state, he was unsettled to discover that he was having trouble holding on to an understanding of her identity. Second by second he was ceasing to care who she was: the only thing that mattered now was that she was female—and prey.

He turned away from the window and tried to reach the door, but his metamorphosing legs collapsed beneath him. Again, for a time, he squirmed and writhed upon the motel floor, the changefire hotter than ever within him.

His genes and chromosomes, once the undisputed regulators—the masters—of his very form and function, had become plastic themselves. They were no longer primarily re-creating previous stages in human evolution but were exploring utterly alien forms that had nothing to do with the physiological history of the human species. They were mutating either randomly or in response to inexplicable forces and patterns he could not perceive. And as they mutated, they directed his body to produce the mad flood of hormones and proteins with which his flesh was molded.

He was becoming something that had never before walked the earth and that had never been meant to walk it.

◑　　　◑

The Marine Corps twin-engine turboprop transport from Twentynine Palms landed in driving rain at Mc-Carren International Airport in Las Vegas at 9:03 P.M. Tuesday. It was only ten minutes ahead of the estimated time of arrival for the scheduled airline flight from Orange County on which Julio Verdad and Reese Hagerstrom were passengers.

Harold Ince, a DSA agent in the Nevada office, met Anson Sharp, Jerry Peake, and Nelson Gosser at the debarkation gate.

Gosser immediately headed for another gate, where the incoming flight from Orange County would unload. It would be his job to run a discreet tail on Verdad and Hagerstrom until they had left the terminal, whereupon they would become the responsibility of the surveillance team that would be waiting outside.

Ince said, "Mr. Sharp, sir, we're cutting it awful close."

"Tell me something I don't know," Sharp said, walking swiftly across the waiting area that served the gate, toward the long corridor that led to the front of the terminal.

Peake hurried after Sharp, and Ince—a much shorter man than Sharp—hustled to stay at his side. "Sir, the car's waiting for you out front, discreetly at the end of the taxi line, as you requested."

"Good. But what if they don't take a cab?"

"One rental-car desk is still open. If they stop to make those arrangements, I'll warn you at once."

"Good."

They reached the moving walkway and stepped onto the rubber belt. No other flights had landed recently or were about to take off, so the corridor was deserted. On the speaker system that served the long hall, taped messages from Vegas showroom performers—Joan Rivers, Paul Anka, Rodney Dangerfield, Tom Dreesen, Bill Cosby, and others—offered lame jokes and, mostly, advice about safety on the pedway: Please use the moving handrail, stay to the right, allow other passengers to pass on the left, and be careful not to trip at the end of the moving belt.

Dissatisfied with the leisurely speed of the walkway, striding along between the moving handrails, Sharp glanced down and slightly back at Ince and said, "How's your relationship with the Las Vegas police?"

"They're cooperative, sir."

"That's all?"

"Well, maybe better than that," Ince said. "They're good guys. They have a hell of a job to do in this city, what with all the hoods and transients, and they handle it well. Got to give them credit. They're not soft, and because they know how hard it is to keep the peace, they have a lot of respect for cops of all kinds."

"Like us?"

"Like us."

"If there's shooting," Sharp said, "and if someone reports it, and if the Vegas uniforms arrive before we've been able to mop up, can we count on them to conform their reports to our needs?"

Ince blinked in surprise. "Well, I . . . maybe."

"I see," Sharp said coldly. They reached the end of the moving walkway. As they strode into the main lobby of the terminal, he said, "Ince, in days to come, you better build a tighter relationship with the local agencies. Next time, I don't want to hear 'maybe.' "

"Yes, sir. But—"

"You stay here, maybe over by the newsstand. Make yourself as inconspicuous as possible."

"That's why I'm dressed this way," Ince said. He was wearing a green polyester leisure suit and an orange Banlon shirt.

Leaving Ince behind, Sharp pushed through a glass door and went outside, where rain was blowing under the overhanging roof.

Jerry Peake caught up with him at last.

"How long do we have, Jerry?"

Glancing at his watch, Peake said, "They land in five minutes."

The taxi line was short at this hour—only four cabs. Their car was parked at the curb marked ARRIVALS— UNLOADING ONLY, about fifty feet behind the last taxi. It was one of the agency's standard crap-brown Fords that might as well have had UNMARKED LAW-ENFORCEMENT SEDAN painted on the sides in foot-tall block letters. Fortunately, the rain would disguise the institutional nature of the car and would make it more difficult for Verdad and Hagerstrom to spot a tail.

Peake got behind the wheel, and Sharp sat in the passenger's seat, putting his attaché case on his lap. He said, "If they take a cab, get close enough to read its plates, then fall way back. Then if we lose it, we can get a quick fix on its destination from the taxi company."

Peake nodded.

Their car was half sheltered by the overhang and half exposed to the storm. Rain hammered only on Sharp's side, and only his windows were blurred by the sheeting water.

He opened the attaché case and removed the two pistols whose registration numbers could be traced neither to him nor to the DSA. One of the silencers was fresh, the other too well used when they had pursued Shadway at Lake Arrowhead. He fitted the fresh one to a pistol, keeping that weapon for himself. He gave the other gun to Peake, who seemed to accept it with reluctance.

"Something wrong?" Sharp asked.

Peake said, "Well . . . sir . . . do you still want to kill Shadway?"

Sharp gave him a narrow look. "It isn't what I want, Jerry. Those are my orders: terminate him. Orders from authorities so high up the ladder that *I* sure as hell am not going to buck them."

"But . . ."

"What is it?"

"If Verdad and Hagerstrom lead us to Shadway and Mrs. Leben, if they're right *there,* you can't terminate anyone in front of them. I mean, sir, those detectives won't keep their mouths shut. Not them."

"I'm pretty sure I can make Verdad and Hagerstrom back off," Sharp assured him. He pulled the clip out of the pistol to make sure it was fully loaded. "The bastards are supposed to stay out of this, and they know it. When I catch them red-handed in the middle of it, they're going to realize that their careers and pensions are in jeopardy. They'll back off. And when they're gone, we'll take out Shadway and the woman."

"If they don't back off?"

"Then we take them out, too," Sharp said. With the heel of his hand, he slammed the clip back into the pistol.

❖   ❖

The refrigerator hummed noisily.

The damp air still smelled stale, with a hint of decay.

They hunched over the old kitchen table like two conspirators in one of those old war movies about the anti-Nazi underground in Europe. Rachael's thirty-two pistol lay on the cigarette-scarred Formica, within easy reach, though she did not really believe she would need it—at least not tonight.

Whitney Gavis had absorbed her story—in a condensed form—with remarkably little shock and without skepticism, which surprised her. He did not seem to be a gullible man. He would not believe just any crazy tale he was told. Yet he had believed her wild narrative. Maybe he trusted her implicitly because Benny loved her.

"Benny showed you pictures of me?" she had asked. And Whitney had said, "Yeah, kid, the last couple months, you're all he can talk about." So she said, "Then he knew that what we had together was special, knew it before I did." Whitney said, "No, he told me that you knew the relationship was special, too, but you were afraid to admit it just yet; he said you'd come around, and he was right." She said, "If he showed you pictures of me, why didn't he show me pictures of you or at least *talk* about you, since you're his best friend?" And Whitney had said, "Benny and me are committed to each other, have been ever since Nam, as good as brothers, better than brothers, so we share everything. But until recently, you hadn't committed to him, kid, and until you did, he wasn't going to share everything with you. Don't hold that against him. It's Nam that made him that way."

Vietnam was probably another reason that Whitney Gavis believed her incredible tale, even the part about being pursued by a mutant beast in the Mojave Desert. After a man had been through the madness of Vietnam, maybe nothing strained his credulity anymore.

Now Whitney said, "But you don't know for certain that those snakes killed him."

"No," Rachael admitted.

"If he came back from the dead after being hit by the truck, is it possible he could come back after dying of multiple snakebites?"

"Yes. I suppose so."

"And if he doesn't stay dead, you can't be certain he'll just degenerate into something that'll remain out there on the desert, living pretty much an animal's existence."

"No," she said, "of course, I can't guarantee that, either."

He frowned, and the scarred side of his otherwise handsome face puckered and creased as if it were paper.

Outside, the night was marked by ominous noises, though all were related to the storm: the fronds of a palm tree scraped against the roof; the motel sign, stirred by the wind, creaked on corroded hinges; a loose section of downspouting popped and rattled against its braces. Rachael listened for sounds that could not be explained by the wind and rain, heard none, but kept listening anyway.

Whitney said, "The really disturbing thing is that Eric must've overheard Benny telling you about this place."

"Maybe," Rachael said uneasily.

"Almost certainly, kid."

"All right. But considering his appearance when I last saw him, he won't be able to just stand out along the road and hitch a ride. Besides, he seemed to be devolving mentally and emotionally, not just physically. I mean . . . Whitney, if you could've seen him with those snakes, you'd realize how unlikely it is that he'd have the mental capacity to find a path out of the desert and somehow get all the way here to Vegas."

"Unlikely, but not impossible," he said. "Nothing's impossible, kid. After I had my run-in with an anti-personnel mine in Nam, they told my family I couldn't possibly live. But I did. So they told me I couldn't possibly regain enough muscle control of my damaged face to speak without impairment. But I did. Hell, they had a whole list of things that were impossible—but none of them turned out to be. And I didn't have your husband's advantage—this genetic business."

"If you can call it an advantage," she said, remembering the hideous notched ridge of bone on Eric's forehead, the nascent horns, the inhuman eyes, the fierce hands . . .

"I should arrange other accommodations for you."

"No," she said quickly. "This is where Benny's expecting to find me. If I'm not here—"

"Don't sweat it, kid. He'll find you through me."

"No. If he shows up, I want to be here."

"But—"

"I want to be here," she insisted sharply, determined not to be talked into another course of action. "As soon as he gets here, I want to . . . I have to . . . see him. I have to *see* him."

Whitney Gavis studied her for a moment. He had a discomfitingly intense gaze. Finally he said, "God, you really love him, don't you?"

"Yes," she said tremulously.

"I mean *really* love him."

"Yes," she repeated, trying to prevent her voice from cracking with emotion. "And I'm worried about him . . . so very worried."

"He'll be all right. He's a survivor."

"If anything happens to him—"

"Nothing will," Whitney said. "But I guess there's not much danger in you staying here tonight, at least. Even if your husband . . . even if Eric gets to Vegas, it sounds as if he's going to have to stay out of sight and make a slow and careful journey of it. Probably won't arrive for a few days—"

"If ever."

"—so we can wait until tomorrow to find another place for you. You can stay here and wait for Benny tonight. And he'll come. I know he will, Rachael."

Tears shimmered in her eyes. Not trusting herself to speak, she merely nodded.

With the good grace not to remark upon her tears and the good sense not to try to comfort her, Whitney pushed himself up from the kitchen table and said, "Yes, well, all right, then! If you're going to spend even one night in this dump, we've got to make the place more comfortable. For one thing, although there may be towels and some sheets in the linen closet, they're probably dusty, mildewed or even crawling with disease. So what I'll do is, I'll go buy a set of sheets, towels . . . and how about some food?"

"I'm starved," she said. "I only had an Egg McMuffin early this morning and a couple of candy bars later, but I've burned all that off half a dozen times over. I made a quick stop in Baker, but that was after my encounter with Eric, and I didn't have much appetite. Just picked up a six-pack of diet soda 'cause I was feeling so dehydrated."

"I'll bring back some grub, too. You want to give me a dinner order, or do you trust me?"

She stood up and wearily pushed a pale and trembling hand through her hair. "I'll eat almost anything except turnips and squid."

He smiled. "Lucky for you, this is Vegas. Any other town, the only store open at this hour would be the turnip and squid emporium. But hardly anything in Vegas ever closes. You want to come with me?"

"I shouldn't be showing my face."

He nodded. "You're right. Well, I ought to be back in an hour. You be okay here?"

"Really," she said, "I'm safer here than anywhere else I've been since yesterday morning."

◊   ◊

In the velvety blackness of room 15, Eric crawled aimlessly across the floor, first one way and then another, twitching, kicking spasmodically, hitching and shuddering and squirming like a broken-backed cockroach.

"Rachael . . ."

He heard himself speak that word and only that word, each time with a different intonation, as if it constituted his entire vocabulary. Although his voice was thick as mud, those two syllables were always clear. Sometimes he knew what the word meant, remembered who she was, but at other times it had no meaning for him. However, regardless of whether or not he knew what it meant, the name predictably engendered precisely the same response in him each time he spoke it: mindless, icy fury.

"Rachael . . ."

Caught helplessly in the tides of change, he groaned, hissed, gagged, whimpered, and sometimes he laughed softly in the back of his throat. He coughed and choked and gasped for breath. He lay on his back, shaking and bucking as the changes surged through him, clawing at the air with hands twice as large as his hands had been in his previous life.

Buttons popped off his red plaid shirt. One of the shoulder seams split as his body swelled and bent into a grotesque new form.

"Rachael . . ."

During the past several hours, as his feet had grown larger and smaller and then larger again, his boots periodically pinched. Now they were painfully confining, crippling, and he could not bear them any longer. He literally tore them off, frenziedly ripped away the soles and heels, wrenched with his powerful hands until the sturdily stitched seams split, used his razored claws to puncture and shred the leather.

His unshod feet proved to have changed as completely as his hands had done. They were broader, flatter, with an exceptionally gnarled and bony bridge, the toes as long as fingers, terminating in claws as sharp as those on his hands.

"Rachael . . ."

Change *smashed* through him as if it were a bolt of lightning blasting through a tree, the current entering at the highest point of the highest limb and sizzling out through the hair-fine tips of the deepest roots.

He twitched and spasmed.

He drummed his heels against the floor.

Hot tears flooded from his eyes, and rivulets of thick saliva streamed from his mouth.

Sweating copiously, being burned alive by the change-fire within him, he was nevertheless cold at the core. There was ice in both his heart and mind.

He squirmed into a corner and curled up, hugging himself. His breastbone cracked, shuddered, swelled larger, and sought a new shape. His spine creaked, and he felt it shifting within him to accommodate other alterations in his form.

Only seconds later, he skittered out of the corner in a crablike crawl. He stopped in the middle of the room and rose onto his knees. Gasping, moaning deep in his throat, he knelt for a moment with his head hung low, letting the dizziness flow out with his rancid sweat.

The changefire had finally cooled. For the moment, his form had stabilized.

He stood, swaying.

"Rachael . . ."

He opened his eyes and looked around the motel room, and he was not surprised to discover that his vision was nearly as good in the dark as it had ever been in full daylight. Furthermore, his field of vision had dramatically increased: when he looked straight ahead, objects on both his left and right sides were as clear and as sharply detailed as those things immediately in front of him.

He went to the door. Parts of his mutated body seemed ill formed and dysfunctional, forcing him to hitch along like some hard-shelled crustacean that had only recently developed the ability to stand upright like a man. Yet he was not crippled; he could move quickly and silently, and he had a sense of tremendous strength far greater than anything he had ever known before.

Making a soft hissing noise that was lost in the sounds of wind and drizzling rain, he opened the door and stepped into the night, which welcomed him.

◊ 35 ◊

SOMETHING THAT
LOVES THE DARK

Whitney left the manager's apartment at the Golden Sand Inn by way of the rear door of the kitchen. It opened into a dusty garage where, earlier, they had put the black Mercedes. Now the 560 SEL stood in small puddles of rainwater that had dripped from it. His own car was outside, in the serviceway behind the motel.

Turning to Rachael, who stood on the threshold between kitchen and garage, Whitney said, "You lock this door behind me and sit tight. I'll be back as soon as I can."

"Don't worry. I'll be fine," she said. "I've got to get the Wildcard file in order. That'll keep me busy."

He had no trouble understanding why Ben had fallen so hard for her. Even as disheveled as she was, pale with exhaustion and worry, Rachael was gorgeous. But her beauty was not her only attribute. She was caring, perceptive, smart, and tough—not a common mix of qualities.

"Ben will probably show up before I do," he assured her.

She smiled thinly, grateful for his attempt to cheer her. She nodded, bit her lower lip, but could not speak because, obviously, she was still more than half convinced that she would never again see Ben alive.

Whitney motioned her back from the threshold and pulled the door shut between them. He waited until he heard her engage the dead-bolt lock. Then he crossed the grease- and oil-stained concrete floor, passing the front of the Mercedes, not bothering to put up the big rear door, but heading toward the side entrance.

The three-car garage, illuminated by a single bare bulb dangling on a cord from a crossbeam, was filthy and musty, a badly cluttered repository of old and poorly maintained maintenance equipment plus a lot of stuff that was just plain junk: rusting buckets; tattered brooms; ragged, motheaten mops; a broken outdoor vacuum cleaner; several motel-room chairs with broken legs or torn upholstery, which the previous owners had intended to repair and put back into service; scraps of lumber; coils of wire and coiled hoses; a bathroom sink; spare brass sprinkler heads spilling from an overturned cardboard box; one cotton gardening glove lying palm up like a severed hand; cans of paint and lacquer, their contents almost surely thickened and dried beyond usefulness. This trash was piled along the walls, scattered over portions of the floor, and stacked precariously in the loft.

Just as he unlocked the dead bolt on the side door of the garage, before he actually opened the door, Whitney heard a rattling in the garage behind him. The noise was short-lived; in fact, it stopped even as he turned to see what it was.

Frowning, he let his gaze travel over the piles of junk, the Mercedes, the gas furnace in the far corner, the sagging workbench, and the hot-water heater. He saw nothing out of the ordinary.

He listened.

The only sounds were the many voices of the wind in the eaves and the rain on the roof.

He turned away from the door, walked slowly to the car, circled it, but found nothing that could have caused the noise.

Maybe one of the piles of junk had shifted under its own weight—or had been disturbed by a rat. He would not be surprised to discover that the moldering old building was rat-infested, though he had not previously seen evidence of such an infestation. The trash was piled so haphazardly that he could not discern if it was all in the same position as it had been a moment ago.

He returned to the door again, took one last look around, then went out into the storm.

Even as the wind-harried rain slashed at him, he belatedly realized what he had heard in the garage: someone trying to pull open the big rear door from outside. But it was an electric door that could not be operated manually while in its automatic mode, and was therefore secure against prowlers. Whoever had tried it must have realized, at once, that he could not get in that way, which explained why the rattling had lasted only a moment.

Whitney limped warily toward the corner of the garage and the serviceway beyond it to see if anyone was still there. The rain was falling hard, making a crisp sound on the walk, a sloppier sound on the earth, spilling off the corner of the roof where the downspout was missing. All that wet noise effectively masked his own footsteps, as it would mask the activities of anyone behind the garage, and though he listened intently to the night, he did not at first hear anything unusual. He took six or eight steps, pausing twice to listen, before the patter and susurration of the rain was cut by a frightening noise. *Behind* him. It was partly a hiss like escaping steam, partly a thin catlike whine, partly a thick and menacing growl, and it put the hair up on the back of his neck.

He turned quickly, cried out, and stumbled backward when he saw the thing looming over him in the gloom. Incomprehensibly strange eyes looked down at him from a height of six and a half feet or more. They were bulging, mismatched eyes, each as large as an egg, one pale green and the other orange, iridescent like the eyes of some animals, one rather like the eye of a hyperthyroid cat, the other featuring a mean slit-shaped iris reminiscent

of a serpent, both *beveled* and many-faceted, for God's
sake, like the eyes of an insect.

For a moment Whit stood transfixed. Suddenly a
powerful arm lashed out at him, backhanded him across
the face, and knocked him down. He fell onto the
concrete walk, hurting his tailbone, and rolled into mud
and weeds.

The creature's arm—*Leben's* arm, Whit knew
that it had to be Eric Leben transformed beyond
understanding—had appeared not to be hinged like
a human arm. It seemed to be segmented, equipped
with three or four smaller, elbowlike joints that could
lock in any combination and that gave it tremendous
flexibility. Now, stunned by the vicious blow he had
taken, half paralyzed by terror, looking up at the
beast as it approached him, he saw that it was
slump-shouldered and hunchbacked yet possessed a
queer sort of grace, perhaps because its legs, mostly
concealed by tattered jeans, were similar in design to
the powerful, segmented arms.

Whit realized he was screaming. He had screamed—
really screamed—only once before in his life, in Nam,
when the antipersonnel mine had blown up beneath
him, when he had lain on the jungle floor and had
seen the bottom half of his own leg lying five yards
away, the bloody mangled toes poking through burnt
and blasted boot leather. Now he screamed again and
could not stop.

Over his own screams, he heard a shrill keening
sound from his adversary, what might have been a cry
of triumph.

Its head rolled and bobbled strangely, and for a moment
Whit had a glimpse of terrible hooked teeth.

He tried to scoot backward across the sodden earth,
propelling himself with his good right arm and the
stump of the other, but he was unable to move fast.
He did not have time to get his legs under him. He
managed to retreat only a couple of yards before
Leben reached him and bent down and grabbed him
by the foot of his left leg, fortunately the artificial

leg, and began to drag him toward the open door of the garage.

Even in the night shadows and rain, Whit could see enough of the man-thing's hand to know that it was as thoroughly inhuman as the rest of the beast. And huge. And powerful.

Frantically Whit Gavis kicked out with his good foot, putting all the force he had into the blow, and connected solidly with Leben's leg. The man-thing shrieked, though apparently not in pain as much as in anger. In response, it wrenched his artificial leg so hard that the securing straps tore loose of their buckles. With a brief agony that robbed Whit of breath, the prosthetic limb came loose, leaving him at an even greater disadvantage.

◑   ◑

In the cramped kitchen of the motel manager's apartment, Rachael had just opened the plastic garbage bag and had removed one handful of rumpled, soiled Xeroxes from the disorganized Wildcard file when she heard the first scream. She knew immediately that it was Whitney, and she also knew instinctively that there could be only one cause of it: Eric.

She threw the papers aside and plucked the thirty-two pistol off the table. She went to the rear door, hesitated, then unlocked it.

Stepping into the dank garage, she paused again, for there was movement on all sides of her. A strong draft swept in through the open side door from the raging night beyond, swinging the single dirty light bulb on its cord. The motion of the light made shadows leap up and fall back and leap up again in every corner. She looked around warily at the stacks of eerily illuminated trash and old furniture, all of which seemed alive amidst the animated shadows.

Whitney's screaming was coming from outside, so she figured that Eric was out there, too, rather than in the garage. She abandoned caution and hurried past the black Mercedes, stepping over a couple of paint cans and around a pile of coiled garden hoses.

A piercing, blood-freezing shriek cut through Whitney's screams, and Rachael knew without doubt that it was Eric, for that shrill cry was similar to the one he'd made while pursuing her across the desert earlier in the day. But it was more fierce and furious than she remembered, more powerful, and even less human and more alien than it had been before. Hearing that monstrous voice, she almost turned and ran. Almost. But, after all, she was not capable of abandoning Whitney Gavis.

She plunged through the open door, into the night and tempest, the pistol held out in front of her. The Eric-thing was only a few yards away, its back to her. She cried out in shock because she saw that it was holding Whitney's leg, which it seemed to have torn from him.

An instant later, she realized that it was the artificial leg, but by then she had drawn the beast's attention. It threw the fake limb aside and turned toward her, its impossible eyes gleaming.

Its appearance was so numbingly horrific that 'she, unlike Whitney, was unable to scream; she tried, but her voice failed her. The darkness and rain mercifully concealed many details of the mutant form, but she had an impression of a massive and misshapen head, jaws that resembled a cross between those of a wolf and a crocodile, and an abundance of deadly teeth. Shirtless and shoeless, clad only in jeans, it was a few inches taller than Eric had been, and its spine curved up into hunched and deformed shoulders. There was an immense expanse of breastbone that looked as if it might be covered with horns or spines of some sort, and with rounded knobby excrescences. Long and strangely jointed arms hung almost to its knees. The hands were surely just like the hands of demons who, in the fiery depths of hell, cracked open human souls and ate the meat of them.

"Rachael . . . Rachael . . . come for you . . . Rachael," the Eric-thing said in a vile and whispery voice, slowly forming each word with care, as if the knowledge and use of language were nearly forgotten. The creature's throat and mouth and tongue and lips were no longer designed for the production of human speech; the formation of each syllable obviously required tremendous effort and perhaps some pain. "Come . . . for . . . you . . ."

It took a step toward her, its arms swinging against its sides with a scraping, clicking, chitinous sound.

It.

She could no longer think of him as Eric, as her husband. Now, he was just a thing, an abomination, that by its very existence made a mockery of everything else in God's creation.

She fired point-blank at its chest.

It did not even flinch at the impact of the slug. It emitted a high-pitched squeal that seemed more an expression of eagerness than pain, and it took another step.

She fired again, then a third time, and a fourth.

The multiple impacts of the slugs made the beast stagger slightly to one side, but it did not go down.

"Rachael . . . Rachael . . ."

Whitney shouted, "Shoot it, kill it!"

The pistol's clip held ten rounds. She squeezed off the last six as fast as she could, certain that she hit the thing every time in the gut and chest and even in the face.

It finally roared in pain and collapsed onto its knees, then toppled facedown in the mud.

"Thank God," she said shakily, "thank God," and she was suddenly so weak that she had to lean against the outside wall of the garage.

The Eric-thing retched, gagged, twitched, and pushed up onto hands and knees.

"No," she said disbelievingly.

It raised its grisly head and stared fiercely at her with cold, mismatched lantern eyes. Slowly lids slid down over the eyes, then slowly up, and when revealed again, those radiant ovals seemed brighter than before.

Even if its altered genetic structure provided for incredibly rapid healing and for resurrection after death, surely it could not recover *this* fast. If it could repair and reanimate itself in seconds after succumbing to ten bullet wounds, it was not just a quick healer, and not just potentially immortal, but virtually invincible.

"Die, damn you," she said.

It shuddered and spat something into the mud, then lurched up from the ground, all the way to its feet.

"Run!" Whitney shouted. "For ███████ sake, Rachael, *run*!"

She had no hope of saving Whitney. There was no point in staying to be killed with him.

"Rachael," the creature said, and in its gravelly mucus-thick voice were anger and hunger and hatred and dark need.

No more bullets in the gun. There were boxes of ammunition in the Mercedes, but she could never reach them in time to reload. She dropped the pistol.

"Run!" Whit Gavis shouted again.

Heart hammering, Rachael sprinted back into the garage, leaping over the paint cans and garden hoses. A twinge of pain shot through the ankle she had twisted earlier in the day, and the claw punctures in her thigh began to burn as if they were fresh wounds.

The demon shrieked behind her.

As she went, Rachael toppled a set of freestanding metal shelves laden with tools and boxes of nails, hoping to delay the thing if it pursued her immediately instead of finishing Whitney Gavis first. The shelves went over with a resounding crash, and by the time she reached the open kitchen door, she heard the beast clambering through the debris. It had, indeed, left Whitney alive, for it was in a frenzy to put its hands upon her.

She bounded across the threshold, slammed the kitchen door, but before she could engage the dead-bolt latch, the door was thrown open with tremendous force. She was propelled across the kitchen, nearly fell, somehow stayed on her feet, but struck her hip against the edge of a counter and slammed backward into the refrigerator hard enough to send a brief though intense current of pain from the small of her back to the base of her neck.

It came in from the garage. In the kitchen light, it appeared immense and was more hideous than she had wanted to believe.

For a moment, it stood just inside the door, glaring across the small dusty kitchen. It lifted its head and expanded its chest as if giving her an opportunity to admire it. Its flesh was mottled brown-gray-green-black, with lighter patches that almost resembled human skin, though it was mostly pebbled like elephant hide and scaly in some places. The head was pear-shaped, set at a slant on the thick muscular neck, with the round end at the top and the slimmer end at the bottom of the face. The entire narrow part of the "pear" was composed of a snoutlike protrusion and jaws. When it opened its enormous mouth to hiss, the pointed teeth within were sharklike in their sharpness and profusion. The darting tongue was dark and quick and utterly inhuman. Its entire face was lumpy; in addition to a pair of hornlike knobs on its forehead, there were odd convexities and concavities that seemed to have no biological purpose, plus tumorous knots of bone or other tissue. On its brow and radiating downward from its eyes, throbbing arteries and swollen veins shone just beneath the skin.

In the Mojave, earlier in the day, she had thought that Eric was undergoing retrograde evolution, that his genetically altered body was becoming a sort of patchwork of ancient racial forms. But this thing owed nothing to human physiological history. This was the nightmare product of genetic chaos, a creature that went neither backward nor forward along the chain of human evolution. It was embarked upon a sidewise biological *re*volution—and had severed most if not all links with the human seed from which it sprang. Some of Eric's consciousness evidently still existed within the dreadful hulk, although Rachael suspected only the faintest trace of his personality and intellect remained and that soon even this spark of Eric would be extinguished forever.

"See . . . me . . ." it said, reinforcing her feeling that it was preening before her.

She edged away from the refrigerator, toward the open door between the kitchen and the living room.

It raised one murderous hand, palm out, as if to tell her she must stop retreating. The segmented arm appeared capable of bending backward or forward at four places, and each of those bizarre joints was protected by hard brown-black plates of tissue that seemed similar in substance to a beetle's carapace. The long, claw-tipped fingers were frightening, but something worse lay in the center of its palm: a round, sucker-shaped orifice as large as a half-dollar. As she stared in horror at this Dantean apparition, the orifice in its palm opened and closed slowly, opened and closed like a raw wound, opened and closed. The function of the mouth-in-hand was in part mysterious and in part too dreadfully clear; as she stared, it grew red and moist with an obscene hunger.

Panicked, she made a break for the nearby doorway and heard the beast's feet clicking like cloven hooves on the linoleum as it rushed after her. Five or six steps into the living room, heading toward the door that opened into the motel office, with eight or ten steps to go, she saw the beast looming at her right side.

It moved so *fast*!

Screaming, she threw herself to the floor and rolled to escape its grasp. She collided with an armchair, shot to her feet, and put the chair between her and the enemy.

When she changed directions, the creature had not immediately followed. It was standing in the center of the room, watching her, apparently aware that it had cut her off from her only route of escape and that it could take time to relish her terror before it closed in for the kill.

She began to back toward the bedroom.

It said, "Raysheeeel, Raysheeeel," no longer capable of speaking her name clearly.

The tumorous lumps across the beast's forehead rippled and reformed. Right before her eyes, one of its small horns melted away entirely as another minor wave of change passed through the creature, and a new vein traced a path across its face much like a slow-moving fissure forming in the earth.

She continued to edge backward.

It moved toward her with slow, easy steps.

"Raysheeeel . . ."

◗   ◗

Convinced that a dying wife lay in an intensive-care ward waiting for her husband, Amos Tate wanted to drive Ben all the way to Sunrise Hospital, which would have taken him too far away from the Golden Sand Inn. Ben had to insist strenuously on being dropped at the corner of Las Vegas Boulevard and Tropicana. And as there was no good reason to refuse Amos's generous offer, Ben was reduced to admitting that he had lied about the wife, though he offered no explanation. He flung off the blanket, threw open the cab door, jumped down to the street, and ran east on Tropicana, past the Tropicana Hotel, leaving the startled trucker staring after him in puzzlement.

The Golden Sand Inn was approximately a mile ahead, a distance he could ordinarily cover in six minutes or less. But in the heavy rain, he did not want to risk sprinting at top speed, for if he fell and broke an arm or leg, he would not be in any condition to help Rachael if, in fact, she needed help. (God, please, let her be warm and safe and sound and in need of no help at all!) He ran along the shoulder of the broad boulevard, the revolver digging into his flesh where it was tucked under his waistband. He splashed through puddles that filled every depression in the macadam. Only a few cars passed him; several of the drivers slowed to stare, but none offered him a lift. He did not bother trying to hitch a ride, for he sensed that he had no time to waste.

A mile was not a great distance, but tonight it seemed like a journey to the far end of the world.

◊　　◊

Julio and Reese had been able to board the plane in Orange County with their service revolvers holstered under their coats because they had presented their police credentials to the attendant at the metal-detecting security gate. Now, having landed at McCarran International in Las Vegas, they used their ID again to obtain swift service from the clerk at the rental-car desk, an attractive brunette named Ruth. Instead of just handing them the keys and sending them out to the lot to locate their designated rental on their own, she telephoned a night-duty mechanic to pick it up and drive it around to the front entrance of the terminal.

Since they had not come dressed for rain, they stood inside the terminal at a set of glass doors until they saw the Dodge pull up at the curb, then went out into the storm. The mechanic, more suitably dressed for the foul weather in a vinyl raincoat with a vinyl hood, quickly checked their rental papers and turned the car over to them.

Although clouds had claimed the sky late in the day in Orange County, Reese had not realized things would be worse to the east and had not bargained for a landing in a rainstorm. Though their descent and touchdown had been as smooth as glass, he had gripped the arms of his seat so tightly that his hands were still slightly stiff and achy.

Safely on the ground, he should have been relieved, but he could not forget Teddy Bertlesman, the tall pink lady, and he could also not forget little Esther waiting at home for him. This morning, he'd had only his Esther to live for, just that one small blessing, which was not a sufficient abundance to tempt the cruelty of fate. But now there was also the glorious real-estate saleswoman, and Reese was acutely aware that when a man had more reason to live he was more likely to die.

Superstitious nonsense, perhaps.

But the rain, when he had expected a clear desert night, seemed like a bad omen, and he was uneasy.

As Julio drove away from the terminal, Reese wiped the rain off his face and said, "What about all those TV commercials for Vegas on the L.A. stations?"

"What about them?"

"Where's the sunshine? Where're all those girls in tiny little bikinis?"

"What do you care about girls in bikinis when you have a date with Teddy Bertlesman on Saturday?"

Don't talk about that, Reese thought superstitiously.

He said, "Hell, this doesn't look like Vegas. This looks more like Seattle."

◗   ◗

Rachael slammed the bedroom door and thumbed in the button to engage the flimsy lock. She ran to the only window, pulled open the rotting drapes, found it had jalousie panes, and realized that, because of those metal cross-ribs, there was no easy exit.

Looking around for something that could be used as a weapon, she saw only the bed, two nightstands, one lamp, and a chair.

She expected the door to crash inward, but it did not.

She heard nothing from the creature in the living room, and its silence, while welcome, was also unnerving. What was it up to?

She ran to the closet, slid the door open, and looked inside. Nothing of use. Just a tier of empty shelves in one corner and then a rod and empty hangers. She could not fashion a weapon out of a few wire hangers.

The doorknob rattled.

"Raysheeeel," the thing hissed tauntingly.

A fragment of Eric's consciousness evidently did remain within the mutant, for it was that Eric-part that wanted to make her sweat and wanted her to have plenty of time to contemplate what he was going to do to her.

She would die here, and it would be a slow and terrible death.

In frustration, she started to turn away from the empty clothes rod and hangers, but noticed a trap in the closet ceiling, an access to the attic.

The creature thumped a heavy hand against the door, then again and again. "Raysheeeel . . ."

She slipped inside the closet and tugged on the shelves to test their sturdiness. To her relief, they were built in, screwed to the wall studs, so she was able to climb them as if they were a ladder. She stood on the fourth tier, her head only a foot below the ceiling. Holding the adjacent rod with one hand, she reached out and up to one side with her free hand, beyond the shelves, and quietly pushed up the hinged trap.

"Raysheeeel, Raysheeeel," it crooned, dragging its claws down the outside of the locked bedroom door, then throwing itself lightly—almost teasingly—against that barrier.

In the closet, Rachael climbed one more step, got a grip on two edges of the overhead opening, swung off the shelves, dangled for a moment with the rod against her breasts, then muscled herself up and into the attic. There was no flooring, just two-by-four beams sixteen inches apart, with sheathed pads of Fiberglas insulation laid between those supports. In the wan yellow light that rose through the open trap, she saw the attic ceiling was very low, providing only a four-foot-high space, with roofing nails poking through in a lot of places, and with larger exposed rafter nails lancing out here and there. To her surprise, the attic was not limited to the area over the office and the manager's apartment, but led off across the ceilings of all the rooms in that long wing.

Below, something crashed so hard that she felt the reverberation through the bedroom-ceiling beams on which she knelt. Another crash was accompanied by the dry splintering of wood and the hard sharp snap of breaking metal.

She quickly closed the trap, plunging the attic into perfect darkness. She crawled as silently as possible along a parallel pair of two-by-fours, one hand and one knee on each of them, until she was about eight feet from the trap. There she stopped and waited in the high lightless chamber.

Anxiously she listened for movement in the room below. With the trap closed, she could not easily hear what was happening down there, for the heavy rain was hammering on the motel's roof only inches above her head.

She prayed that, in his degenerate state, with an IQ closer to that of an animal than a man, the Eric-thing would be unable to puzzle out her route of escape.

◊   ◊

With only one arm and one leg, Whitney Gavis had first dragged himself toward the garage in dogged pursuit of the departing creature that had torn off his artificial leg.

But by the time he reached the open door, he knew that he was fooling himself: with his handicaps, he could do nothing to help Rachael. Handicaps—that's what they were. Earlier, he had jokingly called his amputations "peculiarities" and had told Rachael that he refused to use the word "handicaps." In the current situation, however, there was no room for self-delusion; the painful truth had to be faced. Handicaps. He was furious with himself for his limitations, furious with the long-ago war and the Vietcong and life in general, and for a moment he was almost overcome by tears.

But being angry did no good, and Whit Gavis did not waste time and energy on either fruitless activities or self-pity. "Put a lid on it, Whit," he said aloud. He turned away from the garage and began to haul himself laboriously along the muddy ground toward the paved alley, intending to crawl all the way out to Tropicana and into the middle of that boulevard, where the sight of him would surely stop even the most unsympathetic motorist.

He had gone only six or eight yards when his face, which had been numbed by a blow from the beast's club-hard hand, suddenly began to burn and sting. He flopped on his back, face turned up into the cold rain, raised his good hand, and felt his disfigured cheek. He found deep lacerations cutting through the scar tissue that was part of his Vietnam legacy.

He was sure that Leben had not clawed him, that the blow that knocked him down was delivered with the back of the immense, bony hand. But he was undeniably cut in four or five places, and he was bleeding freely, especially from one laceration that extended up into his left temple. Did that damn fugitive from a Halloween party have spurs on its knuckles or something? His probing fingers set off little detonations of pain in his face, and he immediately dropped his hand.

Rolling onto his belly again, he continued dragging himself toward the street.

"Doesn't matter," he said. "That side of your face is never going to win you any beauty contests, anyway."

He refused to think about the thick, swift stream of blood that he had felt flowing down from his temple.

◗   ◗

Crouching in the lightless attic, Rachael began to believe that she had fooled the Eric-thing. Its degeneration was apparently mental as well as physical, just as she had suspected, and it did not possess sufficient intellectual capacity to figure out what had happened to her. Her heart continued to pound wildly, and she was still shaking, but she dared to hope.

Then the plyboard trapdoor in the closet ceiling swung upward, and light from below speared into the attic. The mutant's hideous hands reached through the opening. Then its head came into view, and it pulled itself into the upper chamber, turning its mad eyes upon her as it came.

She scuttled across the attic as fast as she dared go. She was acutely aware of the nails lancing down just inches above her head. She also knew that she must not put her weight down on the insulated hollows between the two-by-fours because there was no flooring; if she misstepped, shifting her weight off the beams for even a second, she would crash through the Sheetrock that formed the ceilings of the rooms below, tumbling into one of those chambers. Even if she did not tear loose electrical wires and fixtures in the fall—and thus escaped electrocution—she might break a leg or even snap her spine when she hit the floor below. Then she would be able only to lie immobile while the beast descended and took its sweet time with her.

She went about thirty feet, with at least another hundred and fifty feet of the motel attic ahead of her, before she glanced back. The thing had clambered all the way through the trap and was staring after her.

"Rayeeshuuuul," it said, the quality of its speech declining by the minute.

It slammed the trapdoor shut, plunging them into total darkness, where it had all the advantages.

◑   ◑

Ben's soggy Adidas running shoes were so thoroughly saturated that they began to slip on his feet. He felt the mild irritation of an incipient blister on his left heel.

When at last he came within sight of the Golden Sand Inn, where lights shone in the office windows, he slowed down long enough to shove one hand under his rain-soaked shirt and pull the Combat Magnum out of the waistband at the hollow of his back.

He wished he had the Remington shotgun that he had left behind in the disabled Merkur.

As he reached the motel's entrance drive, he saw a man crawling away from the place, toward Tropicana. An instant later he realized it was Whit Gavis without the artificial leg and, apparently, injured.

◑   ◑

He had become something that loved the dark. He did not know what he was, did not clearly remember what—or who—he had once been, did not know where he was ultimately bound or for what purpose he existed, but he knew that his rightful place was now in darkness, where he not only thrived but ruled.

Ahead, the prey made her way cautiously through the blackness, effectively blinded and moving too slowly to stay out of his reach much longer. Unlike her, he was not hampered by the lack of light. He could see her clearly, and he could see most details of the place through which they crept.

He was, however, slightly confused as to his whereabouts. He knew that he had climbed up into this long tunnel, and from the smell of it he also knew its walls were made of wood, yet he felt as if he should be deep under the earth. The place was similar to moist dark burrows which he vaguely remembered from another age and which he found appealing for reasons he did not entirely comprehend.

Around him, shadowfires sprang to life, flourished for a moment, then faded away. He knew that he had once been afraid of them, but he could not recall the reason for his fear. Now the phantom flames seemed of no consequence to him, harmless as long as he ignored them.

The prey's female scent was pungent, and it inflamed him. Lust made him reckless, and he had to struggle against the urge to rush forward and throw himself upon her. He sensed that the footing here was perilous, yet caution had far less appeal than the prospect of sexual release.

Somehow he knew that it was dangerous to stray off the beams and into the hollow spaces, though he did not know why. Keeping to those safe tracks was easier for him than for the prey, because in spite of his size he was more agile than she. Besides, he could see where he was going, and she could not.

Each time she started to look back, he squinted so she would not be able to pinpoint his position by spotting his radiant eyes. When she paused to listen, she could surely hear him coming, but her inability to get a visual fix had her obviously terrified.

The stink of her acute terror was as strong as her femaleness, though sour. The former scent sparked his blood lust as effectively as the latter incited his sexual desire. He longed to feel her blood spurting against his lips, to taste it on his tongue, to push his mouth within her slashed abdomen in search of the rich and satisfying flesh of her liver.

He was twenty feet behind her.

Fifteen.

Ten.

◗   ◗

Ben helped Whit sit up against a four-foot-high retaining wall that enclosed a tangle of weeds where once had been a bed of flowers. Above them, the motel sign scraped and creaked in the wind.

"Don't worry about me," Whit said, pushing him away.

"Your face—"

"Help *her*. Help Rachael."

"You're bleeding."

"I'll live, I'll live. But it's after Rachael," Whit said with that unnervingly familiar note of purest horror and desperation that Ben had not heard in anyone's voice since Vietnam. "It left me, and it went after her."

"It?"

"You have a gun? Good. A Magnum. Good."

"It?" Ben repeated.

Abruptly the wind wailed louder, and the rain fell as if a dam had broken above them, and Whit raised his voice to be heard over the storm. "Leben. It's Leben, but he's changed. My God, he's changed. Not really Leben anymore. Genetic chaos, she calls it. Retrograde evolution, devolution, she says. Massive mutations. Hurry, Ben! The manager's apartment!"

Unable to understand what the hell Whit was talking about, but sensing that Rachael was in even graver danger than he had feared, Ben left his old friend propped against the retaining wall and ran toward the entrance to the motel office.

◑   ◑

Blind, half deafened by the thunderous impact of the rain upon the roof, Rachael crawled through the mine-dark attic as fast as she dared. Though she was afraid that she was moving too slowly to escape the beast, she came to the end of the long chamber sooner than she'd expected, bumping up against the outer wall at the end of the motel's first wing.

Crazily, she had given no thought to what she would do when she reached a dead end. Her mind had been focused so intently upon the need to stay beyond the reach of the Eric-thing that she had proceeded as if the attic would go on forever.

She let out a whimper of despair when she discovered that she was cornered. She shuffled to her right, hoping that the attic made a turn and continued over the middle wing of the U-shaped building. In fact, it must have done just that, but she encountered a concrete-block partition between the two wings, perhaps a fire wall. Searching frantically in the darkness, she could feel the cool, rough surface of the blocks and the lines of mortar, and she knew there would be no pass-through in such a barrier.

Behind her, the Eric-thing issued a wordless cry of triumph and obscene hunger that pierced the curtain of rain noise and seemed to originate only inches from her ear.

She gasped and snapped her head around, shocked by the nearness of the demonic voice. She'd thought she had a minute to scheme, half a minute at least. But for the first time since the beast had cast the attic into absolute darkness by closing the trap door, Rachael saw its murderous eyes. The radiant pale green orb was undergoing changes that would no doubt make it more like the orange serpent's eye. She was so close that she could see the unspeakable hatred in that alien gaze. It . . . *it* was no more than six feet from her.

Its breath reeked.

She somehow knew that it could see her clearly.

And it was reaching for her in the darkness.

She sensed its grotesque hand straining toward her.

She pressed back against the concrete blocks.

Think, *think*.

Cornered, she could do nothing except embrace one of the very dangers that she had thus far been striving to avoid: Instead of clinging precariously to the beams, she threw herself to one side, into the insulated hollow between a pair of two-by-fours, and the old Sheetrock cracked and collapsed beneath her. She fell straight out of the attic, down through the ceiling of one of the motel rooms, praying that she would not land on the edge of a dresser or chair, would not break her back, praying that she would not become easy meat—

—and she dropped smack into the middle of a bed with broken springs and a mattress that had become a breeding ground for mold and fungus. Those cold and slimy growths burst beneath her, spewing spores, oozing sticky fluids, and exuding a noxious odor almost as bad as rotten eggs, though she breathed deeply of it without complaint because she was alive and unhurt.

Above, the Eric-thing started down through the ceiling in a less radical fashion than she had chosen, clinging to the ceiling beams and kicking out more Sheetrock to make a wider passageway for itself.

She rolled off the bed and stumbled across the dark motel room in search of the door.

◊   ◊

In the manager's apartment, Ben found the shattered bedroom door, but the bedroom itself was deserted, as were the living room and the kitchen. He looked in the garage as well, but neither Rachael nor Eric was there. Finding nothing was better than finding a lot of blood or her battered corpse, though not *much* better.

With Whitney's urgent warnings still echoing in his mind, Ben quickly retraced his path through the apartment to the motel office and out into the courtyard. From the corner of his eye, he saw movement down at the end of the first wing.

Rachael. Even in the gloom, there was no mistaking her.

She came out of one of the motel rooms, moving fast, and with immense relief Ben called her name. She looked up, then ran toward him along the awning-covered promenade. At first he thought her attitude was one of ordinary excitement or perhaps joy at the sight of him, but almost at once he realized she was propelled by terror.

"Benny, run!" she shouted as she approached. "Run, for ███'s sake, run!"

Of course, he would not run because he could not abandon Whit out there against the wall of the weed-choked flower bed, and he could not carry Whit and run at the same time, so he stood his ground. However, when he saw the thing that came out of that motel room behind her, he *wanted* to run, no doubt of that; all courage fled him in an instant, even though the darkness allowed him to see only a fraction of the nightmare that pursued her.

Genetic chaos, Whit had said. Devolution. Moments ago, those words had meant little or nothing to Ben. Now, on his first glimpse of the thing that Eric Leben had become, he understood as much as he needed to understand for the moment. Leben was both Dr. Frankenstein and the Frankenstein monster, both the experimenter and the unlucky subject of the experiment, a genius and a damned soul.

Rachael reached Ben, grabbed him by the arm, and said, "Come on, come on, hurry."

"I can't leave Whit," he said. "Stand back. Let me get a clear shot at it."

"No! That's no good, no good. I shot it ten times, and it got right up again."

"This is a hell of a lot more powerful weapon than yours," he insisted.

The hideous Grendelesque figure raced toward them—virtually galloped in long graceful strides—along the canopied promenade, not in the awkward shamble that Ben had expected when first catching sight of it, but with startling and dismaying speed. Even in the weak gray light, parts of its body appeared to glisten like polished obsidian armor, not unlike the shells of certain insects, while in other places there was the scintillant silvery sheen of scales.

Ben barely had time to spread his legs in a shooter's stance, raise the Combat Magnum in both hands, and squeeze off a shot. The revolver roared, and fire flashed from its muzzle.

Fifteen feet away, the creature was jolted by the impact of the slug, stumbled, but did not go down. Hell, it didn't even stop; it came forward with less speed but still too fast.

He squeezed off a second shot, a third.

The beast screamed—a sound like nothing Ben had ever heard, and like nothing he wanted to hear again—and was at last halted. It fell against one of the steel poles that held up the aluminum awning and clung to that support.

Ben fired again, hitting it in the throat this time.

The impact of the .357 Magnum blew it away from the awning post and sent it staggering backward.

The fifth shot knocked it down at last, although only to its knees. It put one shovel-size hand to the front of its throat, and its other arm bent in an impossible fashion until it had put its other hand against the back of its neck.

"Again, again!" Rachael urged.

He pumped the sixth and final shot into the kneeling creature, and it pitched backward on the concrete, flopped onto its side, lay silent, motionless.

The Combat Magnum had a roar only slightly less impressive than a cannon's. In the comparative stillness that followed the dwindling echo of the last gunshot, the drumming rain sounded hardly louder than a whisper.

"Do you have more bullets?" Rachael demanded, still in a state of acute terror.

"It's all right," Ben said shakily. "It's dead, it's dead."

"If you have more cartridges, *load them!*" she shouted.

He was not shocked by her tone or by the panic in her voice, but he *was* shocked when he realized that she was not really hysterical—scared, yes, damn scared, but not out of control. She knew what she was talking about; she was terrified but not irrational, and she believed he would need to reload quickly.

This morning—an eternity ago—on the way to Eric's cabin above Lake Arrowhead, Ben had stuffed some extra rounds into his pockets along with a few spare shells for the shotgun. He had discarded the shotgun ammo when he had left the 12-gauge in the Merkur along I-15. Now, checking his pockets, he turned up only two revolver cartridges where he had expected to find half a dozen, and he figured that the others had spilled out with the shotgun shells when he had discarded those.

But it was all right, everything was okay, nothing to fear: the creature on the promenade had not moved and was not going to move.

"Hurry," Rachael urged.

His hands were shaking. He broke out the revolver's cylinder and slipped one cartridge into a chamber.

"*Benny*," she said warningly.

He looked up and saw the beast moving. It had gotten its huge hands under itself and was trying to push up from the concrete.

"Holy shit," he said. He fumbled the second round into the gun, snapped the cylinder back into place.

Incredibly, the beast had already risen to its knees and reached out to another awning post.

Ben aimed carefully, squeezed the trigger. The Combat Magnum boomed again.

The thing was jolted as the slug tore into it, but it held fast to the post, emitting an ungodly screech. It turned luminous eyes on Ben, and in them he thought he saw a challenge and an indestructible hatred.

Ben's hands were shaking so bad that he was afraid he was going to miss with the next—and last—shot. He had not been this rattled since his first combat mission in Nam.

It clawed for handholds on the post and heaved onto its feet.

His confidence shattered, but unwilling to admit that a weapon as devastatingly powerful as the .357 Magnum was inadequate, Ben fired the final round.

Again the beast went down, but this time it was not still for even a few seconds. It writhed and squealed and kicked in agony, the carapace-hard portions of its body scraping and clicking against the concrete.

Ben would have liked to believe that it was in its death throes, but by now he knew no ordinary gun would cut it down; an Uzi rigged for fully automatic fire, perhaps, or a fully automatic AK-91 assault rifle, or the equivalent, but not an ordinary gun.

Rachael pulled at him, wanting him to run before the beast got onto its feet again, but there was still the problem of Whit Gavis. Ben could save himself and Rachael by running, but in order to save Whit, he had to stay and fight and go on fighting until either he or the mutant Leben was dead.

Perhaps because he felt as if he were in the midst of a war again, he thought of Vietnam and of the particularly cruel weapon that had been such a special and infamous part of that brutal conflict: napalm. Napalm was jellied gasoline, and for the most part it killed whatever it touched, eating through flesh all the way to the bone, scoring the bone all the way to the marrow. In Nam, the stuff had been dreaded because, once unleashed, it brought inescapable death. Given enough time, he possessed the knowledge to manufacture a serviceable homemade version of napalm; he did *not* have the time, of course, although he realized that he could put his hands on gasoline in its mundane liquid form. Though the jellied brand was preferable, the ordinary stuff was effective in its own right.

As the mutant stopped screeching and writhing, as it began to struggle onto its knees once more, Ben grabbed Rachael by the shoulder and said, "The Mercedes—where is it?"

"The garage."

He glanced toward the street and saw that Whit had presciently dragged himself around the corner of the retaining wall, where he was hidden from the motel. The wisdom of Nam: Help your buddies as much as possible, then cover your own ass as soon as you can. Initiates of that war never forgot the lessons it taught them. As long as Leben believed that Ben and Rachael were on the motel property, he was not likely to go out toward Tropicana and accidentally find the helpless man hiding against the wall. For a few more minutes, anyway, Whit was fairly safe where he was.

Casting aside the useless revolver, Ben grabbed Rachael's hand and said, "Come on!"

They ran around the side of the office toward the garage at the back of the motel, where the gusting wind was repeatedly banging the open door against the wall.

• 36 •

THE MANY
FORMS OF FIRE

Slumped against the retaining wall, facing out toward Tropicana, Whitney Gavis felt that the rain was washing him away. He was a man made of mud, and the rain was dissolving him. Moment by moment, he grew weaker, too weak to raise a hand to check the bleeding from his cheek and temple, too weak to shout at the dishearteningly few cars that whisked by on the wide boulevard. He was lying in a shadowed area, thirty feet back from the roadway, where their headlights did not sweep across him, and he supposed none of the drivers noticed him.

He had watched Ben empty the Combat Magnum into Leben's mutated hulk, and he had seen the mutant rise up again. As there was nothing he could do to help, he had concentrated upon pulling himself around the corner of the four-foot-high wall of the flower bed, intending to make himself more visible to those passing on the boulevard, hoping someone would spot him and stop. He even dared to hope for a passing patrol car and a couple of well-armed cops, but merely hoping for help was not going to be good enough.

Behind him, he had heard Ben fire two more shots, heard him and Rachael talking frantically, then running footsteps. He knew that Ben would never bug out on him, so he figured they'd thought of something else that might stop Leben. The problem was that, weak as he felt, he did not know if he was going to last long enough to find out what new strategy they had devised.

He saw another car coming west on Tropicana. He tried to call out but failed; he tried to raise one arm from his lap so he could wave to attract attention, but the arm seemed nailed to his thigh.

Then he noticed this car was moving far slower than previous traffic, and it was approaching half in its lane and half on the shoulder of the road. The closer it got, the slower it moved.

Medevac, he thought, and that thought spooked him a little because this wasn't Nam, for God's sake, this was Vegas, and they didn't have Medevac units in Vegas. Besides, this was a car, not a helicopter.

He shook his head to clear it, and when he looked again the car was closer.

They're going to pull right into the motel, Whit thought, and he would have been excited except he suddenly didn't have sufficient energy for excitement. And the already deep black night seemed to be getting blacker.

◗   ◗

As soon as Ben and Rachael had entered the garage, they'd closed and locked the outer door. She did not have the keys with her, and there was no thumb latch on this side of the kitchen door, so they had to leave that one standing open and just hope that Leben came at them from the other direction.

"No door will keep it out, anyway," Rachael said. "It'll get in if it knows we're here."

Ben had recalled garden hoses among the heaps of junk that the former owners had left behind: "Existing supplies, tools, materials, and sundry useful items," they had called the trash when trying to boost the sales price of the place. He found a pair of rusted hedge clippers, intending to use them to chop a length of hose that might work as a siphon, but then he saw a coil of narrow, flexible rubber tubing hanging from a hook on the wall, which was even more suitable.

He snatched the tubing off the hook and hastily stuffed one end into the Mercedes's fuel tank. He sucked on the other end and barely avoided getting a mouthful of gasoline.

Rachael had been busy searching through the junk for a container without a hole in the bottom. She slipped a galvanized bucket under the siphon only seconds before the gasoline began to flow.

"I never knew gas fumes could smell so sweet," he said as he watched the golden fluid streaming into the bucket.

"Even this might not stop it," she said worriedly.

"If we saturate it, the damage from fire will be much more extensive than—"

"You have matches?" Rachael interrupted.

He blinked. "No."

"Me neither."

"Damn."

Looking around the cluttered garage, she said, "Would there be any here?"

Before he could answer, the knob on the side door of the garage rattled violently. Evidently the Leben-thing had seen them go around the motel or had followed their trail by scent—only God knew what its capabilities were, and in this case maybe even God was in the dark—and already it had arrived.

"The kitchen," Ben said urgently. "They didn't bother taking anything or cleaning out the drawers. Maybe you'll find some matches there."

Rachael ran to the end of the garage and disappeared into the apartment.

The beast threw itself against the outside door, which was not a hollow-core model like the one it had easily smashed through in the bedroom. This more solid barrier would not immediately collapse, but it shuddered and clattered in its loosely fitted jamb. The mutant hit it again, and the door gave out a dry-wood splintering sound but still held, and then it was hit a third time.

Half a minute, Ben thought, glancing back and forth from the door to the gasoline collecting in the bucket. Please, God, let it hold just half a minute more.

The beast hit the door again.

◊   ◊

Whit Gavis didn't know who the two men were. They had stopped their car along the boulevard and had run to him. The big man was taking his pulse, and the smaller guy—he looked Mexican—was using one of those detachable glove-compartment flashlights to examine the lacerations in Whitney's face and temple. Their dark suits had quickly gotten darker as the rain soaked them.

They might have been some of the federal agents who were after Ben and Rachael, but at this point Whitney didn't care if they were lieutenants in the devil's own army, because surely no one could pose a greater danger than the deadly creature that was stalking the motel grounds. Against that enemy, all men ought to be united in a common cause. Even federal agents, even DSA men, would be welcome allies in this battle. They would have to give up the idea of keeping the Wildcard Project a secret; they would see that there was no way this particular line of life-extension research could be safely carried on; and they would stop trying to silence Ben and Rachael, would help stop the thing that Leben had become, yes, that was certainly what they would do, so Whitney told them what was happening, urged them to help Ben and Rachael, alerted them to the nature of the danger that they faced . . .

"What's he saying?" the big one asked.

"I can't make it out exactly," the small, well-dressed, Mexican-looking man said. He had stopped examining the cuts and had fished Whitney's wallet out of his trousers.

The big man carefully felt Whitney's left leg. "This isn't a recent injury. He lost the leg a long time ago. The same time he lost the arm, I guess."

Whitney realized that his voice was no louder than a whisper and that it was mostly drowned out by the patter, splash, and gurgle of the rain. He tried again.

"I think he's delirious," the big man said.

I'm not delirious, damn it, just weak, Whitney tried to say. But no words came from him at all this time, which scared him.

"It's Gavis," the smaller man said, studying the driver's license in Whitney's wallet. "Shadway's friend. The man Teddy Bertlesman told us about."

"He's in a bad way, Julio."

"You've got to take him in the car and get him to a hospital."

"Me?" the bigger man said. "What about you?"

"I'll be all right here."

"You can't go in alone," the big man said, his face carved by lines of worry and bejeweled with rain.

"Reese, there's not going to be trouble here," the smaller man said. "It's only Shadway and Mrs. Leben. They're no danger to me."

"Bullshit," the bigger man said. "Julio, there's someone else. Neither Shadway nor Mrs. Leben did this to Gavis."

"*Leben!*" Whitney managed to expel the name loud enough for it to carry above the sound of the rain.

The two men looked at him, puzzled.

"Leben," he managed again.

"Eric Leben?" Julio asked.

"Yes," Whitney breathed. "Genetic . . . chaos . . . chaos, mutation . . . guns . . . guns . . ."

"What about guns?" the bigger man—Reese—asked.

" . . . won't . . . stop . . . him," Whitney finished, exhausted.

"Get him into the car, Reese," Julio said. "If he isn't in a hospital in ten or fifteen minutes, he's not going to make it."

"What's he mean that guns won't stop Leben?" Reese asked.

"He's delirious," Julio said. "Now *move!*"

Frowning, Reese scooped Whitney up as easily as a father might lift a small child.

The one named Julio hurried ahead, splashing through puddles of dirty water, and opened the back door of their car.

Reese maneuvered Whitney gently onto the seat, then turned to Julio. "I don't like this."

"Just go," Julio said.

"I swore I'd never cut and run on you, that I'd always be there when you needed me, any way you needed me, no matter what."

"Right now," Julio said sharply, "I need you to take this man to a hospital." He slammed the rear door.

A moment later, Reese opened the front door and got in behind the wheel. To Julio, he said, "I'll be back as soon as I can."

Lying on the rear seat, Whitney said, "Chaos . . . chaos . . . chaos . . . chaos." He was trying to say a lot of other things, convey a more specific warning, but only that one word would come out.

Then the car began to move.

◑   ◑

Peake had pulled to the side of Tropicana Boulevard and had switched off the headlights when Hagerstrom and Verdad had coasted to a stop along the shoulder about a quarter of a mile ahead.

Leaning forward, squinting through the smeary windshield past the monotonously thumping wipers, Sharp twice rubbed a stubborn patch of condensation from the glass and at last said, "Looks like . . . they've found someone lying in front of that place. What *is* that place?"

"Seems like it's out of business, a deserted motel," Peake said. "Can't quite read that old sign from here. Golden . . . something."

"What're they doing here?" Sharp wondered.

What am I doing here? Peake wondered silently.

"Could this be where Shadway and the Leben bitch are hiding out?" Sharp wondered.

Dear God, I hope not, Peake thought. I hope we never find them. I hope they're on a beach in Tahiti.

"Whoever those bastards have found," Sharp said, "they're putting him in their car."

Peake had given up all hope of becoming a legend. He had also given up all hope of becoming one of Anson Sharp's favorite agents. All he wanted was to get through this night alive, to prevent whatever killing he could, and to avoid humiliating himself.

◖   ◖

At the side of the garage, the battered door cracked again, from top to bottom this time, and the jamb splintered, too, and one hinge tore loose, and the lock finally exploded, and everything crashed inward, and there was Leben, the beast, coming through like something that had broken out of a bad dream into the real world.

Ben grabbed the bucket—which was more than half full—and headed toward the kitchen door, trying to move fast without spilling any of the precious gasoline.

The creature saw him and let loose a shriek of such intense hatred and rage that the sound seemed to penetrate deep into Ben's bones and vibrate there. It kicked aside an outdoor vacuum cleaner and clambered over the piles of trash—including a fallen set of metal shelves—with arachnoid grace, as if it were an immense spider.

Entering the kitchen, Ben heard the thing close behind him. He dared not look back.

Half the cupboard doors and drawers were open, and just as Ben entered, Rachael pulled out another drawer. She cried—"There!"—and snatched up a box of matches.

"Run!" Ben said. "Outside!"

They absolutely had to put more distance between themselves and the beast, gain time and room to pull the trick they had in mind.

He followed her out of the kitchen into the living room, and some of the gasoline slopped over the edge of the pail, spattering the carpet and his shoes.

Behind them, the mutant crashed through the kitchen, slamming shut cupboard doors, heaving aside the small kitchen table and chairs even though that furniture wasn't in its way, snarling and shrieking, apparently in the grip of a destructive frenzy.

Ben felt as if he were moving in slow motion, fighting his way through air as thick as syrup. The living room seemed as long as a football field. Then, finally nearing the end of the room, he was suddenly afraid that the door to the motel office was going to be locked, that they were going to be halted here, with no time or room to set fire to the beast, at least not without serious risk of immolating themselves in the process. Then Rachael threw open the door, and Ben almost shouted with relief. They rushed into the motel office, through the swinging gate in one end of the check-in counter, across the small public area, through the outer glass door, into the night beneath the breezeway—and nearly collided with Detective Verdad, whom they had last seen on Monday evening, at the morgue in Santa Ana.

"What in the name of God?" Verdad said as the beast shrieked in the motel office behind them.

Ben saw that the rain-soaked policeman had a revolver in his hand. He said, "Back off and shoot it when it comes through the door. You can't kill it, but maybe you can slow it down."

◊　　　◊

It wanted the female prey, it wanted blood, it was full of a cold rage, it was burning with hot desire, and it would not be stopped, not by guns or doors, not by anything, not until it had taken the female, buried its aching member inside her, not until it had killed both of them and fed upon them, it wanted to chew out their soft sweet eyes, bury its muzzle in their torn and spurting throats, it wanted to feed on the bloody pulsing muscle of their hearts, wanted to burrow through their eviscerated corpses in search of their rich livers and kidneys, it felt that overwhelming hunger beginning to grow within it again, the changefire within it needed more fuel, a mild hunger now but soon to get worse, like before, an all-consuming hunger that could not be denied, it needed *meat,* and it pushed through the glass door, out into the night wind and blowing rain, and there was another male, a smaller one, and fire flashed from something in the smaller male's hand, and a brief sharp pain stung its chest, and fire flashed again, and another pain, so it roared a furious challenge at its pathetic assailant—

◑   ◑

Just this morning, when he had been at the library doing research related to the unofficial investigation he intended to conduct with Reese, Julio had read several magazine and journal articles Eric Leben had written about genetic engineering and about the prospects for the success of life extension by means of genetic manipulation. Later, he had spoken with Dr. Easton Solberg at UCI, had done a lot of thinking since then, and had just heard Whitney Gavis's disjointed ramblings about genetic chaos and mutation. He was not a stupid man, so when he saw the nightmare creature that followed Shadway and Mrs. Leben out of the motel office, he quickly determined that something had gone terribly wrong with Eric Leben's experiment and that this monstrosity was, in fact, the scientist himself.

As Julio unhesitatingly opened fire on the creature, Mrs. Leben and Shadway—who, judging from the smell of it, was carrying a bucket full of gasoline—hurried from beneath the cover of the breezeway into the rainy courtyard. The first two rounds did not faze the mutant, though it stopped for a moment as if baffled by Julio's sudden and unexpected appearance. To his astonishment, he saw that he might not be able to bring it down with the revolver.

It lurched forward, hissing, and swung one multiple-jointed arm at him as if to knock his head off his shoulders.

Julio barely ducked under the blow, felt the arm brush through his hair, and fired up into the beast's chest, which bristled with spines and strangely shaped lumps of tissue. If it embraced him, he would be impaled upon those breast spikes, and that realization brought his finger to bear upon the trigger again and again.

Those three shots finally drove the thing backward until it collided with the wall by the office door, where it stood for a moment, clawing at the air.

Julio fired the sixth and final round in the revolver, hitting his target again, but still it remained standing— hurt and maybe even dazed, but standing. He always carried a few extra cartridges in his jacket pocket, even though he had never before needed spare rounds in all his years of police work, and now he fumbled for them.

The creature shoved away from the motel wall, apparently having already recuperated from the six rounds it had just taken. It cut loose a cry so savage and furious that Julio turned away from it at once and ran into the courtyard, where Shadway and Mrs. Leben were standing at the far end of the swimming pool.

◊   ◊

Peake had hoped that Sharp would send him off after Hagerstrom and the unknown man that the cop had loaded into the back seat of the rental car. Then, if shooting took place at the abandoned motel, it would be entirely Sharp's responsibility.

But Sharp said, "Let Hagerstrom go. Looks to me like he's taking that guy to a doctor. Anyway, Verdad is the real brains of the team. If Verdad's staying here, then this is where the action is; this is where we'll find Shadway and the woman."

When Lieutenant Verdad headed back along the motel driveway toward the lighted office, Sharp told Peake to pull down there and park in front of the place. By the time they stopped again on the shoulder of the boulevard in front of the dilapidated sign—GOLDEN SAND INN—they heard the first gunshots.

Oh, hell, Peake thought miserably.

◊   ◊

Lieutenant Verdad stood on one side of Benny, hastily reloading his revolver.

Rachael stood on the other side, sheltering the box of wooden matches from the relentless rain. She had withdrawn one match and had been holding it and the box in her cupped hands, silently cursing the wind and water that would try to extinguish the flame the moment it was struck.

From the front of the motel courtyard, backlit by the amber light spilling through the office windows, the Eric-thing approached in that frighteningly swift, darkly graceful stride that seemed entirely at odds with its size and with its cumbersome, gnarled appearance. It emitted a shrill, ululant cry as it raced toward them. Clearly, it had no fear.

Rachael was afraid that its reckless advance was justified, that the fire would do it no more damage than the bullets.

It was already halfway along the forty-foot length of the pool. When it reached the end, it would only have to turn the corner and come another fifteen feet before it would be upon them.

The lieutenant had not finished reloading his revolver, but he snapped the cylinder into place anyway, apparently deciding that he didn't have time to slip the last two cartridges into their chambers.

The beast reached the corner of the pool.

Benny gripped the bucket of gasoline with both hands, one on the rim and the other on the bottom. He swung it back at his side, brought it forward, and threw the contents all over the face and chest of the mutant as it leaped across the last fifteen feet of concrete decking.

◊   ◊

At a run, Peake followed Sharp past the motel office and into the courtyard just in time to see Shadway throw a bucket full of something into the face of—

Of what? ~~Christ,~~ what *was* that thing?

Sharp, too, halted in amazement.

The creature screamed in fury and staggered back from Shadway. It wiped at its monstrous face—Peake saw eyes that glowed orange like a pair of hot coals—and pawed at its chest, trying to remove whatever Shadway had thrown on it.

"Leben," Sharp said. "Holy shit, it must be Leben."

Jerry Peake understood at once, even though he didn't *want* to understand, did not want to know, for this was a secret that it would be dangerous to know, dangerous not only to his physical well-being but to his sanity.

◊   ◊

The gasoline seemed to have choked and temporarily blinded it, but Rachael knew that it would recover from this assault as quickly as it had recovered from being shot. So, as Benny dropped the empty bucket and stepped out of the way, she struck the match and only then realized she should have had a torch, something she could have set aflame and then thrown at the creature. Now she had no choice but to step in close with the short-stemmed match.

The Eric-thing had stopped shrieking and, temporarily overcome by the gasoline fumes, was hunched over, wheezing noisily, gasping for air.

She took only three steps toward it before the wind or the rain—or both—extinguished the match.

Making a strange terrified mewling that she could not control, she slid open the box, took out another match, and struck it. This time she had not even taken one step before the flame went out.

The demonic mutant seemed to be breathing easier, and it began to straighten up, raising its monstrous head again.

The rain, Rachael thought desperately, the rain is washing the gasoline off its body.

As she shakily withdrew a third match, Benny said, "Here," and he turned the empty bucket upright on the concrete at her feet.

She understood. She rasped the third match against the striking pad on the side of the box, couldn't get it to light.

The creature drew in a deep breath at last, another. Recovering, it shrieked at them.

She scraped the match against the box again and let out a cry of relief when the flame spurted up. The instant the match was lit, she dropped it straight into the bucket, and the residue of gasoline burst into flames.

Lieutenant Verdad, who had been waiting to do his part, stepped in fast and kicked the bucket at the Eric-thing.

The flaming pail struck one of the beast's jean-clad thighs, where some of the gasoline had landed when Benny had thrown it. The fire leaped out of the bucket onto the jeans and raced up over the creature's spiny chest, swiftly enveloped the misshapen head.

The fire did not stop it.

Screaming in pain, a pillar of flame, the thing nevertheless came forward faster than Rachael would have believed possible. In the red-orange light of the leaping fire, she saw its outreaching hands, saw what appeared to be *mouths* in the palms, and then it had its hands on her. Hell could be no worse than having those hands on her; she almost died right there from the horror of it. The thing seized her by one arm and by the neck, and she felt those orifices within its hands eating into her flesh, and she felt the fire reaching out for her, and she saw the spikes on the mutant's huge chest where she could be so quickly and easily impaled—a multitude of possible deaths—and now it lifted her, and she knew she was certainly dead, finished, but Verdad appeared and opened fire with his revolver, squeezing off two shots that hit the Eric-thing in the head, but even before he could pull off a third shot, Benny came in at a flying leap, in some crazy karate movement, airborne, driving both feet into the monster's shoulder, and Rachael felt it let go of her with one hand, so she wrenched and kicked at its flaming chest, and suddenly she was free, the creature was toppling into the shallow end of the empty swimming pool, she fell to the concrete decking, free, free—except that her shoes were on fire.

◊   ◊

Ben delivered the kick and threw himself to the left, hit the decking, rolled, and came immediately onto his feet in time to see the creature falling into the shallow end of the empty pool. He also saw that Rachael's shoes were afire

502 ◐ DEAN KOONTZ

from gasoline, and he dove for her, threw himself upon her, and smothered the flames.

For a moment, she clung fiercely to him, and he held her tightly with an equal need of reassurance. He had never before felt anything half as good as her heart's frantic pounding, which was conveyed through her breast to his.

"Are you all right?"

"Good enough," she said shakily.

He hugged her again, then gave her a quick examination. There was a bleeding circlet on her arm and another on her neck, where the mouths in the mutant's hands had attached themselves to her, but neither wound looked serious.

In the pool, the creature was screaming in a way it had not screamed before, and Ben was sure that these must be its death cries—although he would not have taken any bets on it.

Together, with his arm around her waist and her arm encircling him, they went to the edge of the pool, where Lieutenant Verdad was already standing.

Burning as if it were made of the purest candle tallow, the beast staggered down the sloping floor of the pool, perhaps trying to reach the collected rainwater at the deep end. But the falling rain did nothing to quench the flames, and Ben suspected that the puddle below would be equally ineffective. The fire was inexplicably intense, as if the gasoline were not the only fuel, as if something in the mutant's body chemistry were also feeding the flames. At the halfway point, the creature collapsed onto its knees, clawing at the air and then at the wet concrete before it. It continued to the bottom, crawling, then slithering along on its belly, finally dragging itself laboriously toward hoped-for salvation.

◐   ◐

The shadowfire burned within the water, down under the cooling surface, and he was drawn toward it, not merely to extinguish the flames that were consuming his body but to snuff out the changefire within him, too. The

unbearable pain of immolation had jolted what remained
of his human consciousness, had bestirred him from the
trancelike state into which he had retreated when the
savage alien part of him had gained dominance. For a
moment he knew who he was, what he had become, and
what was happening to him. But he also knew that the
knowledge was tenuous, that awareness would fade, that
the small remaining portion of his intellect and personality
would eventually be completely destroyed in the process
of growth and change, and that the only hope for him
was death.

Death.

He had striven hard to avoid death, had taken insane
risks to save himself from the grave, but now he welcomed Charon.

Eaten alive by fire, he dragged himself down, down
toward the shadowfire beneath the water, the strange fire
burning on a far shore.

He stopped screaming. He had traveled beyond pain
and terror, into a great lonely calm.

He knew that the flaming gasoline would not kill him,
not that alone. The changefire within him was worse
than the external fire. The changefire was blazing very
brightly now, burning in every cell, *raging,* and he was
overwhelmed by a painful hunger a thousand times more
demanding and excruciating than any he had known
before. He was desperate for fuel, for carbohydrates
and proteins and vitamins and minerals with which to
support his uncontrolled metabolism. But because he
was in no condition to stalk and kill and feed, he could
not provide his system with the fuel it needed. Therefore,
his body started to cannibalize itself; the changefire did
not subside but began to burn up some of his tissues in
order to obtain the enormous amounts of energy required
to transform those tissues that it did *not* consume as fuel.
Second by second, his body weight rapidly declined, not
because the gasoline was feeding on it but because *he*
was feeding on himself, devouring himself from within.
He felt his head changing shape, felt his arms shrinking
and a second pair of arms extruding from his lower rib

cage. Each change consumed more of him, yet the fires of mutation did not subside.

At last he could not pull himself any closer to the shadowfire that burned beneath the water. He stopped and lay still, choking and twitching.

But to his surprise, he saw the shadowfire rise out of the water ahead. It moved toward him until it encircled him, until his world was all aflame, inside and out.

In his dying agony, Eric finally understood that the mysterious shadowfires had been neither gateways to hell nor merely meaningless illusions generated by misfiring synapses in the brain. They were illusions, yes. Or, more accurately, they were hallucinations cast off by his subconscious, meant to warn him of the terrible destiny toward which he had been plunging ever since he had arisen from that slab in the morgue. His damaged brain had functioned too poorly for him to grasp the logical progression of his fate, at least on a conscious level. But his subconscious mind had known the truth and had tried to provide clues by creating the phantom shadowfires: *fire* (his subconscious had been telling him), fire is your destiny, the insatiable inner fire of a superheated metabolism, and sooner or later it is going to burn you up alive.

His neck dwindled until his head sat almost directly upon his shoulders.

He felt his spine lengthening into a tail.

His eyes sank back under a suddenly more massive brow.

He sensed that he had more than two legs.

Then he sensed nothing at all as the changefire swept through him, consuming the last fuel it could find. He descended into the many kinds of fire.

◗　　◗

Before Ben's eyes, in only a minute or less, the creature burned—the flames leaped high into the air, seethed, *roared*—until there was nothing left of the corpse but a small bubbling pool of sludge, a few little flickering flames down there in the darkness that reclaimed the empty swimming pool. Uncomprehending, Ben stood in silence, unable to speak. Lieutenant Verdad and Rachael seemed equally amazed, for they did not break the silence, either.

It was broken, at last, by Anson Sharp. He was coming slowly around the edge of the pool. He had a gun, and he looked as if he would use it. "What the hell happened to him? What the *hell*?"

Startled, not having seen the DSA agents until now, Ben stared at his old enemy and said, "Same thing that's going to happen to you, Sharp. He did to himself what you'll do to yourself sooner or later, though in a different way."

"What're you talking about?" Sharp demanded.

Holding Rachael and trying to ease his body between her and Sharp, Ben said, "He didn't like the world the way he found it, so he set out to make it conform to his own twisted expectations. But instead of making a paradise for himself, he made a living hell. It's what you'll make for yourself, given time."

"Shit," Anson Sharp said, "you've gone off the deep end, Shadway. Way off the deep end." To Verdad, he said, "Lieutenant, please put down your revolver."

Verdad said, "What? What're you talking about? I—"

Sharp shot Verdad, and the detective was flung off the concrete into the mud by the impact of the bullet.

◗　　◗

Jerry Peake—a devoted reader of mysteries, given to dreams of legendary achievement—had a habit of thinking in melodramatic terms. Watching Eric Leben's monstrously mutated body burning away to nothing in the empty swimming pool, he was shocked, horrified, and frightened; but he was also thinking at an unusually furious pace for him. First, he made a mental list of the similarities between Eric Leben and Anson Sharp: They loved power, thrived on it; they were cold-blooded and capable of anything; they had a perverse taste for young girls . . . Then Jerry listened to what Ben Shadway said about how a man could make his own hell on earth, and he thought about that, too. Then he looked down at the smoldering remnants of the mutant Leben, and it seemed to him that he was at a crossroads between his own earthly paradise and hell: He could cooperate with Sharp, let murder be done, and live with the guilt forever, damned in this life as well as in the next; *or* he could resist Sharp, retain his integrity and self-respect, and feel good about himself no matter what happened to his career in the DSA. The choice was his. Which did he want to be—the thing down there in the pool or a *man*?

Sharp ordered Lieutenant Verdad to put down the gun, and Verdad began to question the order, and Sharp shot him, just shot him, with no argument or hesitation.

So Jerry Peake drew his own gun and shot Sharp. The slug hit the deputy director in the shoulder.

Sharp seemed to have sensed the impending betrayal, because he had started to turn toward Jerry even as Jerry shot him. He squeezed off a round of his own, and Jerry took the bullet in the leg, though he fired simultaneously. As he fell, he had the enormous pleasure of seeing Anson Sharp's head explode.

◊   ◊

Rachael stripped the jacket and shirt off Lieutenant Verdad and examined the bullet wound in his shoulder.

"I'll live," he said. "It hurts like the devil, but I'll live."

In the distance, the mournful sound of sirens arose, drawing rapidly nearer.

"That'll be Reese's doing," Verdad said. "As soon as he got Gavis to the hospital, he'll have called the locals."

"There really isn't too much bleeding," she said, relieved to be able to confirm his own assessment of his condition.

"I told you," Verdad said. "Heck, I can't die. I intend to stay around long enough to see my partner marry the pink lady." He laughed at her puzzlement and said, "Don't worry, Mrs. Leben. I'm not out of my head."

◗   ◗

Peake was flat on his back on the concrete decking, his head raised somewhat on the hard pillow of the pool coping.

With a wide strip of his own torn shirt, Ben had fashioned a tourniquet for Peake's leg. The only thing he could find to twist it with was the barrel of Anson Sharp's discarded, silencer-equipped pistol, which was perfect for the job.

"I don't think you really need a tourniquet," he told Peake as the sirens drew steadily nearer, gradually overwhelming the patter of the rain, "but better safe than sorry. There's a lot of blood, but I didn't see any spurting, no torn artery. Must hurt like the devil, though."

"Funny," Peake said, "but it doesn't hurt much at all."

"Shock," Ben said worriedly.

"No," Peake said, shaking his head. "No, I don't think I'm going into shock. I've got none of the symptoms—and I know them. You know what I think maybe it is?"

"What?"

"What I just did—shooting my own boss when he went bad—is going to make me a legend in the agency. Damned if it isn't. I didn't see it that way until he was dead. So, anyway, maybe a legend just doesn't feel pain as much as other people do." He grinned at Ben.

Ben returned a frown for the grin. "Relax. Just try to relax—"

Jerry Peake laughed. "I'm not delirious, Mr. Shadway. Really, I'm not. Don't you see? Not only am I a legend, but I can still laugh at myself! Which means that maybe I really do have what it takes. I mean, see, maybe I can make a big reputation for myself and not let it go to my head. Isn't that a nice thing to learn about yourself?"

"It's a nice thing," Ben agreed.

The night was filled with screaming sirens, then the bark of brakes, and then the sirens died as running footsteps sounded on the motel driveway.

◐   ◐

Soon there would be questions—thousands of them—from police officers in Las Vegas, Palm Springs, Lake Arrowhead, Santa Ana, Placentia, and other places.

Following that ordeal, the media would have questions of their own. ("How do you *feel*, Mrs. Leben? Please? How do you *feel* about your husband's murderous spree, about nearly dying at his hands, how do you *feel*?") They would be even more persistent than the police—and far less courteous.

But now, as Jerry Peake and Julio Verdad were loaded into the paramedics' van and as the uniformed Las Vegas officers kept a watch on Sharp's corpse to make certain no one touched it before the police coroner arrived, Rachael and Ben had a moment together, just the two of them. Detective Hagerstrom had reported that Whitney Gavis had made it to the hospital in time and was going to pull through, and now he was getting into the emergency van with Julio Verdad. They were blessedly alone. They stood under the promenade awning, holding each other, neither of them speaking at first. Then they seemed to realize simultaneously that they would not be alone together again for long, frustrating hours, and they both tried to speak at once.

"You first," he said, holding her almost at arm's length, looking into her eyes.

"No, you. What were you going to say?"

"I was wondering . . ."

"What?"

" . . . if you remembered."

"Ah," she said because she knew instinctively what he meant.

"When we stopped along the road to Palm Springs," he said.

"I remember," she said.

"I proposed."

"Yes."

"Marriage."

"Yes."

"I've never done that before."

"I'm glad."

"It wasn't very romantic, was it?"

"You did just fine," she said. "Is the offer still open?"

"Yes. Is it still appealing?"

"Immensely appealing," she said.

He pulled her close again.

She put her arms around him, and she felt protected, yet suddenly a shiver passed through her.

"It's all right," he said. "It's over."

"Yeah, it's over," she said, putting her head against his chest. "We'll go back to Orange County, where it's always summer, and we'll get married, and I'll start collecting trains with you. I think I could get *into* trains, you know? We'll listen to old swing music, and we'll watch old movies on the VCR, and together we'll make a better world for ourselves, won't we?"

"We'll make a better world," he agreed softly. "But not that way. Not by hiding from the world as it really is. Together, we don't need to hide. Together, we've got the power, don't you think?"

"I don't think," she said. "I *know*."

The rain had tailed off to a light drizzle. The storm was moving eastward, and the mad voice of the wind was stilled for now.

Author of the #1
New York Times Bestseller

HIDEAWAY
and
DRAGON TEARS

Dean Koontz

____HIDEAWAY	0-425-13525-X/$5.99
____THE HOUSE OF THUNDER	0-425-13295-1/$6.99
____COLD FIRE	0-425-13071-1/$6.99
____WATCHERS	0-425-10746-9/$6.99
____WHISPERS	0-425-09760-9/$6.99
____NIGHT CHILLS	0-425-09864-8/$5.99
____PHANTOMS	0-425-10145-2/$6.99
____SHATTERED	0-425-09933-4/$5.99
____DARKFALL	0-425-10434-6/$5.99
____THE FACE OF FEAR	0-425-11984-X/$5.99
____THE VISION	0-425-09860-5/$5.99
____TWILIGHT EYES	0-425-10065-0/$5.99
____STRANGERS	0-425-11992-0/$5.99
____THE MASK	0-425-12758-3/$5.99
____LIGHTNING	0-425-11580-1/$5.99
____MIDNIGHT	0-425-11870-3/$5.99
____THE SERVANTS OF TWILIGHT	0-425-12125-9/$5.99
____THE BAD PLACE	0-425-12434-7/$6.99
____THE VOICE OF THE NIGHT	0-425-12816-4/$6.99

For Visa , MasterCard and American Express orders ($15 minimum) call: 1-800-631-8571

FOR MAIL ORDERS: CHECK BOOK(S). FILL OUT COUPON. SEND TO:

BERKLEY PUBLISHING GROUP
390 Murray Hill Pkwy., Dept. B
East Rutherford, NJ 07073

NAME_____

ADDRESS _____

CITY_____

STATE_____ZIP_____

PLEASE ALLOW 6 WEEKS FOR DELIVERY.
PRICES ARE SUBJECT TO CHANGE WITHOUT NOTICE.

POSTAGE AND HANDLING:
$1.75 for one book, 75¢ for each additional. Do not exceed $5.50.

BOOK TOTAL	$ _____
POSTAGE & HANDLING	$ _____
APPLICABLE SALES TAX	$ _____
(CA, NJ, NY, PA)	
TOTAL AMOUNT DUE	$ _____

PAYABLE IN US FUNDS.
(No cash orders accepted.)

227d